WE ARE BESIEGED

WE ARE BESIEGED

Barbara Fitzgerald

SOMERVILLE PRESS

Somerville Press,
Dromore, Bantry,
Co. Cork, Ireland

© Literary Executors, Dr Julian Somerville
and Mrs Christina Hoare 2011

First published 1946
This reprint 2011

Designed by Jane Stark
Typeset in Adobe Garamond
seamistgraphics@gmail.com

ISBN: 978-0-9562231-3-5

Printed and bound in Spain
by GraphyCems, Villatuerta, Navarra

'We may remain, as aliens besieged, in a land that has lost its welcome.'

CHAPTER ONE

In an upper window of the big house, a light was burning; it flickered slightly, warm and yellow, between the half-drawn curtains. Shadows passed and repassed, the monstrous shadows thrown by human beings in candle-light. Then the window was flung up, there was a soft murmur of voices and the light went out.

Outside, the November mist lay like a net, man-high. The chestnut trees looked as if they were detached from earth; they thrust their tangled fingers downwards, dipping into the silvery nothingness below; their tortured pattern was stamped, motionless and a little blurred, on the pale walls and against the unlit windows by the light of the sickle moon, riding in from the sea over the Scotch firs on the hill. Across the lawn, the rhododendrons huddled darkly, crowning the mist.

From the distance came the lap-lap of calm water against the rocks. An occasional dead leaf went spiralling down through the still air to fall with a soft brush amongst the others on the ground. A fox barked once, a high-pitched unearthly cry, away in the cold heather.

Then, from the mist, came sounds of creeping footsteps and laboured breathing. From out of the woods, from behind the rhododendrons, over the sunken fence in front of the house, invisible men approached with slow and cautious movements. They took cover in the bushes, they leant against the chestnut trees, they entered the yard. The hostile gravel and the rustling leaves betrayed their careful feet but the people in the house could not have heard them, for no light sprang up, no voice of alarm sounded, no head peered from a window into the moonlit mist. Silence again, and then a hoarse despairing whisper:

'Oh, my God, she's jammed on me again!'

Somebody caught his breath and hissed: 'For the love of God, man, will ye hold yer tongue.' A tense and listening moment, an expiration of relief and then, more gently: 'Here, give her to me; I'm the only one undherstands her.'

Inside the house, a dog barked, the deep full-throated baying of a large dog proclaiming the menace of strangers.

'Now, boys!'

Men flung themselves across the gravel to the door, kicking against it with their boots, banging with the knocker. They shouted and the dog barked incessantly within. Clamour rocketed through the night.

Above the door, a window opened noisily; a man leant out but he could see nothing in the mist below.

'What do you want?'

His voice was weary, for the question was merely formal. In 1920, every householder in Ireland knew the answer, but still they asked the question, hoping for a miracle.

The racket ceased; only the dog went on barking.

'Captain Butler?'

'Yes. Who are you?' The second question was as useless as the first.

'In the name of the I-rish Republican Army we have ordhers to burn down the house. Ye have ten minyits to clear out and save what stuff ye can. Open the door!'

The voice from the window became bantering: 'Ah, take it easy now, take it easy; go on back to your beds and we'll talk it over in the morning.'

There was uneasy laughter below, guiltily stilled when the spokesman's harsh voice shouted irascibly:

'That's enough now, them's our ordhers. Will ye open the door or would ye like us to break it in? Quick now, or there'll be throuble—an will ye tie up yer dog?'

A short pause. The man in the window held out his hand as though he were bargaining for time.

'All right, I'll open the door. Give me a moment to get some clothes on.'

He disappeared. The men below felt easier now, the job was as good as done. They stood around talking, swinging their revolvers, lolling up against the pillars; one of them whistled a jaunty little tune.

Soon a light flickered in the porch, there was a sound of fumbling at the bolts and the men rushed the door. Archie Butler found himself surrounded, the candlestick dashed from his hand and his arms jerked above his head. Someone shone a torch brutally into his eyes and dug a revolver into his ribs.

'Are y'armed? Have ye a gun in the house?' Rough hands felt him up and down.

'You know very well,' he said bitterly, 'I haven't even a rook rifle left me, or you wouldn't be here.'

They hustled him into the hall; other men were coming up the steps with tins of petrol and bundles of straw.

'Light that lamp. Have ye the dog tied up?'

'I have. And put those damned guns down, can't you see they make me nervous?' He turned on the invaders in exasperation and marked their anonymous uniform: trench coats, black masks and soft hats pulled low over their eyes. They had the voices of strangers. At least his own men had not turned against him. Shamefacedly, they lowered the guns. He went to the lamp, struck a match and lit it, trying to keep his fingers steady; it was turned too high and began to smoke; he turned it down.

'Leave that; there'll be more than lamps smokin' in a minyit.'

The speaker guffawed hoarsely and took out a watch.

'Ten minyits,' he announced, 'to get all the people out and what stuff ye can save.'

Archie turned and ran up the dark staircase.

Upstairs, in a back room, a child lay asleep in the great posted bed, the smooth contour of the coverings hardly broken by her small body. Through the open window came the washing sound of the tide against the rocks. The moonlight lay in a pool on the floor and was spilled over the bed, lighting up the thin pale face half-hidden in a cloud of hair on the gleaming pillow. When the fox barked, she stirred, but while the invaders crept towards the house from out of the woods and over the lawn, from behind the rhododendrons and over the sunken fence, she never moved; a step on the gravel roused her and she muttered and slept again. Then the big dog began to bark and she awoke, sitting tense and upright.

The shouting and the knocking began and she clenched her hands in terror, pushing them into her eyes. A cold film sweat broke out on her face and hands and, gradually, over her whole body. In a furtive movement, as though she were already under the eye of the enemy, she slipped out of bed and with clammy trembling hands started to pull on her clothes.

'They've come,' she thought; 'they've come at last! It's always like this.'

She knew. She read the newspapers. It was happening all over the country and it was always the same.

With all her heart she wished herself at home in Dublin, safe with her parents and dear comfortable Miss O'Connor, and Isabel. If she had not had measles, she would have been at home.

She dared not light a candle, fearing that if she showed a light someone might shoot at the window. She stood in the moonlight on the floor and struggled with garments that had become monsters of intricacy; her knees began to give way under her and she sat down, plunging both feet into one knicker-leg so that when she stood up again to reach for her skirt she fell, a harmless rolling fall, but it added to her panic. She fought with her clothes, tearing at them and tugging as though they were rigid casings of metal that must be beaten into shape. Then, dressed, she leant against the end of the bed and beat upon it with her hands.

'Why doesn't someone come?' she screamed, only no voice came and all she uttered was a little gasping sob; 'Have they forgotten me? Oh, why doesn't someone come?'

Footsteps were coming along the passage, hurrying female footsteps, and a light shone under the door; this would be Aunt Moira; she ran to the door, opened it and stood, still grasping the handle, staring at her Aunt.

Moira Butler, dressed in a tweed suit and a fur coat, her dark hair still in plaits down her back, held a candle in one hand and clutched her jewel case and a handbag against her bosom with the other; a number of brooches, ill-concealed by a silk scarf which hung loosely round her neck, was pinned at random over the front of her woollen jumper.

'Dressed? Caroline darling, you're grand!' Her voice was full of admiration.

'It's the Sinn Feiners, isn't it?' Caroline's huge grey eyes looked almost black and the dark surrounding rings enlarged them; in that moment Moira had a vision, which was to haunt her all her life, of a pair of enormous terrified eyes in that small white patch of face.

She nodded. 'Don't be frightened, darling, they won't do us any harm, they only want to burn the house. We have ten minutes to get out; collect what clothes you can, then you can help us; we're trying to save some of the silver and the pictures. Here, let me light your candle for you.' She took the silver candlestick from beside the bed and lit it from her own. 'I must run, be as quick as you can. You'll be all right, won't you? And put on lots of warm clothes.'

She turned and went hurrying down the passage.

Caroline could only stare after her speechlessly. She was alone again, all alone. Panic returned. She would be burnt with the house, she was sure of it. She saw the hungry flames creeping along the passage, up between the floor-boards, and herself trapped in her room, shrieking at the window, alone within the red-hot walls. How they would mourn for her and what tortures of remorse they would suffer because they had left her alone to die! How her parents would reproach Aunt Moira for not looking after her! Her eyes filled with tears, but the necessity for immediate action steadied her. No one would help her: she must save herself.

Clothes! What should she take?—what did it matter, after all? She dived under the bed and brought out a suitcase. One of the locks would not open, so she gave it a kick and it sprang open with a click that made her jump. Flinging open drawers and cupboards, she hurled things into the suitcase: shoes, her night clothes and a dripping sponge; a hat, her hairbrush and a paint-box, the blue velveteen dress she wore at dinner and a single long black stocking; the cold and flabby hot-water bottle from her bed. She threw her hated woollen combinations away; she would not take them—let them burn! The case would hold no more; she tried to shut it, but the brim of the hat was in the way and the lid would not close. She pulled out the hat and sent it flying across the room; it sailed through the window and she gave a little nervous giggle. The case would shut now; she dragged it to the door and out into the dark passage, then dashed back to fetch the candle. The room might have been rifled by burglars: every drawer was open and one was upside down upon the floor, its contents strewn widely over the carpet; the cupboard doors stood wide. In a moment of clarity she saw that she would need her coat; she pulled it off its hanger in the wardrobe, threw it over her arm and set off with it and the candle, back to the suitcase in the passage.

It was terribly heavy; a dressing-gown sleeve was hanging out and kept tripping her up but she could not stop to stuff it in; candle-grease dripped steadily on her coat but at last she reached the stairs. There was a terrible smell of burning: they had set the house on fire and she was trapped! She tried to scream but no sound came; her hair was in her eyes and she tossed her head to get it out of the way; as she did so, she realised that a lock of it had been singeing in the candle flame. So that was the cause of the smell! In her relief she stumbled against the suitcase and it tipped over the first stair and went crashing and bundling down to the bottom.

'Mother of God!' It was a soft rich voice, vibrant with terror. A torch shone up from the floor below; Caroline came down a few steps and, holding the candle out, leant cautiously over the bannisters; the torch was lowered and she found herself looking into a revolver held by an open-mouthed youth. He looked terribly young and harmless, in spite of his weapon and the sinister mask and clothes. She was frightened no longer.

'I'm sorry,' she said, 'I was bringing down my things.'

He put the gun in his pocket.

'Ye put the heart across me,' he said, wiping his mouth on the back of his hand, 'with the row ye were kickin' up. I'll give ye a hand with the case as far as here, Miss, but I couldn't take it any farther, y'undherstand. Them's me ordhers, that I'm not to leave here.'

He brought the suitcase down the second flight and pushed it through the door into the hall; there was a light here and men were standing about and throwing straw over the carpet; Caroline put down the candle and half-pushed, half-dragged the heavy case towards the porch. Nobody offered to help her. She groped her way down the shallow steps and across the gravel in the mist, feeling with her feet for the grass edge; she could hear the maids gibbering in the bushes and the dog, still barking, evidently tied to a tree somewhere. She became aware of heavy breathing quite close to her but the mist and the shadow of the house made it impossible to see anything; she put out a hand and it touched something soft and warm; there was a frenzied snort and, plunging and rearing, a group of horses clattered off under the trees. She fell forward and her coat and suitcase went flying through the darkness. Terrified and hurt, she began to cry silently, creeping about on the grass, looking for her things; she found her coat and put it on; abandoning the suitcase, she wiped her eyes on her sleeve and made her way back to the faint block of light that was the hall door.

As she reached it, there was a snarling, rushing sound behind her and Otto, the Great Dane, shot past her into the house; he went straight for the men in the hall and there were shouts of 'Oah, my God!' and 'Shoot that bloody dog.' He had one man down on the floor, a writhing mass of arms and legs and stifled cries; somebody drew a revolver and shot. There was a roar of pain: the man was hit and the dog unhurt. Another shot and silence; Otto fell over and lay on his side, blood pouring from a huge hole in his chest, the pleading eyes still open in pained surprise.

Moira and Archie came running out from the drawing-room; the man began to groan.

'Oh, I'm kilt,' he said, 'I'm kilt.'

He had been shot in the leg; they propped him up against a chair and told him he was all right. Caroline was seized with sudden nausea: doubled up and retching, she stumbled out to the porch and was sick down the grass bank of the area. The cold air made her feel better and she went back into the house. Moira had disappeared and the men were accusing Archie of having set the dog on them. He lost his temper.

'Don't you think I've enough to do without giving you an excuse to shoot my dog?' he blazed.

'Well, how are we to get this fella away, will ye tell me that? Don't ye know it's a damned awkward thing havin' a wounded man on a job like this?'

'Oh, for God's sake,' cried Archie in exasperation, 'take the wheel-barrow out of the tool-shed and wheel him down to the car. Surely to goodness you have a car on the avenue? And I hope he dies on you!' he muttered to himself as he hurried off to fetch more papers from his study.

A man was sent off to fetch the barrow; the rest were bending over the injured man, who was still groaning and looking round him with a dazed expression. Averting her head so that she would not have to see the dead dog and the pool of blood, Caroline went up to them.

'Where's Mrs. Butler?' she asked boldly.

A man looked up and stared at her between the slitty eye-holes of his mask; he jerked his head towards the drawing-room and made no answer. Caroline went to the door and looked in.

Watched over by a dreadfully embarrassed youth, Moira was collecting her Persian rugs in a little heap on the floor; she was trying to pull one out from under the piano-leg.

'Wait, Ma'am, I'll give ye a hand with that.'

The raider bent down to extricate it, revealing as he did so the back of a head of flaming red hair. Moira's mouth opened and she gazed at him in fascinated horror; as he stood up to hand her the rug, she snatched it from him and shook it in his face.

'Mickey Cavanagh,' she gasped, 'may God forgive you! If your mother knew what you were up to tonight, it would kill her. I thought you had enough decent feeling not to come burning people out of their houses that have known you since you could crawl and employed you as soon as you could walk.'

There was a terrible silent pause and she saw that he was weeping; his great shoulders shook and the tears rolled down his face beneath the black mask.

'Oh, Ma'am,' he sobbed, 'I swear to ye before God and all the blessed Saints it was only with a revolver stuck in me ribs they got me here tonight. I wouldn't do it, Ma'am, and they said they'd shoot me; they said they must have someone who knew the place and the house, so what could I do, only come along?'

Moira shook her head hopelessly.

'Listen to me, Mickey,' she said in a strange little dry voice, her eyes very bright, 'if ever you get the chance to clear out and go to America, take it and start to live a decent life again; and take your mother with you.'

She bent down, shouldered the bundle of rugs and turned to leave the room; she caught sight of Caroline hovering in the doorway:

'Darling, try and get out some of the dining-room chairs; I'll come and help when I've dumped these.'

They were carrying out the last of the chairs when a man came blustering in from the hall.

'What's going on here? Come on, Lady, yer time's up.'

There was a smell of petrol; the hall lamp had been put out and the men were working with torches, throwing petrol all over the place.

'Out of the house, now, out of the house. Have ye all the people out?'

Archie appeared. 'Yes,' he said in a dead voice; he led them across the gravel to the lawn, which was littered with an extraordinary collection of things; silver glittered in the light of his torch, chairs had been thrown down anyhow, pictures lay about on the grass.

'Better move these things further away; the heat will be very severe.' They lifted the things down over the sunken fence. They could hear windows being thrown open in the house to give the fire a chance to take hold; men came running out of the hall door. There was a sudden flash and the last man, he who had been left to start the fire by throwing in a lighted wad of stuff, came down the steps as though the Devil were after him.

'God,' he exclaimed, coughing, 'there's enough pethrol in there to burn the city of Cork!'

They waited to see the fire well started, fidgeting, anxious to be off. The wheel-barrow with the injured man creaked down the avenue. The whole of the ground floor lit up, flames climbing up the curtains and licking at the window frames. Somebody must have driven the horses up towards the house for there was a sudden thundering stampede and they charged past the burning building in a mad gallop, over the grass, into the darkness and away down the back avenue until the pounding of their hoofs became a vibration in the distance.

There was a high-pitched 'Oah!' from the maids, crouching in the bushes. Moira went over and fetched them, each clutching her little bundle of possessions; they all stood in the dry ditch, leaning up against the wall of the ha-ha, waiting for the men to go.

'Oah!' gasped the maids again as flame spouted from the windows and the crackling became a roar. Archie bent his head and would not watch; he had the stricken look of a man who discovers that all he has lived for has been taken away from him. Moira took his arm and squeezed it gently; he turned and smiled at her and for a moment the lost expression dropped from his face.

'Thank God,' he said quietly, 'none of our own men were mixed up in this: that would have been . . .' and he shook his head.

She dropped his arm and glanced at Caroline. 'Yes,' she murmured, shutting her eyes, for she could not keep up the lie and face Caroline's unwavering stare. 'I think we'd better go to the O'Hara's until morning,' she added quickly; 'do you think the car will be all right?'

'The tyres'll be flat—they always do that; by the way, where's Ryan?'

She put her hands up to her face in sudden horror: 'Oh, Archie, I'd forgotten all about him and Mrs. Ryan!'

The men and the mist had melted away together; from the distance came the sound of a Ford engine being started; Archie threw out a hand in the direction of the avenue.

'They've gone,' he said, and sighed. 'I'll go and see what's been happening in the yard; you wait here.'

He climbed the fence and disappeared into the bushes.

Caroline stood with her chin resting on the grass above the fence; the whole world was roaring, glaring red, with turbulent pillars of black smoke thrusting far into the sky; the smoke caught the reflection of the blaze and it looked as if the air itself were on fire. The upper storey was alight now and there was a tremendous rending crash as a floor gave way and all the contents of a room went hurtling into the conflagration below; she ducked involuntarily and Moira came close and drew her to her.

'Poor darling,' she said, and kissed her; 'I wish we had something to eat; how silly of me not to have thought of that!'

'Why didn't you want Uncle Archie to know?'

'Because he need never know and it would have broken his heart,' broke in Moira quickly; 'he's got enough to bear without that, so you won't say a word, will you?'

Caroline shook her head, fingering one of her Aunt's long dark plaits. Moira's hands flew to her head.

'Oh, my hair,' she wailed, 'and I've no hairpins!'

She began to wind the plaits round her head, trying to tie them together so that they would stay up.

Brigid, the cook, came slowly forward: 'I have one I can spare ye, Ma'am, if ye wouldn't have any objection to it comin' outa me own head, like.'

She plucked a huge black hairpin from her hair and wiped it on the bosom of her coat; Moira took it gratefully.

Archie reappeared and his face was grim.

'They'd tied the Ryans to their beds, both of them,' he said, 'and told them they could burn with the stables; it can only have been a joke as there isn't a trace of fire there. I cut them loose and we went to have a look at the car; they've let the air out of the tyres and I must go back and help him to jack it up. Mrs. Ryan's making some tea, so you'd all better come along.'

The heat seemed to rush at them as they clambered up the fence; the smoke billowed upwards like an escaping monster; sparks lit upon the branches of the trees and fell among the dead leaves to smoulder and start little separate fires that ran along the ground.

They began to run; panting, they reached the yard; there was a dim light in the little house at the end; a wizened little woman with grey locks hanging round her shoulders rushed out and caught Moira by the hand: sobbing, she drew her into the little kitchen.

'Oh, Ma'am,' she said, 'that's a terrible night's work!'

The table was set; there was a loaf of soda-bread and a pound of butter; a big brown tea-pot stood at one side of the tiny range.

'How clever of you, Mrs. Ryan, to have enough cups,' said Moira cheerfully. Mrs. Ryan wiped her eyes on her voluminous black skirt.

'I do have them for the brother's family, Ma'am,' she wept; 'when they do all come over there does be a big crowd. Oah!' she screamed, as the whole house shook with the vibration of a hideous crumbling roar.

'It's all right; that'll be the roof falling in,' said Moira in a slightly shaking voice.

The tea was very black and hot; they stirred sugar into it by the spoonful and sipped it gratefully, sitting two to a chair and eating great slices of thickly buttered bread. Afterwards, Caroline slept a little, head bent over her arms on the table.

'Arrah!' said Brigid, 'look at the poor little thing and she dhrunk with the sleep.' They lifted her on to the settle where she dozed again, her eyes closed, but retaining enough consciousness to know what was going on.

Archie came in, wiping his hands on a piece of rag.

'We've brought all the stuff into the stables,' he said; 'the car's ready and loaded with our clothes and somebody's suitcase, I imagine it's Caroline's. We might as well go now; Ryan wants to come with us.'

Caroline sat up; Mrs. Ryan looked as though she might break down again; Moira turned to the maids:

'I want you all to stay here tonight with Mrs. Ryan; tomorrow you had better go back to your homes; the master will give you some money in the morning. I'm afraid,' she added, shaking her head sadly, 'you'll all have to look out for new places. Goodbye. Goodbye, Mrs. Ryan, and thank you.'

They began to weep, standing in a little line against the wall; Brigid, the cook, stepped forward, the tears streaming down her heavy old cheeks.

'Oh, take me with ye, Ma'am; I've been with ye sixtheen years and ye're a lovely Misthress. I . . . I'd even go t'England with ye, Ma'am.'

Moira was deeply moved; she found it hard to control her voice as she wrung Brigid's fat hand and said:

'Bless you, Brigid! It will have to be England, I'm afraid; I'll write to you as soon as I know where I am.'

'Goodbye, Ma'am, and God bless ye!'

'Goodbye!' Moira bent her head and, seizing Caroline by the hand, rushed out into the yard; she bundled Caroline into the back of the car and got in beside her; Archie was already in the driver's seat, with Ryan next to him. They rattled out of the yard and down the drive; half-way, where there was a gap in the trees, Archie stopped the car and, as though it had been agreed between them, in one movement they all turned back to look at the burning house. The moon had set now; in the midst of darkness the house stood in an aura of rosy light; the turmoil of smoke had subsided and the walls glowed like living coals, throwing a red glare far into the sky.

Appalled by the beauty of it, no one spoke a word. Archie let in the clutch and they drove on.

CHAPTER TWO

Caroline's tawny curls bobbed up and down as she sat bolt upright beside Moira in a frowsy Dublin cab, staring out at the darkening river with wide grey eyes; she was dead tired but the dingy upholstery was so evil-smelling that she could not bring herself to lie back against it and relax. The perpetual muttering song of the train still dinned in her ears. It had been a long and tiresome journey with many delays and some uncertainty about reaching Dublin at all, for the Sinn Feiners had been busy on the line and broken it in several places. Their train was the first to crawl over a bridge that had been blown up a day or two before and she recalled with a little shiver the signs of relief and the burst of pleased conversation in the carriage when they had passed over it safely.

'Praise be to God,' the commercial traveller had burst out, 'I never thought she'd do it!' and he had gone on to tell them a hair-raising tale of how the village where his old mother lived had been burnt by the Black and Tans and of the campaign of burning and murder that these men were spreading round the countryside.

'Aunt Moira?'

'Mm?' Her aunt's voice was weak from fatigue.

'Why do the Sinn Feiners hate us?'

'Oh, my darling!' Moira sat up, startled.

'But why do they? We've done nothing to them, have we?'

'No, of course we haven't.'

'Well, why did they have to burn Butler's Hill?'

Moira stretched out her tired legs and fearfully considered how she should reply; on her answer might depend the life-long attitude of this child towards the country of her birth and those who ruled it; at all costs she must not be sent out on her journey through the troubled years to come with bitterness in her heart, for before very long there would be a new government in Ireland and people would have to take their choice of loyalties. Only those, she felt sure, who could regard the changing world around them with clear eyes could hope for health and happiness in the new Ireland that would emerge from the present fire and turmoil.

'It's a long story,' she began, 'and in Ireland we have long memories. The English first came here seven hundred years ago, but they couldn't conquer the whole country and they settled on the eastern fringe; those were the Normans and the Butlers are descended from them. There were always attempts to put them out, but some of them became Irish and fought against the English. Terrible things happened in Tudor times; conquest was the spirit of that age and because the Irish had their own ancient and different way of doing things, the Tudors saw them as primitive savages who must be made modern by colonisation. Later on, the Irish were loyal to the Stuarts and Cromwell marched through the country, burning and killing; he paid his soldiers off with Irish land, where they settled down, and their descendants are still here, now more than half-Irish themselves, for they married Irish women and many of them changed their religion. When the Stuarts had gone, King William had to come with his armies and batter them into subjection again; they hated the Protestant English, who would not let them keep their own religion or live on their own land, and they've hated them ever since. There have always been Irishmen working to get the English out of the country, raising rebellions that were never quite big enough to be successful; but all through, from the very beginning, there have been Protestant descendants of these English who have seen the injustice of the way the Irish were treated and who have worked with them and for them; some of them held land in their own names for Roman Catholic neighbours, as a trust, because those people were not allowed to own it. I've only touched on the very edge of the question, but that will give you a rough idea of why the English are hated here. The Penal Laws against the Roman Catholics were only repealed less than a century ago; such laws sound appalling to us now, as indeed they were, but tolerance is a modern virtue and, if you think of it, the same laws were applied against the Protestants in France. Up to about a hundred years ago, history everywhere was conquest, war and oppression and Ireland got more than her share of it.'

'Yes, but we aren't English: why did they have to come and burn Butler's Hill?'

Moira sighed; she saw that she was going to get no respite.

'Well,' she went on, 'while the War was on, the Irish thought it was a good moment for another rebellion: they thought the British were so busy fighting the Germans that they wouldn't have time to bother about this country. However, the rebellion was suppressed: you might just remember it—Easter 1916. After that, the Irish started raiding houses for arms and trying to build up a proper army; then the police went and took everybody's arms away, so that the Sinn Feiners shouldn't get them, but they managed to get a good many from various sources—some even from outside the country, and now they're fighting the British again, trying to root out every vestige of British rule. That's why they're shooting policemen and burning their barracks: those policemen are British servants. Then, as you know, the Black and Tans came; that was the most terrible mistake the British ever made—they started the reprisal system. If the Sinn Feiners kill a policeman or ambush some troops, the Black and Tans burn down the nearest village, but there's no justice in that because nine times out of ten the men who did it came from some other part of the country; and in revenge for the burning of the village the Sinn Feiners go and burn down one of the big houses where the descendants of the early invaders are still living; that's why they came to Butler's Hill. And because the police had taken away all our arms, we were absolutely helpless.'

Moira paused, exhausted, and glanced at the small profile set in its halo of dancing curls. 'Well, *I* think,' said Caroline with conviction, 'the Sinn Feiners are quite right.'

Moira quailed; she thought of her sister Helen, Caroline's mother, and her loathing of the Nationalists. She would never be forgiven if she had turned the child into a rebel!

'There's a lot of right on both sides,' she said; 'you're only nine, Caroline, and there are many things you'll understand later on, when you've learnt more about the whole story. For many years the British have honestly tried to do their best with Ireland, but it was too late, neither side could trust the other and there were terrible mistakes.'

'If I was grown-up, I'd fight against the British.' Caroline's head was high, her mouth set in a firm little line.

'We're just the people the Sinn Feiners want to get rid of, darling,' said Moira quietly; 'they don't want us here.'

The cab swung round the corner from Baggot Street and up into Fitzwilliam Square; they were almost there. The driver was crawling now, peering at the numbers on the doors; he stopped and climbed down stiffly; at the same moment, light shone out on the pavement and a voice called:

'Come in, come in, my dears; we thought you were never coming.'

Caroline was home. Her mother caught her and kissed her almost fiercely.

'My darling child!' She squeezed her so tightly that Caroline could hardly breathe; then she turned to kiss her sister.

'My dear, you look *awful!* Leave those things and come up and have some tea, there's a roaring fire upstairs for you. Caroline, Miss O'Connor's kept some tea for you in the schoolroom. Aunt Moira and I will have a lot to talk about. And what about bed when you've had something to eat?'

The indignity of being sent to bed early could not be endured without protest.

'Oh, please no, Mummy.'

'Yes, I think so; run along, like a good child.'

'Hallo!' said a voice from the stairs and Caroline's elder sister, Isabel, came dancing down to greet them; she stared at them in awe, rather as if they were dead people come back to life. She was strikingly different from Caroline, with dark hair flowing out behind her like a mane and rich dark eyes that shone with vitality.

'Oh, Isabel darling, kiss me,' said Moira.

Isabel threw her arms round her aunt's neck in a tight hug.

They went slowly up to the drawing-room; Helen Adair paused in the doorway:

'Now, run along upstairs, children,' she said, and firmly closed the door.

Isabel flew up the stairs, dragging Caroline behind her; in the schoolroom at the top of the house, their governess, Miss O'Connor, was sitting by the fire.

'They've come, Miss O'Connor, and Caroline saved her suitcase!'

Miss O'Connor took no notice of Isabel; she rose from her seat and gathered Caroline in her arms:

'My poor little darling Caroline,' she was saying; and Caroline, unaccountably, had begun to cry.

The big drawing-room was the best feature of the house; on the first floor, its three long windows faced the Square while on the other side massive double doors opened into a room nearly as large which looked over a tiny town garden. On occasions when the doors were opened the two rooms became one, making a magnificent L-shaped expanse, perfect for a reception. The days of great entertaining in Dublin were over but Mrs. Adair was proud of her fine Georgian room with its panelled walls and lovely ceiling, the Italian fireplace of carved white marble and the Waterford glass chandelier which, dusty though it was, could still throw out a glory of opalescent fire from its thousand drops.

The walls were grey-green and white; the pelmetted curtains, accentuating the height of the room, of heavy old-gold brocade; everything in the room was plain except the mellowed Asiatic carpet which glowed with rich and patterned colour. Some superb pieces of Waterford and Cork glass stood alone upon the mantelshelf, jealously kept apart from even the Dresden china, which was relegated to the cabinet in the corner.

Helen led her sister to a big chair at the fireplace and, while the maid brought fresh tea, she tried to shut out the gloom of the November evening by drawing the curtains and heaping yet more logs upon the blazing fire. Her hair was dark, like Moira's, but here the resemblance ended; whereas Moira possessed that colouring which is called Irish, with deep blue eyes and a fair skin, Helen's eyes were brown with a curious burning quality, which, combined with the acute thinness of her body and an expression of bitter determination, gave her the look of a fanatic; she was the taller and looked the elder, although in fact she was three years younger than Moira. She dressed badly, in shapeless tweeds and coarse grey stockings; she wore a necklace of real pearls with her badly-knitted jumper, and her straight hair, rapidly greying, was pinned unbecomingly at the back of her head.

The maid had gone and the door was shut; Moira looked up and said: 'When did you get my wire?'

'Only just after lunch today; you poor things, we're all so dreadfully sorry for you; do you feel able to talk about it now, or would you rather wait until Guy comes back and you've had a rest? He won't be in till fairly late, I'm afraid, there's an architects' conference on and he was to meet some Englishman after it and take him to the Club.'

'I think I'd better tell you about it now; you can tell Guy yourself, later on. It was all so dreadful, such appalling, terrible unnecessary *waste*. Think of that lovely house . . .'

'Oh, my dear, don't!'

Already Moira had lost count of the times she had had to relate her story; it was becoming a kind of set narrative, rather like a recitation, which she could tell now, almost without feeling, as though it had happened to somebody else in another age.

When she had finished, there was a pause; Helen leant forward and dug savagely at the glowing embers, vengeance in her action:

'And they got away?'

'Of course they got away: what could we do, six miles from anywhere? We had no telephone and even if we had had, they would have cut the wires. Archie went in to report it in the morning and old Ryan went with him; they had to go a long way as the barracks at Ballinsaggart were burnt down last week. Now, heaven only knows what the Black and Tans will do as a reprisal!'

'I hope they catch them and burn them. Shooting's too good for the Sinn Feiners!'

Moira looked away, shocked by the bitterness in her sister's voice; even she, who had suffered so much, could not feel hatred like that; she wondered, as she gazed into the fire, whether it was because she was so tired that she could not hate, or whether she had a weaker character than Helen's.

'Were any of your own men with them?'

Moira hesitated for a split second. 'No,' she said, firmly.

Helen's piercing eyes were fixed on her face.

'You're telling me a lie,' she snapped.

Moira did not answer; she spread jam carefully over a piece of wafer-thin bread and butter and made a tiny sandwich.

'Isn't it just like them,' Helen went on, 'to bite the hand that fed them! No one could have been a better landlord than Archie, and they must turn on him like this. For sheer treachery. . .'

'There was only one,' broke in Moira quietly, 'a young lad from the farm and he was forced into it against his will. I spoke to him and he told me they were going to shoot him if he didn't come; he was crying, Helen, so what could I say?'

'Crying indeed. Crocodile's tears, my dear! They've no tears left, these people; they'd betray their own mothers if they thought they had the faintest sympathy with any Unionist. Well, let's hope the Black and Tans have dealt with him by now.' She paused and looked at Moira with sudden suspicion: 'Of course Archie reported him?' she queried.

'Archie doesn't know about it and he's not going to: it would break his heart. And I'm not going to report him.' Moira faced her sister boldly.

Helen peered at her as if she feared for her reason:

'You're not . . . ?' she gasped; 'but you must be mad!'

'Oh, Helen, don't let us have an argument; listen, this is the way I see it: what good could possibly come of reporting it? That boy'll be on the run anyway, now, and they'd never catch him; if we informed on him, somebody'd get shot for it, probably Archie, and it isn't as if it would stop there; there'd be reprisals and shootings, ambushes and burnings, an eye for an eye and a tooth for a tooth, long after everybody'd forgotten the cause of all the trouble. And where would the boy be all the time? Out on the mountains, as wild as a hare and as free as the birds.'

Helen laughed bitterly. 'Perhaps it means nothing to you, my dear—after all you're leaving the country in a day or two—that you're leaving a dangerous criminal at large without lifting a finger to stop him doing more damage, but it means a lot to me. I've got to go on living here. Why, you must be devoid of moral sense to keep quiet about a thing like that; it's your plain duty to report him.'

'But don't you see, Helen, he's not a criminal; he's an unfortunate youth who was forced into it at the end of a revolver; if he's on the run he can do no harm anyway, whereas if he gets caught by the

Black and Tans and survives it, which is unlikely, he'll be a confirmed Republican for life.'

Helen shrugged her shoulders. 'You're behaving just like a Sinn Feiner yourself,' she said, her eyes blazing and her face very flushed. 'If the day comes when the British walk out of this country, and please God it never will, you'll only have yourself to thank and others like you.'

Moira leant back in her chair and regarded her sister calmly.

'Don't deceive yourself, Helen,' she said quietly; 'that day is coming very soon; your children will grow up hardly able to remember what it was like when the British were here.'

Helen shrank back as though a bitter blast of wind had come to shrivel her up.

'Don't talk like that,' she almost screamed; 'they couldn't leave us at the mercy of these people, it's not possible!' The hand that held her cup was shaking and she had to rest it on the table. 'The British would exterminate the Irish, after what's happening now, rather than leave us in their power. Think of the loyalty of the Unionists and of our sons and husbands and brothers, killed in the War! We gave them everything we had then and they can never forget that.' Her voice was confident again. 'I've brought the children up to loathe everything to do with Sinn Fein and the National Movement and they've been taught to hate and despise every one of these traitors who would burn the lot of us tomorrow, if they could.'

Moira thought of Caroline in the cab and almost smiled, but she felt very close to tears. 'Why teach them to hate, my dear, and turn them into exiles in their own land?' she said softly; 'in a few years it'll be we, Protestants and Unionists, who will be against the Government.' She went on, as if she were speaking in a dream: 'We're fighting against something that is stronger than we are, stronger than the British and that you cannot fight with arms and men. The country is losing something today that it will not recover in a life-time or in a hundred years: I mean the happy relationship between gentry and people.

A loyalty that we have not understood and to which we could not subscribe has made us strangers to them in a night. The land has risen up and possessed the people and they have turned against us, whose loyalty is outside the land. So the country that we had foolishly come to think our own has rejected us for the people and there is no striving against it. We go back to an England that has lost all knowledge of us and that can never be our home, or we may remain, as aliens besieged, in a land that has lost its welcome. That is how I see it.'

There was a silence that became intolerable, frightening; Helen rose sharply to her feet:

'I must see to Caroline,' she said, and shivered.

CHAPTER THREE

The high red houses of Fitzwilliam Square were lit up by the westering sun; they glowed tranquilly in the warm light and upper windows threw back a fiery gleam. The roadway was almost empty; a flower woman hurried past, shawl clutched tightly to her and ill-fitting shoes click-clacking on the pavement; a blind man tapped his way home, his dog beside him, unalert; a cat darted from the shelter of some area railings and streaked, belly to ground, across the road; it reached the pathway, hesitated, looked back and was gone, a shadow among shadows. The dog bristled, growled and resumed his trot beside his master.

Inside the Square, the plane trees stood almost naked; only a few pale leaves still clung, limply hanging, to the branches, waiting for a breath of wind to dislodge them. On the ground there were leaves everywhere; they lay thickly on the paths and were strewn untidily over the great lawn. Children shuffled noisily along, scattering showers of gold as they went and their shouts rang out in the still air. Inside the dusty railings, evergreens, jaded after the long summer, showed grimy and dishevelled.

Nursemaids and governesses were stirring and calling to the children to come home to tea; perambulators were making for the gates; old gentlemen rose stiffly, nodded to the children and clanged the gates behind them; soon the place would be deserted, lights would spring up behind drawn blinds and the Square would be submerged in that translucent city twilight, so stringently blue that streets and houses seemed to belong to a motionless submarine world of dark shapes and blue light.

'Can't we go home now?' Isabel sat down on the seat beside Miss O'Connor and kicked the gravel until there was a little bare patch under her feet.

'Yes, dear; where's Caroline?'

'Oh, somewhere. Why won't Mummy let us play with the Joyces, Miss O'Connor? All the other children do and it means we can't play with anybody.'

Miss O'Connor's short-sighted eyes were scanning the Square through her thick glasses: 'It's your mother's wish, dear; she has her own reasons.'

'But they're nice.'

'Go and find Caroline, dear, and we'll go in; your mother wishes you to go down to the drawing-room after tea.'

'Oh, all those awful people: I hate relations.'

'Ssh!' But the old governess gave her a sympathetic little smile.

Isabel went off, truculently, to look for Caroline and it was some minutes before they reappeared; Caroline came spinning across the lawn like a skater, arms out and hair flying, to collapse on the grass in sudden giddiness, laughing among the golden leaves; Isabel caught her hands and they swung round again, feet pivoting together, only to fall again in helpless exhaustion.

'Now what have you two been up to, over there in the bushes?' asked Miss O'Connor gently.

Isabel grimaced: 'Talking to Denis Joyce,' and she smiled rebelliously; 'we couldn't help it, he came up and spoke to us; it wasn't our fault, really it wasn't.'

Miss O'Connor shook her head: 'We'll just have to give up coming to the square, that's all; it's a great pity, but your mother's wishes must be obeyed.' She took the key out of her bag and they walked silently across to the house.

Hair brushed and wearing their blue velveteen frocks, the children crept down the stairs to the drawing-room; they could hear the buzz of conversation outside; giggling a little, they straightened their long black stockings, composed their faces and went in.

Their father came over to the door to meet them; he was a broadly-built man of medium height with a magnificent head; his hair, once the same colour as Caroline's, was grey and he wore it rather long; heavy eyebrows accentuated the brilliance of his blue eyes; his face, with its firm mouth and dominant chin, had a look of culture and intelligence.

He put an arm round each of his daughters: 'I was nearly coming up to look for you,' he said smiling.

'Ah, the dear children, how quickly they grow, Helen!' came a voice from the end of the room; 'Caroline, come here, child, and let me see that you're none the worse for your experience.'

Obediently, Caroline went and stood before her elderly cousin, Catha O'Brien; she was a stocky woman, always dressed in black, with iron-grey hair drawn uncompromisingly back; her face was pink and flushed easily and she was sitting bolt upright on the sofa; she extended a well-padded cheek and caught Caroline's hand in her heavily-ringed grasp:

'No bad effects, child?'

'No thank you, Cousin Catha.'

'That's right, show these people they can't frighten us, that's what I always say, Helen. How very like poor dear Frances the child is growing! Of course, it doesn't follow that she'll be subject to the same delicacy—so very tragic, wasn't it? You don't see it? Quite extraordinary, the likeness is unmistakable! Alec!' She turned to her brother, but he did not hear her; he was listening to the woman beside him who was recounting in a rich brogue the latest of her adventures. She was Eileen Hunt, a lively widow of about fifty with dark blue eyes and a charming spirited face, who, in her youth, had been the despair and inspiration of half the men in County Clare.

'There I was, Alec,' she was saying, 'standing in the hall with not a stitch on me but me shimmy-shirt and two men between me and me bedroom!' Catha's eyes opened wide; one never knew what Eileen would say next and there was Alec, gazing at her like a schoolboy and looking as if he would like to propose to her again that very moment; and now everybody had stopped talking to listen. 'So what d'you think I did? 'Right about turn,' I says, 'faces to the wall, there's good men; ye have me retreat cut off and here I am, dancing about in me nightie until ye let me past.' And the decent creatures turned about like clockwork, hands across their eyes as though they were warding off the plague, while I stepped past them, as bold as brass, into me bedroom! 'Ma'am,' said one of them, 'if you was as naked as the day God made ye, we couldn't take advantage of ye, and you in such disthress! Oh, you've no idea what we go through in our flats, you people who live comfortably in houses!"

There was general laughter; even Moira looked up and smiled; she had been cornered at a chilly distance from the fire by a clergyman who looked like a shabby old bird of prey; bald head cocked enquiringly and watery eyes fixed hungrily on her face, he had been listening to her story, wagging his head mournfully and emitting distressful sounds.

'I must go.' Eileen rose abruptly. 'Goodbye, my dear, I've enjoyed meself,' she said to Helen. Alec O'Brien was still chuckling with an expression on his face of mingled enjoyment and regret. Eileen tapped Catha on the shoulder:

'Don't grudge him a good laugh,' she said; 'sure, didn't he cut his teeth on me and the Morgan girls thirty years ago—I wouldn't take him from you now.'

'Eileen!' Catha blushed hotly and tried to look bewildered, horrified that her thoughts should have been so apparent; but she smiled as the widow kissed her affectionately on the cheek and passed on to take both Moira's hands in hers.

'I haven't had a chance to speak to you, my dear; come and lunch with me tomorrow at the flat? Good.'

The old clergyman loomed up to say goodbye:

'A sad business, a sad business,' he repeated gloomily, wagging his head dejectedly and shaking Moira's hand again and again.

Soon they had all gone; the family hurried back to the warmth of the drawing-room; Moira sat on the long low fender-stool and spread out her hands to the fire.

'What an old ghoul old Canon Cooper is,' she said with amusement; 'really, Helen, it was all I could do not to giggle as I watched his head shaking—it never seemed to stop! Catha's exactly the same, and will be till she dies. She'll be keeping an eye on Alec now for weeks; he shouldn't let her see how smitten he still is. Eileen's a darling, isn't she? She doesn't sound very well off—I wonder if that wild husband of hers gambled all the family fortunes away, they used to be rich people.'

'She's as poor as a church mouse now, but she seems to enjoy it,' said Helen.

'Oh, I really am perished,' and Moira shivered. 'I had a letter from Archie by the afternoon post: he's coming up tomorrow and will stay here for the night, if you can have us both, and then we'll cross over the next night.'

'Of course he must come here, my dear, and don't hurry away.'

'We've got to go somewhere, some time, and I feel that the sooner we get on to our feet again, the better.'

Guy smiled down at her: 'What an awful problem, having to decide where you'll live when you have the whole world to choose from! Do you think you could ever come back—rebuild Butler's Hill and settle down there again when things have become quieter?'

'Oh, I don't think so, Guy; it isn't as if we had children to leave it to; there's only young David Butler, Archie's nephew, you know, and he's not sixteen yet; it's impossible to know if he'd even want to live there . . . and yet, it seems so dreadful to let a lovely place like that go to pieces; I know Archie'd be miserable anywhere else.' Suddenly she turned to Caroline: 'Caroline, you've seen Butler's Hill as it was and as it now is, in ruins: if you were Uncle Archie and me, would you ever want to go back?'

Caroline meditated; Butler's Hill rose before her, burning to the skies, the rolling column of smoke belching up to reflect the glare of the flames; the sickening reek of petrol, the gun-men who watched it burn, the lawn littered with silver and pictures. But that vision faded and in its place she saw the chestnut trees which stood around the house, tangled in winter, resplendent in summer; the rhododendrons glowing with crimson and purple in the spring; the soft green lawns, fir trees silhouetted against the moonlit sky, and the sea, satin-grey and faintly rippled in the dip of the gorse-covered hill. She heard the wild swans clanging overhead and the perpetual murmur of the waves against the rocks; she saw the radiant opalescent light of winter mornings, cool and soft, as the sun withdrew the enfolding mist from earth and trees; she could smell the buttery scent of the gorse on warm summer days and the salty whiff of the sea, the cool damp smell of newly ploughed earth. She felt exalted, triumphant, in a sudden realisation, independent of time and space, people and ownership, that she possessed a passion for the land itself.

Smiling, exulting, she looked up at the surrounding faces.

'I'd have to go back,' she said.

They were all looking at her; Guy with surprise and interest, Helen with dismay. Moira leant over and kissed her. Guy spoke first:

'God forbid that she's going to turn into an Irish patriot! She's got that look in her eye already; how old are you, Caroline?'

'Nine.'

'Nine,' repeated Moira, smiling, 'and I believe the child's right, Guy; we've been here so long that we do belong to this country and it supplies us with something that we really need to keep ourselves alive. And they want to thrust us out as foreigners! I wish I knew which was right—of course we both are, but if there was room for us both there wouldn't be all this trouble now. Don't you feel, though, that we represent something they might be the poorer for losing—a sort of oasis of culture, a little reserve of leisure? They might at least have a kind of Unionists' National Park where we could live unmolested in our natural surroundings . . . I hate to think of our lawns being turned into potato patches and our houses into lunatic asylums.'

They all laughed and Guy said:

'Perhaps the North will supply what you want?' There was a gleam of malice in his eye.

Moira snorted: 'The North! don't talk to me about the North; I'd rather live in England.'

Doran, the old parlour-maid, had appeared at the door, a salver in her hand.

'A telegram,' said Helen, 'how I hate telegrams! Who's it for, Doran?'

'Mrs. Butler, Ma'am.'

Moira tore open the envelope quickly: Archie had been delayed, he would not be in Dublin for a few days; there was no explanation.

Moira had become very quiet; she handed the telegram to Helen and went up slowly to get ready for dinner.

The next morning she slipped downstairs before the rest of the family to examine the post: nothing for her. She opened the paper and glanced through it: more burnings, another ambush; then she gave an exclamation of horror and sat down suddenly: old Ryan, their yard-man at Butler's Hill, had been shot by the Sinn Feiners as an informer. So he must have seen the Cavanagh boy or recognised one of the men! She saw now how it all fitted in; she had wondered why he had been so anxious to go with Archie to the barracks when he went to report the fire; he was not going to tell Archie what he had seen and expose him to danger; he was going to do it himself and now he had paid the price. Her eyes filled with tears as she thought of the faithful old man. And what would happen now? She groaned: the Black and Tans would come roaring through the countryside in their lorries, shooting and kidnapping people who were quite unconnected with the crime; then there would be more vengeance: would Archie be the next to suffer? She sat back in her chair and stared wild-eyed at Doran who was bringing in the porridge. Doran put down her tray and scurried upstairs to tell Helen that Mrs. Butler had been taken ill in the dining-room.

All that day the house seemed to be full of secrets; tongues clicked and heads shook; wherever Caroline encountered her mother she found her in low-voiced conversation with Moira; once or twice Miss O'Connor was called into confabulation, but she would say nothing to enlighten the children. Finally, Caroline, as her habit was, secured the newspaper. 'Riddled with bullets', she read and the phrase haunted her all day; Ryan had taught her to ride the fat pony at Butler's Hill and to row a boat; she could not rid her mind of the picture of his dead body by the roadside, steeped in blood. 'Riddled with bullets' gripped her even when she slept and a nightmare awakened her, sobbing and shivering, her bed-clothes in knots around her. Isabel heard her and, feeling frightened herself, told her harshly to shut up. Caroline turned over and lay sweating until she fell again into a feverish, disturbed sleep.

Monday's newspaper brought tales of shootings and ambushes; roads had been trenched, a bridge blown up, a lorry of Black and Tans attacked and two policemen shot at.

Three days later, Archie came; he drove up in a cab just as the Adairs were sitting down to a late tea. Moira was at the window before the others had heard a sound.

'It's Archie!' she said, and sped down the stairs to open the door; a moment later she was in his arms.

'Oh, my darling, are you all right?' There were tears in her voice.

The astonished cabman placed a suitcase in the hall, gave Archie a knowing wink and hastily departed.

'I'm all right, my love,' and he kissed her tenderly, 'but I think we might be wise to catch the mail-boat in the morning.'

'I . . . I thought I should never see you again!' Moira smiled helplessly at him, tears streaming down her cheeks.

'I knew I should get back to you—I had to; you and I are all we have left for each other,' he said softly, wiping the tears from her face. Arm in arm, they went slowly up the stairs.

As soon as their schoolroom tea was over, the children hurried down to the drawing-room; they could hear their uncle's voice, but the moment they opened the door all conversation ceased and Helen said in a tone of forced brightness:

'Ah, here come the children!'

'Good!' said Archie; 'now we can talk about something nice.'

Long legs stretched out before him, he sat in an easy chair by the fire. He was a tall, thin man with a narrow face and highly-arched eyebrows; there was in his expression and the mildness of his grey eye a pleasant charm typical of the Irish country gentleman; slightly indolent, humorously procrastinating and lacking something in his make-up of force and energy, he was, partly in spite of, partly because of these characteristics, a delightful companion, easy to be with, difficult to offend and always ready to talk.

'Well, Caroline,' he went on, 'you're looking very fit on your adventures. Good gracious me, Helen, Isabel's going to be grown-up in about five minutes! Why, when you were with us in the summer she was only a little girl.'

Isabel was indeed growing up; she was tall and well-formed and already her childish frock was becoming too tight for her developing figure; enchanted by this remark, she danced about smilingly before her uncle.

'I'm going to school soon,' she announced, 'and then I'm to go to Paris, and then I'll come out and Mummy'll give a dance for me, won't you, Mummy?'

'I never said anything so rash', Helen smiled indulgently; she was looking forward with tremendous pleasure to bringing out such an attractive creature as her elder daughter.

'Well, and when you've had your dance, what are you going to do then?' enquired Archie.

'Oh, I'll get married to one of the officers from the Castle and go and live in a big house and have lots more dances,' announced Isabel, without a trace of self-consciousness.

Archie sighed: 'By the time you come out, my dear, there won't be any officers at the Castle, at least of the kind you'd want to dance with, I'm afraid, and it doesn't look as if there'll be any big houses left either.' Suddenly his eyes twinkled: 'So what'll you do then?'

'Oh, I'll marry an Englishman; there are plenty of big houses in England.'

'Oh ho! she's going to have her dances, even if she has to travel for them; what a scheming little baggage you are, Isabel! So all you want is a good time and a big house, eh?'

Isabel grimaced prettily and her uncle turned to Caroline:

'And are you going to marry one of these unfortunate Englishmen for his money too, Caroline?'

'Oh no, not an Englishman,' said Caroline with distaste; 'what, and have to go and live in England?'

'This is interesting,' her uncle encouraged her; 'and why not an Englishman, Caroline?'

'I hate the English; they think we're quaint.'

'Don't be silly, Caroline,' corrected Helen; 'you hardly know any; lots of them are very nice.'

'Well,' Caroline pinioned her mother, 'you know when you say someone's very English you don't mean they're nice, do you?'

Helen bit her lip, annoyed by the general laughter. 'I . . . just mean they're different from us,' she said lamely.

'That woman who stayed with us for the Horse Show,' went on Caroline contemptuously, 'said she thought Doran was "love-ly",' and she mimicked the tone of voice.

'She wasn't a woman, she was a lady,' snapped Helen; 'Caroline, you're getting beyond yourself.'

'I'm afraid Caroline wins,' said Guy laughing; 'no one but an Englishwoman could call poor Doran lovely, even in their wildest moments!'

'Mummy,' said Isabel's voice from the window, 'that soldier's still there.'

'What soldier, darling?' Helen was glad of the diversion.

'His car broke down, while we were having tea, just outside the Joyces.'

'Guy, shouldn't we ask him in or try to help him in some way?'

'It's a wonder he hasn't been shot by now,' said Guy; 'shall we go and have a look at him, Archie, and see what we can do?'

Archie nodded: 'I think we'd be wise to proceed with caution—he might mistake our intentions: these chaps are all as nervous as cats, especially in the dark.'

Helen and Moira went to watch from one window, the children from another; they saw the two men approach the car slowly, stop and speak; a second later they sprang back and threw up their hands. Helen drew in her breath: 'Oh,' she whispered, 'I wish they hadn't gone!'

But there were sounds of laughter coming from the pavement now; in the light of the street-lamp they saw the soldier leave the car and stand talking to Guy and Archie, then the two men turned and walked back to the house.

'Decent little fellow,' said Archie as they came in, 'Cockney; relief car's coming for him any moment; he said the people in that house were very decent to him—Joyce did you say they were? they let him use the telephone and sent food out to him.'

'The Joyces!' Helen's face was a study. 'But they're the hottest Nationalists in Dublin!' She felt insanely angry that these people whom she was determined to dislike should have shown themselves kindly, forestalled her belated hospitality and usurped her privilege— that of helping a stranded British soldier.

'Sorry for a fellow who's down on his luck, that's all,' said Archie, regarding her with some amusement.

'Mummy,' said Isabel hopefully, 'can we play with the Joyces now?'

'Certainly not,' blazed Helen.

'But don't you feel differently about them now?'

'Not in the least, they're not our sort of people and I don't want you to know them; now don't bring the subject up again.'

'Well, we just can't go into the Square any more, then; everybody else plays with them and we aren't going to go and be made fools of.' Large tears brimmed on Isabel's dark lashes.

'Very well; don't play in the Square; go for walks instead.' Helen was not to be moved; she turned to Guy and said indignantly: 'I do think it's intolerable, Guy, that our children should be blackmailed out of the Square like that, don't you?'

He shrugged his shoulders: 'We can't have it every way,' he said; 'either we've got to keep ourselves to ourselves or we've got to mix with the rag-tag and bobtail with whom we're out of sympathy politically and religiously. After all, we are a minority, although that fact is only being forced on us slowly and painfully; as things are at present I see no advantage in cultivating the other side—there's too much bitterness about; when the country's settled down it may be different.'

So it was that Isabel and Caroline ceased almost entirely to enter Fitzwilliam Square.

CHAPTER FOUR

The Butlers left for England, and very dejected and forsaken they looked and felt as they drove off to catch the mail train; they left the country with a sense of guilt that the simple fact of their existence should have unloosed a campaign of violence and terror in the neighbourhood they had left, and a hopeless conviction that nothing would make it possible for them ever to return.

It was Sunday morning, the 21st of November, and the Adair family were sitting at breakfast, arguing about Church; Helen had a streaming cold and was not going out, but, she announced firmly, the children must go.

'Who'll come with me to Christ Church Cathedral?' said Guy.

'Not me,' Isabel made a face; 'it's too long.'

'Caroline?'

'All right.' The tawny curls bobbed up and down; it would be very long, but she liked going with her father.

'Caroline darling, run up and get me a clean handkerchief out of my drawer.' Helen pressed a wet rag to her nose.

Caroline left the room and started to run up the stairs; one always felt different on Sundays, she reflected, with clean clothes on, smelling of soap and the hot-air-press, and one's Sunday frock and best pair of shoes, rather too big; soon it would be time for Catechism with Miss O'Connor in the schoolroom, then a rush to get ready for Church and, when one returned, a delicious smell of roast meat permeating the house. Heavens, what was that? Shots, one after another, shattered the calm of the morning. Again! She ran to the window of her mother's room, which looked on to the square, but there was nothing to be seen, not a soul in the streets. She collected the handkerchief and turned-to run downstairs. More shots; no cry, not a shout, and another short burst of firing. She ran up another flight to the bedroom she shared with Isabel and leant out of the wide-open window; all was silent as the grave. Then, suddenly, came the sound of running feet; through the gap in the roofs she saw a little band of men pounding desperately along the lane behind the houses; the roofs hid them again and the clatter of their feet died away. Silence, so still that it frightened her, returned and she drew back into the room, trembling. Something awful must have happened: grown men did not flee like that unless they were running for their lives.

The bedroom was cold and empty-looking with bedclothes strewn over the chairs to air; Caroline felt an urgent need of human society; she hurried back to the dining-room. Everybody looked very subdued.

'What's happened?' she asked nervously; she knew nobody could tell her but she felt she must break the silence.

Helen sighed wearily. 'It may be nothing,' she said, feigning cheerfulness; 'let's hope so, anyway.'

'I saw men running down the lane,' said Caroline; she felt braver now that she was with other people.

'What!' her father almost snapped at her; 'is that really so, Caroline?'

'Yes, they were in an awful hurry and . . .'

'Look here,' her father interrupted her; 'that shooting may have been nothing, on the other hand it may have been something very serious and until I give you permission you are not to mention what you saw to anybody—to *anybody*, you understand?' His usually calm voice was sharp with anxiety and Caroline stared at him, too surprised to answer.

'Do you understand?' he repeated irritably.

'Yes, Daddy.'

He turned to Helen. 'We couldn't have the child called as a witness, that would be too much. Would you know any of them again, Caroline?'

'Oh no, they were much too far away, and besides I hardly saw them at all, the stables of the houses got in the way; I couldn't even see how many there were.'

'Thank God for that!' he said piously; 'the less you see of these things the healthier for you, and I think we may have clear consciences about not mentioning what you saw—it wouldn't be much use to anyone.' He sat back in his chair, immensely relieved.

Helen was sitting rigidly upright, her mouth closed in a tight little line. 'It sickens me,' she said bitterly, 'that we can't just live in peace and be left alone; we don't want to be dragged into this and we can't keep out of it: look at Moira and Archie, what have they done to deserve all their troubles?'

'This country's too small,' said Guy, 'for any of us to keep out of it; there simply isn't room and, God knows, we're all in it deep enough, whether we like it or not.'

When he and Caroline set out, the streets were deserted; they walked quickly down Dawson Street and towards College Green; here there seemed to be more activity; two or three little groups of men were talking anxiously, as though they were waiting for something to happen. There was an air of tense expectancy about and men looked behind them as they walked; no laughter, no voices raised in bantering good humour. As Caroline and her father came up, voices were stilled and the talkers observed them covertly, alert and uneasy. An army lorry droned and spluttered along Westmoreland Street and the little groups dissolved into innocent units of men leaning against the railings of the Bank of Ireland, crossing the street or walking harmlessly towards Trinity College; the lorry swung into College Green, bristling with rifles on the knees of the soldiers seated on each side; it passed, charging up Dame Street, and the groups began to re-form.

Caroline started at the sound of her father's voice; she had been lost in a terror of the unknown thing that the other people in the street had feared; death seemed to be at large.

'There's been some very dirty work somewhere, I'm afraid,' he said uneasily; 'there's a sort of guilty look about everything. I wish we could get some news.'

'Somebody at the Cathedral may know.'

They hurried on; as they passed the Castle, they saw that the place was alive with soldiers coming and going; armoured cars were driving out of the Yard; a policeman was standing near them and Guy went up to him.

'Anything happened?' he enquired.

The policeman swayed on his heels, thumbs tucked into his belt, as he summed them up.

'God! and did ye not hear, Sir?' he said pityingly.

'Not a word, but from the look of the place you'd think the trump of doom had sounded.'

'Well now!' The man leant forward, shaking his head. 'There's been fourteen British officers murdhered in their beds this mornin',' he uttered in a hoarse whisper, wishing to spare Caroline; 'that's what's happened,' he said aloud and leant back on his heels again.

'Good God! Fourteen!'

'Fourteen, sir; and the lads that did it is the lads as want to govern this country; ah, they're a choice lot!'

'Choice is the word! Thanks,' and they hurried on.

The sound of the Cathedral bells came to them down the hill, pealing merrily.

'Damn those bells,' said Guy vengefully; 'did you hear what he said, Caroline?'

'Yes,' she said quietly; she felt cold and numb; 'that's what we heard then?'

'Must have been, I suppose; what an awful world we've brought you into, haven't we? First the War and now this—and Heaven only knows where it will end.' He took her hand and she left it in his for comfort.

Outside the Cathedral, people were gathered in gloomy little knots, talking in hushed whispers; everybody seemed to know what had happened and all were overcome with horror and indignation.

The bells ceased and Caroline drew a deep breath of satisfaction.

'Don't you like them either?' asked Guy, and she shook her head; they entered the building and took their seats; the congregation was small but the air was electric with feeling.

Never had Caroline felt so unreal; here they were, she and her father, sitting in Church as though nothing had happened, waiting for a service to begin; there were perhaps a hundred other people there, but there was the same thought in the mind of each; even the clergy, robing in the vestry, were certain to be sharing that thought: fourteen British officers murdered.

The processional hymn was announced and the choir entered; boys' clear voices were raised in praise, the congregation stood. Fourteen, thought Caroline, and I've seen their murderers! I wonder we didn't hear a shout or anything. She tried to remember how many shots she had heard. Did people die silently, then? Oh God, don't let it have happened! How silly she was being: even God couldn't stop it now it had happened. One, two, three . . . you couldn't count up to fourteen when you remembered that each one was a man who had been alive a few hours ago.

Her father touched her on the sleeve; to her confusion she found that she should be kneeling; she blushed hotly and knelt on the hard little hassock that slipped about on the tiles; her mind was tumultuous with thoughts; would some awful doom overtake the murderers? 'They that take the sword shall perish by the sword,' she had heard a lot of people say that lately. Perhaps it didn't count with guns. She looked at Guy; he was not attending to the service; head sunk on his breast, he was staring through the back of the empty chair in front of him at the hassock on the seat.

They did not wait to speak to anyone after the service; Guy was anxious to get home. They climbed the little slope up to the street;

the Cathedral is in a slum district and the people were all out of their houses now, lounging about the streets, waiting to see what was going to happen. They muttered in subdued tones, quietly apprehensive. Dublin was in disgrace and her citizens were desperately aware that the bounds of endurance had been exceeded. Reprisals there would be and what form they would take was the question in everybody's mind.

The sound of a motor approached and an army lorry came thrusting round the corner from a slum street; the people stood watching, waiting. Oh! Oh, God! More shooting! Six explosions rang out, deafening, terrifying. The street was full of running figures; women screamed, people bolted into doorways, some threw up their hands and stood; a man on the pavement knelt down and clasped his hands in prayer, face uplifted in supplication; never would Caroline forget the sight of that pale beseeching figure with its lips moving in agony, aware that the Judgment Day had come.

The lorry passed; her father whispered:

'It's all right—they're only backfires, they do that to frighten people.' He caught her hand in his and she clung to it for her knees felt weak and her heart was pounding. The kneeling man stood up; swaying on his feet, he caught at the railings for support and lay back against them, eyes closed. The people were talking again.

'God, I thought we were killed!'

'Them fellas'd put the heart across ya.'

Hand in hand, Caroline and her father walked soberly home.

Retribution was swift and fearful; there was a football match that afternoon and the authorities had reason to believe that the murderers were mingling with the crowd; men were sent to make arrests and there was resistance. The crowd was fired on and the innocent suffered for the guilty. This cold-blooded action evoked nearly as much censure as the crime it avenged; opinion hardened and the war was continued with renewed bitterness on both sides.

CHAPTER FIVE

By the Spring of 1921 the situation in Ireland had become so grave that hope of a settlement, flickering like a candle-flame in a draught, finally dwindled and died. The only prospect was one of gathering horror: more murder, more revenge, more hate. Comedy, the malevolent god-mother of Irish destiny, having twisted events into contortions from which she alone could free them, had departed, exorcised by sheer intensity of passion. There is nothing comic in potential martyrs, no matter what their faith, and the country was bristling with believers who pursued with the single-heartedness of holy warfare their incompatible ideals.

It had long been recognised by Britain that the only end to this ancient struggle could be some form of self-government for Ireland; a Free State had been suggested, with an independent parliament in Dublin, freely elected by the people, the country to remain in the Empire, owning sovereignty to the King. The Southern Unionists, hating the idea, had nevertheless sacrificed their connexion with England to the obvious expediency of a just and lasting peace, but the Northern Unionists, on the other hand, had declared themselves prepared to go to war with Britain rather than suffer embodiment in a state that was to be independent of her.

Faced with this deadlock and abandoning all hope of establishing her single offspring, the Mother of Parliaments had, in the Government of Ireland Bill of 1920, reluctantly given birth to twins which she presented to the Irish people, one for the South, the other for the North;

and though the Northerners grimly agreed to accept their infant, the Southerners proclaimed that the twins constituted an abortion and rejected them with rancour. Sinn Fein demanded that Ireland be left whole, a geographical and logical entity; the North, embarrassingly loyal, insisted that no power on earth should detach it from Britain and the war was continued with ever-increasing bitterness. To add to the troubles, the Northern and Southern loyalists now glared at each other with undisguised animosity for, said the Southerners, if the North had only played fair and given in a little we should have had peace and a united Ireland long ago, while the Northerners deplored the treachery of the South in accepting the idea of a Free State in the first place and in refusing to agree to partition in the second place; righteously aloof, they repeated their slogan: 'Not an inch'.

Capitulation was out of the question and in May Britain determined to bring Sinn Fein to its knees, a project easier to envisage than accomplish; she was dealing with an invisible enemy, as elusive and as dangerous as flame. Sinn Fein was, moreover, well organised by now and its army, though small, was astonishingly mobile owing to the brilliance and industry of the military leader of the party, Michael Collins; it was he who had so undermined the British Secret Service that that weapon was blunted beyond repair, he who had drilled and disciplined, he who had organised the flying columns that were the bane of the British. The hero of his own people and the curse of the British, few men can have been so loved and so hated at one time.

In June British policy changed abruptly; the Irish were to be conciliated at all costs. De Valera, President of Dail Eireann, the Irish House of Commons, was summoned to London by Lloyd George and a truce was arranged to tide over the negotiations. By mid-July a settlement seemed to be in view, but De Valera and the Dail rejected the proposals which included agreements for the partition of Ireland, leaving the North free to remain part of the United Kingdom, and for the retention by Britain of certain strategic ports in Southern territory.

Later in the year, Michael Collins, Arthur Griffiths and other leading Sinn Feiners went to London to work out terms for an acceptable treaty. While Michael Collins sat at these discussions in London a reward of £10,000 was still being offered in Dublin Castle for his capture, dead or alive. Two fruitless months passed. Finally, on December 5th, an ultimatum was handed to the delegates; the Treaty was to be signed instantly or there would be an immediate renewal of the war. It was signed in the small hours of the morning. The members of the Delegation then sailed back to Dublin to be told that they had betrayed Sinn Fein. De Valera and his Cabinet resigned when the Dail ratified the Treaty by a majority of seven. Arthur Griffiths became President and formed a Provisional Government. The British began to leave the country.

Seven hundred years of bitter, unsuccessful and continuous revolt had at last borne fruit, but it brought little sweetness to the mouths of those who tasted it: Sinn Fein was outraged by partition and objected to remaining within the British Empire; the Moderates, while hoping that the Treaty would prove to be an instrument of peace, doubted the intention of the Extremists to abide by it; the North was contemptuous and distrustful, despising the Southern Unionists who, they felt, had sold themselves and the country to a bunch of rebels. Many of the Unionists were afraid to envisage the future.

It was late afternoon on Christmas Day, 1921. The blue mist of the city twilight was creeping across Fitzwilliam Square, encircling the plane trees and engulfing bushes and railings in its rising tide. There was not a breath of wind, not a footstep to be heard on the pavements, but very faintly from behind the drawn blinds of a first-floor drawing-room came the tinkling one-two-three, one-two-three of a waltz played on the piano.

Caroline, her hair brushed in a burnished cloud, hands washed and wearing her green frock, could just hear it as she leant out of the schoolroom window before going down to the drawing-room; one-two-three, one-two-three it went and she began to dance round the room, humming softly to herself. Miss O'Connor, settling down to enjoy herself at the fire, said warningly:

'Better hurry, dear.'

Slide-two-three, slide-two-three went Caroline, out into the lobby and to the head of the stairs; she pirouetted frantically on the top step and almost lost her balance so that she had to stampede down, three steps at a time. Out of breath and laughing, she tried to peep into the drawing-room without being seen; she knew that Eileen Hunt was bringing some friends to tea and that they had a little girl called Olga. Caroline did not know many little girls and she was rather excited at the thought of meeting Olga.

She could see Helen and Mrs. Tom Butler, who was known in the family as Aunt Emma, laughing together at some remark. Aunt Emma was actually no relation, being the widow of Archie's only brother. Her only son, David, aged seventeen, was standing beside the fire, talking to Isabel, his fair head and her dark one close together. Those must be the Hendersons with Eileen Hunt and Guy; there was a lanky little girl with them but Caroline could not see her face, only a mass of fuzzy mouse-coloured hair and a short red frock, much shorter and smarter than anything she was allowed to wear. Catha and Alec O'Brien were there too, and a funny old Professor Pritchard who came occasionally to the house.

Caroline felt suddenly shy and made for her father.

'Hallo, Puss,' said Eileen, 'here's somebody for you to talk to.'

'This is Caroline,' announced Guy, and she shook hands with all three Hendersons.

'And this is Olga,' said Mrs. Henderson in a soft slow voice. Caroline looked up at her for a moment and her mouth opened with astonishment: Mrs. Henderson was the most beautiful person she had ever seen. She was a golden creature with honey-coloured hair and soft brown eyes; she had a look of leisure and gentleness about her as though she could never be in a hurry. She began to smile at Caroline who lost her shyness and smiled back.

'Take Olga off and talk to her,' said Guy.

David and Isabel made room for them at the fireplace and continued their private conversation; they were discussing school. Isabel, who was going to school in England in January, could think and talk of nothing else and David, who was a naval cadet, was to her a sort of god-like authority.

'How old are you?' whispered Caroline suddenly.

'Eleven; how old are you?'

'So'm I—eleven, I mean; I've just had a birthday; Isabel's fourteen.'

'Do you go to school?'

'No, we have a governess. But Isabel's going to school in January and I shall have to do lessons by myself; it'll be awfully dull.'

'I had a governess for a bit in France; she was quite nice but she used to hit me with a ruler.'

'In France!' Caroline thought this was tremendously romantic. 'Do you speak French?'

'I had to.'

'Why were you there?'

'Leonard was painting there; I've been in Spain too.'

'Goodness! Who's Leonard?'

'He's my father. Anne's my mother. I always call them by their Christian names, they like me to.'

Caroline was so startled that she could think of nothing to say; she decided that Olga was a most daring and talented creature and that she would like to get to know her better. Suddenly she had an idea: why should not Olga come and do lessons with her? She turned to her quickly.

'You ought to come and do lessons with me!' Then she blushed hotly, in case Olga might reject her proposal with scorn; but it was all right, Olga was enthusiastic. They settled down to plot in whispers how this might be accomplished.

A political discussion was raging just behind them; Professor Pritchard was depicting the future to Catha and Alec O'Brien.

'It means annihilation for us,' he said, throwing out his hands with a hopeless gesture; 'we shall be an unprotected minority in a hostile country; the Government will never be able to suppress the I.R.A. Just think of it—no army, no police force! How can they imagine they're going to do it? Their policy will be to destroy the gentry and eradicate the Protestants and if they pursue it the whole country will be illiterate inside a quarter of a century. Trinity College might as well close down. And they'll impose their beastly Irish language on the schools and we shall be powerless to stop them.'

Alec cocked an eye at the Professor. 'I seem to remember that this country was called the Island of Saints and Scholars before either gentry or Protestants existed,' he murmured.

Guy, who had been listening, broke into the conversation.

'We can survive if we adapt ourselves, Professor. The British don't want us to sulk in corners over their departure; as you say, our power of effective opposition will have gone with them: it's to our advantage to make the Free State a success—it's no use being diehards now.'

'The mammon of unrighteousness!' snapped Catha. 'How can you even think of these people as human beings, Guy? To me they're monsters and will never be anything else.'

'It can't be a success,' argued the Professor; 'the thing's impossible. No one has any confidence in this so-called Government: how can they have, when every member of it's an ex-gunman? Within a year they'll be begging the British on their bended knees to come back and restore order; but the British won't come back: they've washed their hands of this country and I don't blame them.'

'Your ex-gunmen are idealists, Professor; they may surprise us by becoming model citizens,' said Alec softly.

'Idealists!' snorted the Professor; 'fanatics is the word, O'Brien, fanatics! And you want us to adapt ourselves to them?' he turned to Guy; 'murderers and rebels who will turn this country into a third-class state on the edge of the map, who will alienate us so thoroughly from the English that when we cross the water we shall be looked upon as foreigners, or worse still, as Colonials. I tell you that if we do adapt ourselves, as you call it, they'll suspect us and impose upon us. They'll never trust us: look at our tradition—our sons in British regiments or out in the Colonies, and it'll still be the same. There'll be no job in this country that a decent young man would look at, and even if there were, do you think they'd let our sons have the jobs? Not a bit of it, they'll keep the best jobs for good Catholics and rebels. As for hob-nobbing with them, I'd never be able to hold up my head again if I shook hands with one of these blighters.'

Guy smiled. 'I wasn't suggesting that we should hob-nob with them, I must confess the idea doesn't appeal to me. But I wouldn't refuse to shake hands with them: I think they're honest and believed they were at war with Britain; murder to us was war to them; in their own minds they were not murderers, but simply soldiers. It's a matter of labels but in this case the rose does not smell as sweet by its other name.'

'But it *was* murder, downright bloody murder!' The Professor was almost shouting; 'You've only got to look at the . . .'

'Black and Tans,' interrupted Alec mildly, with a barely perceptible wink at Guy. The Professor stared at him distastefully for a moment.

'I admit that the Black and Tans were an unfortunate experiment,' he said stiffly.

'I think,' put in Guy, 'you'll find these boys will settle down; they've had a lot of nasty responsibilities pushed on to them and that'll sober them quicker than anything. Why should they take it out of us? They've won their war now and can afford to be generous. Besides, we can be useful to them; we've still got land, some of us have money and can give employment.'

'Before long,' replied the Professor, 'they'll have turned our people out of the big houses and shared the land out among the peasants. I'm convinced they'll do everything in their power to get us out.'

'Back to Cromwell, or Paradise Regained? It was theirs before Cromwell paid off his soldiers with it: British mercenaries, paid off with Irish land. I can quite see why our patriots feel so sore about it, but I don't think they'll take our land from us provided we live on it and farm it. Absentee landlords are another matter,' said Alec, serious at last.

Caroline looked round to see Catha, very red in the face, stand up and draw herself erect.

'They will,' she said with great dignity; 'they'll take away our land and our money; I expect to be persecuted like the Jews were in Europe, until my life is a burden and I am driven from the country. I am a Protestant and a Unionist and I shall never alter or pretend to be anything else.' Her voice rose a little as she went on: 'But what is more, I shall not go: they will not get me out. I will not allow these people to defeat me.' Her hand trembled slightly as she wiped first her eyes and then the end of her nose.

In all her dealings with her cousin Catha, Caroline had never once felt sympathetic towards her; but now, as she watched her standing there in her dowdy black dress, red-faced and uncompromising, she felt a sudden affectionate admiration for her. There was something about her attitude that reminded one of an early Christian in the arena with the wild beasts.

Guy was deeply touched and ashamed of a slight feeling of amusement which he could not suppress: 'My dear,' he said gently and with great gravity, 'you are a very brave woman. But I think you're mistaken in thinking that these people still hate us. Our importance to them is past; they must search their own ranks for enemies far more potent than we can be. Far from being honoured with their attentions I fear that we may rather perish from their neglect.'

He looked round hopelessly: Catha must be stopped. The Professor must be stopped. Someone must come and talk to them about birds and butterflies, local gossip or world affairs. At all costs they must be prevented from uttering another word about Irish politics. Everyone was talking gaily and no one was even looking in their direction. He sighed and glanced at Alec. Alec was dumb, looking at the carpet and fingering the loose change in his pocket with little clinking noises. But help was at hand: the starched figure of Doran appeared to announce that tea was ready. Before the Professor could open his mouth again Guy grasped Catha firmly by the arm:

'You must be starving,' he said quickly; 'come down and have some tea.' Helen, who generally had to remind him several times when meals were ready, watched in amusement as he hustled everybody out of the room and down the stairs, overtaking the stately Doran in her unhurried downward course. Poor Doran, engulfed by guests, cast such a look of perturbation and reproach at her mistress that Helen, deep in conversation with Aunt Emma about the appalling cost of school uniforms, gave a little involuntary giggle.

The curtains had been drawn in the dining-room and there was a blazing coal fire in the grate; candles flickered and were reflected in polished woodwork and in shining silver; a mountainous snowy cake stood at one end of the table and a ring of holly surrounded a huge, bowl of white chrysanthemums in the centre; Helen, entrenched behind a tray of tea-pots, jugs and kettles, sat at the end. The rest of the table was covered with plates of food, dishes of sweets and crackers. Guy had thankfully placed Catha beside Leonard Henderson; he would not talk politics to her. Anne Henderson, with the Professor on one side and Alec on the other, was charming them both; Guy slipped in beside Eileen Hunt and sighed with relief; peace and goodwill had come back. He sighed again and devoted himself to his tea.

CHAPTER SIX

In January 1922, the British left Southern Ireland. People stood on the Dublin quays and watched the troops leading their horses to the waiting ships. The Lord Lieutenant handed over the keys of Dublin Castle to Michael Collins: that same Dublin Castle where, little over a month before, £10,000 had been offered for his capture. General Mulcahy, so lately a guerrilla leader against the British, was raising a new green-clad National Army. The Royal Irish Constabulary was disbanded, and instead of that efficient semi-military symbol of enforced peace there grew up, conceived in faith and reared in turmoil, the unarmed Civic Guard. The Red, White and Blue was hauled down from the roof-tops and in its place there fluttered from public buildings the brave new flag, the Green, White and Gold. 'God Save the King' was now only to be heard in Protestant churches and behind locked doors; a new song with an unfamiliar tune and words disturbing to Unionists' ears, words that spoke of 'the Saxon foe', was played at public gatherings; it was called the 'Soldiers' Song' and was chosen to be the National Anthem of the new Free State.

But in spite of these signs of nationhood, the peace had not crystalised; all the forces of order had been removed and the temper of the people was still in a molten state. Where there was hope there was also disillusionment. The Republicans who had never recognised the Treaty began to organise themselves in opposition to the Government. There was no minister in this government whose life was not threatened; the Executive Council of the Dail met and conducted its business in underground cellars.

The Unionists clung to what remained of the outward signs of loyalty. There were still people who would not see that the British had really gone for good; these saw the Free State as an unruly and difficult child and they hoped, because they wanted to hope, that when the child discovered that it was really all alone at last it would cry for its parent to come back again and that the parent, forgiving, would return. Then, they thought, the rule of glory would begin anew, with a penitent Ireland embraced by a loving Britain. It was a blind hope, an empty dream, for they shut their eyes to the hard and bitter purpose that impelled the men of the new Ireland.

Union Jacks were folded away to await a better day; British uniforms were stowed in attics; sons came home on leave in mufti. Daughters found that they had no one to dance with; mothers wrung their hands in despair, for whom could their daughters marry, now that there were no more officers? Dublin was shedding its glamour; there would be no more grand dinner parties at the Castle, no more glittering balls, no more Vice-Regal drawing-rooms. Hostesses found that there were no young men in Dublin, they were all away in their ships or with their regiments, in England or abroad. There remained the middle-aged, the elderly, the very young and an abundance of daughters.

In this uneasy world people tried to live a normal life. Society turned inwards and entertained itself, but there was a chill in the air like that of an empty house. The good old days were gone.

In the Adairs' small world there was little apparent change; Catha O'Brien refused to post her letters in the new green pillar-boxes and doggedly tramped the streets in search of those that were still red and loyal; she objected also to the stamps, over-printed in Irish which she could not understand; anything that effaced the King's head was to her treason and she made Alec stick them on, saying that she would have nothing to do with them.

Eileen Hunt laughed and said that she would learn Irish so as to be able to read the new street names which were soon going to be put up; Catha looked askance at her and Alec for taking things too easily.

Guy was busy: architects were needed just now, for there was a new Ireland to be planned and built. Helen was very unhappy; for years she had refused to see that the day of Home Rule must come; she had shut her eyes to the volcanic moral forces erupting in the country and seen only the sordid battles of armed men. Now she was left with the facts: the unthinkable had happened—the British had gone.

She peered warily into the future; there was no light, no hope; she had been left behind in an empty house, groping in the darkness. People tried to be kind to her; she and Catha and Aunt Emma would sit in gloomy conclave over their tea-cups; Eileen Hunt sought her advice about redecorating her flat; Guy wrote to Moira, in England, asking her if she would invite Helen over for a visit. Moira wrote but Helen would not go; she would not be pitied.

As the days passed, she withdrew behind a facade of resignation. She saw her friends, went shopping, began to chat to Guy about his work. But she was not resigned; all the time her mind was restless, probing, seeking an object on which to pin the future. And slowly, as she took stock of her position, she discovered that she could still fight. She had a weapon, two weapons: Isabel and Caroline.

If she could deprive this upstart state of their allegiance; if she could rear her daughters to be militant Unionists, owing no loyalty save to Britain and the King; if she could burn into their hearts the Northern slogan of 'No Surrender!', then she would have revenged herself upon the Irish. Hate would breed hate and their children's children would still be her revenge.

Grimly she began to plan. The next few years were vital; once the girls were grown up they would be safe, their minds would have hardened. Now, now was the time! She would have to be very clever; the children must never suspect her purpose for them; if they were conscious of the leading-rein they would rebel. Their literature, their friends, their interests must all be chosen for them without their knowledge. They must be prisoners behind invisible walls, thinking themselves free. But there was one obstacle between her and success; it was not an obstacle that could be stormed or surmounted; it must be circumvented by guile. The obstacle was her husband.

In her innermost heart, Helen felt that Guy had betrayed her; not wilfully or consciously, but by that quality in his nature which led him to trust the unknown. How dared he hope that there would now be peace? Helen saw faith and hope in these days as the final, unforgivable treachery. But she would not say a word to him; let him go on believing in his outrageous faith until he learnt wisdom from events, if, indeed, he was capable of learning. Cynically, she saw that this very quality of faith which he possessed could be made to work in her favour; so long as he was unaware of her plans she could discount his influence with the children. Not unless she blundered hopelessly would it occur to him that she was working against him.

His company became unbearable to her at times; she would lie beside him at night, her body rigid with repugnance, but she suffered his advances with closed eyes and a rebellious heart. At last she made insomnia her excuse to consign him to his dressing-room, determining that henceforth her bedroom would be her impregnable fortress.

Isabel, she foresaw, would be no problem. She was already a snob, which was a great asset. She would see nothing romantic or attractive in shock-headed young patriots with accents, but would always prefer uniforms and gaiety and charming young men who told her how attractive she was. Ideas bored her. Anyway, her future was already planned in the most satisfactory way; she would be at school in England for nearly three years, perhaps in Paris for a year. Then she would be eighteen and looking forward to dashing about the country to Hunt Balls and house parties. But she must marry an Irishman; if she went off to England, half Helen's plan would collapse. There were plenty of handsome young Irishmen in the Army or Navy who would have to retire when their fathers died and they inherited family places. Some of them were very well off. Isabel could be happy with any of them. Helen did not overrate her elder daughter's delicacy of feeling.

Caroline was going to be more difficult; she was more like Guy. She, of course, would be going to school in England too, but not for several years. She was less ambitious than Isabel and made friends with everybody, which was a danger. She read too much and her head was always full of wild romantic ideas; but this was no harm: Helen knew that if Caroline could be persuaded to think of herself as a crusader her battle was won.

She made a little mental list of her children's friends; it was pathetically short. Now that Isabel was at school, Caroline would need more outside companionship. She had some wild scheme of doing lessons with Anne Henderson's little girl, but of course that was quite impossible, the child had already started school. But she might make a suitable friend for Caroline. Leonard and Anne should be sound enough; she had known them both, years ago, when they had all been children together. Leonard was a younger son of an old country family; his father had wanted him to go into the army although Leonard had always been determined to be an artist, and there had been great friction in the family; he had become an artist, but he had fought all through the War, hating it. Anne was his cousin; Helen remembered her as a golden little girl with hair so long that she could sit on it; she had always been a 'different' child, sitting apart, chewing daisy stems and watching the other children. Leonard had worshipped her, even then, perhaps because she had always been lovely. They had been abroad since the War and now they had come back to settle down in Dublin as they had always meant to do. Of course they were all right, thought Helen, rather doubtfully; Leonard had told Guy that he was going to have nothing to do with politics, he was sick of the whole business.

That meant that they would avoid the Nationalist literary crowd who were wildly political and full of romantic ideas about Ireland's destiny. Olga would be brought up in the right tradition.

Helen sat down and wrote a note to Anne; would she come to tea and bring Olga? It was so many years since they had met and she had not had a chance to talk to her on Christmas Day; Caroline had so few little friends and would love to get to know Olga who, perhaps, did not know many children here yet.

They came; Olga disappeared upstairs for schoolroom tea; Anne and Helen sat lazily in front of the fire and talked about when they had been children, of Leonard's brothers, who were all soldiers, of Eileen Hunt and her charming impossible husband, who had been killed in the War. They decided that it would be a mistake for Moira and Archie to come back to Ireland. They sadly discussed the many gaps the War had left in families they both knew. Not a word was spoken about politics, but Helen was perfectly satisfied; she saw that Anne lived in a world of her own, intangible and unassailable; she was a person whom events could not touch, who would always go on tranquilly in her own way as though nothing had happened. And this, thought Helen, was admirable; Caroline could see Olga as often as she liked.

Caroline came to look upon the Hendersons' unfashionable little house in Pembroke Road as a sort of promised land. Here everything was different from the ordered life she knew. Anne did all the cooking and the hours of meals varied widely. Olga and Caroline did the washing-up and sometimes Anne would leave them in the kitchen, alone with a recipe book and some provisions, telling them to make what they liked. Olga was no mean cook, having lived this sort of life as long as she could remember, and Caroline was perfectly happy to act as kitchen-maid, sifting flour and washing bowls, wrapped up in an old overall of Anne's; they would bring in the fruits of their labour and eat them, with Anne, in front of the living-room fire, sharing the hearth-rug with two immense purring marmalade cats.

The furniture in the room was low and dark and old; instead of a glaring centre light, a standard lamp near the fireplace gave out a warm subdued glow. The room was full of books; they had overflowed from the book-cases on to the tables, from the tables on to the chairs and from there to the floor; soon, if anybody was to be able to sit down at all, something drastic would have to be done. There were books in English, French, German and Spanish, bound in cloth and leather, flimsy yellow paper or stiff cardboard with exciting designs; books of all colours, shapes and sizes, on every subject under the sun from Chinese painting to modern French poetry. There was only one picture in the room and the first time Caroline saw it she stood open-mouthed, beset by emotion. It was of a bull-fight, but there was no movement; the artist had impaled a static moment. The bull was gathering his forces for the charge, the matador was tense and immobile; only the sand, churned up in action, was hazy round his feet. The combination of colour and panache in this picture affected Caroline and she could not stop looking at it; Leonard, she decided, must have painted it and she conceived a passionate hero-worship for him. One day she plucked up courage to ask Olga if it was her father's work.

'Good Lord, no,' said Olga.

Anne smiled. 'He says he won't sit in a room where he has to look at his own work, it's too depressing. That was painted by a friend of ours, a Frenchman we knew in Spain. It's rather lovely, isn't it?'

'I think it's tremendous,' said Caroline gravely, disappointed that Leonard should have failed her.

He suddenly appeared in the doorway.

'What's tremendous?' he asked; 'you all seem very serious.'

'René's bull-fight,' said Anne; 'Caroline wanted to know if you'd painted it.'

'I wish I had! Caroline, have you ever seen a studio?'

'Oh, no. I'd love to.'

Leonard told Olga to bring her up.

The studio was the most exciting room Caroline had ever seen. A huge window filled in the end wall; canvasses were stacked on every side; a still life was arranged on a table. On top of a pile of papers on a stool near the fire was curled one of the marmalade cats; the mantel-piece was littered with little bottles, tubes of paint, jam-jars full of brushes, pencils, drawing-pins, books and dusty papers. Little tables round the room were covered with paraphernalia; a half-finished canvas stood on one easel while three or four finished ones were piled precariously on another. Caroline stood just inside the door and sniffed with delight.

'Leonard's doing some lovely posters,' said Olga. 'They're not funny or anything, they're just pictures really, only simpler. Can I show her, Leonard?'

Struggling into overalls, he nodded and Olga fetched a roll of papers from behind the cat; she knelt down and pushed the roll away from her, to open it up. 'These are the Donegal ones,' she explained, 'they haven't been printed or anything yet.'

'What she means is,' said Leonard, 'that nobody'll have them.'

There were eight of them; they showed turf-cutters at work on a showery day, straw-thatched farms, their roofs lashed down against the winter storms, a steep little field, low-walled, under the plough, sulky little hills and lakes; there was one of Errigal, superb, seen from across a little reedy lake, sapphire-dark. Another was of a horse and cart on wet sands on a windy day. Bare and strong and clean, they held the cool rain-washed western air, the brooding colour and the racing winds of Donegal.

'The sort of posters you see about,' explained Leonard, 'make me absolutely sick; I want people to be able to see places as they really are, not dramatised or romanticised or whitewashed; trippers won't go there anyway, unless there are piers and esplanades and bathing-boxes, so what's the use of pretending you'll find Blackpool in the west of Ireland? But nobody wants them, they say they're not romantic enough, couldn't I stick in a pretty girl or two?' He mimicked their voices: '"Oh, they're very artistic, I'm sure, Mr. Henderson, we don't deny that, but if ye could do us a nice little one of the hotel, with perhaps a mixed foursome on the golf-course, it'd be more in our line." God help me if I ever find myself doing one of a pretty girl at the seaside; I'd rather starve.'

'Bloody fools,' muttered Olga and Caroline fiercely agreed with her.

'They're not commercial, that's what's wrong with them,' went on Leonard; 'they don't tell you there's an hotel there with h. and c. in every bedroom, or that there's dancing after dinner and that you'll find society clustered there in August in smart tweeds, with pretty girls to flirt with whenever you're not in the bar, drinking yourself silly. Oh, I know what they want, all right, blast their little money-grabbing souls, but they'll have to get one of their tame commercial artists to do it for them, I won't.'

Olga rolled up the posters and replaced them carefully behind the cat; Leonard turned to them:

'Go along now, the pair of you, and take the bowl of fruit from the still life before it all goes bad, I'm finished with it. If you saw what Miss Conroy made out of it last Tuesday you'd never want to set eyes on it again, the same as me.'

'Miss Conroy's one of his pupils,' whispered Olga as they fled from the room.

Downstairs, Anne had tea ready on a low table by the fire; a dish of crumpets was keeping warm in the hearth.

'Oh dear, let me look at those!' she said to Caroline, holding out her hand for the bowl. Fetching a clean napkin from a drawer, she dusted and wiped the fruit carefully before handing it back. 'They've been there for a fortnight,' she explained, smiling, 'and I haven't even flicked them with a duster!'

By this small action, Anne endeared herself for ever to Caroline; she had admitted her into their world, into that carefree liberated sphere where the meticulous observance of such things as regular dusting was a minor slavery to which they could not submit; she was so open about it, so entirely without embarrassment or apology. How lovely to be like that, thought Caroline, to do things when they needed doing and not just out of habit.

Later on, when the light began to fade, Leonard came down and joined them. They had finished tea, but the things were still there and he sat back in his chair, eating crumpets that dripped with butter and drinking large cupfuls of half-cold stewed tea which he said he liked better than anything else and was never allowed to have. Caroline sat on the hearth-rug, running her hand over a long supple sweep of marmalade fur in a dreamy continuous movement. She was completely happy; she knew that in a very few minutes this peace would be broken by the arrival of Miss O'Connor to fetch her home, but that only intensified her delight in the moment. Extending a forefinger, she gently rubbed the cat's wind-pipe; it stretched and relaxed, paws out, white throat and chin in a straight line, a shell-like tip of pink tongue just showing.

Leonard had been watching her. 'Silly things,' he said as he put out his hand to stroke the vibrating flank; 'silly things,' he repeated affectionately; 'I wish people purred.'

'Some people do,' said Caroline, 'don't you think?'

'By Jove, you're right!' He chuckled and looked at Anne, leaning back in her chair, lovely and smiling. She gave a little gurgle of laughter.

'I can't help it,' she said; 'I always have.'

The door bell rang; nobody moved for a moment, then Olga jumped up and ran out. Caroline sat up and straightened her stockings; Leonard put himself between her and Anne and, bending down, kissed his wife.

Miss O'Connor was being ushered in by Olga; Caroline stood up with a jerk; she was back in a world where time mattered.

Isabel wrote from school: 'All the girls ask me if I'm a Sinn Feiner, they seem to think all the Irish are; they were awfully surprised when

I told them lots of people weren't; and they can't understand why I haven't got an accent; if I put one on, just for fun, they think it's lovely and roar with laughter.'

Caroline burned with indignation when she read this letter, the more so because it greatly amused her parents. They had never realised, as had Caroline, that apart from themselves and Anne Henderson, there was no one in their small circle whose speech was entirely free from accent; even Moira spoke with an intonation that could never be mistaken for English. So Isabel had got too grand for them now and was making fun of them to her new English friends! And here was an added source of bitterness: Isabel could no more assume an accent than she could fly, being one of those people whose mode of speech, once acquired, is fixed for life; she lacked the musical ear essential to the successful linguist. And here she was, parading her false outrageous stage-Irish brogue before the simple English who, poor fools, had not the wit to see through her. Caroline was nearly sick with rage.

She herself had a natural aptitude for mimicry and could produce at will an accent of no mean proportions, so she set about perfecting this so that when the time came for her to go to school the English might have a taste of the real thing. Besides, there was always the prospect of shaming Isabel before her English friends if, as she was already planning, some of them were to come over during the holidays. So, despite repeated admonitions from Miss O'Connor she developed the habit of speaking in a rich Dublin accent. Helen did not notice this at once, but one day at lunch she pulled her up sharply:

'I can't think where you learnt to speak like that, Caroline. Goodness knows, I've taken enough trouble to surround you with people who speak nicely.' She looked accusingly across the table at Miss O'Connor who, convinced that she spoke as though she had lived in England all her life, replied:

'Caroline can speak quite nicely when she likes, Mrs. Adair.'

'Caroline, say "I did not" properly.' Helen looked stern.

'I did naht.'

'Not, not nart.' Helen rapped on the table; she herself was no mimic.

Guy suddenly burst out laughing: 'What's the use of correcting the child's accent when she says things like that? You'd never hear anyone outside this country say "I did not".' He blew his nose and went on: 'But seriously, Caroline, that accent of yours is a bit too much; I don't mind as long as you know you're doing it, but I should hate to see it becoming chronic. However, if you possess this profane gift of mimicry, I suppose you'll be able to speak like a duchess when you want to. Why did you pick it up?'

Caroline squirmed; she could not bear reproof from her father.

'I don't know . . . it's fun.'

Helen was not going to miss her opportunity; for once Guy was on her side.

'I do know,' she said; 'you want to be able to show off and one of these days you'll find yourself permanently handicapped with a low accent and you'll have no one but yourself to thank. That accent is to be dropped, do you hear?'

'Yes, Mother.' Caroline would not look at her, but she returned Guy's smile gratefully as he left the table to go back to his office.

Helen was a little startled: Caroline had never called her 'Mother' before.

'Caroline will be up in a minute. Miss O'Connor,' she said and the old governess hastily took the hint and left the room.

'Caroline dear, look at me.'

Caroline edged herself further on to her chair and looked up suspiciously.

'Now I don't want you to feel cross but you must see that people like us have simply got to keep up our traditions. We've been left behind here and we must never give in, never become Irish.'

'Why?'

'Because there's no one else left to keep up the British cause in

Ireland and we must never let it die out!'

'Why?'

Helen began to feel exasperated.

'Don't keep saying "why", darling. Daddy and I are both agreed about this as you saw just now. There are a lot of things you're still too young to understand, but you're quite old enough to realise that loyalty to a great cause is . . . well, that it's a very noble quality. Surely you can see that?'

'Yes.'

'Well then, I want you always to remember that you're a loyalist, one of the people entrusted with the British tradition in this country. The Government here would like to get rid of us and everything we stand for; they'd be just as pleased if they could make us like themselves, but we mustn't let them do either. So we have to set a very high standard for ourselves. We're like soldiers, really, with enemies all round us. Now do you see why I'm so particular about the way you speak?'

'Yes,' said Caroline grudgingly.

'Now kiss me and run upstairs.'

Caroline held out her cheek as she passed, but it was Helen who had to do the kissing.

Nevertheless, within a week, her accent had disappeared.

Civil war broke out in June between the Government forces, known as the Regulars or Free Staters, and the Irregulars or Republicans. In April, the Republicans had seized and made their headquarters in the Four Courts, as the Dublin Law Courts were called. Now, snipers lay on the roofs of pleasant Georgian houses in the city squares and streets, fed by sympathetic hands through skylights. Desperate little forces of fighting men were besieged in public buildings. At night, horrid sounds of sudden death stabbed the darkness and died away.

Sentries were posted at the street corners to search passers-by for arms and ammunition, but in spite of this, supplies reached the Irregulars waiting in back rooms, in cellars, on roof-tops and in empty forgotten houses. Babies were wheeled across the city, bouncing merrily on layers of bombs or belts of machine-gun ammunition. Women cracked jokes with the sentries and walked boldly past them, slung round with revolvers under their clothes. A country youth who had been brought up to respect women, with that peculiar niceness of feeling inbred in the Irish peasant, could not bring himself to submit a shrinking female to the close handling which thorough searching demands; women had their hats removed, their hair let down, their coats opened and pockets and handbags turned out, but their persons were not prodded for suspicious unyielding bulges. A hint of impropriety, delivered with a blushing cheek and downcast eye, would bring a flaming tide to the face of the searcher and his hands to his sides. So, more and more, women were used as couriers.

In the country, the War was fought at cross-roads, from houses in the village streets, and on the mountains. Roads were mined, bridges blown up and all forms of transport commandeered. Big private houses were occupied and, if attacked by the opposing side, burnt by the out-going force. But although this was a dirty bloody war, as all civil wars must be, there were strange and human moments. Rough country youths, caked in mud up to the waist, guns in their hands and their pockets bulging with grenades, would creep along corridors on tip-toe, under orders from Nannie not to wake the baby; the lady of the house, respectfully addressed as Ma'am, would be asked to provide food for twenty or thirty starving men; the family would live unmolested, so long as there was floor-space on which the men could sleep. Articles needed for equipment were commandeered, but generally there was respect for property. But the men brought the mud and grime of war into houses and when they left, if the house was spared, it took weeks of feverish spring-cleaning to remove their traces.

The Adairs spent their summer holidays that year in Devon, with Moira and Archie; they had all meant to go together to the west of

Ireland but the civil war made this impossible since no trains ran to schedule and hotels were, in many cases, occupied by one of the opposing armies. At the end of September, when Isabel returned to school, they came back to Dublin.

During that autumn and winter Caroline bitterly came to realise that nothing was safe; there was no one thing amongst the present horrors from which any of them could count themselves exempt.

One night, her father came in to dinner covered with mud; he had had to throw himself down in the gutter when a party of Irregulars in ambush attacked a passing lorryful of soldiers; a grenade had hit the pavement quite close to him, but when it failed to explode he picked himself up hurriedly and ran for his life. Doran, on a peaceful tram-ride through the city on her day out, was shocked to find herself flattened, with the other passengers, on the floor of the vehicle while bullets shattered the glass and ripped through the woodwork. Olga came pounding home from school one day, her face white with terror, having seen a man shot in the street. After that, neither she nor Caroline were allowed out by themselves, not even for the shortest distances.

If Guy was five minutes later than usual coming home from the Club, Helen and Caroline would peer anxiously out of the windows, listening for any disturbing sounds. Neither of them ever admitted that they were afraid; Helen would say brightly: 'Daddy must have got caught by some of his bridge-friends at the Club,' and Caroline would say: 'Yes, or perhaps he's met someone he knows and can't get away.' If both parents were out together Caroline would wait in utter misery for them to return; she had visions of the telephone ringing and a strange voice saying: 'Mr. and Mrs. Adair have both been killed in an ambush'; if that happened, what could she do? What would become of her, all alone in a big house with only Miss O'Connor between her and the world? It was a terrible thought. Then, when they were safely home again, she would relax and shut herself into the present, where everything was all right.

But it was the sniper who caused Caroline the deepest terror. Only three doors away, a sniper was one day seen on the roof; once there, he had a free run over the roof-tops of perhaps fifty houses, half-way round the block until a vacant lot or a small side-street broke the succession. He was not seen again but that was worse than knowing where he was. In the daytime the thought of him was not so frightening, but when darkness fell panic returned. Caroline would stumble leadenly up to bed, turning on all the lights as she went; she slept at the very top of the house and she was alone there until Miss O'Connor came up, which was quite a long time after dinner. Caroline used to dawdle endlessly over her undressing but the time would come when she would have to turn out the lights and get into bed. She would stand against the wall and reach out a long arm to let the blind go up with a snap that made her jump inches from the floor; then she had to peep round to make sure that there was no sinister form on the window-sill. That done, she would rush out to the lobby and lean over the staircase in the hope of hearing some reassuring household noise below, Doran with the coffee tray or her father and mother talking in the drawing-room with the door open; only rarely did such comfort come her way. If it did, she could not bear to leave the stairs until all was quiet again. Then she would shut her mouth tightly in a firm little line and go back to her room, finger the electric light switch lovingly for a moment, and in one bounding movement turn out the light and take a running jump on to her bed, in case the Republican might be concealed beneath it with his gun. She would lie curled up in a ball beneath the bed-clothes for a few minutes, listening intently, then bring out her head and peer round the room. When nothing stirred and she found she could identify all the shapes in the darkness, she could stretch out her feet and relax; the worst was over: there was something safe about bed.

No one in the house had any idea of the imaginative terror that Caroline endured; she would rather have died than admit that she was frightened and besides, in the day-time, fear receded, imagination subsided and it was impossible to believe that, only a few hours ago, she had known that there was a Republican on the window-sill. How could there have been? He could not get there and, even if he could, why should he want to sit on a window-sill or lie under her bed? It was all silly nonsense, she convinced herself; but as bed-time approached again, the familiar visions returned and she would try and devise excuses for staying up later. Secretively, she would drop stitches in her knitting and pull them down grimly so that they would take a long time to pick up again; or she would ask to be allowed to finish a chapter in her book, knowing that there were at least twenty pages to read. She would beg Miss O'Connor to hurry upstairs after dinner and not to dawdle in the kitchen when she went down to fill her hot water bottle. But nothing made any difference: stolen minutes only prolonged the agony, for bed-time was inescapable.

Her sleep was jumpy and she often had terrifying dreams. Sometimes a huge explosion would shake the night and she would sleep through it; but the lesser, more intimate noises of shots and screams or, running footsteps on the pavement would bring her to dry-mouthed wide-eyed consciousness and she would lie, head up, clutching the bed-clothes tensely until silence swam round her again.

She had one refuge: Butler's Hill was an enchanted kingdom to which she could escape. The very fact that the place was ruined and deserted made it hers to think about and brood over. Even if Moira and Archie never came back and strangers went to live there, it could never be taken wholly from her. It was the centre around which she wove the passionate dreams of childhood, her private and impregnable world.

CHAPTER SEVEN

B y the end of 1926, the new State could be described as well-
established; much had been accomplished in five years and
the fears of the Unionists that they would be singled out for harsh
treatment had been proved baseless, although many of them continued to voice their disapproval of the trend of events, which showed
an increasing preoccupation with national, as against imperial affairs.
Nevertheless, representatives of the Government had attended the
Imperial Conference and the Free State was now a member of the
League of Nations; what disturbed the Unionists were the tariffs
imposed on British goods for the protection of infant Irish industries,
and the fact that land purchase had been placed on a new footing
which imperilled the estates of landowners.

A new national coinage was being devised, a fine network of
roads was being built, tourism was becoming a national industry;
electricity, through the scheme for harnessing the Shannon, was to
be made available to both cities and provinces, Dublin possessed its
own broadcasting station; the Government was working to improve
agriculture and had revived the study of the complicated and moribund
Irish language, plans for abolishing slums were in the air. Things, in
fact, were moving; whether backwards or forwards was a matter of
opinion which provoked discussions of the first magnitude, but no one
could accuse the Government of having stood still.

There remained the old familiar undercurrent of trouble; in 1925, the
I.R.A. had withdrawn its allegiance from its acknowledged leader, De

Valera, and from any party or control, thus becoming an armed force
acting on its own initiative. The Guards had made many seizures of arms,
ammunition and documents which proved that this illegal army was
organising itself against some future crisis. Successive Public Safety Acts
showed that the Government was aware of the danger, but the threat
remained. This underground struggle did not, however, affect the ordinary
citizen, and life in Dublin was pleasant, peaceful and comfortable.

Isabel was at home again. She had spent a year in Paris, where Guy
said she had learnt nothing but nonsense, and a season in London.
She had been presented, she was eighteen, she was grown-up. Helen
was already sifting out the names of possible young men from a list
that she and Aunt Emma had drawn up for the dance that she was
giving in December; in the meantime, she was interviewing caterers and
musicians and dutifully accompanying Isabel to race meetings, which
bored her. She had been surprised to learn that young girls now went
about unchaperoned, but it was a relief to know that she would not have
to go to all the Christmas dances, hunt balls and other entertainments to
which Isabel was looking forward with such relish. All the same, she felt
very anxious: there was no telling whom the child might get to know,
and she was so young, so inexperienced and innocent. Dublin society
had gone to pieces in the last five years; people who, in the old days,
would not have dared to appear at one of the better subscription dances
were now invited, actually invited, to the best houses. Perhaps it was
better in the country; several people had written to her saying that they
hoped Isabel would be able to come down and stay for a few days when
the Hunt Ball was on; there they would all go in their own parties and
there might not be so much risk of her getting into this strange new set.

Helen was immensely proud of her pretty daughter; Isabel was
slim but not tall; she wore her hair short now, shingled neatly to her
shapely head; she was a dark-eyed dancing little person, charged with

vitality and absolutely tireless. Beside her, Caroline felt awkward and despairing; she was tall and still skinny, with long arms and legs that seemed to come in contact with everything; she could not sit down at a table without jolting it and if she tried to skirt round a chair she knocked against it. Her face was as thin as ever, but her nose had grown straighter and a little longer and her cheek-bones stood out more. Her hair was short, too, but Helen made her keep it in a bob, telling her that it would be time enough to have it shingled when she was grown-up. She hated her school-girl clothes, bunchy skirts and woolly jumpers, long black stockings and gym tunics; it was her turn to go to school now, in January, and she was almost glad; she would not have to watch and envy this new and soignée sister whose appearance was a continual reprimand to her.

They were standing in the drawing-room, dressed ready to go out. It was Armistice Day and Catha O'Brien had invited them to listen to the broadcast of the Whitehall ceremony; she had a new and expensive wireless set of which she was very proud; Alec, she said, was quite an expert now and was going to work the thing. Helen was handing out the poppies; they were silk ones, costing a shilling each, for she never bought any others; it was the one day in the year when she could make a public statement of her views, and penny or threepenny poppies would not have the same symbolic value. Wearing a poppy in Dublin was as good as wearing a Union Jack and Helen was careful to choose the largest and grandest that could be worn without absurdity; the cost was immaterial—she subscribed liberally to the Haig Fund—but the emblem worn must be impressive, worthy of her burning loyalty. Guy always bought his own, a penny one.

Caroline peeped enviously at Isabel, pinning her poppy just below the fur collar of her brown coat; she had put some powder on and as much lip-stick as she dared, for Helen had old-fashioned ideas about cosmetics and was always warning her against what she called 'that fast look' which she said was so undesirable. Caroline longed for the day when her head would be neat and shining, when she could powder her nose and wear lovely clothes and little dashing grown-up hats.

A motor-horn tooted mildly outside; Guy had brought round the car. They went downstairs, Helen and Isabel arm in arm, Caroline and Miss O'Connor behind.

This was a big day for Catha; she received her guests just inside the drawing-room door. Chairs, each bearing a little card with a name inscribed, were arranged as for a lecture. The wireless set stood on a small table near the fire, draped with a Union Jack; Alec was seated beside it, watch in hand, ready to tune in at the right moment; on the mantel-shelf had been placed a photograph of the King and Queen, with poppies edging the frame.

When the Adairs arrived, most of the seats were already occupied; Catha, a little fussed, kissed Helen and her daughters, patted Guy's shoulder and shook Miss O'Connor by the hand, then, waving vaguely towards the fireplace, sent them on their way to find their own seats. People were talking in whispers, as though they were in church, but Eileen Hunt, squeezed up against the wall in the second row, stood up and made frantic signs.

'Here you, are, my dears,' she almost screamed, pointing to five vacant chairs beside her; everybody turned to look as they filed in; Guy absent-mindedly leant forward and covered his face with his hands, as though to pray, but recollected himself and smiled awkwardly at Caroline, who wanted to giggle.

Helen sat bolt upright, her face sharp and tense; this, she thought, was the way to celebrate Armistice Day in Ireland. The Armistice itself had little meaning in this country, where war had not ceased until 1923; their tribute to the fallen must be not merely proud remembrance, but a rededication to the Cause, an exercise of loyalty, a gesture of defiance against the facts. She glanced round the room. There were few people there whose families had emerged from the War unscathed; she herself had lost two brothers, one in the Navy, the other in the Army; Eileen's husband had been killed in Mesopotamia, Aunt Emma's in France; an old lady in the front row had lost her three sons, all in 1918. Now, what was left, in Ireland, of all they had so gladly died for? Only the loyalty of their women-folk and their sons, a pitiful few, but with what strength of purpose! From that short, endless silence, soon to come, each heart would pluck the courage to fight on.

Catha looked anxiously towards Alec, who beckoned; she walked sedately up the room, took her seat and held out her hand, demanding silence. Alec began to fiddle with the wireless; it squeaked for a moment and was still. Gingerly, he lifted a corner of the Union Jack and put his head underneath; a soprano voice flooded the room and was abruptly cut off. There was a nervous little current of movement through the room, almost a titter. Alec cursed silently and, as he brought his head out again, solemnly and unmistakably winked at Guy. A male voice, wrapped in the mists of distance, spoke, but no words could be distinguished. The voice got louder, it boomed. The ceremony had begun.

During the Two Minutes' Silence, they stood, with bowed heads; Alec was still twiddling knobs.

It was soon over and Alec stood up, relieved; Catha announced:

'God Save the King!' They sang it unaccompanied; afterwards, there was dead silence; nobody knew what to do next, nobody would be the first to speak.

There was a sudden shocking indrawn sob; Catha put her hands to her face: 'They let us down,' she said brokenly; 'the British let us down.' She sat down heavily and wept.

Caroline stared in horror, unaccustomed to the calamity of grown-up tears. There was a gentle sniff behind her which made her look up; Aunt Emma was weeping silently into her handkerchief.

Alec's head was again buried in the Union Jack and he was the last to realise what was happening; people had crowded round Catha before he could get to her; he waved them all away and leant over her, patting her arm:

'There, there,' he said helplessly; 'there, there.'

Caroline glanced along their row; Helen's face was stony, lifted high in contempt of those who wept as though the fight were over and the battle lost. Isabel was looking straight in front of her in a dreamy sort of way, waiting for this tiresome interlude to be over so that she could return to her own private, not unhappy, thoughts. Miss O'Connor's head was bowed; she was being compelled to witness things which she, as an employee, a governess, ought not to see. Caroline knew that, like the family quarrels, this episode would never be mentioned by Miss O'Connor. Guy edged past them, summoned by a look from Alec. Eileen Hunt smiled at Caroline who was a little shocked that anyone could smile in such awful circumstances; but Eileen looked so normal that Caroline began to feel better and smiled faintly back. She suddenly realised that Guy was speaking:

'. . . downstairs, please; if you will all follow me.' People started moving thankfully towards the door, clumsily, not speaking; speech began after they had shuffled out to the stairway. Caroline looked back as she was leaving the room; all the chairs were out of line, the neatly printed slips of paper were now lying about on the floor or crumpled on the seats; the Union Jack had slipped off the wireless set and lay in an untidy heap on the carpet, where Alec had tripped up in it on his way to comfort Catha; somebody's poppy lay flattened on the floor. Across a sea of chairs, Caroline could see Catha, bent a little forward in her chair, and Alec, a huge white handkerchief in his hand, glancing back, longing for them all to be gone. Serene in their frame upon the mantel-shelf, the King and Queen surveyed an empty and dishevelled room.

Eileen Hunt caught at Caroline's arm and pulled her out of the doorway:

'Come on,' she whispered, and lit a cigarette; 'there'll be something to eat downstairs.' There was a cheerful popping of corks in the dining-room; maids were handing round champagne in glasses and there were mountains of sandwiches and plates of biscuits on the table; everyone settled down with relief to the business of eating and drinking.

Alec appeared at the doorway and beckoned to Guy; they disappeared for a moment, whispering, and came back together. Alec nodded to the servants, who left the room; he held up his hand:

'Ladies and Gentlemen . . . '

Someone was trying to open the door; Alec stopped and looked round as Catha entered slowly, flushed and tear-stained but restored.

'I apologise to you all,' she said clearly. 'Forgive the weakness of an old woman.' She bowed stiffly to the company. Guy seized a glass and handed it to her. Alec began again:

'Ladies and Gentlemen, the King!'

'The King!' echoed the room, 'God bless him.'

Conversation buzzed again. Caroline ate steadily, awkwardly holding her glass of champagne and wondering how she could dispose of it without drinking it. She had taken one gulp which had tickled the back of her nose and made her splutter and feel foolish. Now, to make matters worse, Alec came along with a bottle and insisted on filling up her glass until it was almost overflowing.

'Do you good,' he muttered, 'drink it up.'

She smiled desperately at him and took a little sip, trying hard not to make a face; she wished Olga were here. Olga was worldy-wise and could deal with any social occasion; she probably even liked champagne. She turned to look at Isabel who was enjoying herself, glass in hand, flirting mildly with a courtly old gentleman in the window; she could hear her well-bred little voice, charged with synthetic longing, saying how much she longed to live in the country.

'It's dreadful,' she went on, 'not having a garden. I can't live without flowers!' Her eyelashes fluttered pathetically. The old gentleman was responding beautifully; he was deeply touched and in a moment he would be patting her shoulder.

'Beastly liar!' Caroline almost spat out the words, fuming with contempt. The only kind of country life that appealed to Isabel was, she knew, playing tennis in country houses in brilliant sunshine, or eating strawberries and cream, dressed in delicious clothes and surrounded by admiring young men; the moment a drop of rain fell Isabel would begin to fret for the city streets and amusements.

'*What* did you say?' asked a surprised voice beside her. Caroline turned guiltily and saw her father looking at her in great amusement.

'Nothing,' she said boldly, a scarlet wave of shame rising to the roots of her hair.

'Hm! Well, perhaps you may be right, but don't tell anybody I said so!' And they both laughed. 'Drink up that stuff,' he went on; 'it's time we went home.'

'I can't, Daddy, I simply can't; I hate it.' She looked at him with an agonised expression.

'Here, give it to me, I loathe the stuff too.' He took her glass and tipped the champagne neatly into a flower vase when nobody was looking.

'Now, where's your mother? Say good-bye and we'll get out of this. You get Isabel. Now come on.' Before they knew where they were, they were in the car, driving home.

'Helen,' said Guy, turning round in the driving seat, 'we all need a bit of comic relief after this bloody awful morning; we're going to the pictures this afternoon, all of us.'

'Do look where you're going, there's a car coming,' hissed Helen.

'The funniest, most vulgar picture we can find,' he continued blandly, keeping one eye on the road.

Helen shrugged her shoulders; she wished Guy would behave with better taste, especially in front of the children.

'I can't come; I've got Mrs. Hodges coming to tea, but you can take the children.'

'Isabel?'

Isabel looked doubtful; if nothing more exciting turned up, she would go. Perhaps the telephone would ring and one of her young men would want to take her out.

'I'm not quite sure, I half . . .' She would not commit herself; it would be awful to be left to have tea with her mother and the inexpressibly boring Mrs. Hodges.

'I see, I see,' said Guy quickly, 'but Caroline will come.'

'Oh yes, I'll come.' Caroline rarely went to the pictures; she hoped guiltily that Isabel would have a more pressing engagement.

After lunch, when she went up to get ready, Isabel called her into her room, for she had now been promoted to having a room to herself.

'Look here, I can't come,' she said self-consciously; 'I'm going out.' She was sitting at her dressing-table, surrounded by small bottles, pots and boxes, making up her face.

'What time?' enquired Caroline, determined not to give her the pleasure of being asked with whom she was going out.

'Fourish,' replied Isabel; 'why?'

'Oh, I just wondered; I was hoping you'd have time to get your face fixed up!' She made a grimace and fled down the stairs.

The day of the dance, had come at last and the house was in a turmoil. The front door was wide open, letting in the wet wild December wind, while the caterer's men made endless journeys from their lorries to the pantries, carrying tables, chairs, bottles, pails and china. The drawing-room had been emptied and stripped of its carpet; powder had been sprinkled liberally on the floor and Caroline had been given the job of sliding it in. Helen's feelings had been hurt by Isabel's pronouncement that the floor was not really fit to dance on: what would people say when they found their shoes being torn to ribbons on those awful nails that were sticking up everywhere? Helen's answer had been to hand Isabel a hammer, with a cutting little remark about the ingratitude of children when one spent one's life trying to please them; when she was a girl, people weren't so particular about having everything up to professional standard. Most of the nails turned out to be screws and no one could find the screw-driver; finally Isabel approached Caroline:

'Look, it's pouring rain and it doesn't matter about your hair, just run out and see if it's in the garage.'

Caroline bounced off happily; she would have done anything for anybody today, she was so pleased and excited. When the time had come to decide what she was to wear, it was found, as Helen put it, that the child hadn't a stitch she could put on; so she had a new frock; nothing like as grand as Isabel's, of course, which had been specially made for her in Grafton Street and consisted of incredible quantities of ice-blue chiffon; but it was new, it was pretty and above all, it was grown-up, a proper evening-dress. The little family dressmaker had made it, of apple-green taffeta, fitting at the waist and actually sleeveless. Besides that, Caroline had new silver shoes with high heels and a pair of real silk stockings. She was convinced that the moment she put on these glorious garments, she would shed all her school-girl awkwardness and become indistinguishable from the dazzling and graceful creatures of eighteen and over who were Isabel's contemporaries.

She trotted up with the screw-driver, panting and shaking the rain-drops out of her tawny curls.

'Thanks awfully, you are a dear,' said Isabel gratefully as she set to work.

Helen came in to talk to the pianist about supper for the band; she was annoyed with him because he had been so rude about the schoolroom piano which she had thought would have been quite good enough for a jazz-band; but he had thought otherwise and announced that he could not possibly use it; it had not been tuned for years and the loud pedal would not work; the only thing that piano was good for was as a photograph stand, he said. So there had been endless telephoning and he was sitting around now, waiting for his piano to arrive, humming syncopated tunes and dropping cigarette ash on the arm of his chair, even though Miss O'Connor had thoughtfully provided him with an ash-tray. Just as Helen was talking to him, the men came toiling up the stairs with the piano and he directed them to put it in the corner near the fire. There had been heated arguments in the family about where the band was to be put and no one had thought of consulting the musicians themselves; Helen had decided to have it in the corner near the end window, so she was greatly taken aback when the pianist assumed command; she was so surprised that she did not even protest.

The big double doors into the back drawing-room were to be kept closed; the room was to be used for sitting out and the sofa and some of the chairs from the drawing-room had been squeezed into it; there was so much furniture there now that it was almost impossible to move. Guy had fled for the day and was lunching at his club; his study was going to be used as a bridge-room and all his things were being tidied, with the result, as he said plaintively, that he would never find anything again.

When Isabel discovered that Guy was not going to be in until nearly dinner-time, she began to look thoughtful. There was something she wanted to tell him and now she would have to tell it to her mother instead; Helen was not a person who could be wheedled and she felt more and more apprehensive as the morning wore on; she was, she had discovered, better at dealing with men than women.

Lunch was a scrappy meal of cold meat and bread and butter; everybody in the kitchen was too busy to cook potatoes and vegetables. When they had finished and were sitting round the table, Isabel began as nonchalantly as possible:

'Oh Mother, I hope you don't mind, but I had to ask Denis Joyce to come tonight.'

Helen looked stunned; she stared open-mouthed at Isabel and was speechless.

'I had to, Mother; he was in the party at the dance on Friday and the others were all coming and talking about it; besides, he's nice.'

'"Had to", oh Isabel!' Helen's voice was heart-broken and Isabel felt far more guilty than if her mother had been downright angry. 'Oh Isabel, how could you, how *could* you? It was most dishonourable of you to do such a thing behind my back. You know your Aunt Emma and I took the greatest trouble over the invitations, so as to have only really nice people. And then you go and ask a . . . a nobody, a rapscallion like one of the Joyces by word of mouth. How dare you do such a thing?'

'I sent him an invitation, Mother;' Isabel was looking at the table; 'and he's nice, I tell you.'

Helen's wrath overflowed: 'You sent him an invitation in *my* name! You made it look as though I were inviting him to come to *my* house! Really child, I think you must be mad.' She gave a little pitying laugh: 'But the young man seems to have no manners, because I've not had any reply; perhaps he doesn't know the meaning of R.S.V.P.?' She shrugged her shoulders and added: 'I presume he's not coming, then?'

'Oh yes, he's coming,' said Isabel, rather shame-facedly; 'he gave me the reply; he was coming to drop it and I . . . was at the door, so he gave it to me.'

'It's the deception of it,' wailed Helen, 'it's enough to break my heart. If you can do a thing like this, what are you going to stop at? But I suppose my feelings don't matter, I'm only your mother. Where did you meet this young man? I thought you were with the MacNamaras on Friday.'

'Yes, I was.'

'And they had invited him?'

'Yes, of course.'

'One can't trust anybody these days. I shall never forgive Hettie MacNamara, never. And to think that she was a Cunningham!'

'But,' protested Isabel, 'I've known him for ages; he's at almost all the parties; it wasn't just there I met him.'

'That doesn't make it any better; people must know that all that family are rabid Republicans; do you mean to say that my friends have sunk to asking Republicans to their dances?'

'But don't you see, Mother? That's all over now: you can't pretend the British are still here after all these years.'

Helen lost all control: 'We are the British,' she blazed, 'and we're still here; we shall never give in, never forgive these Nationalists for what they've done to us: they've killed our men and burnt out houses and turned us into exiles in our own land. They hate us, don't you see? They're trying to destroy us now by making friends with us and taking away our will to resist them.'

'Oh Mother, how can you be so vile!' Isabel was in a flaming temper now. 'Denis isn't a bit like that; he likes people and they like him; there's no politics in it.'

Poor Miss O'Connor, who had been fidgeting on the edge of her chair for some time, now hastily excused herself and bolted, making signs to Caroline to accompany her. Caroline ignored the signs; she was going to hear this out to the end.

Helen folded her napkin and pushed her chair back. 'Well, he's not coming to this house, do you hear me? You'll have to put him off. I won't have one of that family inside my house; that's final.'

'But Mother,' Isabel almost screamed, 'you can't put people off like that. What on earth am I to say?'

'You'll have to think up something: you got yourself into this position, you'll have to get yourself out of it. If he does see through the excuse, so much the better!'

Isabel sat straight up: 'I'm not going to do it.'

Helen was half-way to the door; she pretended not to hear.

'Mother, do you hear? I won't do it.'

At the door, Helen turned round. 'Very well, I shall have to do it myself, then,' she said lightly, watching the effect of her words.

'Oh, you can't, you mustn't; I won't have it!' Isabel banged on the table with rage, large tears in her eyes.

'Well, it's either you or me; you'd better make up your mind quickly.' Helen sat down on the chair in the hall beside the telephone.

'I shall wait here,' she announced.

'Well, of all the damned . . . ! She means to listen to what I say,' cried Isabel, and burst into tears.

Caroline was thinking hard: 'Isabel!' she hissed across the table.

'Oh, go to hell. What's this got to do with you?'

'Ring up Daddy at the Club—he'll still be there if you're quick. Mother can't stop you doing that.'

'Oh, can't she?' Isabel looked up quickly; 'it's worth trying, though.'

They went together into the hall and Isabel began to study the telephone directory; she picked up the receiver and asked for a number. Helen was reading the *Irish Times* and was apparently oblivious of her presence. Eventually, a voice replied; watching her mother, Isabel said quietly:

'Can I speak to Mr. Adair, please?'

Helen was on her feet in a moment, furious: 'Isabel!' she cried, 'how dare you appeal to your father! You know he'll support me. Put that thing down at once, I say.'

'Oh, Daddy? Do come home at once, quickly, just for a minute, it's urgent. No, I can't tell you now. It really is urgent. Oh, you will? Thank you.'

Isabel put down the receiver and faced her mother squarely:

'I'll do what Daddy says—he's reasonable,' she said, and raced up the stairs to put her face in order; she felt triumphant: Daddy was easy to deal with.

Guy was in a state of considerable alarm when he let himself in at the front door, together with three of the caterer's men who were staggering under the weight of pots of palms. The four of them filed into the hall; Helen was still sitting beside the telephone; opposite her, leaning against the wall, chin up, was Isabel.

'What in the name of Heaven . . . ?' he began.

Helen waved the men and their palm-trees into the dining-room:

'Come into the study,' she said grimly.

'Is somebody ill?'

'No, nobody is ill.'

He stood at the door to let them pass; as Isabel went by, she turned a pleading face of anguish to him: 'Don't send me out of the room,' she whispered. He looked at her in utter amazement as he shut the door.

'Well, what's happened?' he said, when they were all seated.

Helen began calmly enough: 'Isabel has chosen to invite a most undesirable person to come to the dance—one of the Joyces. She actually sent him an invitation without consulting me. I've told her that I won't have him in the house and that she must put him off; she has absolutely refused to do it.'

'I had to ask him, Daddy; he's been at all the parties I've been at and the other night everybody was talking about tonight, so I just asked him too. Besides, isn't this my dance, can't I have my own friends at it?'

Guy grimaced and took out his pipe. He did not say a word; he turned the pipe over and over in his hand and felt in his pocket for his tobacco pouch.

'Never in my life have I been so flagrantly defied, and by my own daughter, too!' said Helen bitterly.

'What sort of a young man is he?' said Guy to Isabel; 'what does he do?'

'He's twenty-two, he's in Trinity and he's going to be a lawyer.'

'In Trinity? Not at the National University?'

'Oh no.'

Guy smiled; it was unusual for people who were Nationalists and Roman Catholics to choose to send their sons to Trinity. 'Well, well,' he said and turned to Helen: 'Have you seen this young man?'

She gave a little snort: 'Certainly not.'

'Well, mightn't it be a good thing if we had a look at him? He seems to be among the child's set of friends,' he said tentatively.

'It's unthinkable; I should never be able to hold up my head again if one of that family was to be seen in my house, I . . .'

'It was very silly of you to ask him, child, knowing your mother's views on these things,' broke in Guy severely, 'it was most wrong.'

Isabel was blushing. 'I never thought she'd take it like this,' she muttered.

'Well, your mother won't have him in the house and you won't put him off: what do you expect me to do? Ring him up and tell him we won't let him darken our door?'

Isabel gave a little giggle.

'All I can say is, if he comes, I shan't appear,' snapped Helen.

'And if you put him off, I shan't,' echoed Isabel angrily.

'Oh, my God!' groaned Guy, and scowled at Isabel for her insubordination.

'But he's got to come; he's fetching the Moores and they haven't got a car,' said Isabel desperately.

'What, all the way from Foxrock?'

'You don't mean to tell me that Mrs. Moore lets her girls go about with people like that?' exclaimed Helen.

'Of course she does; everybody does, except a few bigoted old women like . . .'

'Control yourself, Isabel.' Guy was getting angry now.

Isabel bit her lip; that last remark had undone a lot of good work. How could she make them give in? As if in answer to a prayer, inspiration came; she looked covertly at her parents.

'As a matter of fact,' she said slowly, 'I think he's more or less engaged to Juliet Moore, only of course nobody's supposed to know.' This was an appalling but expedient lie and she told it bravely; for a moment she doubted its effect, but when she saw the almost comic expression of relief that spread over both faces, she began to hope again.

'Oh, Isabel, you really are very tiresome; why didn't you tell me this before? It makes the whole thing completely different,' said Helen irritably.

Guy was looking thoughtful; he shifted his position and relit his pipe.

'Listen to me, Isabel,' he said sternly; 'you've placed your mother in such a false position that she's forced to choose between two impossible alternatives; if the young man comes, she must deny all her principles of loyalty by receiving him in public as her invited guest; unfortunately, we can't tell people that he was asked without her knowledge. Her friends will be entitled to say that she has thrown over her traditions, by inviting a member of one of the most prominent Nationalist families in Dublin to dance with her daughter and her daughter's friends; the parents of many of the girls who are coming tonight will be justified in feeling the deepest resentment against your mother for introducing their girls to a man of this type. I'm not saying anything against him—he may be most charming and intelligent, but he bears the stamp of something with which your mother has had, and will have, no dealings. Now, on the other hand, if we were to put him off, your mother would, in the eyes of the world, be guilty of unpardonable discourtesy; I quite agree with you that it can't be done, especially in view of this, er, engagement; but if you had acted openly in the first place, this situation would never have arisen. You knew that if you asked your mother to invite him, she would refuse, so you took the law into your own hands and faced her with the problem at the last minute, when it was too late to do anything. That's blackmail, Isabel, and I won't have your mother blackmailed.'

Tears of shame and anger hung on Isabel's lashes: 'But it's her own fault,' she wailed, 'if she'd only let me have my own friends!'

'You're entitled to choose your friends, but your mother has the right to choose her guests. I know you think we're old-fashioned and straitlaced, but you must remember that there's more than mere class distinction in this; even if you've forgotten that you grew up under the British, it's hurtful for older people to have their traditions flouted and their loyalties ignored. Now, when you've apologised to your mother, I'll tell you what I suggest.'

Isabel was silent; she looked from one to the other, a look of hunted misery; there was no comfort, no escape. Guy was watching her narrowly, with a hard appraising look in his eye that made her feel uncomfortably guilty; she had a feeling that he knew she was lying about the engagement, that he could see through her protests and excuses to the fact that, of all things, she wanted to conceal, that she was in love with Denis Joyce.

'I'm sorry, Mother,' she mumbled, without looking up.

Guy nodded. 'Now,' he said, 'this is my suggestion; since, as you say, this young man is engaged to Juliet Moore and is to bring her and her sister here tonight, I think he must come, but only on the condition that you give your mother a solemn undertaking, to be kept whole-heartedly by you, that you'll never invite him to this house again or go to his house without the consent of either your mother or me. This double dealing has got to cease. What do you say, Helen?'

Isabel drew in her breath sharply: so he did guess! Otherwise, why should he imagine that she would ever want to go to the Joyces' house? It would never have occurred to him if he had really believed her story about the engagement.

Helen threw out her hands hopelessly: 'I hate the whole idea of it,' she said vehemently; 'that my friends should see a Republican in my house—I shall never get over it! One thing's certain, anyway—I shall never give another dance; there's been nothing but trouble over this one from the very beginning. I suppose this is what people like Hettie MacNamara call moving with the times!'

'But do you agree?' asked Guy patiently.

'Oh, I suppose the young man will have to come, this once; but never again, Isabel, do you understand? And Juliet Moore doesn't come inside this house again either—not that that will make her change her mind, of course, but still . . .'

'Isabel?' Guy was still watching her closely, his voice faintly enquiring.

'Oh, I agree,' said Isabel sullenly. It was a pity about Juliet, but she wouldn't miss much and anyway she need never know; probably, one of these days, she would go and get herself engaged to one of those terribly decent dull young men she was always going about with, and then Helen would think she had come back to the fold and all would be well. As to asking Denis to the house again, Heaven knew she would never attempt to do that, after all this fuss; she had promised not to go to his house, but they couldn't always ask her where she was going and she could lie, if necessary; from now on she was going to lie, shamelessly, gladly: they had driven her to it. Her head tilted up rebelliously but Guy's penetrating gaze assailed her and she realised despairingly that none of her lies would deceive him. She kicked her leg backwards and forwards, hitting her chair savagely; he would pretend to believe every word she said, but all the time he would know the truth and show her, by the inflexion of his voice or the expression in his eyes, that all her deception was useless. He was still looking at her: why couldn't he leave her alone? She got up quickly and left the room.

Guy shook his head wearily and turned to put on his coat; he bent to kiss his wife as he went out and was horrified at the look of utter exhaustion on her face.

'You're looking rotten, my dear,' he said gently; 'couldn't you go and lie down and leave the rest to Miss O'Connor and the children? Surely they can manage?'

Helen looked down quickly to hide the animosity in her eyes; she had been gratified by his support, but she had no illusions. He had upheld her principles out of loyalty to her alone, because she was his wife; if she were dead, every Republican in Dublin could come to the house and Guy would talk to them and find them interesting. As these thoughts passed through her mind, she realised how bitterly lonely she was and she remembered a dream that had come to her again and again a few years ago; she was on a deserted shore and the tide that had brought her there was rushing out, leaving her alone on a waste of cold wet empty sand. She was indeed alone now; Guy was bound to her only by duty, Isabel almost hated her, one by one her friends were giving in to the pressure of circumstances. There was only Caroline; she had not lost her yet. Suddenly she remembered that Guy was waiting for an answer.

'I'm all right,' she said quietly; 'the arrangements are nothing; everything's done.'

When he had gone, she sat there for a moment, hands behind her head; then she stood up, to watch him pass the window, holding the brim of his hat in the high wind.

'There goes a traitor,' she whispered to herself, 'and he's my husband!'

She went to his desk and, taking a little knife, began to sharpen the bridge pencils carefully, over the fire, so as not to make a mess. She wiped the blade in a piece of waste paper and replaced the knife. Then, walking erectly, she went out to the pantry to see about the claret cup. There was still Caroline.

Miss O'Connor was getting Caroline ready for the dance; she stood there, in her old bronze lace evening dress, busy with little gold safety pins with which she was trying to ensnare Caroline's errant shoulder-straps.

'Stand still, dear,' she murmured patiently as Caroline bent low to catch a glimpse of herself in the dressing-table mirror. 'How can I do anything if you keep bobbing about? Now—oh no, I'm afraid that can't have gone right through.' She took out the little pin and put it in her mouth while she took a firm grip, breathing heavily between Caroline's shoulder-blades.

'That's right, this time,' she said triumphantly; 'now let me get at your hair.'

'I don't want one of those great ugly slides,' said Caroline; 'let me have one of these little things, they don't show.' She produced a battered clip, salvaged from Isabel's waste-paper basket. Miss O'Connor nodded as she brushed fiercely at the red-gold curls. Caroline inspected her nails and sighed; they were short, but clean, she would have liked to see them long and pointed, like Isabel's. She held her hands above her head.

'That makes them white, doesn't it?' she asked.

'What, your hands? It's supposed to, I believe.' The old governess laughed. 'You've got nicely shaped hands, you ought to take care of them.'

'I'm going to,' said Caroline seriously; 'I'm going to look after my appearance from now on; I'm old enough, don't you think?'

Miss O'Connor sighed: 'Yes, dear, quite old enough,' she replied solemnly; in a month, she was thinking, I shall have left and Caroline will be going to school and perhaps I shall never see her again. It was hard to imagine the new life that would begin in January, going into a strange household, after eight years here, growing fond of new children who at first would regard her suspiciously, as all children did with a new governess, until they came to see that she was no fearsome tyrant but a kind and lonely old woman who wished them well. But never, she thought, would she love any child as she had loved Caroline; little Caroline who had been only seven when she came and who was now almost grown-up, who had teased her and tormented her and treated her all the time as a valued friend.

Caroline seemed to know what she was thinking, for she kissed her suddenly, a tiny gentle kiss on the cheek:

'You must come and see me in the holidays, promise you will?'

'Of course I will dear, if I can possibly manage it.'

Isabel came dancing in to show them her new frock.

'Am I all right behind?' she asked, knowing that she was perfect.

'Turn round, dear; yes, quite all right; that really is a lovely dress.'

'I must go down,' said Isabel breathlessly; 'they'll all be arriving in a minute.' She was gone, leaving little perfumed wafts behind her on the air.

Caroline sniffed enviously: 'I wish I had some scent; I think it's lovely, don't you?'

'A little goes a long way,' said Miss O'Connor, who thought that Isabel used too much; 'now, run along dear, your mother will be expecting you downstairs.'

Caroline darted out into the passage and hung for a moment over the banisters; all was quiet, Isabel must have gone down. Cautiously, she crept down to the next floor and into Isabel's empty bedroom; everything was tidy and impersonal, except for the faint entrancing smell of scent which Isabel had left behind her. Caroline shut the door carefully, for Miss O'Connor might come down the stairs and ask her awkward questions.

She stood in front of the long mirror and surveyed herself critically; her figure, she decided, was good; her waist was slim and she was long from hip to toe; she turned sideways; thank goodness she was growing some bosom at last! The evening-dress made her neck look very long, in spite of the simple little string of pearls which Helen had lent her to cover this nakedness, but it was a lovely dress and the colour was perfect, it made her skin look whiter and her hair redder and it turned her grey eyes to green. She twirled round to make the skirt fly out, then, remembering her purpose, she sat down quickly at the dressing-table; if she did not hurry, someone might begin to wonder where she was.

She picked up a little pot of foundation cream and smelt it, dipping in her finger, she smoothed it all over her face; she knew just what to do, having watched Isabel many times. Then she dabbed the powder puff lightly on her nose, but there was too much powder on it so she had to wipe it off and start again. After the powder, the rouge; one had to be careful with rouge, she knew, or it made one look about fifty. Something had gone wrong; she looked like a Dutch doll, with a brilliant red spot on each cheek of a dead-white mask. Wash it off and start again. Oh, that was lovely! She rubbed the patches of rouge busily at the edges until the friction made her cheeks scarlet and she could not tell where the rouge ended or began. Now for some of that eye-lash stuff, the directions said to use water, but Isabel always spat on it; Caroline spat fastidiously, trying not to think how often Isabel had done the same thing. Some of the stuff got into her eye and made it water; it hurt horribly and a little black puddle formed underneath her eye; she had to keep mopping to prevent it becoming a trickle down her cheek. The pain subsided and she tried again, this time successfully. Goodness, what long eyelashes she had!

There were plenty of lipsticks to choose from; she took the brightest and set to work; eventually she was satisfied. She picked up the hand-mirror and examined herself from every angle; the results were certainly most gratifying: to look at her, nobody could know that she was not grown-up. Even her hair was smooth and shining.

She tidied everything away and went down, taking care to keep out of Helen's way; she squeezed past the dancing couples, walking very slowly and smiling at the people she knew.

David Butler and her father were talking at the fire-place; she slipped her arm inside Guy's and said with a brilliant smile:

'Hallo, David!'

David, now a sub-lieutenant and home on leave, took one look at her and gasped:

'Good Lord, Caroline, are you grown-up now?'

'Well, nearly,' murmured Caroline, terrified that Guy would give her away, but he did not; he gave her a side-long glance, opened his eyes wide and blinked; then he said:

'You two had better go and dance, I think. How's your programme, child? Have you any dances left?'

'Oh!' exclaimed Caroline, 'I haven't got a programme, I forgot.' An empty future loomed hideously before her; she had spent so much time making up her face that now everybody would be booked up and no one would ask her to dance. She very nearly burst into tears.

'Keep the supper-dance for me,' said Guy. She nodded gratefully. David led her off and fetched her a programme.

'I got here too late to book many dances,' he said, 'so when in doubt, come to me. That is, if you're not bored.' He looked a little frightened of this strange new creature whom he had been accustomed to see in a gym-tunic, showing quantities of spindly black leg. 'I only got back tonight,' he explained, 'and Mother couldn't find me any boiled shirts; that's why I'm so late.'

'Thanks awfully,' she replied, filled with gratitude. They began to dance and she tried to put into practice all Isabel had shown her of the fox-trot; she thought ruefully of her childhood dancing classes, where she had been taught nothing but hornpipes, polkas, and Grecian dances—why couldn't they have taught her something useful?

'Do you know all these people?' asked David.

'Some of them. Oh, I'm sorry!' She had got out of time.

'My fault,' lied David gallantly. 'By the way, how old *are* you? I always thought you were six years younger than me.'

'I'm afraid I am still, David,' said Caroline, depressed at being caught out so early in the evening. 'I'm sixteen, actually, *just.*'

'Well, I must say, you've managed to conceal it pretty effectively!' They both laughed. 'Who's that gorgeous beast dancing with Isabel?'

The music stopped and Caroline saw Isabel walking off with a tall young man, dark and broad-shouldered.

'It's someone called Denis Joyce,' she said.

'Denis Joyce! But they're all Sinn Feiners, aren't they? What the hell's he doing in your house?' David looked quite angry.

'Oh, Isabel says she's known him for ages; she asked him to come and Mother was furious; there was an awful row. That's why Mother wasn't there to shake hands with people when they came; she wouldn't shake hands with him.'

'I don't blame her, I'm sure there was a row; if I'd been your father I'd have kicked him down the steps. Does Isabel know many of that crowd? Damn good-looking chap, blast him.'

'I don't think so; she says he's at all the parties.'

'Come in after them, I must get Isabel to give me a dance, I haven't been able to get near her.' He pushed Caroline firmly in front of him into the back drawing-room, sat her down in a chair and went up to where Isabel and Denis, in complete silence, were staring dreamily at each other on the sofa.

'Hallo, David,' said Isabel warily; 'so you did come! I'd almost given you up.'

'Couldn't help it, my dear, I'm awfully sorry—I only got back tonight. May I have a dance?'

Isabel pretended to consult her programme, knowing perfectly well that it was full; she held it up carefully so that he should not see how frequently the initial 'D' appeared on it; she knew that she was foolish to dance so often with Denis, but she felt reckless after the quarrel with her parents and if she could not deceive Guy she could at least defy Helen. Besides, she wanted to dance with Denis more than anything else.

'Sorry,' she said, 'I'm afraid you've missed the boat.' She shook her head regretfully and smiled up at him.

'Ah, come on Lizzie,' David jokingly burst into a broad Dublin accent and, bending down, took her hand; 'don't be so hard-hearted, spare a little wan for an old pal, willya?'

She pulled her hand away and looked at him as though he had struck her; an expression of horror came over her face. Denis had quite a considerable accent and if he were to open his mouth David would roar with laughter, thinking that he too was trying to be funny. It was terrible to think of his Celtic sensibility being bruised by ridicule. She frowned at David to make him behave, but his eyebrows shot up and he looked as if he might, out of pure devilment, ask what was wrong, so she said hastily:

'No, I haven't got one, I tell you; not even an extra.'

'Damn,' said David, but he did not go away; he squatted on his heels and looked at her quizzically. 'Don't be cross, Lizzie,' he said gently.

'I'm not cross,' she protested smiling coldly. Great blundering idiot, why couldn't he go away. She thought of a way to get rid of him.

'David, have you met Mr. Joyce? Denis, this is Mr. Butler.'

David drew himself up and glared; Denis nodded cheerfully.

Isabel stifled a yawn and waited, but the devil had entered into David.

'There was a chap called Joyce in my term at Dartmouth,' he said to Denis; 'he might be some relation of yours—lives in England, but they used to be in Wexford; burnt out in the bad times, you know.'

Isabel squirmed with embarrassment: this was frightful! She looked at Denis in agony, but he was quite unperturbed; he glanced knowingly at David, with a glint of amusement in his blue eyes, and answered:

'I've no relations in England; they're still all in this country, thank God!'

David was disarmed. 'I just wondered,' he said lamely. He grimaced at Isabel: 'Sorry you won't dance with me, Lizzie,' and made his way back to Caroline.

He and Caroline spent the greater part of the evening together; they had their several reasons for avoiding Helen, Caroline because she did not want to be sent off in ignominy to wash her face, and David because whenever Helen caught sight of him she would lead him off to dance with some dowdy, thoroughly nice girl. Returning from one such mission, he mopped his face and announced that he was damned if he was going to cart any more wall-flowers round the room. 'That one was like towing a heavy gun,' he said, 'and the one before was like trying to bicycle against a high wind; isn't there anywhere we can go where I shall be safe?'

'We could go and have something to eat,' said Caroline, 'or, if you like, we could go up to the schoolroom and roast chestnuts.'

His face lit up: 'I'm all for the chestnuts; you wait here and I'll dash down and get us some drinks; what'll you have?'

'Ooh, I don't know; they were making some claret cup this afternoon . . .'

'I'll see what I can do.' He sped down for the drinks and was back in a moment; side by side, they ran up the stairs, weaving their way past dim couples sitting out, laughing like a pair of excited children.

'Your claret cup only just missed going down someone's neck,' said David, panting, when they reached the lobby; they peered into the schoolroom.

'Don't let's turn on the light—it's much more fun with just the fire,' said Caroline.

Suddenly they perceived a dark shape in the arm-chair; there was a sound of gentle snoring. They stood still, listening, and Caroline began to giggle. It was Miss O'Connor, fast asleep, recovering from an exhausting day.

Caroline put her finger to her lips and gave David a little push to make him stay where he was; she crept forward, looked back mischievously, and kissed the old woman on the very tip of her nose. Miss O'Connor awoke with a guilty start.

'Caroline, dear,' she said reproachfully, 'you gave me such a fright!' She patted her hair apprehensively, afraid that Caroline might have removed the pins, and smoothed down her skirts.

'David's here,' whispered Caroline; 'we've come to roast chestnuts.'

'Oh dear!' Miss O'Connor struggled to her feet, greatly fluttered; 'Dear me, I'm so sorry David, come and sit down—such a long time since we saw you.'

They settled down in the firelight, Miss O'Connor in her chair, David and Caroline on the floor; from below came the faint sound of music. Soon the room was filled with the aroma of roasting chestnuts; David peeled them gingerly and handed them to the others. Caroline leant against Miss O'Connor's knees, head on one side, staring dreamily into the fire and nibbling chestnuts as they were handed to her; she had become quite a different person. Only yesterday she would have stuffed them into her mouth, like a child, making little panting noises to avoid getting burnt. Miss O'Connor glanced at David, his fair head bent over his hands; he looked up and smiled, holding out the chestnut he had been peeling, but she shook her head:

'Eat it yourself, I've had enough.'

Lazily chewing, he stretched himself and grinned. 'This is grand,' he said contentedly; 'I haven't done anything so nice for ages.'

There was a faint rustling in the lobby, and a sound of slow footsteps; a couple turned into the room, so engrossed in one another that they did not see the little group round the fire; three heads were lifted, watching them as they kissed in the doorway. A sinister little spurt of flame lit up the room for a moment: Isabel and Denis.

David turned away and carefully knocked over the fire-irons; Miss O'Connor gave a little warning cough; Caroline just stared.

Isabel drew in her breath sharply: 'Oh God, who is it?' she said in an anguished whisper.

David's face looked puce in the firelight: 'Sorry you've been troubled,' he said stiffly, not looking up.

Isabel caught hold of Denis's hand and pulled him out of the room. 'Come on out of here,' she whispered desperately. The others could hear them making their way down the stairs. Tum-ti-tum, came the sound of the band gaily from below, tum-ti-tum-ti-tum.

David stood up: 'Your father'll be looking for you for the supper-dance,' he said sternly, 'and I must wash, I'm filthy. Aren't you coming to have some supper. Miss O'Connor?'

'Yes,' she said absentmindedly; 'Oh yes, I must go down for it. You two go on and I'll follow in just a minute.'

Guy was standing at the drawing-room door, waiting for Caroline. 'Good,' he said; 'I wondered where you were.'

The band began to play an old-fashioned waltz: 'Ah,' he said, 'this is something I know how to do.' He tucked his arm. round Caroline's waist and whirled her round and round the room. 'Can you reverse?' he asked, and she shook her head. 'Got to,' he laughed, 'or you'll fall flat on your face.' He whisked her almost off her feet in the opposite direction; on and on they went; Caroline was gasping with excitement and exhaustion. 'Don't stop, don't stop,' warned Guy, as they spun round and round. At last the music stopped. Laughing and panting,

Caroline slipped her arm in his; he smiled down at her:

'That's what a waltz *should* be like; in the old days your mother and I used to dance like that; it was great fun.'

Her eyes opened wide in astonishment and he laughed: 'Yes, I know it's hard to imagine that we were ever young, but it's true.'

The stairs were thronged with people making their way down to supper; she tugged at his arm: 'Do you remember, once, years ago, Isabel said that when she had her dance she'd have all the officers from the Castle, and Uncle Archie said there wouldn't be any officers then?'

'Ah yes! That must have been in the old days, before the British left. Well?'

'It would have been more fun if things had been like that, with uniforms and things, wouldn't it?'

Guy sighed: 'Perhaps,' he said quietly.

'I'd like to have seen a dance at the Castle, just to know what it was like,' went on Caroline; 'everybody says dances here will never be the same again.'

'Ever heard of nostalgia?' he asked her, smiling.

'Mm.'

'Well, things can change without necessarily becoming worse, you know, but people forget that. What they grew up with is best.'

They were swept into the dining-room; there was a seething throng round the long tables, men coming and going with plates of food, or carefully juggling their way between the people with full glasses in their hands. Round the walls, sat the girls, laughing and talking, waiting for their partners to bring them food. Installed in an arm-chair at the end of the room, sat Catha; she neither danced nor played bridge, but she would not allow that to prevent her from coming to Isabel's dance.

'Come here, child,' she beckoned to Caroline, 'kiss me.'

Caroline obediently bent down.

'Now let me look at you. Quite grown-up, aren't you dear?'

Eileen Hunt, who had been playing bridge, playfully jerked one of Caroline's curls as she went past.

'You look lovely, duckie,' she whispered in her ear. Almost overcome by gratitude, Caroline beamed at her disappearing form.

'Well, this really is delightful,' said Catha, smiling with satisfaction; 'now tell me, where is Isabel? I haven't been able to admire her new dress properly yet, but I'm sure she has no time to waste on old ladies on an occasion like this.'

Caroline pointed her out, the centre of a little knot of admirers, near the door. Catha fumbled for her lorgnette, which hung on a long gold chain round her neck.

'Ah yes! She seems to be very popular, but that is hardly surprising. What a beautiful frock—but your dear mother has such good taste! She really does look lovely, don't you think?'

'Yes,' agreed Caroline; 'she chose the frock herself.'

'Indeed! How very nice. She looks a trifle tired, I think; all the excitement, no doubt.'

Guy and Alec appeared with plates of food, but Alec spotted Eileen, fending for herself at the buffet table, and deserted them to look after her.

'This is most delicious, Guy,' said Catha, consuming a lobster patty with relish; 'I do think Helen has been so clever over the whole thing. Now who is that very handsome young man talking to Isabel, over there? Such a good-looking fellow!'

Guy looked round and gave Caroline's arm a little squeeze as he answered: 'Oh, that's some friend of hers that I haven't met yet— these modern daughters, you know! Now, let me get you another of those things.'

'Well,' bridled Catha, 'I mustn't be greedy, but they really are so very good; if you could just get me a tiny one, Guy dear, a very tiny one.'

Guy went off to select the largest patty he could find and take a good look at the unspeakable Denis Joyce on his way.

'I said a tiny one,' said Catha, immensely pleased, when he returned.

She started to eat, as though she were afraid Guy might take her at her word. 'And there's dear David, looking so handsome too, just like his father at that age!' She pulled Guy's sleeve to make him bend down, and whispered loudly: 'Now, wouldn't it be very nice if he and Isabel . . .'

Guy gave a wry little smile: 'Of course it would be delightful, but . . .'

'Perhaps she prefers someone else, is that it? Well, well, there's time enough, they're all so young. It looks to me as if that dark young man was rather a favourite—what did you say his name was?'

'Daughters don't tell fathers, these days, where their affections lie,' said Guy laughing; 'perhaps when Isabel actually gets herself engaged to someone, she'll find it convenient to let me know who it is. Now, let me get you something to drink—I know just what you'd like,' and he was off again before Catha could ask him more awkward questions.

Caroline wandered away and found herself pursued by a pale young man with a bony face and mouse-coloured hair.

'I say,' he stammered, 'I'm sure you don't remember who I am, but do you think you could possibly dance with me? I'm Gilbert Hamilton; you came over to Kilmurry once when you were staying with your Aunt at Butler's Hill, you were only very small then . . .'

Caroline smiled: 'Of course I remember.' The Hamilton family had been rather a joke with the Butlers; Sir Hercules Hamilton was a fiery old widower with this painfully shy, studious small boy and a large and buxom daughter; everyone said that it was Marion who should have been the boy.

'I'd love to dance,' she added.

She watched him as they climbed the stairs; he had not changed much; he still had the same diffident gauche look, as though he suffered continually from the knowledge that he was not like most people; he was probably horribly boring, except when he was being learned, and he looked the sort of person who would never allow himself to speak about things that really interested him, for fear of boring others. This was the kind of young man that Isabel heartily despised; she liked only successful confident people, but Caroline felt sorry for him and smiled at him to put him at his ease.

'How's Marion?' she asked.

'She's in London, making a career for herself at interior decorating; she's doing frightfully well.'

She would be, thought Caroline. 'And you?' she said.

'I'm at Woolwich.'

'Do you like it?'

'Oh, it's all right,' he said, and she knew he loathed it.

Few people had come up from supper yet and the band was playing to an almost empty room; awkwardly, they began to dance. Caroline was not an accomplished dancer, but Gilbert was hopeless and they stumbled along miserably.

'I'm afraid I'm a rotten dancer,' said Gilbert unhappily; 'would you like to stop?'

'No, it's me,' said Caroline reassuringly, 'don't let's stop.'

He smiled gratefully and said: 'Oh no, I think you're . . .' and did not finish the sentence.

When the music stopped, they went into the back drawing-room. Isabel was there, pretending to listen to some young man who was giving a highly-coloured description of a motor-cycle race. She would not look at Caroline, but stared moodily at her evening bag as she kept playing with the clasp.

'Terrific, wasn't it?' said her partner.

She looked at him blankly; she had not the remotest idea what he was talking about. 'It must have been,' she said slowly, hoping that she was saying the right thing.

'But, can you believe it, the chap wasn't killed!' he said, and went on with his interminable story.

'Who . . . stole my heart away, Who . . . makes me dream all day?' began the band and Denis came in to fetch Isabel; she looked at him uncertainly, as though she were afraid to dance with him again. Her whole evening had been ruined: was Miss O'Connor going to be a beast and give her away? Denis gripped her elbow and led her off. David was standing at the door; as they passed, he bowed:

'The schoolroom's empty now,' he said stiffly; 'Miss O'Connor's gone to bed. Just thought you'd like to know.'

Isabel shot him a look of intense loathing; Denis lingered for a moment, as though he were about to say something, but she tugged at his hand.

'Come on,' she urged, 'don't take any notice of him—he's drunk.'

But Denis laughed: 'Jealous sort of fella, isn't he?' he said.

Isabel dealt with Caroline before she went to bed and extracted a promise from her that she would tell no one of the scene at the schoolroom door; actually, this was quite unnecessary, as Caroline was rather impressed by this romantic incident and would never have thought of talking about it; but Isabel slept badly: there was still Miss O'Connor to be silenced.

At breakfast, heavy-eyed and unhappy, she watched the old woman anxiously but could read nothing in her face; she took pains to be very polite to her and smiled whenever she caught her eye, but without response. Miss O'Connor was very quiet, but then she never did talk much; perhaps she was making up her mind. Isabel knew that if she considered it her duty to tell Helen of what she had seen, nothing would stop her, and old-fashioned people had such a peculiar sense of duty, one never knew what they would find themselves impelled to do. She wished the old governess was safely out of the house in her new post.

When the others had left the table, she stayed there, hunched up miserably, thinking, but Miss O'Connor's voice outside brought her suddenly to her feet.

'Could I speak to you for a moment, please, Mrs. Adair, when you're not too busy?'

Helen's reply was a relief: 'Yes, of course, if you could just wait until I've done the housekeeping.' She heard Miss O'Connor trot off, up the stairs; she darted out and followed her to the schoolroom; mercifully, Caroline was not there. She stood facing her: 'I want to talk to you about something,' she said.

'Well?' queried Miss O'Connor, sadly and a little wearily.

'About last night.'

'Yes?' Isabel saw that she was going to get no help.

'You're not going to tell Mother about . . . I mean, are you?'

'About what happened in here?'

'Yes,' said Isabel, relieved to have had it expressed at last. 'It's nothing to do with me, dear, you're no longer in my charge, but I do think it would cause your mother a great deal of pain if she knew that you were . . . carrying on, shall we call it, with that particular young man, especially in her house. What I mean is, is *it fair*, dear?'

'But you're not going to tell her?'

'I told you, dear, it's nothing to do with me.'

'Oh, thank you,' cried Isabel joyfully; she tried to throw her arms round Miss O'Connor's neck, but found herself being pushed gently away.

'Don't kiss me, dear. Now, what about getting to work on putting all the furniture back? There's a lot to be done and we must try to save your mother.'

Mortified and puzzled, but with a wonderful feeling of liberation, Isabel went down to help put the house to rights.

CHAPTER EIGHT

One dim chilly morning in January, Guy drove Helen and Caroline down to Kingstown, recently given back its old name of Dun Laoghaire, to catch the mail-boat: Caroline was going to school. With a sinking heart she watched her luggage being taken off the car; Isabel's old school trunk, with her initials still on it, packed full of unspeakable school uniform which she would have to wear for at least the next year; the brand-new hockey stick, emblem of the British schoolgirl, which she did not even know how to use, and her precious little brown writing-case, a parting present from Guy; these, with Helen's suitcase, were loaded on to a barrow and taken off towards the ship. Guy parked the car and came with them as far as the gangway. Helen, clutching a book, an umbrella, her fur and her handbag, fumbled for the tickets.

'Here, let me,' said Guy, holding out his arms for some of her things.

'If I let one go, they'll all go,' she wailed, 'and I don't know where to begin!'

'Oh, you women!' said Guy, and gave up the struggle.

'I think I'll leave you here,' he said, when the tickets had been found. He squeezed Caroline's hand: 'It won't be as bad as you think,' he whispered, and she smiled.

'Guy, have you got Caroline's rug?' Helen was doing mental check of all the luggage.

'Must have left it in the car—I'll get it.' He started off, but a scream from Helen made him turn round.

'She's got it herself, it's all right. Caroline, dear, can't you be a little more on the spot?'

From half-way down the pier, Guy raised his hat and laughed; then he turned and was gone.

They climbed on to the boat; there was a smell of paint and rubber flooring that made Caroline feel faintly sick; Helen went straight to the saloon and spread her belongings on a sofa; then she took Caroline down to the ladies' cabin, found a stewardess and located the berths that had been reserved. They went up on deck again to wait for Olga, who was going to travel with them and who was coming by train from Westland Row; she and Caroline were going to school together.

Olga's company, thought Caroline, was the only thing that was going to make this new life bearable. Anne had decided that it might be good for Olga to go to boarding-school for a year and Olga, who hated the idea of it, had agreed to go quietly if she could go with Caroline.

The train came in slowly alongside and people began to pour out of it. Caroline spotted Olga, hair streaming behind her, grappling with a suitcase, and Anne, calm and lovely, vaguely swinging Olga's school hat with the striped band, by its elastic; Leonard went off to the van; they waved at the Adairs and made signals to show that they would come on board in a minute. Looking down, Caroline envied Olga; there was something about her that made her look gay and attractive, even in her school uniform. Anne remembered the hat in her hand and held it out with a questioning smile; Olga took it, whirled it round on one finger and shook her head pityingly. Leonard came up and kissed her, looking quite miserable; he was convinced that Olga would come home with enormous muscles and a hearty manner.

The three of them stayed on deck until Leonard and Anne were out of sight; then Caroline and Olga looked at each other in their thick navy-blue overcoats and black stockings, and laughed.

'What d'you bet they won't make me wear this hat?' said Olga, wrinkling up her nose.

'Not only that, but they'll make you plait your hair,' said Helen; she wondered what they would make of Olga.

The school was in Sussex, and they arrived there late that night, tired, cold and hungry; Helen was going straight back to London.

Tired as she was, Caroline could not help being impressed by the head-mistress, Miss Deane; she was a very little woman and seemed to have concentrated immense force of character into the minimum of space. She had a large head and bright brown eyes that missed nothing; her grey hair, which had a persistent kink, was combed back into a bun and she sat rigidly upright, as though she were unable to relax; when she spoke, her head moved but her body remained motionless; her limbs appeared to be attached to some immovable object which was not really alive; her voice was small, clear and powerful and she never raised it.

She received them in her study, a small square room, lined with bookshelves; she rang a little bell on her desk as soon as the formalities were over.

'Matron will show you your cubicles and give you some supper; after that, I feel sure you will want to go to bed.' She spoke with such authority that it was impossible even to envisage any action contrary to her suggestions.

'Now, Caroline, will you say goodbye to your mother? Perhaps you would like to go into the ante-room, Mrs. Adair?'

'I do hope you'll be happy, darling, and make lots of friends; write to us often.' Helen had her arm round Caroline's shoulders.

'Yes;' Caroline wanted to end the parting.

'There now, you'll be all right.'

'Yes,' said Caroline; 'goodbye.'

Helen kissed her and went back to Miss Deane; Olga appeared with Matron, a massive woman in a blue uniform; they followed her in a sort of daze, through endless corridors and up and down little flights of stairs to a great dining-room where they were given a meal of soup, cold meat, potatoes and bread and butter pudding. School had really begun.

Caroline and Olga found themselves regarded somewhat as curiosities by the other girls; there were no other Irish girls.

The first morning, while they were consuming cocoa and biscuits during the eleven o'clock break, they were approached by a little group of girls.

'You're Irish, aren't you?' said one.

They said they were.

'Where do you come from?'

'Dublin,' said Olga.

'Is that in the north or the south?'

'It's in the south,' she replied, a little pityingly.

'Oh, the south's all right, isn't it, or is it the north?'

'What do you mean, all right?'

'Well, one of them's disloyal or something, isn't it?'

'The south's the Free State, if that's what you're getting at,' said Caroline with dignity.

'Are you Republicans?'

'Yes,' replied Caroline, winking at Olga, 'red-hot ones!'

'Are you really? Oh, I say!' They shuddered in awful admiration.

'You can't be really Irish,' said another; 'you haven't got brogues; we had an Irish maid once and you don't speak a bit like her.'

'You can't be English, then, you haven't got a Cockney accent,' retorted Caroline hotly.

'But only servants and people have Cockney accents; of course I haven't got one.' The girl was quite annoyed.

'Well, we can be Irish without having an accent, just the same as you can be English and not have one.'

'Ooh,' they cried, 'look out, she's got red hair and an Irish temper!' One of them turned to Olga; 'You don't look a bit Irish,' she commented, with a look of disappointment. The girl who spoke was unmistakably Jewish-looking.

'I can't say you look particularly English, for that matter,' was Olga's instantaneous reply. There was a nasty silence.

'Can you speak Irish?' asked someone.

'I had to learn it at school, it's frightfully difficult,' said Olga.

'Do say something.' The girl looked rather puzzled.

Olga said slowly, in Irish: 'It's pigs you are and you give me a pain in the belly!'

'Oh, is it a language?' said the girl, in a bored voice; 'I meant, say something in a brogue. What were you saying?'

'Something silly,' and Olga giggled.

'Do tell us.'

'No.' She was adamant.

'Are you Roman Catholics?' queried another.

'No,' they both said, firmly.

'How extr'ordinary! I thought all the Irish were. What are you, then?'

'Church of Ireland,' said Caroline patiently.

'What on earth's that?'

'Same as Church of England, only Irish.'

They couldn't understand; the bell rang for classes to begin and Olga and Caroline were left alone; they gazed at each other weakly and laughed until the tears came into their eyes.

'What do we do now?' said Caroline.

Olga shook her head: 'I've no idea.'

A young efficient-looking mistress poked her head round the door: 'Now, you two,' she said, very slowly and distinctly, as though she were explaining something to a very young child, 'will you come with me? We must find out how much you know about mathematics.'

'Does she think we're foreigners?' whispered Caroline to Olga.

They sighed and followed her.

One brilliant April day, near the end of the term, Caroline was sitting on her locker, lazily putting on her hockey boots, when she was summoned to Miss Deane's study. 'Oh Lord, what have I done!' she thought as she hurried along the corridors and knocked at the door.

'Come in,' called the small bell-like voice.

She opened the door and found herself faced by Archie and Moira Butler; she stared at them for a moment, unable to believe her eyes, then fell upon her aunt and hugged her greedily. Miss Deane looked on benignly.

'This is a nice surprise, Caroline, is it not? Now, will you take your aunt and uncle round the grounds and then you may bring them to tea in the ante-room; no one will disturb you. You are excused your classes until six o'clock when you will attend preparation.'

'Oh thank you, Miss Deane,' said Caroline beaming with delight. The head-mistress nodded dismissal and Caroline went to the door and held it open. Outside in the ante-room, Archie took hold of her by the shoulders and shook her gently:

'I'm here too,' he said laughing, 'didn't you notice?'

'Yes, of course I did,' and she kissed him affectionately; 'you are sweet to come and see me—you're the first visitors I've had.'

'We've got some news for you,' said Moira; 'we'll tell you when we get outside.'

'Oh now!'

Moira shook her head; she looked excited and happy. There was still not a grey hair to be seen on her head and Caroline thought she looked younger than when she had last seen her two years before. She led them out and they walked under the great elms among the daffodils.

'Now!' she said.

Moira tucked Caroline's arm inside her own and turned to Archie: 'You tell her.'

'No, you, my dear.'

'Well,' said Moira, 'we're on our way over to Ireland; we're going to rebuild Butler's Hill!'

Caroline stopped dead: 'Truly?'

'Yes, truly.'

'Oh, how lovely! How simply lovely!' Caroline's eyes were shining.

'May I come and stay with you?'

'Of course, Darling. I wish you could come and live with us. You love that place, don't you?'

'Better than anywhere else. Oh, Aunt Moira I'm so happy!' And they all laughed.

'Your father's designing it for us,' said Archie. 'He went down to have a look at the house and he says the old walls are undamaged, so there won't be a terrible difference, outside.'

'They never told me,' said Caroline disgustedly; 'they never said a word about it in their letters.'

'We wanted to tell you ourselves; I wanted to hear what you said and to see your face when you heard the news,' explained Moira.

'Oh!' Caroline did not know whether to feel appeased or not. 'Have they begun it yet?'

'Yes, they're working at it now; it'll be ages before it's finished; we're going to live in Ryan's little house in the yard until it's ready,' said Archie, and added sombrely, 'poor old Ryan!'

'The leaves'll be coming out on the chestnuts,' said Caroline.

'Some of the spring and all the summer before us—think of the rhododendrons!' Moira was smiling dreamily.

'And I shall have to be here! Just think of it!' Caroline seethed with indignation.

Archie made a sweep of his hand to show her the fine park with its massive trees, the rambling stone house and the rolling Downs in the distance: 'What's wrong with here?' he asked, to tease her.

'Nothing, except that it's not there.'

'Perhaps,' suggested Moira, 'your mother would let you come down for a bit in the summer holidays; we might be able to squeeze you in.'

'May I really? she must—I couldn't bear it if she didn't.'

Moira smiled: 'I'll talk to her when we're in Dublin; we're going to stay with them tomorrow night. Now, tell me, do you like school?'

Caroline made a face: 'Better than I thought; they think Olga and

I are a little mad—they're awfully ignorant, really. It's all quite true what Isabel used to write home: they expect us to have bombs under our beds and to have no drainage and they think we eat, sleep and live on horseback.'

Archie leant against a tree and rocked with laughter.

'But surely,' protested Moira, 'it's only the most ignorant ones who talk like that? Haven't any of them ever been to Ireland?'

'None of them, ever,' said Caroline. 'One or two of them have Irish grandmothers: they think that's frightfully romantic and gives them the right to have a temper. The mistresses are all right, though, except at the beginning one or two of them seemed quite surprised that we could understand what they said. What on earth sort of people do they think we are?'

Moira waved her hands feebly: 'They were sorry for us, in Devon, until we began to want to go back—they thought of us as political refugees, rather heroic and martyred, but when we said we were thinking of going home, they couldn't understand that at all. They thought we were mad, too, very mad—hopeless!' She broke off with a little ripple of laughter.

Archie went on: 'They told us we'd be murdered in our beds, that gunmen would be waiting for us on Kingstown pier, that it was dangerous to travel in Ireland and I don't know what not. They were very serious, they believed every word of it.' He wiped his eyes with a shaking hand: 'And now,' he was laughing so much that they could hardly hear what he said, 'and now, they think we're terribly, terribly brave and terribly, terribly foolish.' He shook his head gravely, until he was assailed by another gust of laughter.

When they came near the house, they saw the girls coming in, muddy and dishevelled, from their game of hockey. Caroline beckoned to Olga, who darted up to talk to them for a moment.

'Attractive child,' said Archie, when she had gone; 'full of vitality.'

'I remember her mother, years ago,' said Moira, 'she was like someone out of a fairy-tale. She had long golden hair, quite straight, and she never seemed to be quite conscious of other people.'

'She's rather like that still,' said Caroline; 'she's a lovely person.'

Miss Deane had arranged a wonderful tea for them; Caroline poured out from a silver tea-pot. It began to be late; the Butlers remembered that they had a train to catch. Caroline waved them down the avenue, clutching a bulky parcel of sweets which they had thrust into her hands. On her way back through the hall, she met Miss Deane.

'They had to catch a train, Miss Deane, and we couldn't find you, so they asked me to say goodbye to you and to thank you very much. . .'

'They, Caroline? Who are 'they'?'

Caroline blushed. 'My aunt and uncle. . .'

Miss Deane relented and smiled: 'They are very charming people,' she said quietly, and patted Caroline's elbow.

In the summer term, Caroline found that she and Olga were no longer to be in the same dormitory; Miss Deane had decided that they kept too much in each other's company and that it would-be good for them to get to know the other girls better. Speech was forbidden in the dormitories, but there was a good deal of illicit whispering. One by one, the other girls would drop off to sleep and Caroline would lie awake, staring out of the window at the shadows growing blue under the trees, and listening to the rasp of the corn-crake in the meadows.

This was the time of day when she could cease to be one of a crowd of chattering schoolgirls and become herself; always, she would think of Butler's Hill and the cool green glen that led down to the sea; in the glen, one was enclosed in a green world where there was no sky, only the light filtering through the leaves of the small sycamores and silver birches to the water trickling over the rocks. At the bottom of the glen was an ancient graveyard, with a forgotten ruined church and here one came out again into the sun and the world of wind and blue water; sometimes, a funeral would be going on there, the men kneeling stiffly at the grave-side, looking very small and unreal, tiny figures made of wood being moved about by some invisible power in a shapeless pattern on the green grass.

Then she would imagine herself lying back on the heather, watching the moon pulling herself over the breast of the hill, up, up, until she reached the Scotch firs; there would be the sound of lapping water in the calm of the evening and, if one stood up, a shimmering golden path across the sea; beyond the hills, the last chilly yellow light; then, damp with dew, one would stretch and think of going home. Home, to a blackened, ruined house! She could not think how Butler's Hill would look, rebuilt.

Helen had promised that she should go there in August; then it would be nearly seven years from the day when, as a little girl, she had watched the burning house sending great clouds of black and evil smoke far up into the calm November sky. Could they, she wondered, ever undo that night's work, appease the quiet gods for the clamour and the violence, and restore the ancient peace? Slowly, perhaps, the old walls would grow accustomed to the new rooms inside, cease to resent the new roof and, when the bustle and disturbance was done, accept them in forgiveness. All through these six years, Caroline had remembered Butler's Hill as a secret world of her own to which she could withdraw; she had never talked of it, but it had been there, hers; now it was to be a dreamworld no longer, but a new life.

Sometimes, when she had had her fill of dreaming, she would think of her father, whom she loved, but of Helen she hardly ever thought; if she did, it was in connexion with something that had to be done, or to wonder whether she had yet discovered Isabel's love affair with Denis Joyce, never with longing for her presence. At times, she felt guilty because she did not love her mother more: most girls were devoted to their mothers; she would sigh and determine to be more affectionate when she went home again. Strange, that of the three people in her home, there was only one in whose company she felt really happy;

Isabel and she thought no thoughts alike, knew no common interest; she could only see her sister as a hard little person who cared for none of them but set herself ruthlessly to the achievement of her one purpose—that of getting her own way.

It was her last day at Butler's Hill; Caroline stepped out of the boat and paused to look down at her feet, so white and slim as the green sea-weed washed against her toes; little waves lifted the stern of the boat and, receding, bumped it gently on the stones. Archie was already out, his trousers rolled up to the knee, and Moira was gathering together picnic baskets and bundles of bathing clothes. They hauled the boat up a little way and Moira climbed out.

They sat on the stony beach for a moment, lazily putting on their shoes, then carried their things over the crest of the island to a flat place among the rocks, where they lay, deep-cushioned in the long fine sea-grass, to watch the slow blue rollers pushing on towards the coast. Caroline left them there, content and half-dozing in the sun, and went exploring by herself. The island was tiny, not more than a couple of hundred yards long, but she climbed a steep slope westwards until she found herself overlooking a deep pool between jutting walls of rock; there was a small outlet, just big enough for a boat to pass through at high tide, but now the water was sucking round the bare fangs of rock that guarded the entrance. She wormed herself along a ledge and lay, gazing down into the dark blue water to where, from the sea floor, the thick brown arms of great plants reached upwards. Jelly-pink and olive-green sea anemones, abandoned by the sea, clung limply to the rock-face, but under the water she could see huge ones of many strange colours; a small jelly-fish, blue-grey, propelled himself with astonishing speed through the water, closing and opening his transparent parachute with clockwork precision; fish, dark and shadowy, passed in slow motion in and out among the long-tongued leaves. A dip in the rocks admitted a single shaft of sunlight which fell on the far corner of the pool, changing the quality of the water so that, instead of being dark and clear it became opaque and green, almost solid, as though the beam might have been lifted out of the water by someone wielding a giant spoon. In the open water, beyond the rocks, a grey-green head bobbed up, with a merry whiskered face and soft brown eyes; it disappeared, surfaced again and was gone, swimming effortlessly along; it was a seal, seeking his private slope of rock where he could lie, basking in the sun.

Caroline had the sensation that she was seeing all this twice; once now, with the full pleasure of the living scene, and again in the mirror of her mind where she would store it for a day when she was in need of refreshment; then, out of the deep recesses of memory, would come the clean vital smell of the ocean water, the slow suck-suck of the sea round the rocks and the slight heaving movement of the brown glutinous weeds below; those creatures, swimming and creeping around in the blue deep water, were hers; even if she were never to see this place again, she would possess it for ever.

With a feeling of tremendous exultation, she edged her way back to the sunlit grass above; there she stood and looked around her at the rollers sweeping in at their leisure to clash against the rocks in a thin white line; she could see the encroaching gorse in full glory on the hill-sides, the grey ribs of bare rock that pierced the soil and the small stone-walled fields where the cattle cropped a hard living from the short green grass; to the west and east were more little rocky grass-capped islands, each with its ribbon-edge of white; near her, a cormorant stood on a needle of rock, preening herself and shaking her feathers in the sun; crabs rustled over the seaweed, each in his own hurry; a gannet, out to sea, stopped in his flight and dropped like a stone into the water.

Caroline faced the sun; and stood, arms half-extended and palms outward, to salute this shining world.

CHAPTER NINE

In 1928, Caroline spent the Easter holidays in Paris, with the Hendersons; Leonard and Anne had been there for a couple of months, and when Anne wrote to Helen, saying that she was going to fetch Olga in London and that it would be a great pleasure to them if Caroline could come too, Guy insisted that this was an opportunity not to be missed.

In the taxi, on their way from the station to the small studio flat where they lived, on the Left Bank, Anne showed Caroline a letter from Guy: 'Since she is going to be with you for a month,' he wrote, 'she must be properly dressed; it would be cruel to make her go about in Paris in those extraordinary clothes which, it seems, are necessary in English schools. Would you be so good as to buy her some reasonable and attractive clothes, such as a French girl of her own age might wear? Take her to a hairdresser, too, if she wishes it; after all, the child is seventeen and I want her to enjoy herself.'

'There was a cheque with it,' explained Anne; 'a nice one; we ought to be able to do quite well, if we're clever. I think we'll get your hair done first—we'll have to do that before you can choose a hat.'

When Caroline emerged from the hairdresser's, she felt transformed, as though she had been given a new head. Anne chose some powder for her, rouge and lipstick, and made her buy a tiny eyebrow brush to tidy up her face, as she called it. Then she took her to the Galeries Lafayette and fitted her out from top to toe. They took a taxi home, loaded with boxes and parcels.

'Darling Daddy!' thought Caroline as she lifted her new green dress from the enveloping tissue paper. She held it up against herself and peered into the mirror; the dress had a little yellow suede collar and yellow lacing down the front; the coat had a bunch of yellow leather flowers at the neck; brown hat; neat brown shoes with moderately high heels; soft brown suede gloves. She spread all her new belongings on the bed and looked at them lovingly; there were still a couple of little parcels unopened; three pairs of fine silk stockings, tailored underclothes of peach-coloured satin.

She flung off her stained blue skirt and tussore shirt, the long black stockings and blue woollen knickers, and hurled them into a corner; with trembling hands she dressed herself and made up her face. Hastily, she transferred her few possessions from the worn black handbag which she had once thought so grand, to the new flat brown one, bought that morning with her own money. Then, after a final examination in the glass, she walked tremulously in to face Anne and Olga.

'Oh, Caroline, you do look attractive!' exclaimed Olga rapturously; 'you've got such lovely colouring and your figure's perfect, isn't it Anne?'

Anne smiled her slow sweet smile and nodded: 'We'll pack your school clothes away and forget all about them until you have to go back,' she said.

They lived like French people, eating the same food at the same hours, travelling in the Metro or in buses, hardly ever by taxi; they stood in queues for cheap seats at concerts and theatres, sat drinking syrups in cafés and wandered along the river banks, browsing in the little bookstalls on the way. The Hendersons had innumerable friends of every nationality, mostly artists and writers; they would sit and argue stormily in French for hours, sipping aperitifs, or drinking cup after cup of coffee. Caroline would watch them in stupefaction, through a haze of aromatic cigarette smoke; she was amazed at the facility with which the Hendersons, when they were with French people, instantly became French themselves, slipping quite unconsciously into Gallic attitudes and gestures as into some invisible cloak that turned them into strangers before her eyes; then a sudden turn of Anne's head, or a familiar burst of laughter from Olga, would remind her that these were the same people whom she had known in Dublin.

At school, French was considered to be her best subject; she could construct grammatical sentences, read fairly fluently and understand the robust British pronunciation of the language, but here she felt utterly lost. When these people talked, she gazed at them in fascinated admiration as they emitted a ceaseless flow of beautiful incomprehensible sounds. Sometimes, they would try and talk to her, taking immense pains to enunciate slowly, but after a moment, the words would stream out in a torrent and she would be overwhelmed; then Olga would interpret and Caroline would reply in her careful inexpressive French; she felt like a cart-horse, suddenly entered for the Derby.

For ten whole days, she understood hardly a word of what was said around her; then, astonishingly, understanding came to her and sense emerged from the turmoil of language; at the same time, words and sentences took shape, expressions came to mind and she found herself using her hands, her shoulders or her head to supplement her speech. Her new friends nodded and smiled encouragement.

'Ah!' they said, 'elle fait du progrès, cette petite.' She began to listen avidly to their conversation; she exulted in the clarity of their thought and their skill in expression; they unlocked their hearts and spoke their opinions without fumbling or apology; she began to lose some of her British shame about ideas. These people made her think furiously about everything—communism, painting, poetry, politics; they expected her to have opinions and often, with shame, she had to confess that she was too ignorant to have formed any, but when she did express her mind on any subject, she noted with surprise and gratitude that no one laughed.

She picked up some atrocious slang and a great deal of excellent French and, not having sufficient knowledge to adapt her expressions to her company, used both with complete indifference wherever she happened to be, to the intense amusement of the Hendersons. They did, however, warn her that some of her words and expressions would not be acceptable in polite French circles, and these she tried to suppress, but she found it most confusing to differentiate between subjects that were correct in conversation and those that were improper. Her delight knew no bounds when, one day at Versailles, their guide held aloft an entrancing little chamber-pot, announcing with the pride of a connoisseur:

'Et voici, Mesdames et Messieurs, le vase de nuit de Marie Antoinette, en porcelaine de Sèvres, peint a la main!'

Sometimes, in the Bois, at the Louvre or in the more fashionable streets, they would encounter a giggling group of English girls under the dragon-eyed chaperonage of some lean suspicious harridan; Caroline would blush with shame for them and observe them with a sinking heart, always with the thought in her mind that they might come from that finishing school to which Isabel had been sent and to which she herself was to go in the autumn; she was appalled by the prospect of having to submit to that narrow mistrustful supervision, being forced to become like one of these gibbering irresponsible creatures whose only means of self-assertion lay in making eyes at men in the street and in resolutely refusing to absorb any of the culture with which they were so assiduously surrounded.

One day, Anne told her that she had had a letter from the Vicomtesse de la Tour du Vallon, who presided over the school, announcing that Madame Adair had been good enough to inform her that her daughter was in Paris and requesting that Anne and she would give her the extreme pleasure of their presence at five o'clock tea . . . the polite phrases went on and on. Caroline groaned when she read it and looked helplessly at Anne.

'Better get it over, Darling,' said Anne; 'I'm afraid it's got to be done.'

Olga was despatched to some friends for the afternoon and Caroline set out with Anne towards Clichy; the school consisted of an *appartement* in a tall grey house; they entered a minute lift and were whirled up to the third storey. Anne had barely taken her finger off the bell before the door was opened by an elderly maid, immaculately attired in black and white.

The Vicomtesse was seated at a writing table in her white and gilt Louis Seize salon. Her fine snow-white hair was piled on top of her head, where it was held by two glass combs; she wore a black dress with a high neck and a tiny white turned-down collar; the smallest of buttons adorned her dress, in a straight line from neck to hem. She had the face of an ascetic, aquiline and colourless; the only gleam of colour in her entire person came from the light blue hooded eyes whose lids were never fully lifted.

She received them with great politeness; tea was immediately brought in on a huge silver tray; three cups, a tiny silver tea-pot and a plate of little cakes; there was a small dish of sliced lemon. The tea was horrible; it tasted as if it had been steadily boiled for many hours; evidently the Vicomtesse did not make a habit of drinking five o'clock tea and had only thought of it as a compliment to her English guests.

Several times Caroline intercepted the hooded glance directed towards Anne. 'She's sizing her up,' she thought; Anne was looking quite lovely and absurdly young in a bright dark-blue dress with a white hat and white gloves.

'I do not quite understand,' the old lady was saying, 'you live in Montparnasse?'

'Yes,' replied Anne, in her beautiful fluid French; 'my husband is an artist and we have a studio flat there.'

'And your own daughter, she lives with you there, and Mademoiselle Adair?'

'But yes,' protested Anne politely, 'we all live there together.'

'Of course you have a chaperon for them—it would not do for them to meet your husband's friends.'

'They are sensible girls,' replied Anne patiently, 'and I never let them go far from the house by themselves, so they do not need a chaperon;

as for our friends, I do not consider their conversation injurious . . .'

'To live in such a district and have no chaperon!' The Vicomtesse was shocked beyond words; she held out her hand as though to prevent Anne from revealing any further horrors. 'Here, in this delightful part of Paris, inhabited only by the best families, my girls are not allowed to leave the house by themselves for an instant, not even to post a letter across the street; one has no conception of what might happen.' She shrugged her shoulders delicately as though Anne's views were beyond her comprehension. 'You will find things very different here, my little Caroline, for in the society to which we are accustomed it is not considered correct for young girls to run about the streets alone, becoming acquainted, perhaps, with soldiers.'

'I have confidence in my daughter and in Mademoiselle Adair; I know that they would not be so dishonourable as to . . .' but Anne was not allowed to finish her sentence; the old lady broke in:

'I fear that your poor mother must be ignorant of the danger to a young and innocent girl of living in the Latin Quarter amongst anarchists and apaches, in a family where she is not properly supervised and where she is certainly involved in the discussions of artists and Communists and the enemies of Holy Church; all the English are Protestant, as I know, but the enemies of the one would seek to destroy Christianity of whatever sect. . . . You will soon return to your English school?'

'In less than a week,' replied Caroline, hot waves of anger mounting to her face.

'It is good; I trust that no irreparable damage will have been done, although the memories of your first visit to Paris will not be easily effaced; here, in the autumn, you will spend many delightful hours attending lectures on our wonderful civilisation, studying much of the work of our great dramatists and poets, and you will acquire at many of our beautiful galleries a profound knowledge of classical art; there will be expeditions to many places where history and architecture combine to provide a basis for the most interesting study. You have not been to Versailles?'

'But yes; Madame Henderson took us to Versailles last week.'

The Vicomtesse looked surprised. 'You have not then visited the Louvre and our great Cathedral of Notre Dame?'

Caroline told her that they had visited both; the old lady lifted her heavy lids for a moment to glance at Anne.

'Many visits are, of course, necessary before one can fully realise the extent of the treasure in our beautiful capital. You do not speak French badly, my child, but your expressions are not of the best—there is a certain vulgarity. When you come here, you will have the unspeakable advantage of moving in the society of cultured women of a high social order from whose lips you will hear only the purest of French.'

Never once had Caroline seen Anne angry, or even perturbed, but now she sat erect with blazing eyes, her lips set in a thin little line; she was holding her bag and gloves as though she were about to rise, but she neither spoke nor moved. 'Of course,' thought Caroline, 'she can't say anything: she's afraid of spoiling my chances here!' In a moment of clear vision, she saw that life in this prison, with its ceaseless restrictions and impertinent supervision, would be impossible. How could she tolerate the authority of this old woman who had so insulted her adored and lovely Anne?

No good to write home and say that she could not face coming here—Helen would think she was being merely silly. She must do something herself, now. She looked quickly round the room, panic-stricken; time was passing, bearing away this moment of tension and opportunity.

Leaning toward, she shifted her position and gave the tea-table a lusty kick, so that it rocked and the tea slopped out of the cups into the saucers. With a brazen look at Anne, she used an unprintable word loudly, by way of exclamation; Anne's mouth dropped open and she looked as if she might burst into tears or begin to laugh uncontrollably.

Overcome by her own audacity and not far from tears herself, Caroline turned apprehensively to the Vicomtesse; the old lady was lying back in her chair, speechless, with closed eyes.

'Pardon, Madame la Vicomtesse,' she muttered; 'I am so *maladroite.*'

The Vicomtesse rose, with a glance of abhorrence at Anne, as though her presence were a pollution of her salon; the old face was ivory pale, only the lips trembled a little as she clasped her hands in front of her and prepared to speak. Anne stood up and Caroline crossed over to her and took her hand.

'You apologise for being *maladroite* when you have just made use of the most disgusting word in the French language; no doubt you are ignorant of its meaning, my poor child, but after this it will be quite impossible for me to receive you in my school. You understand? Quite impossible. Who knows with what foul expressions you might contaminate my charming and innocent girls? Certainly the disgrace will be a great blow to your poor mother, but she is much to blame in permitting you to come to Paris in such unsuitable company. I shall write to her without delay, making it quite clear why I cannot for a moment contemplate having you for a pupil.' The weighted lids were lifted for an instant as the icy glare was turned on Anne. 'Perhaps you now see, Madame, the result of your negligence? Now, would you be so good as to leave?' She leant over to ring the bell.

She remained standing as they left the room, hands clasped as before, eyes covered, making no attempt to bid them goodbye; outside, the maid was holding open the door on to the main staircase, 'Caroline,' said Anne reproachfully, when they had reached the street, 'you've let me down.' But she squeezed Caroline's hand as she spoke.

'Oh, Anne, I had to do it, I simply had to! After the way she spoke to you, I knew I'd die if I went to that school. I had to prevent it somehow. Are you awfully angry?'

'Not really. Darling, but what on earth am I to say to your mother?' Anne smiled a little woefully. 'Did you really do it on purpose?'

'Yes, I did, and I'm glad, except about you and Mother—I hadn't thought about that. I'll tell her I did it on purpose; I won't let her blame you.' Caroline peered hopefully into her face but Anne shook her head slowly.

'She must blame me, darling, because whatever way you look at it I am to blame; perhaps, in the end, she will see . . .' She did not finish her sentence.

When they got back to the flat, Caroline shut herself into her room and wept bitterly.

CHAPTER TEN

Caroline leant against the side of the mail boat and smiled dreamily at the distant cone-shaped Wicklow hills, smoky-blue in the fine weather haze; it was late July and she was coming home for good.

She had made more friends in this last term at school than in the preceding four; since Olga had left, she had been thrown upon her own resources. She knew that she was popular, in spite of her dislike of team games. The other girls had conceded her the right to be different, because she was Irish and, therefore, a little mad; on the other hand, she had come to realise that they, being English, were also entitled to be odd.

Dalkey Island blocked her view as they approached the harbour; she went to the saloon to fetch her things and returned to take her place in the landing queue; the boat was crowded with school-children and holiday-makers and she found herself tightly wedged on all sides against sweating people, grumbling about the heat, the crowds and the approaching Customs examination.

At last the people began to move along, picking up babies and luggage, coats and thermos flasks and baskets, and setting them down again every few yards, as their progress was halted. The smiling waiter on the train had taken charge of her luggage, handing it over to a steward on the boat who would send it ashore by a third party.

She reached the Customs table and surveyed the bulging heaps of luggage; someone had planted an open suitcase on top of hers; she removed it firmly, with polite apologies. 'Have yez annything to declare? Wines, spirits, cigarettes, tobacco, clothing,' recited the officer monotonously; his voice suddenly came to life: 'Have yez anny new clothing?' He had a large pale face with a loose mouth, and his cap was slightly awry.

'No, nothing.'

'Are ye sure now?'

'Yes, quite sure.' Caroline smiled, trying to look as blameless as she really was.

'Is that a new hat ye have?'

'No, I've had it for months.'

'Whereja get it?'

'In Paris, last April.'

The man scratched his head. 'Paris, is it? And I suppose ye paid a lot for it?'

'I didn't pay for it, I can't quite remember what it cost.'

He winked knowingly: 'Ah, don't be talkin', whatever it was, I'm sure it was twice too much, annyway.' He grinned at her as he chalked her suitcase. 'I suppose ye got the dress there, and the coat an' all? Ah well, it's well for yez.' He nodded his head several times in a contemplative way and passed on to the next person. 'Anything to declare?' began the routine voice again.

Caroline locked her suitcase and the porter carried it to the barrier. Somewhere behind that milling crowd, would be Guy; she caught sight of him and he waved his hat; she made frantic signs at him to show that she still had to find her trunk, which would be with the heavy luggage; when she finally emerged at the little gate, the crowd had nearly gone. Guy kissed her shamelessly and they walked along the pier and up the little hill to the car, where they would have to wait until the luggage barrows were wheeled up.

She settled down beside Guy in the front seat and smiled at him with real pleasure; he beamed back at her and said:

'Lovely to have you home for keeps,' and added, as though he had only just seen her: 'I say, you're looking rather good—-is that what

Paris has done for you?'

She nodded and stretched out her feet: 'It's grand to be home again; how's everyone?'

'Oh, fine. Isabel's gadding in Waterford; she'll be back for the Horse Show.'

When they reached the house, Helen came darting down the stairs and kissed her affectionately: 'How you've changed, Darling—and what lovely clothes!' she exclaimed.

'Paris,' explained Caroline.

'Oh yes, of course, Paris!' echoed Helen in a grim little voice, and Caroline knew that the subject was being shelved for the moment, so as not to spoil her home-coming, but that before long she would have to face an inquisition about Paris.

Doran came pattering up from the basement with a diminutive teapot on a tray:

'Welcome back, Miss Caroline,' she said, her toothy old face wreathed in smiles; 'I'll leave yer tea in the drawing-room, Miss.'

'Thank you, Doran; how's your mother?'

'Not too bad, Miss, thank you, but she does be getting very old now; eighty-seven she is, and her eyes is very bad and she can't put a foot out of bed this long time.'

'Oh dear, I'm so sorry.' Caroline had always thought it miraculous that Doran should have a mother living, for she looked not a day less than eighty herself, and she could never ask her to do anything without feeling guiltily that it was she who ought to be waiting on Doran.

Helen had had her tea, but she poured out for Guy and Caroline and they sat, lazily making plans, long after Doran had cleared away the tea-things.

'After the Horse Show,' said Helen, 'your Aunt Moira wants us all to go down to Butler's Hill for a bit; your Father and I will go for a fortnight, but we thought you and Isabel might like to stay on into September; David will be there some of the time.'

'How sweet of her. Yes, I'd love to go.'

'We'll have to get you some clothes; there'll be several dances in Horse Show Week and besides you'll need some more day clothes, if that's all you've got; but of course a lot depends on what you're going to do in the autumn.' There was a slightly questioning note in Helen's voice.

Caroline came back to earth: 'The autumn? Oh, yes. I know what I want to do,' she announced slowly.

They both looked up; Helen a little anxiously and Guy with an air of surprised amusement, as though he could not really believe that this was Caroline, grown-up and with a mind and plans of her own.

'Well, what is it?' asked Helen, faintly irritated by the delay; and fearing she knew not what.

'I want to go to Trinity and study French.'

'Excellent,' said Guy quickly, 'excellent!'

Helen's face fell: this was the sort of thing she had been trying to stave off for years, and now Guy was encouraging it.

'There are all sorts of curious people there now, I believe,' she faltered; 'it's changed a lot in the last few years. I've heard that there are even Republicans . . .' She stopped, wishing that she could have been more subtle; Guy would certainly try to over-rule her objection.

'Do the child good to mix with people and run up against a few Republicans,' he said briskly; 'she's led too sheltered a life. Besides, if she meets Republicans there, she's bound to meet some Orangemen from the North, and that'll be an education in itself.'

'I've never met any Orangemen,' said Caroline; 'what are they like?'

'Well,' said Guy, smiling, 'they've got red hair and no lips, and the first words they learn in infancy are "To Hell with the Pope" and "No surrender"! They also have a highly developed business sense; if you can gather anything from that picture, you'll have a fairly accurate, but distinctly uncharitable, Southern view of an Orangeman.'

Caroline laughed, but Helen remonstrated: 'Oh, Guy, do be fair; they're loyal.'

Guy was filling his pipe: 'They're so loyal that they have to beat drums on the twelfth of July until their hands bleed, in commemoration of the Battle of the Boyne, when King William, of glorious, pious and immortal memory, defeated poor Catholic James . . . Ah, well, they're a wonderful and successful people. It's the climate that causes their lips to disappear,' he added informatively; 'It's so vile that they have to keep their lips permanently compressed!'

Even Helen had to laugh: 'But you can't help admiring them,' she protested; 'they've never yielded.'

'Not an inch!' said Guy, smiling, 'and I doubt if they ever will; but we're not talking about politics, we're discussing Caroline's future.' He did not want the conversation to become explosive.

'I wanted to present her next season,' said Helen, changing her tactics; 'I'd like the child to go about a bit and have a good time before she goes and buries herself in a university; she'd better wait a year.'

'That elusive occupation known as having a good time,' murmured Guy; 'she can have a perfectly good time here, my dear; she'd be living at home.'

'But she'd have so much work to do, she'd never be able to enjoy herself properly; think of all those exams!'

'Actually,' began Caroline, wondering how she was going to avoid wounding Helen's feelings, 'I don't want to be presented much, although it's awfully nice of you to think of it, Mother.'

A look of genuine mystification came over Helen's face: how could any normal girl be content to refuse such an opportunity? She peered anxiously at Caroline.

'I can't think what's happened to you,' she said irritably; 'first of all you go and make a mess of all my plans for you in Paris, and then you say you don't want to be presented; most girls would give anything for such a chance: I think it's downright ingratitude!'

'Oh, please, Mother, don't think I'm not grateful; I am, only I'd much rather stay here and start work in October; besides, think of all the money it'll save,' added Caroline cheerfully, knowing that this would appeal to Guy.

'By Jove, yes! Isabel's presentation nearly ruined me.'

Helen made an impatient exclamation: 'You know we can afford it,' she said angrily.

'We can afford it, if the child wants it, but as she doesn't, I think it would be a criminal waste of money,' replied Guy, puffing serenely at his pipe.

Helen saw that she was beaten in yet another round of the losing battle that she had been fighting for years; one by one, the invisible battlements that she had built round her children were crumbling away. If Caroline entered Trinity, she would be able to choose her own friends, form her own opinions and be free from protective supervision. Helen had heard most disquieting tales about the disaffection amongst students; some of them, she had been told, actually remained seated while 'God Save the King' was being played.

'If she must go to a university, why not Cambridge?' she enquired suddenly; 'a Cambridge degree . . .!' She dangled the bait hopefully.

'Women aren't given degrees at Cambridge, although, of course, it comes to the same thing,' said Guy; 'but I want to have the child at home, Helen; remember, she hasn't been home for six months and we've hardly seen her for two years; what's the use of having daughters unless you see them sometimes?'

Helen could only object: 'But she'd have been away another year if she'd gone to Paris.' Guy had a maddening trick, she reflected, of making statements that you could not refute without seeming to be wanting in affection, or social sense, or some other quality that no one could admit lacking. 'And while we're on the subject,' she went on, 'I should like to have some explanation of that disgraceful scene with the Vicomtesse.' She picked up a half-finished jumper and began to knit furiously.

'Did Anne come to see you?' asked Caroline.

'She did indeed, and I let her see that I thought she was greatly to blame for what happened; I always thought it was a mistake to let you go to Paris with them, but your father would have it; Dublin's quite different from Paris and I knew quite well they'd be in with all the wrong sort of people there, artists and so on, but men can never see that sort of thing. Two, four, six, eight, ten, decrease,' she added in a whisper.

'What was this obscene expression so frightful that the poor lady couldn't defile her pen by writing it?' enquired Guy, with a gleam of amusement in his eye.

'I don't know the English for it—yet,' admitted Caroline, and Guy roared with laughter; 'but I knew it was pretty bad and I said it on purpose,' she went on. 'The old Vicomtesse had done nothing but insult Anne from the moment we came in, and she kept telling me about the unspeakable advantages of being in her school and meeting only the best people, and hearing only the purest of French, and so on, until I couldn't bear it any longer; I knew that I simply could *not* go there and be under her thumb.'

Guy was still laughing, but Helen looked up acidly: 'I suppose you know it's in the worst of taste to insult foreigners,' she said, 'especially a noble and distinguished woman like the Vicomtesse.'

'Well, she started it,' protested Caroline.

'You could have written to us and explained that you didn't like the school, and the whole thing could have been arranged without any unpleasantness.' Helen began to count stitches again.

'Could have,' said Caroline, standing up; 'but would it? You know you'd have thought I was just being silly and you wouldn't have done anything about it, would you, Mother?'

'Eight, ten, make one; now!' Helen wound up her wool and harpooned the ball savagely on her needles. 'I can't understand what's happened to you, Caroline, I told you before; you've suddenly become so . . . assertive and obstinate. Isabel's the same; you never used to be like that, either of you.'

Caroline picked up her bag and the little brown hat despondently, and stood looking at Helen for a moment; for the first time she saw, shockingly, not the mother who was always there, age-less, unalterable, but a weary middle-aged woman with thin dispirited legs and lifeless grey hair, whose back had lost its spring so that it drooped now in forgetfulness. Helen glanced up, stiffening when she saw the look of scared compassion on her face.

'Why are you looking at me like that?' she said sharply; 'you . . . you frighten me, you looked so odd, suddenly.'

'I'm sorry, Mother.' Caroline bent down to kiss the cold cheek gently, without warmth, shutting her eyes as she did so in an attempt to hide from herself the fact that this was an act, not of affection, but of mercy.

Horse Show Week is Dublin's big social event; it takes place early in August and people flock to it from all over the country and from England. Landladies retire to the squalor of their basements and let their houses for fantastic sums, every spare room has its occupant and the hotels bulge with English visitors; theatres put on special attractions, restaurants are packed, prices soar. The summer road-mending campaign is in full swing and the streets are blocked with traffic and obstacles; the citizens blossom into their best clothes and entertain furiously for these few hectic days, before they flee, exhausted, to the coast for their holidays. All the time, the gaiety goes on: lunch parties, cocktail parties, dinners, dances—no one has time for sleep; like butterflies, people flit from place to place, alighting briefly, now here, now there, never stopping in one place for long.

Everybody goes to the Show. On Tuesday, the attendance is small and business-like; men in tweeds, farmers in leggings, girls in jodhpurs crowd round the rings to watch the judging; children ride round on fiery little ponies; massive slobbering bulls are led about by sunburnt countrymen, spruced up for the occasion in spotless shirts, faces shaven and heads newly cropped; hunters with polished satin coats tittup jerkily and show the whites of their eyes, upset by the strange surroundings; grooms, chewing an end of hay, murmur soft words and, loverlike, pat and coax them into an uneasy calm; there is a peaceful smell, good to the senses, of horses, straw and cattle.

In the afternoons, people dress up and go to watch the jumping and to meet their friends; tailor-mades on Wednesday, silk frocks and dressy hats on Thursday and Friday. Saturday is the cheap day and the place is thronged; country people, brought up to Dublin in special trains, pour out of the trams and move uncertainly past the turnstiles, families sticking together as though, once parted, they would never meet again. The great hall is packed with stands and, outside, there is the constant burr of machinery in motion; bands play under the trees and people sit lengthily over their tea, reluctant to give up their seats and stand on their aching swollen feet. In the jumping enclosure, the fortunate sit in comfort on the stands, under cover, while the rest jostle below. Everywhere, priests, dowagers, officers on leave, green-clad soldiers, fat elderly women with bulging feet stuffed agonisingly into constricting shoes, horsey young women with loud country accents, spare full-blooded racy-looking men in yellow sweaters, and buxom red-faced country girls in gaudy cheap clothes rub shoulders and crack jokes good humouredly. Everyone is out for enjoyment: it is almost a national festival.

Helen bought a new hat and went to the Show with Isabel and Caroline; she seemed to revive suddenly, becoming quite animated as she chatted to people she had not met for years, agreeing with a sigh that this was almost 'like the old days'. Guy went with them, but his progress was slower and he arrived at the jumping enclosure when the afternoon was well advanced. 'I met old Saunders,' he said, 'he's just bought a filly and I had to go and see her, and ran into Billy Garrett and couldn't get away.'

'Oah!' groaned the crowd, as a riderless horse, terrified into a frenzy by the shouts and cheers, tore madly round the course and jumped the railings in a desperate effort to escape; the people surged back in a panic to let him pass, then forward again to surround him when he was caught and held, sweating, wild-eyed and heaving.

'Oh, I wish I could take off my shoes!' sighed Isabel.

'Quick, let's make a dash for home before the shower,' snapped Helen. After the Show, there was always a rush to get home and change into evening dress for the round of gaieties that would continue until the early hours of the morning.

Helen hated cocktail parties, not only because they bored her, but because she was never free from the fear that one of her daughters would disgrace her by coming home, or worse, going on to a dance, roaring drunk; when Isabel had first come out, she had martyred herself by attending them all, but after a while, unwillingly, though with a sense of tremendous relief, she had allowed her to go to them alone. Now, she gave Caroline strict instructions that she was to drink no more than two cocktails and that she was always to eat something with them. When they came home, she always demanded to be told who was there; Isabel would mention a number of people who would meet with her mother's approval, adding: 'There were lots of others, but I didn't know who they were, most of them.' This neat phrasing enabled her to keep Helen in the dark about the names of her particular friends, and Helen, reassured, would lapse into silence.

At first, Caroline had thought that Isabel was glad to have her back, pleased to have someone with whom to discuss the parties and dances, who would confirm her decisions about what she should wear, ask who was going to be there and listen to her advice about the way to do her hair, but before long she had discovered that Isabel resented her intrusion into her private activities. At these parties, Isabel would take no notice of her whatever, beyond introducing her to a few of her less interesting friends; she kept her jealously outside her own special little circle of admirers until, one day, some of them demanded to know her.

Isabel's face expressed acute astonishment: 'Oh, I thought you all knew her,' she replied, and went off to fetch Caroline with a tiny scowl of annoyance.

She brought her up, a protective arm flung round her waist as though she were looking after a little girl at her first party:

'You know Juliet and Brigid; well, this is Mike; and Brian and Hugh and Nick; you've met Denis, haven't you?' Caroline shook herself free: 'Not since we were kids in Fitzwilliam Square,' she said, smiling.

'And you weren't allowed to play with us, in case you might get tainted,' said Denis, disarmingly.

'Now you know everyone,' Isabel put in quickly, in case Caroline might embarrass her helplessly by saying, 'We still aren't,' or something equally trying; Denis and Caroline were grinning at one another as though they might say anything.

They were all very nice to Caroline, offering to fetch her drinks and cigarettes, anything she wanted; they teased Isabel for keeping her beautiful sister out of the way for so long and she, with a tight little smile, repeated furiously that she had thought they all knew her. Mike, who was small, dark and sun-burnt, wanted to take Caroline in his care to the dinner-party to which they all seemed to be going, and later to the dance, but Denis stepped in and said:

'Ah, now, not so fast, not so fast; she's coming with us, isn't she, Isabel?'

Isabel shrugged her shoulders: 'Mike wants to take her,' she argued.

'I know, but she's coming with us, all the same, aren't you?' And he looked at Caroline with such friendliness that she decided to risk Isabel's wrath and accept.

'I'd love to,' she said and added, turning to the disappointed Mike: 'May I go with you another time?'

'By God, you may,' said Mike thickly.

Isabel spread herself over the front seat, beside Denis, so that Caroline would have to climb into the back by herself, but Denis insisted that there was room for three in the front, and made her move up.

'Mike was a bit shot,' he explained, 'and he's not always too safe to drive with when he's like that; hope you didn't mind?' He smiled across at Caroline, and she shook her head.

'Mike's a beautiful driver, however drunk he is; he's safe as houses,' protested Isabel.

'Not with that Bentley, he's not; poor old Mike's all right, but he reached his limit pretty early this evening—he'll be an awful mess before the night's out.'

Isabel could suppress her annoyance no longer: 'Oh, I know you don't like him,' she said, nastily.

Denis looked at her in astonishment: 'I do like him,' he said, 'but I don't like his money, you can't get away from it; and I'd like him a lot more if he wasn't fluthered half the time.'

'I like money,' she said in a gloating voice; 'I wish I had lots of it!'

He looked at her comically, out of the corner of his eye, and drummed lightly on the wheel with his fingers: 'Better marry Mike, then, and you'll have as much as you want; distilling's a gold mine and he's an only son.'

'Oh, don't be silly, you know nothing would induce me to marry him.' She gave him a warning look, so brief that Caroline could hardly be sure that she had seen it; Denis nodded, almost imperceptibly, and turned to smile at her with such adoring intimacy that Caroline began to wish that she had risked death with Mike rather than break in upon the happiness of these two; if she had not been there, his arm would have been round Isabel's waist. Suddenly she felt as she knew Miss O'Connor must often have felt, when family rows had burst around her and she had been compelled to witness them.

When they came home that night, dazed with fatigue, Denis and Isabel lingered in the hall, while she climbed the stairs wearily; but when she was half-undressed, Isabel came into her room, closed the door and sat down firmly on the bed.

'Look here,' she said, unscrewing her ear-rings, 'the sooner you get a boy-friend to take you about, the better; Denis and I don't want you with us all the time; so when somebody asks you to go with them, you've got to go: do you see?'

'Even when they're drunk,' replied Caroline with some bitterness; 'I see; but Denis did ask me, you know; he insisted.'

'Only out of politeness—you know perfectly well he didn't really want you.'

Caroline felt too tired to fight: 'I'm sorry if I spoilt your evening,' she said drily, 'I'll know better next time,' and she began to brush her teeth.

'Mike's all right,' said Isabel invitingly, 'and he's awfully rich.'

Ignoring this remark, Caroline turned and faced her: 'Are you and Denis engaged?' she asked boldly.

Isabel looked nonplussed: 'What on earth makes you think that?' she said, trying to induce a yawn.

'Lots of things—I'm not blind,' replied Caroline mercilessly; 'are you?'

'I don't see what it's got to do with you'—Isabel looked as if she were trying to think quickly—'but, if you must know, we are. Now, perhaps you'll keep out of our way. Does it meet with your approval?' she added sarcastically.

'I think he's a dear,' said Caroline simply, 'but have you thought what the family's going to say about it?'

Isabel melted a little. 'Oh, to hell with the family!' she said; 'It's nothing to do with them—why can't we choose our own husbands? They've nearly driven me to drink already, what with their remarks about mixed marriages and marrying out of one's class, and all the lies I've had to tell them: I hate the family!'

Caroline winced. 'Daddy wouldn't be like that, if it weren't for Mother,' she said, but Isabel pounced on her:

'Oh yes, he would! He's just as bad as she is about marrying Roman Catholics; they've both got an obsession about it.'

With the sudden perception that sometimes comes with acute fatigue, Caroline had a moment of panic; she foresaw Isabel's future with terrifying clarity: endless strife, deception, frustration and unhappiness before she could marry Denis, and afterwards, censure, hostility, social adjustment and perhaps even poverty. Isabel, as yet, saw nothing of all this; she could only see the tiresome and futile opposition of unreasonable parents, opposition which could be overridden as everything that had ever blocked her plans in the past had been overridden.

'Do the Joyces know?' she asked.

'Good Lord, no! Nobody knows, nobody at all, except for some of the others, Mike and that lot, I mean, who've probably guessed by now. Denis is going to break it to his family this summer, while we're at Butler's Hill.'

'I don't expect they'll be particularly pleased,' said Caroline slowly.

'Not pleased? Why ever not? I'm a lot better than they are —they ought to be glad.'

'Well, they're pretty pious, aren't they? They probably feel just as bad about mixed marriages as Mother and Daddy.' Isabel snorted with impatience: 'But I'm not going to try and convert him,' she argued; 'It's not as though I was a rabid Protestant. I'll leave him alone, and he'll leave me alone.'

'*They* won't,' insisted Caroline, 'not if they're pious.'

'But I'm not marrying his family,' cried Isabel in exasperation; 'I'm marrying him, and the less I see of them, the happier I'll be; his mother's an old trout, anyway, with an accent like a cart-horse, although he adores her—I can't think why.' She stood up, smoothing out the creases in her frock with one hand, while with the other she jingled her ear-rings. 'Of course,' she went on, 'we probably won't be able to get married for ages, until he's making some money, but the Joyces are quite well off and, if they're decent, they'll give him a pretty good allowance. I know it's no good expecting anything from *them*!' and she pointed through the floor.

Caroline climbed into bed and lay back on the pillows, hands behind her head.

'Do you remember the row about the dance?' said Isabel.

'Mm.'

'Well, it'll be nothing to the row there's going to be when they find I'm married to Denis, but it'll be too late this time, too, because they're not going to find out until it's over.' She stopped, looked curiously at Caroline and began to laugh softly: Caroline was asleep.

CHAPTER ELEVEN

Driving down to Butler's Hill, surrounded by suitcases, fishing tackle, tennis racquets and all the half-packed accompaniments of a summer holiday by car, Caroline worried about Isabel and Denis; she watched Isabel's hard but pretty little face, staring blindly into Guy's back, unaware of the high white clouds ranging across the sky, the flying hedges and the momentary dappled shadows as they sped past a group of trees. She had an uneasy feeling that Guy knew far more about the affair than Isabel imagined and that he was biding his time, either because he did not quite know what to do, or else because he was waiting to see whether it would all pass over. It was incredible that Isabel could really think that she could keep her parents in the dark for long, in a place like Dublin where anybody's business is everybody else's concern and where one cannot even walk harmlessly down the street without comment. Caroline dreaded the day, certain to come, when someone would come to pay a long call on Helen and drop a hint, maliciously dutiful, about the way in which modern daughters hoodwinked their parents. She could see it all: Helen would look up suspiciously, uncertain whether this remark applied to her or was part of a general tale of woe about Dublin's bright young things. Then would come enlightment: 'I think perhaps you ought to know . . . most painful for me to be the one to tell you . . .' and the whole story would be out. Then, as Caroline put it to herself, the whole house would go up in smoke and there was no knowing what the end would be. But one thing would be certain, and she could think of this only with relief—something would happen and the lies and pretences would be at an end.

Anyway, at Butler's Hill, there would be peace: no Denis, no fear of gossiping tongues, nothing to hide; only the sea and the sun, the stony gorse-covered hills and the dreamy passing of the days. Then, suddenly, with a little jerk, she recollected something that had, up till now, been only a vaguely pleasing prospect: David would be there for some of the time, and unless he was a changed being, there would be no peace after all. He and Isabel were scarcely on speaking terms.

She sighed, stretched her cramped legs and turned to look out of the window. Away to the south, there were mountains now, blue and lusty, hoisting themselves out of the green plain; pressed between green banks, a broad treacly stream passed through a tunnel of trees by a white farm and, liberated, thrust foaming against smooth rocks; a heron, poised on one leg, prepared for flight, thought better of it and resumed her fishing; colour, renewed as though with wine, strengthened under the great cloud shadows as they ploughed across the countryside. Instantly Isabel was forgotten as Caroline, unseen, lifted her hands, palms outward, in the intimate spontaneous movement that was her salute to beauty.

Once off the main road, they rattled along in a hot and sleepy silence occasioned by the quantities of cider they had drunk with lunch; a cloud of white dust swirled behind them, settling again on the grass in a grey sheen; they passed lines of cage-like carts on their way from the bogs, stacked high with chocolate-coloured turf; sheep-dogs, to whom the motor-car was still an enchanted monster, hurled themselves on to the road and pursued them dangerously with enthusiastic barks. This was the country of low loosely-built stone walls and red fuchsia hedges, stony little hills and small reedy lakes where the trout rise lazily and the wild swans sail in unmolested dignity.

'We should,' remarked Helen, pulling herself out of an uncomfortable doze, 'be able to see the sea.'

Guy looked at her reproachfully: 'What can I do, when you choose to go to sleep, sitting on the map?' he enquired, and Helen laughed.

'Better stop and ask,' she said, as more turf-carts came into view.

They drew up alongside the leading cart and an old man, dressed in the peasant's flannel collarless shirt and home-spun trousers, hopped nimbly off and poked his head helpfully in at the window:

'Good evening, sir, are y'in throuble?'

'Good evening,' replied Guy; 'we are.'

'Arrah, them old mother-cars is no good annyway; what ails her?' His voice rose and fell in the rich full-throated country accent of the South-West.

'Oh, the car's all right,' said Guy, 'but we wanted to know, are we all right for Ballinsaggart?'

'You are, sir, ye're all right. Keep right on till ye get to the Creamery at Knock, and go on pasht it until ye get to a little crossroads; go straight on there and it'll bring y'in to Ballinsaggart in the end. If ye was to take the wesht road it'd take ye to the sea, and th' aisht would bring ye back where y'are.'

'Thanks,' said Guy; the old man repeated his directions at length, grinned toothlessly and climbed back on to his cart; touching his hat, he flicked the rope reins gently. Guy was just moving off, when Caroline's voice from the back stopped him:

'He wants to say something more.'

The old man was at the window again; leaning forward, so that his mouth was almost against Guy's ear, he said in a husky confidential tone: 'Would ye be wanting a thorough-bred colt, sir?'

Guy beamed at him in unconcealed delight: 'Not today, thanks; is he a good one?'

'A rale beauty, sir, a rale beauty; if ye was to see him ye'd want him.' His tone was as seductive as a lover's.

'Sorry,' said Guy; 'we've got to get on.'

'Right y'are, sir, right y'are. Michael Greaney is me name, if ye was to think about it later, maybe. Pasht the Creamery and straight on is yer way.'

It was not far to Ballinsaggart; they drove uphill through the small grey village, sniffing the turf-smoke as they passed; up, past the priest's bare new concrete house and in at the open iron gates. Children were playing round the lodge door and the small garden was full of flowers, hollyhocks, sweet williams and asters; pink geraniums covered the tiny house; a young woman dashed out and snatched a baby from the path, then stood smiling and rocking the child in her arms, chiding it gently. Behind the white palings on the avenue, cows stood in the shade of the beech trees, swishing their tails to disperse the flies; beyond, the corn-fields lay golden ripe.

Caroline leant forward to look at the house: in the distance, it seemed surprisingly unchanged. They drew nearer and she saw that the hall-door stood open as it had always done and the same thin plume of smoke curled upwards from one chimney; the great grey block of the house looked no different from the days when she had come here as a little girl. They stopped in front of the door and Guy switched off the engine; nobody moved. Inside the porch, they could see Archie's fishing rods propped up against the wall in their canvas cases, a pair of rowlocks, waders and a broken oar. Caroline experienced a delicious sensation of home-coming.

'Why, Daddy!' she exclaimed, 'It's really just the same— they've even got it untidy again; if the bells don't ring, it'll be perfect.'

Guy laughed. 'We'll see,' he said, climbing stiffly out of the car, but before he could reach the bell, Moira came running out.

'I feel like a bride,' she said excitedly, 'and you're my first visitors! Leave everything in the car and come and have tea; it's on the lawn, under the chestnut tree. Perhaps you'd like to wash first.'

Archie appeared, smiling and unhurried; he peered into the car and grimaced: 'I think we'll leave that to Paddy,' he said, and wandered off into the house with Guy.

Moira led the others through the new, plain rooms where the smell of paint still lingered.

'I'm glad you've got old furniture,' said Helen; 'It's lovely, my dear.'

Moira beamed. 'Well, we've tried hard; I think we've been to every auction in three counties for the last year; we started off with three beds, the dining-room chairs, which we'd saved, and a couple of tables; the rest has been gathered in from all over the countryside. We didn't hurry—we thought we'd rather do without for a bit than get things we didn't like. There's a lot to do still.'

Caroline peeped into what she thought must be the dining-room; it gave her an odd feeling in this familiar house to guess which room was where. The family portraits hung on the walls and the silver looked as if it had stood for years on the polished sideboards. They went upstairs to a sea-green and chromium bathroom; in the old days there had been brass taps, shining copper cans, and a dark mahogany border round the bath; now, even the bedrooms had gleaming white wash-basins and running water; radiators were built in under the windows and cupboards fitted into the walls; the rooms looked bright and large and the whole house was fitted for electric light.

'We're waiting till the Shannon Scheme comes down here,' explained Moira, 'and then we'll have electricity: lovely!'

Helen snorted: 'The Shannon Scheme in Ballinsaggart! Moira, you must be mad to think it'll ever get down here. I don't believe the thing'll even work.'

'It *ought* to work,' Moira looked undismayed; 'they've been rather efficient about it so far.'

'Only because they've got a German firm to do it; once they've gone, they won't be able to keep it going. I'll be surprised if you get your electricity within the next twenty years: can you imagine them running anything like that properly in this country?'

'You know, I think they're getting more business-like over here, slowly, of course, and in their own way, but I do think they are,' said

Moira; 'anyway, even if we don't get it for ages, the house is all ready for it when it does come. Wait till you see my cooker, though; that's something you haven't got, even in Fitzwilliam Square! Caroline, here's your room.'

They passed on, and Caroline stayed to inspect the little rose and white bedroom. From the window she could see the sea, shimmering-silver beyond the Scotch firs; she had hoped for this view, hardly daring to expect it; when she had stayed here as a child, her room had faced the same way; in those days there had been little chintz-covered chairs, a huge posted bed, flowered wallpaper and spotted muslin curtains.

The others came wandering back and they all went down to tea, although it was now so late that it was nearly dinner-time; they sat in wicker chairs, thirstily drinking cup after cup of tea.

'Caroline thinks the bells oughtn't to ring,' said Guy, 'otherwise she says the house is all right.'

Moira smiled: 'I give the bells six months,' she said; 'something happens to those sort of things in the winter here that they can never survive. Don't look at my poor garden,' she went on, turning to Helen. 'It'll take me years to get it back into order as it was a wilderness when we came and it's not much better now.'

A dark, untidy-looking maid came out across the lawn.

'Paddy wants to know what's he to do wid de luggage, Ma'am?'

Guy stood up. 'I'll sort it out,' he said, and went off with the maid.

'That's Minnie,' said Moira; 'she's straight off the bogs and I'm taming her; she has a wonderful expression for when I go out by the back door—"de Mistress is after going out backwards," she says. Archie thought she'd gone mad the first time she told him that, but it's really very logical. Thank Heaven she's never been to a cinema, or she'd never stay; I wonder if they'll ever get one in Ballinsaggart?'

Isabel began to laugh: 'The Ritz, Ballinsaggart: can't you see it?'

'She's terrified of the telephone,' went on Moira, 'she stands dithering in front of it until it stops ringing, and then it's too late to answer it.'

'She did answer it once,' said Archie; 'she came in to me and said there was a fella wanted me on de phone, and I found it was the Bishop!'

'She'll be all right,' said Moira protectively, 'you'll see. You won't know her when I've had her a year; they all start like that.'

Archie, lying indolently back in his chair, legs crossed, looked up with a grin: 'Have you warned them about tomorrow?' he enquired maliciously.

'Oh no.' Moira took a deep breath. 'A big day, tomorrow; the O'Haras are having a regatta and you'll all have to row. I think they may let you off, Helen, but Guy and the young will certainly have to perform.'

Isabel looked down at her soft beautifully-kept little hands; 'Oh dear,' she said ruefully, 'blisters! Must we?'

'I'm afraid you must; it'll be rather fun, really; everybody's coming from miles around and they're going to dance afterwards.'

'What does one wear?' asked Isabel.

'Cottons,' said Moira firmly, 'or trousers, if you have them. You can take a short frock to change into, if you like.' Isabel made a face: she despised cotton frocks and did not fancy herself in trousers.

'You two,' went on Moira, 'look as though you could do with a good night's sleep; have you been very gay at the Horse Show?'

'They have,' put in Helen, pride in her voice as she exulted in the popularity of her daughters; 'I don't believe they've been to bed for a week!'

'What happens if it's wet?' said Isabel, thinking of her newly-set hair; if her waves were to be washed out on the first day of her visit, the prospect would be black indeed; she could not possibly re-set it herself and there was no hairdresser within fifty miles.

'It depends how wet: if it's just showery, we'll have to go, if it pours, we don't.'

Isabel looked dissatisfied: 'It all sounds frightfully hearty,' she complained.

Moira was instantly concerned: 'You're dead tired,' she said kindly;

'if you don't feel up to it in the morning, just stay in bed and Minnie'll look after you.'

Would it be worth enduring the regatta for the sake of the dance to follow? Isabel was trying to calculate; she was about to give some evasive answer when Archie stood up:

'There are sure to be some of the chaps from Spike Island or Bere Haven there,' he said innocently; 'they get about a bit, you know.' He began to stack up the chairs for Paddy to put away.

'Oh, officers?' It was out before it occurred to her to conceal the revival of her interest; 'thanks awfully. Aunt Moira, but really I'm quite all right; I'm sure it'll be great fun.'

Chair in hand, Archie turned to his wife and his eyelid flickered in the least perceptible of winks.

The next day was not wet, but a high wind rose in the night and when Caroline opened her eyes, white clouds were hurtling across the sky, and the sea was deep blue and flecked with white; before she was properly awake, Isabel had dropped in to talk about clothes.

'It's perishing,' she announced, shivering; 'far too cold for cotton frocks; what are you going to wear?'

'Trousers,' murmured Caroline, 'and a shirt and about four jerseys.'

'It's all very well for you—you've got no behind and trousers look all right on you; I think I'll wear my grey flannel skirt and my red sweater; no, I won't, I'll wear the yellow one; oh, that's got a hole in the cuff, I'll have to wear the red one after all.'

Caroline began to giggle: 'You'll wear the whole lot before the day's out,' she said. 'We'll get soaked, rowing in this weather; we'll be lucky if we don't capsize!'

'People will be so beastly strenuous in the country,' complained Isabel, wrinkling her nose distastefully, 'and they never make any allowances for the weather. I think my blue-spotted crepe-de-chine for tonight, don't you? You are lucky to have all those lovely new clothes, mine are all so terribly ancient; somebody spilt sherry all down the front of my red flowered one and it's unwearable.' Her voice became persuasive: 'I suppose you wouldn't lend me that turquoisy one of yours? It's much more my colour.'

'It's not!' protested Caroline indignantly; 'besides,' she added with determination, 'I'm afraid I'm going to wear it myself.' She was rapidly discovering that, unless she acted with great firmness, Isabel would soon purloin her entire wardrobe.

'Oh, don't be mean, you've got lots of others.'

'I'm not being mean: you know my clothes don't really fit you—you split the last thing I lent you.'

'Do be nice; just for once!'

'No. Nobody here knows your things—they'll think they're all brand new. I'll lend you my blue belt, if you like, for tonight.' Caroline fished in a drawer for the belt and held it out.

'Thanks,' said Isabel, unpropitiated; her sole purpose in this visit had been to borrow Caroline's frock, and she returned disappointed to her room.

They set off, soon after eleven o'clock, in two cars, with two suitcases full of spare clothes, baskets of lunch, bundles of bathing things and innumerable rugs and mackintoshes. Archie was taking Isabel and Caroline, while the others were to go with Guy; then, in the evening, if the elders wished to return early, one car could be left for the girls.

'You do look nautical!' commented Guy in an amused tone, as Caroline climbed into the car, 'but still feminine, thank God; I don't know how you do it.' She looked very slim in her dark blue slacks and sweater, with a striped shirt, open at the neck; a Basque beret was tucked over her russet curls and came down over one eye, accentuating the high cheek-bones and the curve of her eyebrows.

'She looks sweet,' said Moira; 'they both do,' but she glanced a little uneasily at Isabel, wondering what would happen to those incredible eyelashes, stiff and blackened with mascara, if they came in contact with salt water.

They drove along the coast road, with the blue sea on one side, whipped up by the south-westerly wind; now and then they bumped over the smooth bones of rock which pierced the road-surface; cows grazed by the wayside and twice they passed bulls, massive and contented, chewing the cud, but they did not move as the car rattled past. They came upon some tinkers, their lean dejected chestnut nag covered with sores, moving along at a snail's pace; an old woman, with jet-black hair, greeted Archie in Irish from her donkey cart.

'She's a great old character,' he explained, waving his hat at her, 'she has three sons in the British navy and two more to help her on the farm. She can speak some English, if she wants to, but she's too shy.'

When they arrived at the O'Haras, the house was deserted; they made their way down to the sea, where people were clustered on the rocks, sitting on rugs and muffled up in overcoats, trying to shelter from the wind. Willie O'Hara, engaged in giving directions to an old boatman, dashed up to greet them; he was a tall, weather-beaten man, dressed in an ancient herring-bone suit.

'A bit of a bobble,' he said, 'but it'll be better when the tide turns; won't be long now. Nina's still up at the house, brewing some potion or other for tonight, but Gerry's down here somewhere. Pat, tell Miss Gerry I want her. Now . . . ' and he burst into a detailed account of the events, for which they all seemed to have been entered.

Gerry came up, a large pleasant girl in uncomely slacks, her dark hair flying about in the wind. Before she knew where she was, Caroline found herself in a boat, paired up with a tiny bird-like woman who talked ceaselessly with a cigarette in her mouth, to row in a ladies' race against four other boats; she could see Isabel, looking her most fastidious, trying not to wet her feet as she scrambled into her boat in the company of a gaunt rugged young woman who looked as though she could have rowed to America unaided. A small boy, almost entirely covered in an immense white sweater, with a couple of inches of grey shorts barely visible above a pair of brown bruised legs, was allotted to them as coxwain; his name, she discovered, was Maurice. He fiddled knowledgeably with the rudder, politely fixed their rowlocks for them and announced that it was just their luck to have drawn the outside berth, adding with a glance at their unimpressive physique, that he was afraid they wouldn't have much chance against the heavy-weights on a day like this, but that they could have a jolly good try. He added, further, that the cox of the winning boat would receive a prize.

The oars seemed to be yards long and to weigh a ton; the sea was unbelievably rough. Helen hovered anxiously on the shore, certain that before the day was out she would be childless and a widow. Caroline almost caught a crab and recovered herself just in time to see Isabel do the same thing and collapse backwards, feet waving in the air.

Maurice was very efficient; he steered them skilfully past the other boats and kept them under the lee of the rocks until they had just time to take their station and the race began. They were pulling against the wind and before they were even under way they were drenched with spray; huge white-capped waves rushed past them and every moment it seemed as though they were going to be engulfed, but they battled on, heaving, with lolling heads, kept going by the thought of Maurice's disappointment if they did not win. They seemed to remain stationary, in spite of all their efforts, but suddenly Caroline noticed that three of the boats had fallen out of the race; Maurice was yelling like a maniac, his entire being concentrated on getting them forward. 'Give her six,' he screamed, 'one, two, three, the heavy-weights are cooked, five, six.' They were not there yet. 'Six more,' yelled Maurice: 'One, two, three . . . ' The heavy-weights had won.

'Bad luck,' shouted Maurice above the roaring of the sea and the cheers of the on-lookers; they rested on their oars and were instantly back beyond the starting-line.

Caroline smiled at the small boy: 'I'm sorry, Maurice,' she said when they were in calm water again; 'I'd have liked you to get that prize.'

'It doesn't matter,' said Maurice philosophically, 'I might get another; anyway, we'll be in the finals, so there's still a chance.'

'Oh will we?' said Caroline ruefully, wishing now that she had not rowed so hard; it was terrible to think of having to go through all that again, her bird-like little partner lit another cigarette; she was completely unruffled.

Helen was waiting for her on the shore with an overcoat, borrowed from Moira; she was convinced that Caroline would catch her death of cold if she sat on the rocks after becoming so over-heated; she was equally sure that she had overdone herself and had better not row any more that day. Caroline tried to soothe her, assuring her that she was neither hot nor tired and that nobody could catch cold from a wetting with salt water. Isabel, she heard, had contrived to damage her wrist and was not going to take part in any more events.

A figure detached itself from a group on the rocks and came up to greet her shyly; it was Gilbert Hamilton, the pale bony-faced young man who had re-introduced himself to her at Isabel's dance. Helen left them together: the Hamiltons were just the right sort of people, not very well off, but Gilbert would be a Baronet some day; they had a big place and his father, old Sir Hercules, was a great old diehard. With a little gurgle of amusement, Caroline suddenly realised that Gilbert's sister, Marion, had been one of the heavy-weights: how furious she would be if she knew! Marion breezed up now and informed her loudly of her success as an interior decorator, her popularity in London and her resentment at having to return annually to the back-of-beyond to see her poor old dad. She soon departed to organise the next event; it was strange, she intimated, that she had not been made a member of the committee, for they seemed incapable of keeping up to schedule and at this rate the regatta would go on till midnight.

Gilbert stuck to Caroline, speaking little, but shadowing her all day like a faithful dog, immensely appreciative of being allowed to bask in her company and perform small tasks to contribute to her comfort. Isabel, her wrist swathed importantly in a large white male handkerchief, was playing the fascinating sufferer to what Caroline could only surmise must be one of the officers from Spike Island or Bere Haven; Caroline guessed that by nightfall the damaged arm would have made a miraculous recovery. Isabel seemed to be having trouble with Marion, who appeared to consider this particular fair-haired and check-coated young man as her especial property, but her self-inflicted duties as an unofficial member of the committee prevented her from keeping him continually at her side. Poor Marion, reflected Caroline—she seemed to be having an unsatisfactory day.

Guy and Archie were with Willie O'Hara; they were sitting on a rock, watching the races and occasionally jumping up to give directions or fire the starting-gun; but in the intervals they sat, heads close together, listening intently as one of them talked and bursting into roars of laughter from time to time: Archie would have a new fund of stories to tell, if he could be induced to repeat them at home.

Helen and Moira, cornered by the Rector and his wife, were making rash promises to exert themselves in helping to run the annual inescapable Church bazaar, which was always timed to take place in August, when there were plenty of visitors. Helen brought the Rector's daughter, a huge, gushing red-faced wench, up to Caroline; Nan, she explained, was going to Trinity next term, too; it would be nice for them to know one another: if the thought of being a fellow-student with Nan did not deter Caroline, nothing would, she decided.

In the afternoon, the wind dropped somewhat and with the turn of the tide the sea had gone down considerably; it was rather pleasant to sit on the rocks, chatting with all sorts of people, occasionally rousing oneself to take some strenuous exercise, then return to smoke a cigarette and relax in the sun; Gilbert was very attentive and, Caroline could see, absolutely happy. A little warning thought came into her mind that, one of these days, he might become a problem, but that need not be faced today; after all, sitting beside him on the rocks to watch an amateur regatta committed her to nothing.

She and her bird-like little partner were again defeated by the heavy-weights, but Maurice was consoled by the fact that the second prize, which they won, was to him more desirable than the first. The prizes were distributed in the evening, on the broad gravel sweep in front of the house, while people stood around or sat on the long low stone wall, drinking sherry and whiskey and sodas.

Then it was time for the girls to change, hopping warily into a cold bath and out again, for the O'Haras' hot-water system had expired early in the day. The lamp-lit bedrooms were loud with the chatter of girls in all the stages of dressing, shaking out flimsy little frocks that had been crushed by packing, pulling on silk stockings over sunburnt legs and lining up before the mirrors to complain of what the weather had done to their hair, and to make up their faces.

Caroline, bathed and dressed, leant her elbows on the wide-open window-sill, awaiting her turn for the mirror. Outside, the light was beginning to fade, long shadows had crept over the lawn and the in-coming tide swelled and lapped over the rocks; there was not a breath of wind and the scent of the marigolds in the flower-beds under the windows rose up pungently; all the strong colour of the day had departed, leaving the water and sky softly grey, no-coloured. She thought of that terrible endless night in November 1920, when she had come to this house with Archie and Moira, homeless wanderers, seeking a night's shelter; there had been difficulty, she remembered, in persuading the O'Haras to open the door, for they had naturally thought that their visitors were raiders, and Mrs. O'Hara had pushed her husband aside and harangued them in fine style, telling them that she would get Father Quinlan to curse them from the pulpit, every mother's son of them. She had a dreamy recollection of slipping down between crisp white sheets in this very room, and awaking in the late afternoon to draw the curtains and be faced with this unforgettable sight of the smooth grey sea, island-dotted. She took a deep breath and turned back into the room; Isabel came up and whispered disgustedly in her ear:

'My dear, It's only a gramophone dance!'

'Well, what did you expect?' replied Caroline impatiently, 'Ambrose and his orchestra?' Isabel really was the limit, sometimes.

The O'Haras were immensely hospitable: downstairs, tables were loaded with an enormous cold supper; hungry after picnic meals and a long day in the open, people ate heartily. Caroline was at last permitted to meet Isabel's new friend, who had finally succeeded in shaking off the adhesive Marion.

'Will you dance with me a lot?' begged Gilbert, emboldened by several whiskeys. Caroline smiled, hoping that his dancing had improved during the last two years; surprisingly, it had, and although he was too unyielding a person ever to be a good dancer, he was now a tolerable partner. He fetched her coat and led her out into the still, chilly night, across the gravel to the wall, where they could be alone.

There was a long silence, which embarrassed neither of them; a tiny crescent moon lit up the dark water and the sky was full of stars; below, unseen, someone was rowing along in the shadows and they could hear the splash of oars and the slight groaning sound of the rowlocks. Gilbert was not looking at her; with that devoted reverential expression that was beginning to disturb her conscience, he was staring out to where the islands lay, patchily dark under the stars.

'Don't you think,' he said suddenly, in a quietly emotional voice, 'that there's nowhere like this in the whole world? I don't mean this place, particularly, but all around here.'

'I do indeed!' Caroline had been thinking the same thing herself. 'I've always thought so.'

He leant forward to look at her face, as though what she had said was of such importance to him that he hardly dared believe it. 'You really mean that?' he said seriously, 'you're not just saying . . . but you wouldn't, you're too honest a person. Marion hates it. I was afraid you might feel the same.'

Caroline smiled at the thought that she could feel the same as Marion about anything.

He was afraid he had hurt her: 'I knew you didn't, but I wanted to hear you say it,' he went on.

'I think it's the loveliest place in the whole world,' reaffirmed Caroline, as though she were repeating a creed; 'I've always felt I belonged here, although I've never really lived here at all, and . . .' She stopped, alarmed at this revelation of her most intimate thoughts to someone who, until a moment ago, had been a stranger to her.

'Go on,' he said softly.

'No; I don't know you well enough.'

'You don't have to tell me,' he said eagerly, 'I know. You *do* belong! Looking at you today, amongst all those people, I noticed it: you were so different, somehow; I had . . . an extraordinary feeling that you'd grown out of the sea and that when you went away you'd still be there . . . I can't explain it any better . . .'

She stared at him, almost in terror; he bent forward and took both her hands gently and, bringing them together between his own, kissed them reverently: 'Oh, Caroline . . . !' he said, and thrust her hands back at her.

'Don't you think,' said Caroline quickly, her emotions in a turmoil, 'that we're getting very serious?'

He bent his head instantly and gripped the edge of the wall, swaying backwards and forwards in silence.

'You're quite right,' he said, smiling suddenly; 'you haven't known me for very long, have you? Listen, I want to go and talk to your uncle about some fishing, one of these days; how long are you going to be there?'

'Oh, ages; until the middle of September, probably.'

'I'll come over a lot, if I may; when Marion goes, I'll be able to get the car.'

Caroline was trembling and her conscience smote her: now was the time to say something, do something to show him that he was wasting his time. He was so vulnerable, so deadly in earnest. But uncertainty uncoiled within her, paralysing her limbs and clamping a deadening finger on her speech. What was this tumult that possessed her? Did this bubbling fluidity of the senses mean that she was in love, or did it spring from the suddenly shared intimacy of their most private thoughts? She felt pursued and trapped, the quarry run down, untamed but captive, motionless in the grip of the pursuer.

'You'd rather I didn't,' stated the quiet voice beside her.

'Oh yes, do come.'

'Are you being polite?' there was accusation in his tone, that she should need to be polite to him.

'No. I don't know. I'm not sure. I wish I knew.'

He put his hands over his face: 'I am a brute to rush you like this! I haven't given you a chance—how could you know?' He brought his hands down and clasped his knees; for a moment he was the diffident awkward person who had sat beside her at the regatta, struggling to refrain from saying things that might bore her, but when he turned to her gravely, hands and feet at rest, she lost this view of him again.

'Listen, Caroline, I want you to know something. I think you really know it already, but I'm not asking you for an answer, do you see? I've been in love with you ever since that dance at your house in Dublin, nearly two years ago. You were only a school-girl then and it would have been wicked to write to you or try to show you what I felt. I've been waiting for this day ever since, half-crazy, sometimes, in case you might have met someone else and fallen in love with him before I could meet you again. I'm not asking you for an engagement: you're still so young that you should have a chance to meet other men and make up your mind calmly, and, besides, you don't really know me yet. All I want, Caroline, is to be allowed to see you and write to you; you can trust me not to bother you . . . too much. As far as I'm concerned, there can never be anyone else but you—you know that now, don't you? I'll wait for you for years, if necessary—the last thing I want to do is to hurry you. I never meant to say all this tonight, but . . . being with you like this was too much for me.'

He paused, and Caroline turned to look him full in the face: 'Thank you,' she said, feeling greatly humbled, and convinced that this reply was hopelessly inadequate.

'Now may I come over to Butler's Hill to see you sometimes? I promise you I shan't pester you to marry me.'

She held out her hand impulsively: 'Yes, do come.'

He took her hand and laid it across his own, seeing nothing but the slim whiteness of it on his palm; his fingers curled round it gently and he kissed it once more, then laid it softly on her knee.

'You mustn't do that,' he said, smiling gratefully, 'if you want me to keep my promise.'

There was a crunching of trodden gravel and a murmur of low voices as a couple walked slowly past them in the shadows, linked together, anonymous, engrossed. Caroline shivered and Gilbert sprang to his feet, embarrassingly contrite.

'You've been frozen all this time, and here I am, keeping you out: why didn't you tell me?'

She stood up: 'I'm not cold,' she said, 'only nearly.'

They walked slowly towards the house; he did not even try to take her arm, and Caroline, who had learnt much about young men in Horse Show Week, was humbled and slightly disappointed by his reticence.

Moira poked her head round the library door: 'Your young man,' she said, 'has come to see you, Caroline; he's in the drawing-room. I asked him to come with us to the picnic—is that all right?'

'Yes, of course,' said Caroline quickly, trying not to look self-conscious; 'isn't he rather early?'

'Yes, very,' said Moira in an amused tone, and withdrew her head.

Archie folded his two-days-old *Times* and placed it on his knee with the air of someone who has endless time to devote to contemplation: 'Damn nice fellow, young Hamilton,' he said; 'he must be badly smitten to turn up an hour after breakfast.'

'Perhaps,' suggested Caroline tentatively, 'he wants to talk to you?'

He bent his head and looked up at her with a grin: 'Mm; perhaps not, my dear; better go and look after him, he'll be suffering torments by himself in the drawing-room.'

'Won't you come too? I'd like it.'

He shook his head: 'I like the fella,' he said; 'besides, he might shoot me.'

'I'll walk him about outside,' said Caroline; she was beginning to get used to these sallies. Gilbert's attachment to her had provoked varying reactions in the family; Moira and Archie, amused and intrigued, teased her gently about it; Isabel despised her openly for wasting her time over a person whom she described as 'a complete wet'. Guy was an on-looker, not always entirely happy, Caroline thought, about the affair; she would catch him looking at her sometimes with a long appraising stare which would turn into an affectionate smile when he saw that he was discovered. Helen was the most dangerous: she refrained from comment so assiduously that her reticence was a perpetual reminder of her satisfaction; she watched Caroline ceaselessly, bridling like a pouting pigeon when she thought Gilbert was making good progress. Caroline knew that her mother already saw her firmly established in the life of the county, a baronet's wife and mistress of Kilmurry.

It was ten days since the regatta and this was the fourth time that Gilbert had come to Butler's Hill; he made no excuses and Minnie admitted him now without demur, hastening to tell Moira that 'de young gentleman was here again to see Miss Caroline, and would he be here for lunch?' Moira invariably replied that he would, and probably for tea and dinner besides. Today, they were all going out to one of the islands for a lunch-picnic, returning in the afternoon so as to be at the house when David arrived. Caroline was dreading the next few days: until her parents went away, she felt that David's presence in the house would be a continual menace; he was quite capable of asking Isabel, across the dinner table, how her Republican boy-friend was getting on.

She had reached the drawing-room now; through the open door she could hear Helen's voice, almost purring as she exchanged civilities with what she fondly imagined to be her son-in-law to be. Gilbert was magnificent with Helen, listening attentively to her tales of his father, whom she had known as a girl. With growing repugnance, Caroline observed this stranger, who was her mother, exerting herself to the utmost to assist his wooing; as soon as she was inside the room, Helen would, she knew, make some absurdly weak excuse to absent herself and leave them conspicuously and embarrassingly alone; not only that, but she would close the door when she went out and, as likely as not, mount guard in the hall to prevent anyone else from entering so that their privacy should not be violated. And Gilbert and Caroline would be left standing shamefully together, stammering nervously, incapable even of looking at one another naturally. Her behaviour reminded Caroline, revoltingly, of the old women who used to prepare the bed-chamber for the consummation of a royal marriage, retiring discreetly at the right moment.

'Caroline, why not take Gilbert down through the glen and meet us at the boats later on? He says he hasn't seen it since he was a boy.' Helen looked up with an artificial smile.

Caroline blushed hotly with rage and shame: Helen had succeeded in making her hate Gilbert; he himself was standing up uncomfortably, unable to look at either of them.

'Very well,' she said stiffly; 'I'll go and collect my things.' She left the room, bending her head to hide the tears of mortification which stood large in her eyes, making the whole room swim before her. 'I'll never marry him,' she vowed to herself, 'never, as long as I live!'

Helen saw them off from the door, smiling secretively and clasping and unclasping her hands; they walked in silence across the lawn to the little gate that led through the wood into the glen. He held it open for her, reverently, and she waited sullenly while he closed it and came up with her again. He began to talk; his leave was nearly over and she became leadenly aware that he was going to make an indirect attempt to get her to agree to an engagement. They were in the glen now, immersed in the green dusk of the translucent summer leaves; the dark water dripped slowly over the rocks and was caught in little shadowed pools, to trickle on in a tiny ribbon to the sea.

Gilbert stopped suddenly: 'Caroline, you're angry—you haven't said a word to me yet.'

'No I'm not,' she lied, and tossed her curls; she started to walk on, but he caught at her hand and held her back.

'What's wrong, then? Darling, I must know: I've never seen you like this before, and I can't bear it.'

She wrenched her hand away and stood facing him: 'Don't touch me!' she snarled; 'I can't ever marry you, and Mother seems to think we . . .' Her shoulders quivered with resistance.

His hands dropped to his sides and he stared at her, very pale; she wanted to hammer that bony greenish-white face which condemned her silently with its expression of unutterable hurt; why couldn't he say something, call her names or shake her, instead of standing there speechlessly, with his mouth open?

'My dear,' he said in tender bewilderment, 'tell me what I've done.'

'You haven't done anything,' she blazed; 'can't you see, it's what you are? You're not human, you make me feel like a snared rabbit: you know too much about me and I could never escape from you.' She clenched her hands and knocked them together: 'And you're so controlled: I know you want to touch me, but you never have, except my hands, that first evening; why don't you try, and let me knock your teeth in?

I'd know you were human then. And Mother's on your side, scheming and plotting to leave us alone together; it makes me sick—but it's done something for me: it's shown me I hate you, before it's too late.'

She drew a deep breath, and stopped, her wide grey eyes fixed on his in horror at what she had just said. He never moved; his stricken eyes still gazed at her miserably, only his hands shredded a leaf into tiny bruised pieces. She turned and fled up the glen, slipping on the moss-covered stones and darting blindly between the tree trunks. She thought she heard him following her and glanced back, but he was still where she had left him, leaning up against a tree, staring at the ground. She became frightened: she had said unforgivable things—suppose he did something terrible? But it was no good trying to put things to rights now. She sank down amongst the fern, under a tree, and burst into a storm of tears, pressing her hot brow against the cool roughness of the bark. There was a slight sound: Gilbert was standing beside her, humbly waiting for her tears to end; she looked up at him, towering above her, knee-deep in fern, and spread out her hands wildly:

'Don't speak to me, after what I said,' she sobbed; 'I'm sorry. Oh, can't you go away and leave me alone?'

'In a moment,' he said firmly, 'but there is something you must hear first. Don't blame yourself, Caroline: I think I always knew you were beyond my grasp, a nymph or a mermaid that slipped out of the sea one day and got lost in the world;' his voice trembled a little; 'to me, you were always someone out of another world, always eluding me, and I felt that if I touched you it would break the spell and you would vanish away, out of my life. My dear, say you don't hate me— can you forgive me? I shan't come near you again.'

She covered her face with her hands, in shame and exasperation: how could he ask her for forgiveness when she deserved that he should wring her neck? She held out an unwilling hand, salty and wet with tears; he knelt down and took it in both of his, covering it with hot dry kisses. She endured it wretchedly, thinking that if he would only pound her head against the tree trunk, or lift her and hurl her into the stream, she could almost like him.

'You lovely thing!' he said, pressing her hand between his own until it hurt; 'you can't think what this means to me.' He stood up stiffly. 'Let me take you back to the house,' he went on; 'the others will have gone; then I'll go down to the boats and tell them you're not coming—that you've got a headache and have gone to lie down, or something.'

'Let me go by myself,' she begged, 'please.'

'Am I so . . . repulsive to you?'

'No, It's not that: I'd like to be by myself.'

'Very well, I shall go down to the slip from here; you won't see me again. Goodbye, dear Caroline.'

'Goodbye.'

He stood looking at her for a moment, watching a dancing shaft of sunlight that fell on her red-gold hair amongst the fern; then he turned and walked off quickly through the trees, without looking back.

Caroline sat there for a while; she felt dazed and shaken, and her hands trembled. It was very quiet in the wood; little splashes of sunshine filtered through the leaves, moving gently as the breeze swayed the branches above; wood-pigeons cooed in the tree-tops, hidden by the thick foliage. She leant back against the great beech-tree and closed her eyes. She must have slept, for when she opened them again she was cold and numb and the sunshine had gone. Her head and neck ached and her eyes felt swollen. Miserably, she got up and made her way back to the house.

Coming silently into the hall, she was confronted by Minnie, reclining in capless and dishevelled comfort in an arm-chair, black-stockinged feet stretched out before her on the fender-stool; she was reading a novel, her face red from exertion as she spelt out the words, syllable by syllable, in the burdensome monotone of the semi-literate peasant.

'Oah, glory be to God!' she screeched when she caught sight of Caroline; gathering up her shoes, which she had been nursing in her lap, she fled for her life, dropping, cinderella-like, one of them at Caroline's feet. A door banged and there was a scurrying noise from the back stairs, followed by squeals of alarm and consternation as she recited her narrative in the safety of the kitchen.

Caroline sat on the arm of the newly-vacated chair and laughed weakly until the tears sprang up again. Poor Minnie would be having fits in case she might tell on her! She picked up the shoe by its strap and gingerly opened the door which led to the back stairs.

'Minnie!' she called softly.

There was an instant cessation of sound below.

'Minnie, come here a minute.'

She leant over the bannisters and was aware of Brigid, the cook, indignantly pushing Minnie before her along the passage.

'I'm after tellin' her, Miss,' announced Brigid in righteous wrath, 'that's no way to be goin' on in decent houses, dhrapin' herself on the sofas and chairs like a lady. Oh, I thought as much, mind ye, when she'd be off with her up the stairs as soon as you was all outa the house, but I'm not one to be spyin' on the girls. Maybe she might be givin' the silver a bit of a polish, I thought to meself, but not a bit of it! I suppose the next thing ye'll be ringin' the bells for thrays of tea,' and she turned on the terrified Minnie, whose eyes were goggling helplessly.

'Sure I never did it, only dis once, Miss; me feeht was painin' me terrible and I was waitin' on de poshtman . . .'

'The postman is it?' echoed Brigid relentlessly; 'It's a queer postman would come here at two o'clock in the afternoon!'

'It's all right, Minnie,' said Caroline quickly; 'I won't say a word to Mrs. Butler this time. Could you boil me an egg, d'you think, Brigid, and send Minnie up with it? I never went to the picnic, I . . . didn't feel very well. Here's your shoe, Minnie,' and she held it out invitingly by the strap. Minnie received a shove from Brigid which propelled her far enough up the stairs to seize the shoe and retire hurriedly, murmuring gratitude.

'What ails y'at all, Miss?' Brigid looked up in concern; 'is it sick y'are? I wouldn't be takin' eggs, Miss, they do be very sourin' to the stomick.'

'No, It's only a headache, Brigid; I'll be in my room.'

Brigid wagged her head as she marched the cowering Minnie back to the kitchen.

'Eggs'd turn yer shtomick,' she muttered gloomily, 'ye'd be heavin' afther them. And let you,' she continued severely, 'dhress yerself like a Christian, the way ye'd be fit to carry up Miss Caroline's thray. It's well for ye it was only Miss Caroline was in it, so it is, and she so nice and gentle. God bless her. There's odthers in this house'd be out scourin' the grounds for the Misthress, to tell on ye.' The kitchen door slammed on Minnie's shuddering groan of woe.

Caroline went up to her room feeling cheered; her huge grey eyes stared back at her from the mirror, underlined by tiny crescent bruises. She pressed a cold sponge to her forehead and wondered what she could say to keep her mother quiet. The story about her headache would not have deceived her for a moment; she would not be able to hasten home quickly enough to find out what had happened; she would come in, full of pretended concern, probing skilfully until she found a reason for this strange behaviour, convinced that tomorrow Gilbert would come again, to be welcomed with open arms.

Minnie came in with the tray: 'Dat's de check hen's egg, Miss; Bridgie'd let you have no oder.'

Caroline discovered that she was hungry; she sat down to devour the check hen's egg and quantities of toast and butter; when she had finished, she made up her face and brushed her hair until it shone: she must be looking normal when the others returned.

She could hear a car groaning up the avenue: that would be David arriving, and the others had not come back from the picnic. Would she remain hidden in her room, or go down and meet him? She decided that she would be safer in public: even Helen could not say much to her in front of David.

Going slowly down the stairs, she saw Paddy bringing in the luggage; his head had an unfamiliar look, for the greasy cloth cap that rarely left it was tucked under his arm; he deposited two suitcases heavily on the floor and wiped the drip from his nose against his sleeve, before taking up his load again to proceed sedately up the stairs.

David came running up the steps, clasping fishing tackle, a tennis racquet and a mackintosh.

'Caroline!' he exclaimed, flinging everything into a chair and coming forward to take both her hands, 'why, you lovely thing!'

'Oh, don't!' she almost screamed: this was horribly like the scene in the wood with Gilbert. She tried to pull her hands out of his grasp, but he held them firmly and shook her gently.

'Now, what's wrong? You're not married or engaged or anything terrible like that, are you?' She shook her head and smiled. 'And you haven't got a jealous lover concealed behind the curtains with a gun?' He looked round the hall. 'Well, then, what's wrong? Nothing at all—all nonsense, isn't it?' He grinned and released her hands: 'Where's Aunt Moira?'

'They're all out at a picnic—they were going to be back before you came. I had a headache and didn't go.'

'A headache?' David's eyebrows shot up; 'Caroline, I don't believe you've ever had a headache in your life! I wish I could get to the bottom of this. . .'

'Look, here they are, go on and meet them.' Caroline tried to push him down the steps, but he turned back to say with a grimace:

'You ought to make a habit of headaches, they suit you, my dear.'

Moira and Helen had nearly reached the steps; David seized their baskets from them, amidst exclamations of greeting and surprise. Helen barely waited long enough to be civil to him before darting into the house to look for Caroline, whom she discovered flattened against the window in a vain attempt to remain unseen.

'Ah, there you are, poor child,' she exclaimed in solicitous tones, 'and how's the head?'   .

'Gone, thank you.'

Helen's eyes lit greedily on the mackintosh in the chair; so Gilbert, she thought, was still here! 'And what,' she enquired coyly, 'have you done with your young man?'

'Which one?' Caroline's voice was sullen and rebellious.

Helen laughed lightly: 'Oh dear, have you so many? Why, Gilbert, of course!'

'You saw him last: he must have gone ages ago.'

'Gone?' Helen's eyes glittered hardly; 'then, whose is that coat?'

'David's.'

Her head jerked back in annoyance: 'Of course, how stupid of me! Then Gilbert didn't come back with you?' Her face became sly and she looked at Caroline with a tender little smile; 'I was hoping, perhaps, you might have something . . . nice to tell me!' and she looked down again quickly.

Caroline stared gloomily out at the gravel; Guy, Archie and Isabel had come up now and they were all talking in a group; they looked as though they might not move for another ten minutes. Damn, she thought angrily, why couldn't they come in and release her from this inquisition? She turned back to Helen.

'I'm never going to marry him, if that's what you're trying to find out,' she said brutally; 'and it's no good asking me why, because you wouldn't understand.'

Helen's jaw dropped: 'You mean you refused him? He proposed and you refused him? Oh, Caroline, you foolish, foolish child!'

'Yes,' blazed Caroline; 'you think I'm foolish because he'll be a baronet one day and own Kilmurry, but I'd rather marry a chimney sweep! You think that because he's a gentleman and has nice manners he's good enough for me: you wouldn't mind if he drank like a fish and spent his time gambling, so long as he was a Protestant and came from a good family of Unionists. You're afraid that I may want to marry someone you don't approve of, later on, that I'll meet the wrong sort of people in Dublin and get out of your power, so you've plotted and schemed to bring this off . . . you've never trusted either of us.'

Helen leant back against the table and beat upon it with trembling hands: 'Stop, stop!' she cried, 'how can you say such things to your own mother? If I thought you believed them . . .! Caroline,' she bent her head and began to weep, 'come here to me, child.' She stretched out her hand and Caroline approached warily. 'Listen, darling, you're hysterical and overwrought just now, you don't realise that I'm working for your happiness, I want the best for you, the very best. I thought you could have been happy with Gilbert: every mother wants her daughters to be well-married and happy . . . that's all I wanted for you—surely there's no crime in that?'

Caroline watched her silently, as she wiped her eyes and tried to smile.

'You can't blame me for that, can you?' queried Helen again.

'No, Mother,' said Caroline; tears, she thought, could make her say anything.

Suddenly, the hall was full of people; Helen melted away upstairs and Caroline was left to face the interested stares and studied absence of comment of her relations.

Helen and Guy had departed to fish in Galway; September had come and brought with it rough weather, dark rolling clouds and the roar of the south-west wind in the woods; soon, the boats would be brought up for the winter and gales would come to sweep the leaves from the trees and the last visitors from the countryside.

At last there came a perfect day, one of those cold windless September mornings when the mist lies late on the ground and, over the sea, the sun slowly sucks the moisture away in opalescent patches; the sea was deep blue and calm, the fishing-boats chugged out, the noise of their engines very loud in the mist; slowly, the day got warmer.

'The last picnic,' said Moira, and hurried away to see about the food.

They rowed out to one of the islands in two boatloads; Moira, Archie and Caroline; Isabel and David. The quarrel over Denis Joyce seemed to have been forgotten, but Isabel was behaving strangely; although she was receiving letters from Denis almost every day, and reading them in secret exultation in her bedroom, she seemed determined that David should belong to no one but her. It was, 'David, what about a single?' or 'David, come for a bathe before lunch;' and she would look at Caroline, as much as to say, 'you keep clear—David and I don't want you.' But the funny thing was, reflected Caroline, that David did seem to want her; she gave a little chuckle of amusement as she watched him rowing, glumly furious, because Isabel had sat herself firmly in his boat when he had already asked Caroline to go with him. 'Oh, never mind,' she had said; 'I'm here now; you can go back together,' and she had refused to budge.

The tide was slack; a yellow ribbon of seaweed edged the cliffs; gulls sat whitely on the rocks, preening themselves in the sun, or rising to mew and wheel for a moment and catch the light on their spread wings; a bumble bee, tiny, loud and resolute, flew past them out to sea on a dead-straight course, dedicated to some little private odyssey that could only end in tragedy; just inshore, a hawk hovered, about to drop on an unsuspecting mouse foraging on the edge of the bracken.

The dew was still on the grass when they reached the island; they spread out rugs and mackintoshes, plunged gasping into the deep cold water and emerged to lie on a sunny little beach, on the shingle, then back on to the rocks to dive again.

Caroline's white shoulders cleft the dark water; she came up again to lie on the surface, her hair spread round her head like the sea-weed that floated round the rocks. David was standing on a needle of rock above her, and she smiled up at him; he dived, and came up beside her and they lay side by side on the water for a moment; then she turned and swam back to the shore as fast as she could go.

'Come back,' he shouted.

'I can't, I'm going in—I'm perished,' she shouted back, and began to dress.

After lunch, they lay basking in the warm sun; first Archie, then Moira, then Isabel fell asleep; Caroline opened sleepy eyes to find David beside her, a finger on his lips for silence. He grasped her hand and pulled her to her feet.

'Come on,' he whispered.

They sped silently away from the others, hand in hand, over the rocks and the long soft grass, up to the crown of the island, where the whole world, east and west and south, was open to their vision. Far away, on the skyline of the hills on the mainland, the cattle stood small and black against the blue; below them, the sea was ruffled with the flooding tide and rising breeze, like some thick and shining fluid jostled in a bowl and crusting as it cooled; a single white sail moved slowly, bowing, and dipping.

They faced each other, laughing and breathless; David drew her to him and kissed her on the mouth; they leant against each other, mouth to mouth, and collapsed laughing on the deep fine grass.

'Darling!' said David, drawing a deep breath of satisfaction;

'I've wanted to do that ever since I saw you in the hall when I arrived, and I've never had a chance.' He kissed her again, fingering her russet-coloured curls. 'Your hair's the same colour as that bracken,' and he pointed to a little patch of it, just turning golden red; 'Oh, you darling!'

She lay in his arms with shining eyes, stroking the fair hair at the back of his head.

'When I saw you floating on the water today, I knew I could never do without you: you were so white and slim, and your hair . . . You were so lovely that you frightened me. Oh, why do we all have to go away?' He shook her gently by the shoulders— 'and I don't believe you mind a bit, you little beast!'

She lay back smiling, and silently raised her lips to his.

'Perhaps you do, a little,' he conceded; 'but I love you, darling, love you, love you . . . you can't love me like that, it's not possible. Or is it?'

'I think it might be.'

'Darling!'

'Look out,' hissed Caroline; 'here's Isabel.'

'Oh, damn Isabel! Why can't she keep to herself?' he muttered.

Isabel was indeed approaching, picking her way over the rocks and stopping every now and then to look around her, calling for them. They lay, face downwards on the grass, and talked in whispers, but she found them in the end and stood over them, open-mouthed.

'Well, you're a nice pair,' she said; 'I've been looking for you all over the island. Uncle Archie says we must get back, the sea's getting up too much, so you'd better come at once. You might have answered when I called.'

'Were you calling?' said David vaguely, and she gave him a look of hatred.

'Yes, yelling; and if you hadn't been so busy you couldn't have helped hearing me!' She turned her back on them and stamped off, down the hill.

David caught Caroline by the hand: 'Let's run,' he said.

They raced over the grass and down the rocks, slipping and falling, picking themselves up to laugh and start again; they passed Isabel, who stopped to stare at them and then began to run after them. Caroline's hair flew out behind her and the wind rushed in her ears. Panting, they reached the boats; Archie and Moira were packing in the rugs and baskets; they looked up, to see David and Caroline, still hand in hand, standing with enchanted faces on the rock above them, like a pair of dishevelled children.

'Oh, my dears,' said Moira, and paused; 'here, get in, you two, and go off; we'll take Isabel.' She and Archie smiled slowly at one another as they rowed away.

'Dear Aunt Moira,' said Caroline; 'you never have to tell her anything!'

She looked back; Isabel was stepping delicately into the other boat.

They had got a good start; when they reached the slip, the other boat was still only a speck on the water; David moored the dinghy with feverish speed: 'We'll go up through the glen,' he said.

'The glen!' Caroline looked up at him wildly; nothing, she felt, could make the glen bearable to her after that hideous morning with Gilbert.

'Why, you silly darling, what's wrong?' David put an arm round her shoulders.

'It . . . it's haunted.'

'You'll be all right with me: don't tell me you believe in ghosts, and in broad daylight too?'

Arm in arm, they started to wander up the glen; the gales had thinned the leaves and dappled sunshine flickered on the ground; the rain had filled the stream, which gushed and foamed over the rocks. David stopped and held her close: was this where Gilbert, too, had stopped and said to her: 'Caroline, you're angry?' She could not tell, and now she found that she no longer cared.

'Darling, the sun on your hair! No one in the world has hair like yours!'

It was a long time before they reached the house.

CHAPTER TWELVE

It was October 1928, and Caroline's first day of lectures was over. She was a student and had worn a gown; she had a Tutor, of whose duties she was completely unaware; she possessed a number of virgin note-books, bearing the College crest, and had acquired the necessary text-books from some vaguely superior being who floated about in a voluminous black-winged garment which she had discovered was a Scholar's gown, symbol of vast erudition and achievement.

With other Junior Freshmen of her sex, she had attended a 'Social', the sole purpose of which appeared to be to involve her in membership of a hundred different societies: would she join this and that? The advantages to be gained were out of all proportion to the trifling subscription; games, missions, social service, debating, languages, dramatics? She would, perhaps, later on; in the meantime, she would wait and see.

She had been allotted a locker and a key, warned not to leave jewellery on the lavatory basins, informed that if she wished to read in the great Library she would have to swear a Latin oath, told that she must leave the College premises by six o'clock each evening, reminded that she must not visit the rooms of students or members of the staff, and asked to attend a prayer meeting, with no obligation to join. Her head swam as she walked out of the Front Gate into College Green and started to make her way homewards.

The streets were crowded; lights had gone up in buildings and offices as the city haze came creeping down; street signs were beginning to glow and flash: ruby and green, blue and yellow and white; the lighted trains groaned to the stopping-place outside the Provost's House, blue flashes darting from their trolleys. 'Heggle or Mail, Heggle or Mail, Dobolin *O*-pinny,' shouted the ragged newsboys. 'Give us a panny for a cupper tea'; barefooted and with streaming noses, they boarded the trams, thrusting the papers at the passengers with husky confidential salesmanship:

'Fin'l, late fin'l, Heggle or Mail; give us a copper, Miss.' Others on the pavements harried the passers-by. Headlights prodded the dusk; suburban housewives hurried home from the pictures to prepare the six o'clock meal; business girls began to pour from the offices.

Caroline walked home; she loved this hour of city twilight, when all around her was rush and noise and colour and she could turn to see the plane trees stand out from the blue mist and, beyond the railings, the great stretch of lawn that might have been some huge slow silent river, wrapped in vapour, flowing between the Nassau Street embankment and the College buildings with their distant quivering lights.

Isabel was out, and Helen was alone in the drawing-room, writing letters on her knee, comfortably installed before the fire.

'You look dead tired,' she remarked cheerfully as Caroline came in to crouch on a low stool by the fender; 'I hope all this College business isn't going to be too much for you!' Although she had apparently given in, she still maintained a flow of propaganda, to discourage Caroline from her university career.

'I'm exhausted,' admitted Caroline, 'but I suppose I shall find out one day what it's all about.'

'Don't let them make you join all those societies, dear; you'll have quite enough to do with your work, and you must have a little time left to enjoy yourself. Have you come across any nice girls yet, in your year? The sort of girls you feel you could make friends with?'

'Well, there's Nan Wilson from Ballinsaggart,' began Caroline: wickedly, knowing that Helen thought Nan was awful, but before

Helen could utter a word of protest the door had opened and Doran was ushering somebody in. 'Mrs. Joyce, Ma'am,' she announced, rigid with disapproval.

They stared at her, open-mouthed, and Caroline gave a little gasp of consternation: so it had come to this! Denis's mother was taking the law into her own hands and Isabel's game was up. With brutal suddenness, Helen would learn the whole sordid history of the past two years, discover how she had been flouted, deceived, ignored. Caroline trembled at the thought and, from beneath her fear, there arose a feeling of intense pity for her mother; it was so appallingly unjust that she should have to hear from the lips of this particular stranger, whom she had always considered her enemy, the tale of the treachery of her own daughter. It was too late to do anything about it now; she stretched out a hand and laid it on her mother's arm.

Wheezing painfully from the exertion of climbing the stairs, a large black figure advanced into the room; Helen sprang to her feet, shaking off Caroline's hand:

'Mrs. Joyce, I don't think . . . '

'No, Mrs. Adair, we've never met before, for all we're near neighbours.'

Caroline pushed forward a chair and Mrs. Joyce sank heavily into it: 'Excuse me, won't you?' she said, 'pouf—the stairs . . . I have to take it easy . . . in me own house they're just the same, but I go at them slower.' She lifted her head and, in a strangely authoritative voice, asked: 'Mrs. Adair, can I speak to you alone?'

Helen was speechless; as the door closed behind Caroline, she stared at the massive ill-corseted figure with its dowdy black clothes and cheap black hat; she noted with distaste the sham diamond brooch and broad gold wedding-ring, the shiny artificial silk stockings and gold-rimmed spectacles, the fat hands and feet and the intelligent red face: this was her enemy, embodiment of all she detested, symbol of the new Ireland that was jostling the Unionists out of their place in the life of the country; if the Joyces were in society now, she was well out of it. But why had this woman come? To gloat over her and remind her that the Protestant ascendancy was at an end? Doran must have been mad to let her in.

'I can't think,' she began coldly, 'what you can have to say,'

Now she felt herself being observed; the bright blue eyes behind the spectacles solemnly scanned her face with a regard of kindly grave concern.

'God forgive me,' said the wheezy voice; 'as if you hadn't suffered enough!'

Helen sat down suddenly: she knew now what was going to happen. Her breath came in short little gasps and the lids flickered over her dark burning eyes; the suspicions of many months were taking monstrous shape. What a fool she had been to believe those lies and excuses! She despised herself that she could have been so deceived. Memories flashed across her mind: the night of the dance and Isabel's last-minute story of Denis's engagement to another girl—that had been the first lie; then she remembered Isabel returning, flushed and triumphant, from parties and dances: 'Who was there, dear?' 'Oh, the usual crowd'; or 'Who brought you home?' 'Oh, nobody you'd know.' Rebellious glances and evasive answers and now, the final ignominy, that Isabel should have left it to this woman to enlighten her. A wave of furious self-pity engulfed her: they were all against her, all deceiving her; Caroline must know, perhaps Guy, too, was in the plot. The blood drummed in her ears and for a moment she thought that she would faint; the knuckles stared white out of her lap as she dug her nails into her palms in a supreme effort at control. Then pride reasserted itself: not for a moment should her enemy see her weaken.

'Come,' she said, in a stifled voice; 'I know why you've come: let us get it over.'

Mrs. Joyce dived into her handbag for a handkerchief and wiped her upper lip:

'I pocketed me pride and me scruples, Mrs. Adair, to come to you. Nobody knows I'm here, and if me husband was to get wind of it, I don't know what would happen to me, the house is that divided.' She paused.

'Yes, yes,' said Helen impatiently: the effrontery of the woman to talk to her of pride!

'You know well enough why I'm here: it's about my son and your daughter. Things have gone on long enough the way they are—either they must get married, or else . . .'

She was dictating to her, to *her*! 'We could never agree to a marriage'; Helen spat out the words.

'Now listen, Mrs. Adair: you're a mother, the same as me, and that's the only bond there can ever be between us, you don't need to tell me that. You're Protestants and Unionists and we're Republicans and Catholics, and only tolerance and time can bridge that gap. You're a lady from a grand family and my father was a small contractor in the County Wexford; he was an honest man, God rest his soul, but not one ever to let on he was one of the gentry, and he'd never let us put on any airs and graces for all the great education he gave us. So I'm not pretending to expect that you'd welcome a marriage between the two families; but I'm proud of me sons, Mrs. Adair, they're all fine boys, and honest boys, and if they are good Catholics, who'd say a word against them for that?' the heavy face trembled a little. 'And your Isabel is a lovely girl, God bless her. Believe me, I want that marriage no more than you do, but I want me boy to be happy, and if you love your daughter, you'll see that nothing else will do them, only to get married.'

'I . . .' began Helen furiously, but Mrs. Joyce put out a hand.

'Hear me out, now, hear me out. Mr. Joyce is dead against it, the same as you, and he has Father Byrne on his side; the two of them have poor Denis half-killed between them, trying to talk him out of it; if you could only see the misery on that boy's face, it'd melt a heart

of stone! But Mr. Joyce is a hard man, if I say it meself, and he can
only see the harm in it, his son rising up against him; he can't see that
all the boy wants is the right of every man to choose his own wife.
Mammy, says Denis to me, I love her, and where's the crime in that?
God knows, you couldn't blame the boy! Now, two years is a long time
to be in love, with nothing to look forward to, and when I see them
together it frightens me, so it does, to think what may happen if we
old people don't give way. You know as well as I do that there comes
a time when human nature won't be denied, Mrs. Adair: remember
the time when you were in love yourself—d'you want your daughter
to be soured by the very name of love?' The bright blue eye was fixed
on Helen's face. 'This isn't a passing affair, believe me, and I'd let all
me scruples go if I could see the two of them settled happily together.
Maybe I'm putting me immortal soul in peril, but I'm willing to take
the risk for me son's happiness.'

She leant back in her chair and wiped her eyes under the spectacles,
unashamed of the tears that had risen while she spoke.

Helen was silent, her compassion unstirred. She felt sickened by all
this sentimental nonsense about love and happiness; stealing a covert
contemptuous glance at her adversary, rage surged within her: how
dared the Joyces resent the marriage! They had no right to object
to her daughter; she would never forgive them that; was it not her
prerogative that all the opposition should have come from her? This
preposterous fool of a woman, with her tears and sloppy talk, what
did she know of pride? And what did she want? This conversation was
leading nowhere, there must be something more to come. She must
keep calm, fool the woman into thinking that she had been won over
and lure her into further confidence. She poked the fire cautiously.

'What do you want me to do?' she asked quietly, without looking
up.

'Ah, this is where the trouble comes;' Mrs. Joyce shook her head
ominously; 'it's the money.' She paused expectantly, but Helen said

nothing, so she went on: 'Denis has nothing but the little he earns and his father won't let him have a penny—sure they're not even on speaking terms now and God knows if I'll ever reconcile them again. If I had anything of me own to give them, they'd be welcome to all I had, but me father lost all his money in a court case the year I was married, and I never came in for anything since. Now, the legal profession is very slow, but Denis is a clever boy and in four or five years he'll be earning enough to keep a wife and family, I've no doubt, but their hearts'd be broken waiting all that time, with everyone against it and all. Now, if you and your husband could make them an allowance of a couple of hundred a year, they could marry now, with what Denis earns, and in five years they'd be independent. Surely, if you could afford that, it's not too big a price to pay for your daughter's happiness?' She looked hopefully at Helen's averted face. 'There's one thing I want you to remember, Mrs. Adair; Denis is a good boy, and if they marry, you needn't be a bit afraid, he'll make her a good husband. They'd have a struggle, but who minds that when they're young and in love?'

Helen bit her lip to keep back the flaming words: 'I'd rather they lived in sin!' and blinked in horror that such a thing should have occurred to her. A good husband, indeed! The last thing she would want Denis to be was a good husband: let him beat Isabel, drink, be unfaithful, make her life unbearable so that she would be compelled to leave him and learn by bitter trial that her mother had known best. The impertinence: first trying to foist this marriage on her and then expecting her to finance it—as if she would lift a finger or part with a penny to make it possible! She choked her anger back and tried to think; suddenly her lips curled in an icy smile of satisfaction: she had the whip hand over them all! She drew a deep breath and turned to Mrs. Joyce.

'Like you,' she lied, 'I have no private means—nothing at all, so I'm quite at the mercy of my husband, you understand? But, if I can persuade him to agree to this marriage, it's possible that he might settle something on Isabel which would permit them to get married at once. You must leave it to me . . . I'll see what I can do.' She stood up, calm and gracious.

'Ah now, I don't know how to thank you!' tears welled up behind the spectacles again as Mrs. Joyce wrung Helen's lifeless hand; 'God bless you, Mrs. Adair, I don't know how to thank you!'

Helen was severely practical: 'You're not going to mention this visit to your son?' she enquired warily.

'You can trust me not to say a word—it's as much as me life is worth; begging, he'd call it, and I doubt he'd ever speak to me again. Oh no, mum's the word!'

'Of course, I shan't say anything to Isabel, either, it would spoil everything. I'll write you a note in a day or two to tell you what my husband says.'

'Better leave it for me at the little cake-shop at the corner, for you never know . . .'

Helen saw her visitor out at the front door and went back to the fire; her face was burning and her hands and feet felt icy cold. She plunged the poker through the bars, digging at the embers and heaping on coal and logs until the blaze roared up the chimney. Then she began to rock herself backwards and forwards on the low stool, planning. Isabel, by her cowardice and treachery, had earned nothing but defeat and she would have her desert: Guy should never know of Mrs. Joyce's visit, never be given the chance to make the marriage possible, and in a few days, perhaps a week, so that Mrs. Joyce should think that she had spent herself in days of fruitless argument, she would write the promised note. The sentences were framing themselves already . . . 'adamant . . . can do nothing with him . . . cannot induce him to contemplate the marriage . . . afraid things are now worse than they were before . . . must wait until your son is in a position to support a wife.' Yes, she could beat them all! If those two knew that they would have to wait five years, it would never come off. Isabel was not the sort of girl to face prolonged opposition and the bleak prospect of poverty thrown in. It was enough to shake the resolve of any girl, and Helen knew her Isabel: popularity was the breath of life to her, she must have her comfort and her pretty clothes, servants to look after her, admiring friends; she would never make a poor man's wife. Within a year, she decided, Isabel would be fancy-free and glad to marry anyone with money and good looks. In the meanwhile, let her see her Denis, taste to the full the hopelessness of the attachment. She would soon sicken of it. She herself need say nothing; all she need do was to continue in apparent ignorance. It was very simple, nothing could go wrong. And Caroline? Yes, she had even thought of a story to keep Caroline quiet.

At that moment, Caroline's head came round the door; sitting miserably before the cheerless electric fire in her father's study, not knowing what to say if he came in, she had heard the stir of the departing visitor, the hall-door softly closing and Helen's quiet step as she had made her way upstairs again. Ever since, she had been bracing herself to meet the storm that must burst in awful fury upon the entire household: what form would it take, she wondered—tears, imprecations, would Isabel be turned out of the house? Nothing was impossible. And what would Guy do? He would be angry, certainly, and desperately hurt, but she doubted whether he would be surprised. She could bear it no longer: she must go up and find out what was happening, then she might be able to warn Isabel when she came in.

'Come here, dear,' called Helen cheerfully; 'such an extraordinary thing!'

Caroline stared at her in amazement from the door: this confident, almost amused manner was the last thing she had been expecting; nervously, she came nearer the fire and sat down, half-wondering if Helen had actually gone out of her mind.

'Do you remember that maid we had—the one we always suspected of taking things?'

'Mollie?' Certainly Helen had gone mad.

'Yes, Mollie, and we could never pin her down to anything; well, it seems she's been in several places since she left us, but, of all people, who d'you think she's with now? The Joyces, those Republicans down the Square, and she seems to have been robbing them right and left— clothes, shoes, money, all sorts of things! That's why Mrs. Joyce came to see me, to find out whether we'd had the same trouble with her; her husband wants to prosecute, but she said she didn't want to do that unless she was a confirmed thief, because the girl's been having a lot of trouble at home and might have needed the things. Of course, I told her that we had no evidence to prove that the girl had taken anything when she was with us—you can't be too careful, you're open all the time to an action, and that's why Mrs. Joyce wanted to speak to me alone. You'd better not mention it to anyone, even to Isabel, because it might get about and I don't want to be dragged into court for libel or defamation of character: better not tell anyone even that she came to see me—they'd want to know why.'

Caroline felt weak with relief; she stretched out her legs and let her hands hang limply:

'No, of course I won't say anything,' she promised.

'That's the first time I've ever spoken to a Republican, to my knowledge,' went on Helen, laughing; 'dreadful old thing, wasn't she?'

'I thought she looked rather a dear.'

Isabel came in, her hard little face sullen and unsmiling; Helen regarded her with satisfaction: that was the expression she wanted to see.

'Had a nice afternoon, dear?' she enquired with an impassive smile.

'Oh, all right, thanks.' Isabel could never be gracious with her mother. She turned to Caroline: 'Well, how d'you like Trinity?' They began to talk together.

Helen sighed; she had acted her part and now she could relax. She put her hands to her face and closed her eyes; she felt desperately tired, in another minute she would be asleep; she brought her hands down to her lap and forced herself to sit erect. The firelight swam before her in a shifting glare; the girls' voices came from far away, she felt herself being slowly sucked into distance; a flock of dancing crows filled her vision, they were coming towards her, roaring all around her and she raised a hand to ward them off. Caroline's clear frightened voice pierced the walls of distance:

'Mother, are you all right? Are you ill?'

'No.' The voice did not seem to be her own, somebody else was speaking for her, bringing out the words that she must say:

'No, I'm all right, let me go.' She was coming back, her flesh pricked uncomfortably and she could feel the blood returning to her face that a moment ago had seemed stretched taut over the bones.

'I'm always all right,' she said harshly; rising to her feet, she squared her thin shoulders and walked quickly out of the room.

Eight days later she left the note at the little cake-shop.

CHAPTER THIRTEEN

The air in the stuffy lecture-room had been breathed and rebreathed, but in spite of the blazing fire it was still cold; outside, rain dripped steadily through the foggy air. In a corner near the door, stood a little collection of umbrellas, their folds flaccid and shining wet; water trickled from them into a swelling pool on the floor. The lecturer was standing very close to the fire: if he stayed there much longer the flowing skirts of his gown would go up in flames; already there was a smell of burning. The students' faces brightened for the first time that morning and they began to nudge one another and giggle in delighted anticipation of a diversion. The lecturer paused, sniffed the air, glanced over his shoulder and, with a reproachful look at his class, hopped nimbly out of danger. Interest waned again as he continued his lecture.

Caroline shook her fountain-pen, making a little comet of ink on the bare boards, and went on with her desultory note-taking. She shifted about, trying to find a position that was even tolerably comfortable on the black wooden bench; her feet were wet and her stockings were splashed up the back; raindrops still glistened in her hair and the back of her collar felt coldly damp, for she had come out unprepared for rain. The man in front of her was drawing faces in his notebook, long-haired glamorous creatures with sweeping eyelashes and high cheek-bones; they were rather good; he showed them to his neighbour and they began to whisper together. The lecturer paused again, stared them into silence and went on in a bored voice.

'Aren't the boys awful?' whispered Nan Wilson beside her, red-faced and giggling, horribly feminine in male company.

How like school it all was, thought Caroline, as she laid down her pen and gave up listening; the lecture was nearly over and she had much to think about.

There was a letter from David in her bag; he had been at Greenwich, now he was in Plymouth, doing a course. He would be home for a week at Christmas-time and was going to hire a car so that they could go where they liked: they would go up to the mountains and walk for miles, they would drive all over the country; in the evenings they would go dancing: not a moment of their precious time would be wasted. That was only three weeks from now; Caroline's eyes shone, but she sighed guiltily as she thought of the examination she would have to take in January. Oh well, what did a week matter? No one could work at Christmas, anyway.

She must have a new evening-frock; at lunch-time she would go up Grafton Street and see what was in the shop windows; perhaps her father would pay for it if she told him that she needed one especially badly just now; he was a darling and had never let her down yet. Or, if he was feeling poor, as he sometimes said he was, perhaps he would make it his Christmas present to her, and let her have it a day or two before the time.

The lecture was over; she collected her things hurriedly and darted back to No. 6, where the women students had their cloakrooms; she hurled her books into her locker, washed the grime from her hands, pulled a hat on over her damp curls and almost ran up Grafton Street. It was after one o'clock and she had another lecture at two; if she was to find a dress and have some lunch besides, she would have to be quick. Half-way up the street, she came to a stand-still: there was a perfect frock in a window, cream-coloured chiffon with a tiny gauged bodice and narrow gold shoulder-straps; she edged round to see if she could catch a glimpse of the back and someone who was striding blindly down the street bumped into her heavily. She lost her balance and put out a hand to save herself from being pitched against the glass, but there was no support and she found herself sitting on the muddy pavement, laughing weakly.

'Caroline!' said a horrified voice; it was Denis. He pulled her to her feet, apologising for his clumsiness, wiping the mud from her clothes and holding out a huge handkerchief.

'It's all right,' she said, retrieving her bag from the gutter, 'don't worry, nothing awful's happened.'

He looked at her seriously: she was still bubbling with laughter.

'Look here,' he said, 'I'm frightfully sorry I knocked you down, but I'm terribly glad I met you: you're just the person I want to see— come and have lunch with me?'

He looked awful, as though he had not slept for a week. 'Thank you,' she said; 'I'd love to.'

'It'll have to be somewhere cheap, me dear, I'm broke: d'ye mind?'

She shook her head and smiled at him: 'I'll pay for myself if you like—I'd have to have lunch anyway.'

'You will not,' he said viciously; 'I haven't sunk to that yet.'

They dived into an underground restaurant and ordered sausages and mashed; the place was crowded, but they managed to find a table for two. Denis leant forward and began in a low voice:

'You know all about Isabel and me, don't you? She said you did.'

'Yes, at least . . .'

'Well, what's happened to her now: she won't speak to me?'

'Won't she?' Caroline looked up, startled; 'why?'

'I wish I knew; I thought she might have told you.'

'Oh, Lord, no: Isabel never tells me anything like that; we're a funny family, none of us ever tells the others anything unless we have to.'

'I'm in one hell of a mess;' he ran his fingers through his dark hair; 'my family are cut to the heart because I want to marry her, and my father won't even speak to me; and now Isabel's gone all queer and won't speak to me either: I can't think what I've done.'

'Poor Denis!' Caroline felt really sorry for him; 'I wish I could help you, but I daren't say a word to Isabel.'

They drank their coffee in silence.

'Perhaps she can't face it,' said Denis slowly, 'and I couldn't blame her; she says she's afraid to tell your people, that your mother would have her life. I wanted to go and see your father, but she got into such a state I had to promise I wouldn't. So what can I do?' He looked desperately at her; she shook her head helplessly and pushed away her empty cup.

'I'm afraid it's no good talking to me about it—she never listens to anything I say and she'd be livid . . .'

'My God, there she is!'

Caroline turned round in her chair; Isabel and Juliet Moore were standing just inside the door, looking for an empty table. She had seen them: she stood stock-still, staring at them with a stony face. Denis stood up and started to go to her, but with a quick movement she grasped Juliet's arm and the two of them were gone. Denis came sheepishly back to the table and spread out his hands in a hopeless gesture:

'You see how it is? Ach, what can I do with her at all?'

He roared for the bill and hustled Caroline quickly into the street.

After her lecture, she sped home; she would light the schoolroom fire and work until dinner time. She was taking Spanish as her second language and, never having studied it before, had a great deal to make up: with the aid of a dictionary she would struggle with 'Dona Perfecta'. She changed out of her damp clothes and crossed the lobby; Isabel was sitting in the schoolroom, curled up in an arm-chair in front of a blazing fire, with a book on her knee; she glared at Caroline as she came in, and sat up rigidly.

'Well!' she said furiously.

Caroline stopped halfway across the room, checked by the anger in her voice: 'Well, what's wrong?'

Isabel stepped out of her chair and leant against the mantelpiece:

'When are you going to stop stealing my boy-friends away from me?'

'I'm not, Isabel, honestly . . . Denis knocked me down in the street and . . .'

'Oh, don't be silly—knocked you down in the street!'

Caroline threw her books on the table with a little nervous giggle: it did sound absurd. 'It's true; I was looking into a shop window and he bumped into me and I sat down on the pavement, so he asked me to have lunch with him. I've never tried to take anyone away from you, honestly; I like Denis, but not like that.'

'Oh, yes you have: first it was David and then it was Mike—he used to be mine too; and now it's Denis. Why can't you leave them alone and marry your wonderful Gilbert?'

'I don't want Denis, I tell you, and he doesn't want anybody but you, and as for Mike . . .'

Isabel's face was very white above her dark red dress. 'Well,' she said, in a tight little voice, 'you're welcome to Denis, actually, I'm finished with him.'

'Isabel!'

'Yes, I'm sick of the sight of him and his beastly family; I wouldn't marry him if he was the last man in the world. You try, and see what you're up against: you'd think I wasn't even a Christian! I'm going . . .'

'Well, you might tell him, he's in an awful state.'

'So you've been discussing me with him, have you?' There was an icy silence.

'No,' said Caroline at length; 'he asked me if I knew why you wouldn't speak to him. and I said I didn't, that's all.'

'Well, next time you have lunch with him, you can tell him I'm engaged to someone else;' she struck out her chin and stared defiantly at Caroline; 'I'm going to marry David.'

Caroline's jaw dropped in amazement; she thought of David's letter in her bag and sudden anger swept over her hotly.

'You're damn well not,' she said, 'you're not engaged to him.'

'He's mine,' sneered Isabel, 'he's always been mine, ever since we were children, so you'd better keep your hands off him. I know you've been trying to take him away from me, but I'm going to marry him, not you.'

'He hasn't asked you to!'

'What makes you think he hasn't?' Isabel's head was on one side and she was smiling oddly.

'Because he's in love with me!' Caroline's grey eyes blazed back at her.

'But he hasn't asked you to marry him, now has he?' Isabel laughed softly. 'You think he's in love with you—you don't know anything about men; he's been in love with me for years and he's only flirting with you to try and make me jealous. You'll see soon enough when he comes home at Christmas who he wants to marry: if I were you, I'd keep out of the way so that you won't feel too much of a fool. Why don't you ask Aunt Moira if you could go down to Butler's Hill for Christmas? Gilbert might be on leave again.'

'How d'you know David's coming home for Christmas?'

'Ah-ha! I can get letters just as much as you, I suppose . . .' She took an envelope out of her pocket and tossed it about in her hands, quickly, so that Caroline should not see it properly.

'I don't believe it's from David.'

'Believe what you like, my dear: how else should I know?'

How else indeed? thought Caroline miserably; she opened her books and pretended to look up a word in the dictionary, seeing nothing. It was true that David had been jealous of Denis, she remembered him at Isabel's dance . . . if he knew that Isabel was free now . . . was it possible that it was she he had wanted all the time? But he had told her that he loved her: 'Darling, the sun on your hair . . . love you, love you . . . you can't love me like that, it's not possible—or is it?' She looked up, reassured again; Isabel was still standing, staring down at the floor, her foot playing with a tiny lump of coal that had fallen out of the scuttle. Caroline shut her book with; a bang and stood up:

'I'm not going to budge,' She said resolutely; 'David's not yours; you lost him when you got engaged to Denis.'

Isabel said nothing; she shrugged her shoulders and smiled pityingly.

Caroline ran to her room and put on a coat; she would go and see Anne. If only Olga had been here! She was so worldly-wise and experienced: but Olga was at a dramatic school in London, a budding actress of great talent.

It was getting dark already; the foggy air still dripped with moisture and the muddy pavements gleamed under the street lamps. Caroline ran most of the way, just as she had done when she had gone to see the Hendersons as a child. Anne's front windows glowed warmly through the drawn blinds; panting, she knocked at the door, the special little knock she always gave at that house. Anne opened the door herself:

'Caroline darling, how lovely! I knew it was you, by your knock.' She pulled her into the warmth and light; there was the marmalade cat on the hearthrug, stretched out in purring luxury. It was like coming home. Anne brought a decanter and glasses.

'We'll have some sherry,' she said; 'you look as if you needed something.'

Caroline sipped it gratefully and smiled at Anne; she did not want to talk; all she needed was to relax in this friendly house. Anne was growing older; her golden hair was beginning to fade, but her calm face was still unfurrowed: she was a tower of strength. She asked Caroline no questions but talked quietly about Olga and Leonard. Leonard was in danger of becoming a fashionable portrait painter, she said, and felt that he was perjuring his soul by perpetuating all the hideous women in the country—they were always the ones with the most money and seemed to have a mania for immortalising themselves. They were getting quite rich now, and she had a maid; she held up some gleaming white satin:

'My Christmas present for Olga: it's an evening dress.'

'How lovely! Did you make it?'

'Yes; I used to make all her clothes; I'm just doing the finishing.'

Caroline thought of the cream chiffon frock with the gold shoulder straps; she wanted it no longer: she did not want any new clothes, ever again.

'How is Olga?'

'Very happy: she loves her work; she's coming home next week, *without* her Russian prince.'

'I hadn't heard about him.' Caroline suddenly realised how little she had seen of the Hendersons lately.

'He's a musician and sends her orchids, and then has to go and eat at coffee stalls because he can't afford to go anywhere else; she says he's too gloomy to marry and she keeps telling him to go away, but the orchids keep on coming.'

They both laughed; Caroline could imagine Olga in London, flitting about among all her strange friends: artists, musicians and actors, down-and-outs, half of them, talking politics in French, discussing art in Spanish and wearing strange clothes that would make anyone else look foolish; she was a person who could only flourish in a city. She began to be rather frightened at the thought of seeing her again: would Olga have become very grand and cosmopolitan, with her acting and her Russian prince, and make her feel terribly young and provincial, or would she be the same enchanting vital Olga who had somehow contrived to avoid wearing the school hat during her entire stay at Miss Deane's?

'You needn't worry,' said Anne; 'she hasn't changed a bit.' Leonard came in and poured himself out a glass of sherry; he had just returned from the West, where he had been staying in a country house, painting the young wife of an old man.

'Of all the hard-faced little so-and-so's,' he said, 'and d'ye know, that old fella wouldn't even let me be in the room with her alone!' He leant one elbow on the mantelpiece and looked down at Caroline: 'I wish you'd let me paint you—will you?'

'What, me?' Caroline pointed to herself in disbelief; 'you're not
serious?'

'Yes I am; perfectly serious.'

She glanced up at Anne, who smiled her slow dreamy smile:

'She'd make a lovely portrait, Leonard, I've often thought so: sitting
on the floor in her emerald green dress, stroking the marmalade cat . . .'

'May I?' pressed Leonard.

'Why, of course; I'd love it.' She blushed with pleasure.

They discussed when he could begin work; Caroline quailed as she
thought of her coming examination.

'After January,' she begged; 'I've got an exam.'

'All right, and you needn't be nervous, I won't send your father a
bill for fifty guineas afterwards!'

Anne chuckled: 'Oh, who did that?' He closed one eye and grinned:
'No one,' he said innocently, 'no one at all; I'm just reassuring her.'

Anne poured out more sherry: 'Stay to dinner, Caroline; there's
plenty.'

'I couldn't, really; Mother would have a fit.'

'Ring-up and tell her—we've got a telephone now: I told you we'd
gone up in the world.'

'I believe I will;' Caroline beamed at Anne; 'may I help you to cook
it, like we used to? Or does the maid cook now?'

Leonard shook his head: 'No, I soon put a stop to that nonsense:
grey potatoes and congealed eggs, and the same soup every night, pale
yellow!'

'He thought I was getting old.' Anne smiled up at him mischievously,
'so he said I must have more leisure; so I did, for a week, and then he
decided that I wasn't as old as all that and I was re-instated in the kitchen.'

Caroline laughed heartily for the first time since she had returned
from Butler's Hill. That night, when she was back in her room she put
her elbows on the dressing-table and stared at herself in the mirror. 'If
Leonard *wants* to paint me,' she thought, 'I can't be so bad-looking.'

She combed the hair back off her high forehead; 'I think I'll get that new frock after all.' The little gold sandals that Helen had bought for her in Horse Show Week would be perfect with it, and her green velvet cloak. She would have her hair set in a new way and buy some varnish for her nails. She shivered with pleasurable anticipation and took David's letter out of her bag: she would write an answer to it now and post it on her way out in the morning.

The house was terribly quiet and silence seemed to close in upon her; she stiffened suddenly and looked furtively round the room as though it contained some hostile watching presence. She got up quickly and shut the door, remembering the days of the sniper, when she used to peer under the bed with a choking heart and expect to find him on the window-sill when she pulled up the blind. It was foolish to feel like that, she told herself, for there was nobody there. Her bed was neatly turned down, pyjamas laid upon the eiderdown, slippers on the rug below; the nursery pictures, 'Bubbles' and 'The Boyhood of Raleigh', that had hung on the faded wall-paper as long as she could remember, the tattered postcard screen beside the wash-stand and the high fire-guard, where a succession of nannies had aired the night-clothes of generations of babies, all proclaimed the customary welcome of familiar things; but all her confidence had gone.

She folded up David's letter and put it away; she could not answer it tonight. With chilly trembling fingers she took off her clothes and crept into bed to sleep uneasily and dream frustrated horrid dreams: Isabel dancing round her, gloating and saying: 'I've won, why don't you go away?' And when she tried to answer her, the tormenting figure would fade and there was nothing there.

The next day, after lunch, she tried to write to David. She sat at the schoolroom table, chewing her pen and making endless false starts on sheet after sheet of paper; the only words that would come were stiff and pompous; she could not bring herself to mention Isabel. Her mind was paralysed: she could feel Isabel's critical presence, as if she were actually there in the room, looking over her shoulder and ridiculing every word she wrote. 'Dear David . . .' That sounded so silly; 'Darling . . . my darling . . . ' But, the mocking voice whispered in her ear: 'Oh, how touching! Go on, make a fool of yourself.' She laid his letter before her on the table and, reading it again, knew that she was right: David did love her. She bent her head to start again and, at that moment, Isabel came into the room.

One glance at the disordered table and at Caroline's agonised face was enough for her: 'Don't mind me,' she said sarcastically, 'I'd hate to disturb you!' She went to the arm-chair and curled herself up in it, pretending to read. Caroline was ceaselessly aware of her probing covert stare. She thought of raising a little barrier of books between them, but even that would not make her feel at ease. It was no good: she could not write in this house. Desperately, she gathered up the papers and threw them on the fire; when the blackened fragments began to flutter up the chimney and into the grate, she screwed up her pen and collected her things.

'Am I driving you away?' Isabel taunted her politely.

Once out of the house, she felt released; she made for the little Post Office in Merrion Row; she could buy a letter-card and write it on the counter. She opened her bag to look for David's new address, but his letter was not there: in her confusion she must have burnt it with all her half-written sheets. On the verge of tears, she took the scratchy Post Office pen and stared hopelessly at the blank card; someone behind her was waiting for the pen.

'Darling David,' she began hurriedly; at the end, she hardly knew what she had written; she addressed it, care of Aunt Emma, and wrote 'please forward,' heavily underlined. The person behind her was getting restive; she handed over the pen and slipped the letter into the box. She felt better now.

Just outside, she ran into Eileen Hunt who was hurrying home, clutching a large bunch of chrysanthemums.

'For Catha,' she said; 'she's ill; does your Mother know? Alec rang up at lunch-time and I'm off to see her the moment I've swallowed me tea.'

'I don't think she knows;' Caroline slowly descended to earth; 'I'm sure she doesn't: is she bad?'

'Baddish: pneumonia, and she's fat, y'know; two nurses and everything. Poor Alec's in a terrible state—men are hopeless in an illness. Come back and have tea with me—I've got crumpets and a walnut cake.'

Caroline went gladly; she was fond of Eileen, and besides, this would save her from having to face Isabel at tea.

'Nurses can be the devil,' went on Eileen; 'ham and eggs and tea at all hours of the day and night; they take possession of the house and the maids get into an uproar! Alec's nearly demented—you'd think she was dead already.'

Eileen's living-room was pleasant, with large windows and a high ceiling; Caroline knelt on the window-seat, looking down at the trams, rising and dipping as they hurtled along Stephen's Green like small illuminated ships; there was still a starred bullet-hole in the glass above her head where a stray shot had entered the room in the Bad Times.

'Tea, Puss,' said Eileen; 'come over to the fire.'

Sarah, the maid, had lit the standard lamp and was drawing the long green curtains; two big comfortable chairs were drawn up close to the fire; Eileen sat back and looked around her with pleasure.

'I love me little flat,' she said; 'it's much better to live in a small space and have a little money left to do what you want, although I must say I'd have liked a little garden; I can't live without flowers— but people are terribly kind.' Indeed, the room was full of flowers; chrysanthemums of every size and colour were arranged in bowls and vases, and the air smelt of violets.

'D'ye know what I think,' she went on, handing the crumpets across the table, 'take two—it's a curious thing, but I can never think of Catha without thinking of your mother in the same breath, and the other way about.'

Caroline wiped a little stream of butter from her chin: 'But why?' she said; she could think of no two people more unlike each other.

'Well, they're both relics; to me, they're the last diehards in Dublin; I know there are others left, but when anybody mentions diehards, I always think of them. They don't live in our world, either of them. Remember the fuss Catha made over the stamps and the green pillarboxes? Well, she's still complaining about the new coinage; I don't know which they've put instead of the King's head,' she said to me, only the other day, 'the harps, or the chickens and horses and pigs, but I know that the King's still King of Ireland, however they insult him, and I won't use a coin that hasn't got his head on it.' So Alec has to collect all the English money he can and hand it over to her; he has a dog's life with her and her fads.'

'It's awful nonsense, isn't it?' exclaimed Caroline hotly, 'but Mother's not a bit like that, you know; of course we all know she doesn't like it, but she never says very much, except about the people we get to know.'

'Isabel and her Republican?' said Eileen, glancing at her sharply; 'my dear, you needn't look at me like that, it's common gossip and I suppose your mother's the only person in Dublin who doesn't know how far it's gone. However, that's none of my business. No, your mother doesn't make a fuss, but it all goes down inside her in a little well of bitterness—I've watched her for years. Catha gets it off her chest in the grand manner, with a big protest, your mother can't, and it's made an old woman of her. D'ye remember her at all before the War, when you were a very small child?'

Caroline searched her memory for early pictures of her mother.

'I remember her coming to kiss us good night in lovely dresses, rustling through the nursery and smelling nice; she was always in a hurry, going out to dinner or something. I hardly remember her in the daytime at all, except during the War, when Daddy was in France and we always had people living with us, to keep the house going; she used to sew things all the time, for the Red Cross, but we never saw much of her—she was so busy.'

'She was a different creature in those days, even during the War,' said Eileen thoughtfully; 'alive and natural; she and your Aunt Moira were considered a beautiful pair of sisters when they were married— the two lovely Miss Wards, they were known as, and they had masses of eligible young men after them. Your mother was married in 1905, I think it was, and she was very gay when she was a bride—you've only got to look at that photograph of her in your drawing-room, and look at her now! Your aunt's still quite a young woman, compared to her: Moira saw what was coming and gave in—-your mother never did and never will.'

Caroline remembered the night she had danced a waltz with her father and he had told her of the times when he and Helen used to waltz together; she had thought it almost unbelievable then; Helen did not look as if she had ever danced in her life.

Eileen held out her hand for Caroline's empty cup: 'Your mother was dragged across the barrier between the two worlds in 1922, but her spirit stayed behind; one of these days, when something forces her to live in the present—it may be Isabel, it may be you, I know nothing about your affairs—it will kill her.'

'Kill her?' echoed Caroline; 'but she's never ill—she's one of the strongest people I know.'

'There's nothing left of her but bones and eyes, you can see that for yourself; she's still got a fire inside those eyes of hers, but if anything happens to put it out, she's finished. Catha won't get over this, I'm not fooling meself for a moment; she knows she's been struggling all this time against something that's too big for her and she's just lost her will to live. I'm not saying that she wanted this illness as an easy way to get out of the world, but I do say she won't fight against it; you'll see.'

There was a long silence and Caroline, for the first time, began to see clearly the difference between Helen's background and her own. Helen was of the old Anglo-Irish who could smile at the English while worshipping the British. In her mouth, the words 'but how English!' were an expression of contempt for a way of life that was chilly, humourless and formal; 'how British!' if she had ever said it, which was unthinkable, for it would have been almost as bad taste as to mention God at a tea-party, would have meant something quite different: it would have been a paean of praise for everything just and good and high-minded. To her, the British were a chosen people with a divine mission to rule; all they did was done in justice and good faith and if it was not without profit to themselves, it conferred inestimable benefits upon the subject races which they ruled with such benevolence. British rule was not domination, but a privilege, and any who strove to reject it were not only doing themselves the greatest material disservice, they were kicking against the will of God and committing unforgivable treachery against their predestined governors. The desire for independence, admirable in some of the smaller continental nations whose masters were, of course, oppressors, was treason if it involved a demand for freedom from British rule.

But Caroline could not see things in the same light; in the first place she hardly remembered what British rule was like and her only memories of it were unpleasant ones of war and tumult. She was prepared to concede that British rule was as just as any other, but that it was divinely inspired she could not believe. One by one, the little nations of the world were becoming aware of their right to an individual destiny, and that it was a right, not merely a rebellious desire, she was hotly convinced. She was Irish, and the Irish had fought for that right, not only ten years ago, but for seven centuries, continually and with bitter though ineffectual determination. Therefore she was glad that at last they had been successful. She did not hate the British: they were a friendly nation across the sea; but what she did hate was the English attitude to the new Ireland; people spoke of the Irish as traitors because they had fought for independence: they were not traitors, but patriots. But that was a thing that, it seemed, the English would never understand.

Nevertheless, she began to feel a little ashamed; what she had angrily called nonsense was loyalty and unwavering faith—fantastic, ludicrous in its manifestations, but as genuine as a crusade. She knew that this faith was a thing that she herself could never possess, but it made her respect her mother and Catha, and others of their generation whose principles would not permit them to accept the change in Ireland. The people with whom she could not sympathise were those of her own age who had grown up, like her, in the new Ireland, only to repudiate their birthright and declare that their sole allegiance was to England and the Crown; if these rejected the closer loyalty they should, in justice, forfeit the privilege of living in the country; if they were honest, they must accept the new regime or go. No one, least of all the departing British, had asked them to deny their nationality and give such blind and useless loyalty; they had implored the Unionists to give their support to the new state, trusting in their adherence to the Empire as well as to the nation. Now that the Free State was established, a self-governing member of the British Commonwealth of Nations, could they not be satisfied?

Eileen was looking at her keenly: 'Have I frightened you Puss? I'm sorry.'

'No, I was only thinking.'

The telephone rang and Eileen ran to answer it—'That'll be Alec, wondering why I haven't come yet—I'm afraid I'll have to run. Hallo . . .?'

It was Alec; Caroline put on her coat and gloves.

'You're right to wear no hat, with that hair,' said Eileen as she kissed her on the door-step; 'don't forget to tell your mother that we've got the nurses and there's nothing more to be done. Tell her Catha's pretty bad, but the doctor says she'll pull through—don't tell her I said she was going to die.'

The house was empty when Caroline reached home; she felt tired and depressed as she crossed the lobby from her bedroom to the school-room in a despairing search for David's letter. She saw it as soon as she entered the room, propped up against her books on the table, neatly folded into its envelope. Isabel must have found it and put it there: certainly she now knew every word of it by heart. It was spoilt for her now; she never wanted to read it again. Tearing off the corner with the address on it, she threw the sheets on the fire and watched them burn.

Catha died within a week; she slipped slowly and calmly out of life; during the last few days, Alec and her friends felt that she had already left them; she had gone beyond their reach, preoccupied and unafraid.

Alec came to beg Guy to help him with the funeral arrangements; he seemed quite stunned and unable to think of anything for himself. The weather was bitter, and on the day of the funeral, the northeast wind sent isolated flakes of dry snow scudding along the frozen street under heavy leaden clouds.

Caroline wrapped herself in coats and scarves: she would go to the burial with her parents; it was the least she could do to make amends for having laughed at Catha. They were surprised, but made no comment.

Eileen went with Alec, the Adairs followed in another car; the church was warm and they gathered strength for the ordeal ahead. Then the coffin was borne out to the hearse; already numb with cold again, they set out for the cemetery at Dean's Grange. Here there was a sprinkling of snow on the ground and the small cypresses were lashed and bent under the burden of the wind, which swept across the open country.

The mourners stood round the gaping grave with its shallow lining of powdery snow-flakes, their faces whipped and stung. The hands of the men who lowered the coffin were stiff and scarcely able to bear its weight. Alec crumbled a handful of frozen earth and let it fall from his bare blue hands, not looking into the abyss. The priest's surplice flapped and billowed whitely over the whitened ground, his head was bent to face the wind. It was over. Helen's face was greenish-white and she stood, huddled into herself like an old woman; Guy touched her arm and they moved off.

Caroline looked back; in spite of the weather, a surprising number of people had come: Catha had been a symbol of something that was disappearing from the country, and in paying a last tribute to her they had honoured what she represented—staunch uncompromising Unionism. Alec and Eileen were still standing by the grave-side; she drew his attention to the friends who had come with them; he nodded once or twice, mechanically; slipping his arm into hers, for comfort, he turned and slowly made his way back to the car.

CHAPTER FOURTEEN

Caroline sat in a Dalkey tram, looking out at the darkening roadway; it was the 23rd of December and she was going to meet David at the boat; she had a cold and a headache, had not slept properly for nights and loathed the new way the hairdresser had set her hair. David, she felt sure, would take one look at her reddened nose and foolish curls and suffer an instant change of heart. If only she could run away! She felt in such despair that she was almost ready to abandon the field to Isabel.

The conductor came along, shaking his satchel of coin. 'Kingstown, please,' said Caroline absent-mindedly. He closed his mouth in a downward grin and put his head on one side: 'Is it Dunlaoghaire yez mean?'

'Oh yes, I'm sorry.' She felt a little annoyed at the correction. 'Could yez not say what yez mean another time?' He clipped the ticket, deliberately slow, and handed it to her as if he were doing her a favour.

It was a beastly day; the tram smelt of babies and wet unclean clothes; a woman beside her, pungently damp, was deep in conversation with a friend of hers across the gangway:

'Ye're coddin' me, I says; I'm not, says he; ah, go on, says I; go on yerself, says he; and is that the way of it? says I; didn't I tell yez, says he.'

They guffawed happily and rocked with merriment. 'Oah, Chaney!' gurgled the friend, 'yez'd be killed laffin' at him!'

When Caroline stepped out of the tram, it was blowing hard and raining; the roadway by the Yacht Club was packed with cars, but there was no shelter for her until she reached the pier; even there, she was only protected from the rain for the gale hurled itself across the pier like an uncaged monster. It was still early, only ten minutes past five, but the mail boat, resplendent with light, was already visible. She walked up and down and stamped her feet, chilled through. As the boat swept into the harbour, all the people from the cars came crowding on to the pier; she took up her place at the Customs barrier, where she could peer between the bars.

People were pressed together like cattle, waiting to get off the boat; there was no sign of David. The Customs men stood around, swinging their arms, muffled up to the ears.

Quite suddenly, Caroline saw David in front of her, through the bars; she called out to him but he could not hear her above the din. She gave up trying to attract his attention and watched him instead: if a person did not know you were looking at him, you could see him much better. He was very good-looking, she decided, in his dark blue overcoat, tall and slim, with his fair head topping everybody else's. How was it you could always tell when a man was a sailor, no matter what he wore? He seemed to be having a joke with the Customs man and Caroline found herself smiling, although she could not hear a word they said. The man chalked his luggage and released him; she pushed her way to the little gateway as he came out.

'Darling! Oh you darling, to come down!'

He caught her by the shoulders and pushed her into the waiting train.

'I haven't got a ticket,' she faltered.

'We'll buy one—we'll buy a hundred if necessary. What'll we do tomorrow?'

'Christmas shopping.'

'Oh hell! I suppose we must.'

The carriage was full of people; he looked at them in furious resentment and turned back to Caroline: 'You're coming to dinner with us tonight—I'll tell Mother you've got to.'

'She'll want to see you alone—she won't want me.'

'Oh yes, she will.'

'No. She'd hate it, you know she would.'

'I'll come round after dinner, then: I've got a lot to say to you.'

'Darling, be reasonable; your first evening—Aunt Emma'd be terribly hurt.'

He scowled at her: 'When am I to see you then? '

'Tomorrow—and tomorrow and tomorrow.'

'You wait till I get you alone,' he muttered, smiling at her.

Caroline sat back and wiped her streaming nose: 'I've got a code.'

'It makes you look better than ever, like your headaches!'

She sat back and laughed with real happiness; it did not seem to matter what she looked like, David still loved her. She felt almost sorry for Isabel.

She awoke the next morning with a burning face and throbbing head; her throat felt parched and sore and the light, when she opened her eyes, sent darting needles of pain through to the back of her neck. Obstinately, she tried to stand up and dress, but the floor heaved at her feet and she had to hold on to the end of the bed to avoid flopping ignominiously. It was no good, she must just give in. Moving painfully, she climbed into bed like an old woman.

She felt too ill to tell anyone what had happened; Isabel slept on the next floor, so did Guy and Helen; they would miss her soon enough at breakfast and come up to see what was wrong. It was 'flu, of course, and she was stuck here, imprisoned, for a week, probably, the whole length of David's leave. Oh, why must this happen to her now, of all times? Tears of weakness, rage and despair coursed down her cheeks as she thought of David and his car, the walks they were to have had on the mountains, the Christmas shopping they were to have done together, the dances they were to have gone to. Her white and gold frock, unworn, was hanging invitingly in the cupboard. Now Isabel would have a free hand with David, and what use she would make of her opportunity!

There was the breakfast gong; she reached for her soaking handkerchief, struggling desperately for control; perhaps she would feel better later on, even be able to get up. If only she had a cool drink! Her tray of morning tea was beside her, untouched, but it must have been there for over an hour and would be stewed and beastly. She could hear the others going downstairs, Helen's quiet fast step, Guy whistling a nimble little tune, Isabel running, a little late. Soon the maids would come, banging up the stairs with carpet-sweepers and dustpans, to do the rooms and make the beds.

From far below came the tinkle of the telephone bell; if it was David, she must speak to him, even if it killed her. Silence. Supposing it was for her and nobody could be bothered to come all the way up to tell her! Ages afterwards, it seemed, Isabel's voice called faintly:

'Caroline!'

She sat on the edge of her bed, struggling into dressing-gown and slippers, then crept slowly to the door, holding on to everything that could support her; the stairs rocked before her as she shuffled out across the lobby and embraced the bannisters.

'*Caroline!*'

'Coming.' Her voice was a kind of croak; Isabel's upturned face was a shifting pinpoint of white at the bottom of a well. She shut her eyes and plunged blindly down the stairs, gripping the rail as a drowning man grips a floating oar; it was minutes before she reached the hall, where an icy draught rushed up from the basement. She collapsed shivering on to the telephone chair and took the receiver in her hand:

'Hallo—David?'

'Darling, what ages you've been.'

'I'm ill, I've got 'flu, I'm in bed: oh, darling, I can't come out!'

'My angel, what a thing to happen: I'll come and see you.'

'Better not; you might catch it.'

'I don't care—I'd like it: if it's yours it must be rather nice. Go straight back to bed and I'll come round.'

'Mother'll probably try to stop you seeing me—you mustn't let her. Don't let anybody stop you.'

'They'd better not try! Go back to bed, now, or you'll get worse. Goodbye, you poor angel.'

'Goodbye.'

She felt terrible; she staggered to the door of the dining-room and opened it, still clutching the handle.

'What on earth . . .?' Guy was gaping at her, a forkful of egg in mid-air.

'I . . . I . . .'

'Quick, she's going to fall down.' He was beside her in a moment, supporting her to a chair near the fire; Helen was searching for the brandy; Isabel, unable to think of anything to do, was sitting open-mouthed at the table. The brandy burnt her tongue and made her splutter, but it did her good. Helen became severely practical:

'Isabel, tell them to get two hot water bottles, quickly; run, child, and then go and get me the thermometer from my drawer.'

Isabel fled from the room.

'I've only got 'flu,' said Caroline weakly.

'Yes, I know, darling.' Helen spoke as if she were humouring a very small child.

'Really, that's all.'

'Of course.'

Caroline gave it up.

Helen's eyebrows went up when she read the thermometer; she handed it to Guy.

'What am I?'

'You've just got a little temperature,' she said cheerfully;

'Isabel, ring up the doctor, dear, and ask him to come round.'

'But I wish you'd tell me what it is—I'd much rather know.'

'Oh, nothing much; now we must get you back to bed; Guy, you help her on one side.'

Caroline glumly submitted to being helped up the stairs again, hating all the mystery and paraphernalia with which people surrounded one when one was ill.

'David's coming round this morning: I want to see him.'

'David? Of course, darling,' replied Helen soothingly: was the child delirious?

'I must see him.'

'Yes, yes; now catch hold of Daddy's arm.'

'You'll let him come up?' persisted Caroline.

'Yes, dear; if he comes.' The humouring tone drove Caroline nearly frantic; she knew how it would be: David would come and be told that she was not fit to see anyone—it would only excite her and make her worse, and they would send him away. Or would they? He was a person of great determination; perhaps he could defeat even Helen.

Back in bed, she slept, in spite of her resolve to remain awake at all costs. The doctor came, and she awoke to discover that the morning was over: David must have come and gone.

She was to be starved and kept quiet; the doctor scribbled a prescription.

'What about visitors?' said Helen.

'In a few days, perhaps; certainly not at present,' he said, ignoring Caroline's pleading eyes.

She called Helen back as she was leaving the room: 'Didn't David come?'

'You were asleep: he can come some other day.'

'Oh, Mother, you promised!'

'You heard what the doctor said.' The door closed behind her.

Caroline fumed in impotent rage; she might as well be in prison, tied and bound; she was cut off from all contact with the outside world, except by letter. She would write a note to David, later on, and get Doran to post it; she was the only hope. It was no good expecting Isabel to do anything. Later on; she felt too weary now, weary and miserable. She slipped back against the pillows and dozed again.

On Christmas morning, she languished fretfully; her bed was littered with paper, string and family presents, but she felt too disheartened even to tidy up the mess. There had been nothing, not even a note, from David and she felt unreasonably neglected and hurt. She had persuaded Doran to go scurrying through the darkness, the night before, with a note from her, so that he should be certain to have something from her this morning. She tried to convince herself that he had not forgotten her, that the day was still early and that he would surely call round himself; but all she could think of was Isabel, gloating because Aunt Emma had asked her to dinner tomorrow night.

The family flitted in and out of her room in various stages of dressing for Church. Isabel, buttoning her coat and arranging the veil of her little hat before the mirror, speechless because of a pin in her mouth; Helen, stretching a pair of newly-washed chamois gloves. Guy padded up irritably in his stockinged feet to complain that his only decent pair of shoes had disappeared: were they merely being cleaned, or was it possible that Helen had given them to the Parish Jumble Sale? How could anyone expect him to be in time for anything, in such a household? Glove-stretchers in hand, Helen hurried off. Guy leant over the end of the bed and smiled at Caroline as she thanked him for his present, an envelope containing five crisp pound notes, and, rather disconsolately, told him he was a darling to have given her the frock as well.

'Poor Puss,' he said; 'it's very hard luck,' and patted her hand.

They went off at last, galvanised into action by frantic screams from Helen in the hall. Caroline lay back and sighed wearily; every time she moved, something fell off the bed. She gave a kick, sending the remaining things sliding to the floor, then turned to the wall and closed her eyes.

There was a delicate little knock at the door and Doran came in, her toothy old face wreathed in smiles; she had something in her hand; Caroline sat up quickly.

'From Master David, Miss; he came himself.'

'Is he still here?' She would see him, there was nobody to stop her.

'The Misthress told him you wasn't well enough for visitors today, Miss, and she sent him away; he does be askin' to see you all the time.'

'Oh, Doran!'

'Ah now. Miss, don't be frettin'; sure, ye're not able for the visitors yet—ye didn't eat a bite this mornin'.'

Caroline grimaced: 'That's only because I'm too fat.'

'Don't be talkin', Miss; ye're as thin as whips, the pair o' ye!' Doran put her head persuasively on one side; 'Would ye drink a nice little cup o' tea now, if I was to bring it up, and a little slice of toast with it?'

'Doran, you're a dear, but I simply couldn't; I'll have one of these oranges.'

Doran glowered balefully: 'There's no good in them old oranges,' she muttered as she left the room.

There was a little package and a bulky letter, eight pages in David's exuberant hand; she tore open the package; it contained a silver flap-jack, enamelled dark blue, with a naval badge; she hugged herself in delight and began to read the letter.

David was furious, she discovered. It seemed that, weeks ago, Isabel had telephoned Aunt Emma to find out if he would be at home for Christmas and had then proceeded to give her a list of the engagements to which she hoped he would escort her: three dances, two parties, a Boxing Day meet. Aunt Emma, delighted that he should have such an opportunity of enjoying himself, had rashly promised that he would be only too pleased to take her about; she had kept the news as a nice surprise for him when he arrived. When he had told her bluntly that the only person he wanted to see was Caroline, she had declared that she was very sorry, but there was no escape; she was terribly hurt, wounded to the heart because her efforts had not pleased him: had she not done her best to arrange a pleasant leave for him? She had always thought that he and Isabel were so fond of one another and now, of course, it was too late to expect the poor girl to find anyone else to partner her. Why could he not have told her about Caroline? Finally, when he refused to give in, she had burst into tears, saying that he was ungrateful and had no manners, and she had never thought she would have to be ashamed of her son. They had both gone to bed, hurt and angry. Now, however, that Caroline was ill, he supposed he had better appease his mother and take Isabel to all these things, but he would be miserable, have a rotten leave and never forgive Isabel for thrusting herself on him like this. Surely to goodness, she must have gathered, when they were all at Butler's Hill, that he and Caroline . . . he couldn't understand it. And now, when he tried to see her, he was sent away: was she really so very ill? He would go on trying until they let him in and none of Isabel's engagements were going to interfere with his efforts to see her.

Caroline was rigid with anger by the time she had finished the letter: of all the dirty tricks! So that was how Isabel had known that David would be home for Christmas! And poor Aunt Emma, no wonder she was hurt—she adored David and must feel terribly injured to think that she knew so little about him that she was capable of spoiling his whole leave by her loving little conspiracy. So now, while she was lying in bed, she would have to watch Isabel dressing up to go out with David, think of her dancing with him, flirting with him, slipping her arm into his in that possessive way she had and looking up at him through her long dark lashes as if she owned him. Well, she could only hope that they would both be bored to tears!

She said nothing to Isabel, who returned triumphantly from church, to announce that David and Aunt Emma had come to share their pew. She did not even rise when Isabel asked her casually what she thought she ought to wear for Aunt Emma's dinner party: 'The best you've got,' she replied bitingly, 'but I shouldn't think it matters much.'

Helen was mystified by this affair between Caroline and David; like Aunt Emma, she felt a little resentful: nobody ever told her anything, she complained to Guy, and she was always the last to hear what her own daughters were doing. At one time, in fact only this summer, she had thought that David and Isabel . . . she noted the little scowl that came over his face as she said this, and did not add that she had been counting on David for Isabel when she was tired of her affair with that unspeakable Joyce boy. Even now, she was not quite sure which of the girls David wanted; although he seemed to be able to think of nothing but Caroline, telephoning two or three times a day and keeping poor Doran endlessly on the run opening the door either to him or to the tradesmen who brought his presents of fruit and flowers, he was taking Isabel to this and that, fulfilling engagements made, according to Isabel, weeks before he came on leave. Was he in love with both of them? It was most puzzling. She had done her best to keep David away from Caroline, but it was no good, Doran came chasing after her: Master David was at the door and could he see Miss Caroline, even for a moment? Finally, she weakened; he might have tea with her that day.

Caroline had been in bed for four days; she was sitting up, hollow-cheeked but cheerful, her huge eyes looking bigger than ever in their frame of tawny golden hair. Isabel brought him up and installed herself comfortably on the edge of the bed. They looked at one another: would she never leave them alone? Neither had the courage to tell her bluntly to clear out. Isabel began to talk brightly about the dance they were going to that night—who would be there, what would the supper be like, would there be champagne? Caroline, watching David's sickened face, found that she was actually enjoying herself.

Doran appeared, trembling from the effort of carrying the heavy tray to the top of the house, her breath coming in wheezy gasps. David took it from her and looked about for somewhere to put it down; Caroline patted the bed, but Isabel cleared a table and brought it up.

Doran held the door open and waited: 'Yer tea's waitin' for you below in the dhrawin'-room, Miss Isabel,' she said severely. Bless Doran, thought Caroline, you could always rely on her.

'I'll come back afterwards—I won't be long,' was Isabel's parting remark.

'Don't hurry yourself,' said David coldly, watching the door.

It was hardly shut before he was on the bed, with Caroline in his arms: 'Darling, you look so sweet in bed, I can't bear it; we must get married quickly,'

She lay back, smiling: 'You haven't asked me yet—I may say no.'

'Don't say things like that: you don't mean it, do you? '

'Try and see.'

'Darling, I love you: will you marry me?'

She nodded seriously: 'Yes.'

He leant over her, caressing her cheek with his lips: 'Oh, my love!' His voice was broken. 'Do you really mean it?'

'Mm,' she answered from the pillows.

'I can't think why you want to;' he raised his head to look at her face.

She grimaced wickedly: 'Because you'll have Butler's Hill one day, that's why.'

'You little devil!' He shook her gently by the shoulders; 'take that back.'

'No.' She raised her lips to his; 'You might get too conceited.'

'If you go on like this, I'll . . .'

'What?'

'Never mind—it might give Isabel a shock.' He stood up reluctantly. 'Have I really got to take her to the MacNamaras' miserable dance tonight? I wish she didn't want to go—I wish she'd get flu!'

'So do I,' said Caroline fervently; 'I'm jealous.'

'You're not really?' He looked at her in astonishment; 'You know, I'm fed to the teeth with her—I can't think how I can ever have imagined I was in love with her, two or three years ago; I must have been mad in those days. Is she going to marry that Republican fella?'

'No,' said Caroline, quietly munching bread and honey; 'she's not going to marry anyone, that I know of.'

'When are we going to get married? I suppose I shall have to ask Uncle Guy formally for your hand. You know, I may be going abroad.'

'You've only got two days left: I don't see how we can manage it this leave.'

Isabel was returning, they could hear her coming up the stairs; she rapped cheerfully on the door and came in.

'Congratulate us,' said David; 'we're engaged.'

She stopped half-way across the room, her face suddenly very red: 'Engaged?' she repeated leadenly: 'Oh, congratulations!'

He looked up at her, puzzled: 'You don't seem very pleased?'

'Of course I'm delighted;' her voice was husky and unreal; 'it's so suitable, isn't it? I mean, everyone will be terribly pleased.' She cleared her throat: 'I came up to tell you, actually . . . I'm not going tonight. I . . . I think I must have got Caroline's 'flu, so that lets you off, doesn't it? Well, I expect you'd rather be alone.' She gave a harsh little laugh that was almost a grimace and, before they could say anything, the door had closed behind her.

'Well, I'm damned!' said David, and they instantly forgot all about her.

CHAPTER FIFTEEN

David had gone to China for two years and Caroline found that she was being handled by her family; she was not to be married until he returned; she was to continue her studies, which would keep her out of mischief, and in the meantime she was to be treated with that curious mixture of respect and conspiratorial bonhomie which left her stranded on a level of her own, between the unmatched girls of her own age and the young married women. She was to languish for her lover, but feel the deepest satisfaction at having caught her man; she was to go to parties and dances as before, but remain detached; she must look radiant, but the men she met must be left for other, less fortunate, girls; at the same time, it was only a compliment to David if all men found her charming and attractive. It was all very difficult.

Elated and a little shy, she had written to Moira and waited nearly a week for her reply. Moira wrote delightedly; she was not really surprised to hear the news, she said, slipping in a sly exclamation mark, but she was truly glad and quite certain that Caroline and David were ideally suited to one another and would be deeply happy; she loved them both dearly and could think of no marriage that would give her such real pleasure as this. She went on to say that she felt Caroline had always belonged to Butler's Hill and that all her doubts about the wisdom of rebuilding it had now been allayed. She had always wondered how David would settle down there, when they were gone, and whether he would be prepared to cut himself off from his career and all his friends to live in the depths of the country;

here was the answer: Caroline would teach him to love the place and the people and when the time came—still far off, she hoped—for them to live there, they could feel that they were coming home. Never again need she be haunted by the thought of Butler's Hill being sold, for Caroline, she knew, would never let it go. Helen, she added, had written to say that she and Guy were delighted by the engagement: what about Isabel? There was a postscript to say that Gilbert had got himself sent to the North-West Frontier of India.

Helen, indeed, was deeply gratified, in spite of the fact that she would now have to think of someone else for Isabel to marry; it gave her great satisfaction to think that one of her daughters, of her own free will, was making a marriage of which she could unreservedly approve; she had begun to be a little nervous about Caroline and some of her Trinity friends, they all seemed so odd—nobodies with queer ideas and terrible politics. Now, she and Aunt Emma, drawn closer by the bond, congratulated each other heartily on their good fortune. Already they were planning the wedding: Caroline must be married in the Cathedral. Aunt Emma brought out the Limerick lace veil which had adorned both her mother and herself: Caroline must wear it too.

She invited Caroline to lunch with her alone, in her little house in Waterloo Road, so that she could envisage her as David's bride instead of as Helen's little Caroline whom she had known from the cradle. She expected a great deal from the girl who married David, she announced, and although the separation was a hardship she thoroughly approved of it, for it would give them both time to be really sure of themselves before they plunged into matrimony. Marriages in these days were too hasty and people seemed to think they could be dissolved as easily as they were undertaken; she hoped—with a sharp look at Caroline— that she did not feel like that. David was her only child, all she had left, and she was determined that he should be happy.

Caroline smiled back at her and assured her that she would do her best; it sounded inadequate, but she was embarrassed by this serious conversation and felt unable to express herself. However, Aunt Emma appeared to be satisfied and patted her hand warmly; when she left, she handed her an old-fashioned diamond brooch which she had been keeping for David's bride. It had been intended for a wedding present, but she was so pleased about the engagement that Caroline was to have it now. She grasped Caroline's left hand and peered short-sightedly at her ring: 'Emeralds suit you, dear,' she said, and kissed her a little tearfully; 'I trust your marriage may be as happy as ours was—never a quarrel or even a cross word, and I miss him still, even though I've been a widow for twelve years. We'll hope there'll be no wars in your time—war is a terrible thing.'

Caroline squeezed the fat hand in sympathy: 'Wars are finished,' she said confidently; 'there won't be any more, I'm sure.'

But Emma was not to be reassured so easily; she sighed and shook her head as she watched Caroline go down the steps.

The Hendersons' house was quite near; Caroline decided that she would drop in. She really ought to go and work, but Olga might be there and she had not seen her yet; besides, Emma's white wine had made her sleepy and disinclined for work.

Olga came running to open the door, and Caroline gasped when she saw her. She was wearing a slim little black dress, high at the neck, and a tiny absurd black hat over one eye; her lashes looked like curling metal brushes and the one eyebrow that was visible swept in an arched and shining line over the grey-blue eye. She had not altered the natural clear pallor of her face, but her mouth, until she smiled, looked like a dark red sea-anemone, and her nails were the same colour; her hair was very short and the long delicate neck looked like a stalk that was not stout enough to bear the flower above it. Caroline felt that she was looking at a black tulip.

'Darling,' said Olga, 'you're looking too marvellous.' She put her arm in Caroline's and drew her into the house.

'You look as if you're just going out'; Caroline felt slightly foolish.

'No; I've just come in, this minute.'

Anne was sitting by the fire, pretending to darn, with an open book beside her.

'Oh, I was hoping you'd come: where's your David? I haven't seen him since he was a schoolboy.'

'He's been sent to China.'

'Poor child! you ought to go and marry him out there.'

'The family won't let me—they think we're too young.'

'Nonsense! Leonard and I were married when he was twenty-two and I was seventeen.'

'Isn't she looking lovely, Anne?' said Olga; 'no wonder Leonard wants to paint her.'

Anne smiled slowly: 'Quite lovely.'

Caroline glanced back at Olga, the slender sophisticated creature who made her feel an awkward child; they had grown into different worlds now.

'You've changed a lot, too,' she said at last; 'you're terrific.'

Anne and Olga both laughed at the awe in her voice. Olga stretched herself like a cat: 'I'm just the same, really,' she said, almost apologetically.

'We're having a dinner party on Friday, the night before Olga leaves: will you come, just to eat and talk?'

'I'd love to.' From what Caroline could remember of Anne's entertaining in Paris, both the dinner and the talk would be of the first quality.

'We're going to be rather grand and change, for once; it makes people talk better, don't you think? They feel they're at a party.'

Caroline agreed; she would at last wear the frock that she had bought for David's leave.

'I'll get somebody to fetch you and take you home: who d'you think, Olga?'

'Brian O'Malley,' said Olga quickly; 'he'd adore Caroline.'

'Do you know him?'

Caroline shook her head.

'That won't matter,' said Anne; 'as soon as you've met him you'll feel you've known him for years—he's that sort of person.'

So, on Friday evening, Caroline waited in her father's study for Brian O'Malley to fetch her, not knowing whether to expect an elderly musician, a doctor of forty or a Communist of her own age. Guy teased her gently:

'It's all wrong, you know, this running off with strange young men when you're nearly a married woman.'

She smiled back at him, over the top of his desk.

'Never mind,' he went on; 'you're young, and you should enjoy yourself; David doesn't expect you to go into purdah while he's away, does he? '

'No; he's not going to, either.'

'Much more sensible—shows you have some confidence in each other. Poor Puss, do you feel very bereft?'

She nodded, her mouth suddenly tremulous.

'I tell you what, we'll make a date, you and I; every Sunday afternoon we'll go off for a drive in the mountains together, just the two of us. How would you like that?'

'Better than anything.'

'Good; that's a bargain, then.'

They could hear a car stopping outside the house; Caroline darted round the desk and kissed him lightly on the cheek before running out into the hall to meet the intriguing Brian O'Malley.

He was a broad little man, with a large pale face and mouse-coloured hair that curled thickly and gave him an unruly look; he might have been thirty-five or forty, perhaps only thirty; he was the sort of person who would look the same for years. Short straight eyelashes, irregular eyebrows and slightly drooping lids framed an astute grey eye; he held out a firm short-fingered hand:

'Well,' he said; 'they didn't deceive me! 'His face wrinkled in a crooked friendly smile and Caroline found her hand being shaken up and down.

'What do you mean?'

'Anne Henderson told me I was to fetch the loveliest girl in Dublin and I didn't believe her; I thought I knew them all, but she was right, after all.'

There was no flattery in his voice and Caroline had to laugh.

'You know Olga?' she said.

'Yes, I know Olga, and I guess she's lovely too.' He held open, the door of an ancient Ford and tucked a rug round her knees. There was something trans-Atlantic about his voice.

'Are you an American?' she asked.

'No, but my mother was and I spent five years there after the War; my father was Irish.'

'What are you doing here? . . . I mean . . .'

'In my spare time I breed dogs; in the rest of my spare time I'm trying to run a tweed industry, and when I'm not doing that I earn my living.'

'What at? Where?'

'Farming; sheep mostly, near Blessington; there should be money in sheep, but there hasn't been in mine, yet.' He shook his head; 'It's a grand country, all the same.'

They were silent as the car rattled and spluttered along Baggot Street; he went on: 'My father would turn in his grave if he saw me settling down in this country; he went North at the time of the Treaty and never came back here before he died; he said he'd never set foot in the South again. But that's not the way I see it: I figure it out this way, if a people wants to be independent, well, there's no more to be said. Maybe you don't feel like that?'

'Oh yes, I do, but I know lots of people who don't—my mother, for instance.'

'I guess people like that must suffer a lot: they just can't help making it a question of loyalties, but it's natural to want to run your own show—nobody wants to stop on at school when they're grown-up.'

They had reached the house; Anne's maid, who was unaccustomed to dinner parties, was lying in wait just inside the door, ready to pounce when she heard the bell; she took their coats, beaming and quite prepared to embark on a lengthy conversation.

Leonard was pouring out sherry: 'Cocktails are filthy things, don't you agree, Brian? Olga thinks I'm old-fashioned, but I like wine, every time.'

Brian held his glass up to the light: 'Wine,' he agreed, 'well, nearly every time; you can't beat it.' He gave Olga a gay little grin and went to greet his hostess. Anne was standing by the fire in a slim brown velvet frock that revealed her golden-skinned shoulders and arms; she wore no jewellery but a pair of pearl ear-rings and her rings; her straight golden hair was knotted at her neck. Caroline marvelled at her: she looked as though she spent her life in leisure, yet there would not be a dish at dinner that had not been prepared and cooked by her. The room was miraculously tidy; where, she wondered, had they managed to stow all the books and papers that usually littered the chairs and tables? Assuredly, no cupboard would bear opening. Olga was wearing the dress that Anne had made for her; she looked dazzling, in a metallic sort of way, with her black-red lips and nails, her shining dusky hair and small ivory face. She was talking earnestly to an olive-skinned young man, obviously a foreigner, with smooth black hair and sorrowful intelligent eyes so human that there was something ape-like about them: was it possible, wondered Caroline, that the Russian prince had scraped together the amount of his railway fare and followed Olga to Dublin? But it was not he; Anne held out her hand to Caroline and said:

'Come and be introduced—you don't know René, do you?'

René . . . the name was familiar: suddenly Caroline remembered.

'Did he paint your bull fight?' She felt rather excited.

'Yes—how clever of you. René . . .?'

'Madame?' He laid his hand on Olga's arm in apology for the interruption and approached politely.

'Monsieur Poliakov: Miss Adair.' He brought his heels together and bowed stiffly.

'Enchanté—I am delight-ed to meet you, mademoiselle.' There was no trace of a smile on his serious face.

'She speaks French,' said Anne.

'Ah!' he bowed again; 'you will for-give me?' and he returned to Olga.

More people were being ushered into the room; a short dark man with a high colour and a tiny bright-eyed woman with thin pale hair; they were a playwright and his wife.

At dinner, Caroline found herself seated between Leonard and René Poliakov, with Olga beyond him; the round table was lit by candle-light and there were flowers floating in a bowl, so that cross-table conversation should not be impeded; the terrified maid brought round the white wine, wrapped in a napkin, and proffered it in a deprecating way, praying almost audibly that it would be refused and she be spared the agony of pouring it out, but no one took any notice of her qualms. Everyone talked gaily; Olga and René were immersed in an argument about a French actress, the playwright was talking farming with Anne and Brian, while his wife was describing to Leonard a recent journey they had made into the interior of Mauretania, where they had narrowly escaped being held up for ransom. Caroline listened with enjoyment: she did not want to talk. On her left she could hear:

'Mais voyons: elle est vieille, elle est laide—alors, c'est fini, n'est-ce pas?' René threw out his hands in emphasis, but Olga was equally emphatic:

'C'est une grande actrice, je dis même la plus grande . . .'

And on the other side, the high-pitched little voice beyond Leonard:

'. . . to find a people so close to Europe and so untamed! Do you know, they still cut off people's ears and fingers and send them to the relatives with little notes! Until I went there, I thought that sort of thing only went on in China, these days . . . and so handsome! I nearly lost my heart: I would have, if they had been cleaner.' She broke off with a little ripple of laughter.

René turned to her at last: 'You are English, mademoiselle?' he enquired gravely.

'Well, Irish.'

'It is the same thing, is it not?' He looked politely incredulous.

'Ah no!' replied Caroline indignantly: 'are you Swiss?'

'Indeed no!' His voice was outraged; 'Je suis français; mon grand-père était polonais.'

'But is it not the same thing?' She smiled at him, to show that she was not angry.

His lips parted in a fleeting smile: 'Bien touché,' he said, with the slightest of bows; 'c'est très profond, ça, très profond. Then you are Nationalist?'

'In a sense . . .'

'I myself am not a politician. You are Catholic?'

'Protestant.'

'Irish and Protestant? Pas possible!' He studied his fish earnestly.

'How long have you been in Dublin?'

'Last night I come from London; tomorrow I go to America; today Mademoiselle 'Enderson show me your city and I see also some of the work of your great Irish painter: formidable! It has made a deep impression on me.'

'Who . . . ?'

'The name is to me impossible: he is the brother of the poet. Working quite by himself he has outstripped the Paris groups; one day he will make your country famous.'

'You're not going to paint here?'

'You do not have the sun,' he said, laying down his fork with an air of finality.

Caroline was grievously disappointed; she had always imagined the painter of the bull fighting scene in the other room to be some hot-blooded European, smelling of the earth; this young man was civilised to the point of frigidity; perhaps something froze in him when he left his native sunshine.

The sorrowful eyes were turned on her again: 'You are very beautiful, mademoiselle; how is it that you are not married?'

'I am going to be married.'

'Ah! That is your fiancé over there?' He was looking at Brian O'Malley with distaste.

'No; my fiancé is in China; he is in the Navy.' Caroline laughed.

René drew himself up wrathfully: 'He is a very foolish fellow: jealousy would not permit me to leave such a one as you to be seduced by other men—I would suffer torments, but the English are cold, perhaps it is different here . . .'

'The Irish,' corrected Caroline gently.

'Pardon, the Irish; they are not so cold, then?' The brief, charming smile flickered again, but the sad eyes still held the burden of suffering humanity. 'In that case, it is very dangerous indeed. You are faithful to him, this man who leaves you?'

'So far,' she said smiling, 'I have managed to be.'

He inclined his head again and turned back to Olga. Perhaps, reflected Caroline, he was not so frigid after all.

'You're not letting René seduce you?' said Leonard's amused voice on her right.

'Not quite.'

'He'll have a good try! Oh dear, what would your mother say? She's never quite forgiven us about the Vicomtesse. I suppose she'd never let you come to France with us again? We might go there next winter; it would be good,' and he grinned, 'for your studies.'

'I wish she would; I wonder . . .' Caroline felt doubtful; perhaps she would be able to persuade Guy to let her go.

'Anne would love it: she misses Olga dreadfully—we both do.'

'I'll try and get my Tutor to say it's essential . . . it might work if I put it like that.'

The maid came round with the Burgundy again; Caroline shook her head, but Leonard nodded encouragingly; she sighed and gave in. Everybody was warming up now and conversation buzzed around her. René was actually laughing at some remark of Olga's. She felt elated and expansive, ready to talk with anyone; this was a pleasant party. The glass and silver reflected the candle flames and firelight, the polished table shimmered with light; the food was delicious, trust Anne to see to that. Thick curtains, closely drawn, kept out the cold dark night. The playwright's wife and Brian O'Malley were discussing the future of his tweeds; she had been a United Irishwoman and seemed to know a great deal about dyes. They were becoming technical; in another minute they had arranged to capture the London and Paris markets, then New York: it could be done, it must be done, they agreed enthusiastically; Caroline and Leonard were drawn into their schemes.

Anne was trying to catch her eye; the playwright's wife was on her feet; René jumped up and held the door open; they filed out, across the passage into the other room.

'They'll be ages,' said Anne; 'Leonard always forgets that there are any ladies to join.'

Sipping strong black coffee, Caroline discovered that she was slightly drunk; she felt tremendously good-tempered and rather sleepy. When Anne led them upstairs, she had to be careful not to trip up on her frock; she found herself talking animatedly to the playwright's wife, laughing at herself as she took care not to slip her words into one another.

Brian made straight for her when the men came in from the dining-room; he wanted her to come and see his farm, his setters and his tweeds. She arranged that she and Guy would go to Blessington one Sunday; she promised to inspect his tweeds in the little shop he was opening in Dublin. She almost promised to buy some when next she wanted to have a suit made and he practically offered her the job of selling them: he wanted someone like her, he said, who was a lady and looked nice; the offer was not quite made and she was not certain whether he was serious or not. She felt greatly tempted to say: 'Do you really mean that?' and accept on the spot, but she held back: decisions were too difficult at this hour of the night when she was not quite sober.

Regretfully, everybody said goodbye; it was very late, long after midnight. She chatted drowsily to Brian on the way home; René had accepted a lift in the back of the car and she could feel him observing her carefully for any hopeful sign of infidelity to her absent fiancé; he was disappointed. Brian dropped her on the doorstep with only a cordial handshake and a reminder that he expected to see her again before long. René bowed gravely over her hand as he shook it: if she was in Dublin when he was on his way back, would she . . . ? She had the impression that he was asking whether she would make it worth his while for him to break his journey. 'Perhaps,' she said, smiling, 'I shall then be in China.'

'Ah! then I shall go straight to Cherbourg.' He was looking at her, eyebrows slightly raised, as if the threat might make her change her mind; but she said nothing. His shoulders lifted almost imperceptibly as he released her hand.

'Au revoir, mademoiselle; it is possible that one day, in France . . .? 'Au revoir. . . .'

Once inside the hall door, she sat down on the telephone chair and began to laugh weakly: the evening had been fun.

CHAPTER SIXTEEN

'All the men fall for you, Caroline,' said Nan hungrily; 'I wish I was pretty!' And she heaved a hot and gusty sigh. 'there's Johnny Campbell,' she went on, 'He's crazy about you and you don't even want him; I wish he'd like me, I think he's ever so nice!'

'He is nice,' said Caroline distastefully. Nan, oozing passion and perspiration at every pore, revolted her. She took her eyes off the road for an instant to glance at the heavy profile; she knew exactly what Nan was looking like: her coarse black hair would be waved in rigid lines, her red face shining through the powder with unfailing soap and water honesty; her white rabbit-fur collar would be slightly grimy, and underneath the black velveteen coat there would be that terrible red georgette frock, stained under the arms and with every seam doing its duty; Nan always looked as if she had been buckled into it.

'They'll all ask you to dance,' went on Nan, 'and I shan't know a soul.'

Caroline did not know what to say: it was only too true. They were going to an inter-University dance where students from Dublin, Belfast, Cork and Galway were to be brought together with a view to encouraging better understanding; she was not looking forward to it, but Nan was; Nan relished every opportunity of meeting men.

'Of course I wouldn't say it to anyone else, only you're me best friend,' came the thick voice again from the darkness, 'but, d'ye know, nobody's ever even tried to kiss me—not that I'd let them, of course.'

Caroline sighed; she had arrived at being Nan's best friend by pure kindness of heart and now she could not shake her off. From the moment when Nan had arrived in Dublin as a student, she had glued herself to Caroline, sat beside her at lectures, kept a table for her at lunch, persecuted her to attend prayer meetings and shown such genuine pain at any rebuff that Caroline had not the heart to be really rude to her.

'Perhaps if you didn't . . .' began Caroline, but she could not go on; it was too cruel. 'Hurl yourself at people,' was what she had been going to say.

'Go on,' panted Nan.

'Oh, nothing. Look, we're there now. I'm sure you'll have a lovely time, Nan,' she said hopefully. She parked the car and they went into the building together.

There was a curious collection at the dance; young men in tweeds were militantly talking Irish with girls in evening frocks; dinner jackets mingled with short dresses; there was a constrained atmosphere about the party: everybody was being very careful to keep political differences under the surface.

A bullet-headed youth in a dark suit jerked his head at Caroline.

'Hullo!' he said. He was Mr. McGuffey from the North, and she had met him that afternoon.

'Oh, hallo.'

'Wull ye dance?'

Mr. McGuffey began to take a proprietary interest in her; he advised her not to dance with those fellas from Galway; they were awful rough, he said as he trod on her toes—Nationalist scum. Better stick to him and his pal, Wully, for the evening. His own name, he added encouragingly, was George, but his pals called him Geordie; he would be awfully pleased if she would let him call her Carrie; he knew a very sweet girl from Ballymena whose name was Carrie.

She saw that he intended to call her Carrie, whatever she said; she looked across the floor at Wully: he had fair curling hair, a bashful smirk and a roving blue eye—would he do for Nan? After that dance she brought Nan over and introduced them; Wully seemed quite pleased and Nan was in giggling ecstasy.

One of the Galway students came up to Caroline; he looked rather ashamed of himself as he asked her to dance; he explained that he was not much of a hand at foreign dances; he wore cow-coloured tweed plus-fours and his hair was the same colour as his clothes; his name was Rory O'Hegarty. Mr. McGuffey stuck a warning elbow into Caroline's ribs and stared in pained surprise as she shuffled off in the clutches of Mr. O'Hegarty.

'I didn't want to dance with you,' began her partner belligerently.

'Oh?' Caroline's eyes opened wide with astonishment; 'then why on earth did you ask me?'

'Well, ye see, you're Trinity, and I was afraid I might get tainted, talking to ye, but I couldn't help meself, if you know what I mean.'

'Tainted! How?'

'Well, all you Trinity people are pro-British, and . . .'

'Are we?'

'Aren't *you*?' and he burst into a torrent of Irish.

Caroline began to laugh helplessly: 'I'm sorry,' she said humbly, 'but I don't speak Irish.'

'Ach! ye're no good—an' you call yerself an Irishwoman?'

'Yes, of course.'

'Do you hate the English?' he asked hopefully.

'No,' said Caroline firmly.

'You're no Irishwoman,' he said, looking at her with disgust; 'you're just one of the ones who plays at it.'

'Now, look here;' Caroline was beginning to feel annoyed; 'is there only one way of being Irish? Have I got to be like you—must I hate the English?'

'Yes, you must,' he said, and his voice became quite different, vibrant and passionate; 'don't you know what they've done to us?' and he began a resumé of seven hundred years of history.

'That's all over now,' said Caroline patiently, when he paused for breath.

'It's not all over—not until we get the North.'

Caroline thought of Mr. McGuffey and would have smiled, had she dared; 'What are you going to do about the North?'

'We'll fight them,' said Mr. O'Hegarty, and he looked ready to invade the North single-handed; 'they've got to come in, they're part of the Irish Nation.'

'Fighting doesn't settle anything,' said 'Caroline wearily; 'let's sit down.'

He led her to a corner and prepared for further battle; 'I see you're engaged to be married; betcha he's a British officer!'

'Right,' said Caroline stiffly; 'a Naval one.'

'I knew it!' He almost screamed his triumph. 'You call yerself an Irishwoman, and you're goin' to marry a man in the pay of a foreign power—a British agent! And is he an Irishman too?'

'Oh, don't talk nonsense;' Caroline wanted to hit him in the face. 'He is Irish, and of course he's not a British agent.'

He looked at her through narrowed contemptuous eyes: 'But if England was at war with us again, he'd fight against us, all the same.'

'Yes,' Caroline bitterly admitted; 'he'd have to.'

'There's an Irishman for ye! And what about yerself—what side would you be on?'

'It depends what it was about.'

'It does not,' said Mr. O'Hegarty; 'you were born British and you'd fight for the British, right or wrong, in spite of all yer great notions that ye're an Irishwoman. It's in yer blood, ye couldn't help it. The old Ascendancy, that's what you are! I'd like to see a brazen wall round Ireland,' and he fashioned it with his hands, 'and every Anglo-Irish bloody Protestant on the other side of it.' He crossed his arms, glowering at her; 'Why can't you and yer like clear out of this country; we don't want you—there's no place for you here.'

Caroline was hurt, and smarting with anger; 'I won't have that,' she said fiercely; 'you make us sound like traitors, and we're not. We all want an Irish nation, but we want to be friends with England too—it's no good keeping up old wrongs. You'll never make a decent country out of this, if you're going to hate your neighbours on principle. And you owe a lot to us, though I don't expect you to admit it; some of the Anglo-Irish have fought for you and with you for years. Anyway, we're not going to clear out of here: this is our home, and we belong here just as much as you do; besides, you need people like us to keep you sane,' she added venomously.

'The British hate us,' he spat.

'Don't be silly: they're bored to tears over the whole Irish question—they're not even interested. Have you ever been to England?'

He looked outraged at the question: 'I have not.'

'Have you ever met any English people?'

'No, thank God.'

'Well, don't talk about things you know nothing about. I'm sure you think you're very grand sitting in Galway, talking Irish and breeding hate against the British, but it's not going to get you anywhere.'

He stood up and thrust his hands into his pockets: 'I'm not going to stay and be insulted,' he said sulkily.

'You began the insults, if you remember,' said Caroline quietly; 'tell me, do many people think like you do?'

'The youth of Ireland,' he said proudly.

'Then, God help Ireland!'

He turned to go. 'I'm sorry we fought,' said Caroline, suddenly penitent; 'can't we forget it?'

'No: you insulted me.'

'You're behaving like a child.'

He shrugged his shoulders and left her. She found Johnny Campbell beside her, asking her to dance.

'Oh, Johnny,' she begged, 'let's just sit and talk. I feel I want to throw things . . . I must cool off for a bit.'

'Has that little tyke from Galway . . .?' began Johnny.

'No, he hasn't; *sit down*! And if I tell you about it, you're not to get angry. We had a political argument—just the sort of thing we were brought here not to have, and we both got rude; he called me an Anglo-Irish bloody Protestant and I found myself championing the British and calling him names too, and . . .'

Johnny was on his feet again: 'By God,' he said, 'I'll . . .'

'No, Johnny, it wouldn't do;' Caroline was deadly serious; 'there can't be a fight at this dance—it absolutely mustn't happen: don't you understand? It'd give them the most frightful grievance against us.'

'Mm. Oh Hell!' 'Johnny sat down stiffly on the edge of his chair. 'I say, look at Nan! Who's she got hold of?'

'That's Wully from Antrim, and I don't know his other name; it looks as if her ambition is about to be realised.'

'What's that?'

'To be kissed,' said Caroline; 'oh, I am being beastly!'

'No, you're not; she's bestial.'

'Well,' said a voice over her shoulder; 'how did ye get ahn?'

It was Mr. McGuffey; he sat down, rubbing his hands in anticipation of the revelations be felt sure were coming; his eagerness was too much for Caroline.

'Damn better relations! about as well as I'd get on with you, I should think,' she snapped, and went off to dance with Johnny.

CHAPTER SEVENTEEN

Every Sunday afternoon, Caroline and her father would drive off to the mountains, to Glencree, Glencullen, Bohernabreena or the Featherbed; at Lough Bray, they would watch the brown water lapping against the stones, then, edging the lake, climb waist-deep in heather to the sunless Upper Lough, black and bottomless under the shadow of Kippure; or they would drive up from Enniskerry and circle Knockree hill on foot, under the bare trees that had looked purple from the road, shimmering in the mid-winter sunlight; across the valley, beyond the wild little river, they could see the Ballyreagh plantation, dark beneath the looming Tonduffs.

In soft weather, great ragged clouds would drift sullenly across the hilltops, or a white, creeping mist would come to veil the turf-stacks and send long probing fingers deep into the bare upper valleys; sometimes, on cold clear days, there would be snow lying patchily in the gullies and crevices, blue-white against the grey-black rock, immaculate, untrodden and out of reach, cooling the still air. If there was a real fall of snow, the hills would glow in the sunlight, rose-gold and gleaming white in dazzling glory, their soft contours rolling and heaving against the sky; there would be ground-mist below in Bohernabreena, blurring the silver trees of Glenasmole and shrouding the long thin lake that, on a clear day, lay like a blue ribbon between the hills.

On their way home, between the last trees which marked the beginning of the mountain road, they could see the city, laid out like a map below them, under its curtain of smoke, blue in fine weather, black when the sky was grey. The car would slip down the long Killakee hill, past the old Hell-Fire Club, into the blue twilight of the city plain.

One day they went to Blessington, and beyond, to where Brian O'Malley's farm overlooked the King's River, rushing frothily between great rocks under pine-clad banks; the house was small, square and Georgian, colour-washed, with an old-fashioned garden, ringed with ancient trees; they could see his sheep, tough little horny creatures, leading a mountain-goat existence on the steep hillside. Red setter dogs hurled themselves from the door and engulfed the car, then Brian himself emerged, shouting to welcome them above the din of barking.

Inside, the house was pleasant, with mellowed polished furniture and good glass and china; huge copper whiskey-measures took the place of vases and mirrored the flickering fire-light. He gave them a mighty tea of home-baked soda-bread, thickly layered with butter and honey in the comb; there were cheese scones and a tall sponge-cake with a golden, crusty top. Greatly pleased to see them, he smiled his friendly crooked smile and proudly showed them his curtains and covers, made from his own tweeds, coarse-woven in a pale neutral colour. Guy was impressed and liked him from the first; this was the sort of person who was needed in the country, he told Caroline afterwards; someone with enterprise, enthusiasm and a determination to make his projects pay; someone who could see what the Government was working for and who had not been embittered from the start; embittered he might become, he added wryly, but that would be the result of experience, not of prejudice.

Caroline sat for her examination in a kind of daze; her fingers felt cramped and cold and, as she looked uneasily round, the sight of all the other students writing busily filled her with panic. She fixed her eyes on the bent head in front of her and tried to concentrate; the invigilator glanced at her sharply and she wrote her name on the virgin page; time was passing and there would be another paper soon. Despairingly, she began to write and in a moment she felt better: her brain was working again. When she went up for her viva voce, fear returned; she felt she could not say even the simplest sentence in French, but the examiner did his best to put her at her ease: had she ever been to France? Suddenly it all came back and she found herself telling him the story of the Vicomtesse, coming to a blushing halt when she reached the point where she had brought out the unmentionable word.

'I can guess, I can guess,' he assured her in French, rocking with delight. He wiped his eyes with a huge handkerchief and sent her back to her seat, sure of a good mark.

But the Spanish was terrible; she had to write an essay in this language that she had studied only for four months; all the verbs became confused in her mind and before the day was out, she felt sure that she had failed. When she emerged, the great bare trees in the Front Square were wrapped in a white and chilly mist and the light was fading; she hurried home, thankful that it was all over, so tired that she did not even care whether she had passed or failed.

That night, Isabel was late for dinner; Helen was annoyed: it was happening too often, she said, and the girls were treating the house like an hotel; unpunctuality was so tiresome and nobody seemed to mind how much trouble they gave the servants, keeping food hot and trotting up and down from the kitchen. If she said nothing, the girls seemed to think it was all right and they could go on being late, and if she protested, they thought she was being unreasonable.

'Sorry, Mother,' said Isabel mildly; Caroline looked across at her in astonishment: Isabel's face was flushed and triumphant; she was not thinking about them at all. She did not speak again until Doran had set the dessert on the table and left the room; then she tilted her chin suddenly and faced her father.

'Daddy!'

They all stared at her.

'Well?' A crimson spiral dangled from Guy's half-peeled apple, poised expectantly in mid-air.

'You've got another wedding on your hands: I'm going to be married too!'

'My God, who to?' Guy's voice was joking, but he looked perturbed. Helen drew in her breath sharply and waited, biting her lips.

'Who do you think?' Isabel threw back her head and smiled at them mockingly. None of them dared speak; the only name that any of them could think of was that of Denis Joyce and nobody would mention it; they looked at her in horrified anticipation and she began to laugh softly.

'Come on, child,' said Guy, almost irritably; 'it isn't fair to keep us waiting.'

'Mike Millar!' She hurled the name at them defiantly. 'He's a Protestant, he's rich and he went to a public school, so I hope you're satisfied.' But, in spite of all her bravado, her under-lip trembled.

'Old Horace Millar's boy: is he in the business?'

She nodded.

'Distilling,' said Guy, for Helen's information; he looked very troubled.

Helen stood up and made for Isabel with both hands extended.

'Darling, I'm so glad!' Her relief was such that she felt she would not have minded if he had been a chimney-sweep and, after all, there was nothing disreputable about distilling. Pride and satisfaction radiated from her: to have two daughters engaged, two weddings to arrange!

But Isabel shrank from her embrace: 'Don't touch me,' she hissed; 'can't you leave me alone?'

Helen's hands sank foolishly to her sides as she goggled at her daughter: 'But I'm . . . delighted about it, I only wanted to . . .'

'Yes, I know,' blazed Isabel, but Guy broke in:

'Come, Isabel: we'll talk it over inside.' He caught hold of her arm and led her firmly into his study, closing the door in case Helen should attempt to follow them. He sat her down before the fire and handed her a cigarette; she kept it limply between her fingers, staring at him as he lit a spill and held it out to her.

'Buck up!' His fingers were in danger of getting burnt.

'Oh, sorry'; she jammed the cigarette between her lips and pulled furiously.

He took out a cigar and lit it slowly; Isabel's feet kicked with impatience: why couldn't he get on with whatever he was going to say! He leant back in his deep chair and surveyed the end of his cigar:

'Are you in love with this fellow?' His voice was kind, unusually gentle.

She observed him from under her eyelashes: 'Do you think I'd marry him if I wasn't?'

'I think you might. Are you?' he repeated patiently, watching her face.

'Naturally!' She shrugged her shoulders slightly.

He lowered his eyes to the floor: 'And he with you?'

'Yes.' Her voice was contemptuous, weary and ashamed.

'I'd like to meet him: when will you bring him here?'

'Whenever you like—he wants to see you.'

'All right.' She was about to stand up, but he motioned to her to stay where she was.

'Good; now listen; I've something to say to you and you won't like it. You say you're in love with this chap, and he with you; I believe the second part, but not the first: I don't believe you care two hoots about him.'

'I *do!*' Her chin was out again, her body rigid with defiance.

'Very well, if you say so, but I haven't finished yet. You know what marriage involves? All girls do, nowadays, I suppose.'

She looked down quickly, pouting her lips: 'Yes.'

'Well, do you know that one of the meanest things a woman can do is to sleep with a man who loves her and think, not of him, but of the other man she loves?'

A scarlet tide rushed to her face and she stood up, fists clenched:

'Daddy, you're disgusting!' She spat out the words, heaving with anger.
'Ethics,' he said quietly, 'but if the cap fits . . .'

'It doesn't,' she almost shouted; 'it doesn't, it doesn't! I'm not in love with anybody else; I'm going to marry him, none of you can stop me, I'm twenty-one.' He shook his head slowly: 'It's for your own happiness as well as his. Think hard, child, before you marry him; if you love him, you have my blessing. You're going to persist in it?'

'Yes, of course.'

'Well, listen; just suppose that between now and your wedding, whenever that may be, you were to find that you wanted to break it off, I'd stand by you and back you up, whatever anybody says— up to the hilt, you understand?'

'Thanks,' she said coldly, 'but you won't have to bother.'

He made a last effort: 'Won't you tell me why you want to marry him? I know he's rich, and presumably a nice sort of a lad, but I'm still not satisfied: are you sure you're not doing it on the rebound?' His voice was very gentle and he was not looking at her.

She glared at him: 'If you knew anything, you wouldn't dare . . .' but she halted and pushed back the bitter words that were seething in her mind. 'Your bigotry, your snobbishness,' she thought, 'your beastly politics have ruined my happiness, but I won't tell you. I'll punish you by marrying someone I don't care tuppence about and I'll make you suffer from a guilty conscience for the rest of your life: you've shown me that you knew about Denis all the time, but you wouldn't lift a finger to help me and now it's too late. I don't know which is the worst, you or mother or Denis's horrible old father, but between you you've wrecked my life; so I'll punish you all, yes and Denis too, and Caroline; I'll make her feel awful because she stole David away from me: I could have been almost happy with David. . .'

'Yes,' said Guy, very quietly; 'go on; if you've got hard words to say, let me hear them.'

As if she would! She turned on him with scorn: 'I'm marrying him because I want to: is that good enough for you?' She gave a vicious little nod and was out of the room before he could reply.

Guy did not move; he inspected his dead cigar and relit it carefully. 'Oh God,' he muttered, 'I wish I knew what was right!' He had been very near relenting: if Isabel had given him her confidence would he have told her to marry her Denis and be damned to the family? Would he? Even now, he could not make up his mind. The marriage could never have been happy, he was convinced of that: religion, politics, class, all different; not much money, and bitter opposition from certainly one family, if not from both—it was a poor look out. And yet, if they loved each other . . .? He shook his head; anyway, it was too late now and there was nothing to be done, nothing at all, except to watch his daughter preparing her own funeral and plunging into another marriage that was also doomed to failure. She did not seem to have had a chance, and for the life of him he could not see who was to blame for that: Isabel herself, perhaps, in part, for not coming into the open, but what good would that have done? He had not been prepared to sanction the marriage and Helen would never have agreed to it; he felt thankful that Helen was ignorant of the whole affair. Was he himself to blame—was he trying to preserve a standard that had fallen out of use?

He watched the lengthening ash on the end of his cigar. One could not let everything go, not if one still cared, and he did care; class he could have passed over, but the religion was the trouble and the politics were all bound up with that. Thank God the same thing had not happened with Caroline: fortunate Caroline to have fallen in love where she could marry! She, at any rate, would be happy. But it was all wrong that it should be a matter of luck; they were out of place in the country, the Protestant star had set when the British left and there was no choice for the children of the old Unionists but to intermarry and retain their loyalties, or else lose their individuality by marrying into the other camp; that was what it involved—losing their individuality, for religion and politics in this country were so intermingled and swollen with bitterness that compromise was impossible. However ready one was to co-operate with the new regime, if one was Protestant, the label Unionist went with it and there could be no peace or fair-play in a mixed marriage of the kind that Isabel had contemplated, where the other family was wildly Nationalist. She would have had to watch her children being brought up Roman Catholics, taught to hate all that her family had stood for, and hating and despising her in the end for being a product of Anglo-Irish stock.

There came a timid knock on the door and Doran came in with a salver:

'The Misthress sent me down with yer coffee, Sir; I'm afraid it is stone cold, it has been up that long.'

'Never mind, Doran; just leave it on the desk.'

He threw the butt of his cigar into the fire and settled down unhappily to work.

Upstairs, in the drawing-room, Caroline sipped her coffee in silent misery, only half aware of Helen's complaints about the ingratitude of her daughters: what was Isabel doing all this time—what could she be doing? She must know that her mother was dying, simply dying to hear all about it; it was just like her not to tell them anything, probably everyone in Dublin knew about it before they did. It wasn't as if she deserved to be treated like that, Helen went on; no mother could be more devoted to her daughters, but they never told her anything.

Caroline let the flood of grievances pass over her. How, she wondered, could Isabel bring herself to marry that drunken little play-boy, Mike? Of course she would be rich and have a lovely house, they could travel and buy expensive cars, tear round the country to all the race-meetings and dash over to London to enjoy themselves whenever the spirit moved them; Isabel could buy all the clothes she wanted and entertain to her heart's content, but how long could she stand Mike? She shuddered, and was suddenly aware that Helen was digging an impatient finger into her knee.

'Caroline, do listen to me, child: do you know him?'

'Who, Mike? '

Helen's tongue clicked with irritation: 'Of course, who else?'

'Oh, yes, a little; he's small and very dark and about twenty-four—quite good-looking if you like that sort of looks, and he's got a marvellous car.'

'Well, Isabel's not very tall; they ought to make a handsome pair, both dark like that. Would you say he was clever?'

'I shouldn't think so: he may be.'

'Of course I know Lady Millar, she was a Lambert—they had money too. The boy's an only son, isn't he—an only child?'

'Yes.'

'They'll come in for a lot of money when the old people die,' announced Helen complacently; 'I'm afraid,' she added with a sympathetic smile, 'they'll be much better off than you and David can ever hope to be.'

Caroline shrugged her shoulders: 'She's welcome to it.'

'I wish Isabel would come up; I expect they'll want to be married at once—there's nothing to stop them.' Helen patted her hair with a preening gesture. 'Do you think I ought to telephone to Lady Millar, or should I wait for her to make the first move?'

'I've no idea.' Caroline stared at her blankly.

'I must talk it over with Daddy. Perhaps I could go and call there tomorrow with Isabel, or it might be better to wait for her to come here: I don't want to look too . . . eager, you know, as if . . . Oh, I do wish Isabel would come, I can't think why Daddy wanted to drag her off like that when I'm longing to hear all about it, but of course men never think of that sort of thing!' She rattled on until at last Isabel came, white-faced and grim.

Helen was up in a moment: 'Sit here, darling, near the fire; and put your feet up—you look dreadfully tired. You must go to bed early and have a good night's sleep: there's nothing so tiring as being in love!'

'I'm not tired.' Isabel sat down gloomily and stared into the fire.

'Of course you are,' said Helen fondly, 'but you just don't know it; I remember feeling just the same. Now, I want to hear all about everything: when do you plan to be married?'

'As soon as possible—early in March, I suppose; and we want a huge wedding with lots of bridesmaids.' Isabel spoke as if she were in a dream.

'In the Cathedral?' suggested Helen eagerly.

'I suppose it's bigger than anywhere else.'

'And where will you go for your honeymoon—or is that a secret?' Caroline squirmed at the coyness in her mother's voice, but Isabel did not seem to notice anything.

'America, I think.'

'America?' echoed Helen, shocked; 'wouldn't you rather choose somewhere a little . . . quieter? Portugal, or perhaps Madeira? I suppose it's too early for Switzerland or the Italian Lakes. America sounds very noisy and full of people, dear!'

Isabel surveyed her mother with stony contempt: that's the sort of honeymoon I should have liked with Denis, she thought, or I could have endured it with David; but with Mike! It would be too terrible to be quite alone with Mike. From now on she was going to surround herself with people, all the time, so that she would never have to think. It was she who had chosen to go to America: there would be people on the ship, millions of them, and she would see to it that they did not stir out of New York, which was crawling with people.

'We both want to go to America,' she announced, and that closed the subject.

'Where shall we get your wedding-dress?' Helen began again.

'In London: Mike wants me to go to Molyneux for all my clothes.'

Helen made a little face: 'I don't know about the expense, dear; Daddy may have something to say to that.'

'Mike says he'll pay for them if Daddy can't.'

'Oh, I don't think Daddy would like that; he wouldn't like that at all.' Helen shook her head and pursed her lips dubiously.

'Why should I have dud clothes when Mike's willing to pay for them? He's got so much money he doesn't know what to do with it all.'

'It's a matter of principle, dear; Daddy's very independent; he wouldn't like to think of your fiancé paying for your trousseau; of course, when you're married, it'll be a different matter. Besides, there's no need for them to be dud clothes, as you call them: you can be beautifully dressed without going to Molyneux.'

Isabel felt too tired to fight: 'Daddy wants Mike to come to dinner tomorrow.'

'Oh!' Helen straightened up; 'now, that will be nice! We'll ask Sir Horace and Lady Millar too, and we'll have a family party. I wonder if I shall be able to get a bit of meat that's been hung long enough, or shall we have a pair of chickens? No, I think ducks—ducks with orange sauce, it's quite a new idea; and clear soup. Oh dear, it's very short notice, but men never think of that; however, we'll manage somehow; I shall have to get the things in early. Daddy will have to see about the wines. They're not teetotallers or anything, are they?' she added anxiously; 'Sometimes brewers and people like that are.'

Isabel's lip curled slightly in an odd little smile:

'No, they're not teetotallers.'

Helen spent the next day in a happy bustle; she brought out the Waterford glass finger-bowls and salt-cellars, opened up little boxes of preserved fruits and harried the butcher until he sent the shin-beef for the clear soup; she drilled the cook in the new recipe for orange sauce with duck, scoured the city for flowers and fruit, implored Guy to get in some champagne for the occasion and wrote out menu-cards in her thin straight hand. She seemed quite tireless and all her weariness and discouragement had fallen away as she stood, straighter than she had been for years, with a faint wash of colour in her cheeks, waiting by the fire with her husband and her daughters for the guests to arrive.

Lady Millar was an ample person with well-dressed grey hair and a pleasant expression; she used lipstick, rouge and powder enough to make her look well-groomed, and her nicely-shaped nails were lacquered shell-pink; she was expensively and plainly dressed in wine-coloured crepe, with little, but valuable jewelry. Helen was frightened of her; she herself had long ago given up any attempt to beautify herself, and she felt shabby and dowdy with her wispy hair, pale lips and badly-made velvet jacket that had begun to wear at the elbows. Sir Horace was a little man with protruding blue eyes and thick white hair which he wore very short; he held both Helen's hands in his own as he told her how happy he was about the engagement and how little his son deserved his luck.

'Young rascal,' he chuckled, 'did it all on the quiet! But it'll be the making of him, settle him down; that's what he needs, responsibility. And he's certainly picked a winner!'

Lady Millar made for Isabel and kissed her warmly.

'My dear,' she said, putting her hands on Isabel's elbows, 'I'm so very happy about it, so very, very happy. Michael needs a wife and you're just the person I would have chosen for him. We must be great friends, you and I.' She gave the elbows a gentle squeeze; 'Won't we?' she smiled.

'Yes,' replied Isabel, in a little terrified voice, not looking at her; 'Oh yes, I hope so.'

'Good: I know we shall. I want you to be the daughter I always longed for, and never had. You're not frightened of me, are you? You won't find me the traditional type of mother-in-law, you know.'

Isabel managed a tiny, suffering smile: 'Oh, not a bit.'

'I know it's a terrible ordeal, my dear; you must feel that we're ready to criticise everything about our son's future wife, but I promise you we're not; we're very, very pleased and proud to think that you're going to marry Michael.'

Isabel was almost wriggling; the traditional mother-in-law would have been infinitely preferable to this open-hearted person who was prepared to love and admire her, and who yearned for her confidence; this woman made her feel a cad and for a moment her heart failed her.

'I hope I'll be able to make him happy,' she said, and at the time she very nearly meant it.

'Of course you will!' Lady Millar was reassured at last; 'He's head over ears in love with you, my dear, and you'll be a tremendously good influence on him. Now I must talk to your mother.' She turned away, and Isabel sighed with relief. Mike was standing dumbly beside Helen, longing to escape, but as soon as Lady Millar had gone, Sir Horace rushed up and Isabel found herself coping with his bantering gallantry until Doran came in to announce that dinner was ready.

Helen had been in a fever about the seating at dinner; they were only seven: ought they to have invited an eighth? If only David had been here! Guy told her she was worrying about trifles: what did it matter if the table was uneven; this was a family party, not a grand occasion. So Isabel was seated between Mike and her future mother-in-law, and Caroline was allotted to Sir Horace.

The old people talked incessantly; the young scarcely uttered. Guy and Lady Millar seemed to find each other particularly sympathetic; they were discussing the historic gun-running episode at Howth, in July, 1914; she had seen the whole thing from their house. Mike was so sober that he was almost speechless; he was going to reform, he had told Isabel, and this was the first evidence of his good intentions. He was going to London, to choose her a ring—nothing in Dublin was good enough: a square-cut diamond, he thought, from Cartier; she agreed that it would be lovely.

The duck with orange sauce created a sensation; Sir Horace swallowed two massive helpings and gazed regretfully after Doran as his plate was swept away. Lady Millar begged for the recipe.

Isabel faced the toasts boldly, trying to wear the correct expression of confused enjoyment as Sir Horace paid her compliment after gallant compliment; Mike felt for her hand under the table and she left it in his, cold, limp and unresisting; his reply was properly humble and enamoured, delivered with a slight stammer and obvious sincerity. Helen bridled at Sir Horace: how delightful it was to see the young people so much in love!

Sir Horace joined the ladies by himself; his son, he explained, was being put through the mill by Guy; it reminded him of the day when he had had to submit to the same thing, 'and *her* father,' he said, pointing to his wife, 'was a lot more terrifying than yours, my dear; he barked at me!'

Little did he guess, thought Isabel gloomily, how formidable her father really was.

Helen was delighted with the success of the party; the Millars were charming people, Mike was so handsome and so very much in love and the dinner had gone off splendidly; the clear soup had been cloudless and had Guy noticed how Sir Horace had appreciated the duck? She was sure he would have had a third helping if he had been given the chance. And fancy going to London to choose the ring! Was not that delightfully romantic, she whispered to Guy. He grunted and went downstairs to lock up the wine.

There was only one thing, Helen confided to Caroline as they went up the stairs to bed, one more thing that she would have liked for Isabel: if only Sir Horace had been a baronet instead of a knight, it would have been something for her to look forward to when the old people . . . that is to say, Sir Horace . . . she ended with a nervous little giggle, aware of Caroline's incredulous stare.

CHAPTER EIGHTEEN

While Caroline attended lectures and began sitting for her portrait, Helen and Isabel organised the wedding. Guy complained that they would ruin him, but his protests were ignored: Helen was going to see that her elder daughter was fittingly married.

A miracle had happened and, months before Helen had dared to hope for success, Isabel had thrown over her illicit lover and replaced him with someone who was not merely acceptable but highly eligible. She swelled with maternal pride and gratitude: for this change of heart Isabel should be rewarded by the gratification of her every whim; nothing was too good for her. Together they bullied and wheedled until Guy was forced to capitulate, and the two of them went off to London to buy clothes. Helen was prepared to sell some shares and dip into her capital if Guy would not pay all the bills: how was he to know that she had a guilty conscience to appease, that she was determined to make it up to Isabel for the note she had left at the little cake-shop only three months before? And how could she bring herself to put into words the fear that was always at the back of her mind: that unless Isabel got exactly what she wanted, she might turn capricious and call off the whole affair? That was a possibility so appalling and unthinkable that Helen did not dare express it, even to herself.

Caroline's portrait was progressing; she wore, not emerald green, but her white and gold frock, and sat, perched on a stool before a brilliant green back-cloth, on a kind of dais in the carefully warmed studio while Leonard sweated silently in his overalls. It was a wearisome business, she found; Leonard spoke only when he wanted to interest her and bring life into her face, and she was thankful for the infrequent rests and for the cups of steaming coffee which Anne would bring up from time to time. Anne never stayed with them; she would open the door quietly and lay down the tray wherever space could be found for it, generally upon the floor, smile at Caroline and go out without speaking a word. Leonard would nod gratefully and, as often as not, forget all about the coffee until Caroline reminded him that she was in need of a rest and sustenance. Then she would climb down stiffly and they would begin to talk.

The day of her final sitting was bitterly cold; an east wind scoured the streets at nearly gale force, the puddles in the gutters were frozen and even the brilliant sunshine had a brittle quality; there was snow to be seen on the mountain tops and people fought their way along, bent double and blue with cold. Nothing could make the studio warm on a day like this and Caroline shivered as she sat in her thin frock, neck, shoulders and back exposed; the fire was piled high with coal and logs, but little gusty draughts belched through the ill-fitting windows. She seemed to have been sitting there a long time, but she had not the heart to tell him that she must come down; then suddenly she knew that she was going to faint. The blood drained from her face, leaving the skin stretched taut over the bones; she felt that she must be swaying on her stool and the whole room swayed with her. 'Leonard!' she gasped urgently.

He was beside her in a second, lifting her down; she was slack in his arms and he was carrying her to the big chair beside the fire; through the mists of limitless distance she could hear his voice murmuring over her:

'Caroline darling; oh, my poor darling, what have I done to you!'

Her eyes were closed; she felt deathly sick and could not open them; she could feel his lips touching her hair, but she never stirred: Leonard thought she was unconscious and instinct told her that she must never let him know that she was aware of what was happening.

He began to curse softly at the clutter of things on the chair; shifting her weight on to one arm, he sent everything flying to the floor and set her gently down. She opened her eyes; he was leaning over her, breathing heavily, a lock of dark hair over his brow; he closed his eyes for a second and stood upright, tossing his hair back into place:

'I'd better get Anne.'

'Leonard, I'm going to be sick; I'm awfully sorry.'

He looked helplessly round the room: 'Oh, my God.' She struggled to her feet and made a dash for the bathroom; when she returned, Anne was in the studio; she threw a coat over Caroline's shoulders:

'It's the cold, darling; you shouldn't have come today.' She soaked a handkerchief with eau de Cologne and handed it to her.

Leonard came in with brandy and glasses; he looked almost as white as Caroline.

'We'll all have some: you need it on a day like this.'

Anne hurried down to make some coffee and Caroline began to feel better; her teeth stopped chattering and sensation crept back into her limbs.

'I'm all right now,' she said shakily.

Leonard had been gazing at her dumbly: 'Did you pass right out?' he enquired anxiously.

She looked at him with steady eyes: 'Right out.'

His head jerked back with relief and his 'Thank God!' was almost audible.

Caroline sat back in her chair and relaxed: that was that. She had saved her friendship with Anne and Leonard; she could forget what had happened, still come to this welcoming and happy house and talk to her beloved Anne, sit on the hearthrug and stroke the purring marmalade cats; if this house had been closed to her, she would have felt indeed bereft.

'The picture is really finished: you won't have to come again.' Leonard's expression was one of unconcealed relief.

She stood up to look at it: 'Am I really like that?' she asked in an awed voice.

'It doesn't do you justice.'

'Oh, Leonard, it does; much more than justice.' Anne came back with a tray:

'You must bring your parents to see it, Caroline. By the way, did Leonard tell you—it's to be our wedding present to you; that is, if you like it?'

'Of course I like it: you are a darling, Anne. I think it's the most lovely present.'

Anne stood back from the portrait: 'I really do think it's good; I'm not saying that because Leonard did it, but he's got something about your expression that a lot of people would have missed. You know, Caroline, you ought to have been one of the ancient queens of Ireland, with your red-gold hair.'

Caroline thought of Mr. O'Hegarty from Galway and his insistence that she had no right to be in the country, and laughed:

'When I was at school,' she said, 'they used to call me carrots and tell me that my only hope was to dye it.'

Helen and Isabel returned triumphantly from London with the precious wedding-dress, an enchanting affair of pearl-spattered satin; even Guy, as he wryly enquired the cost, had to admit that it was lovely. Helen put him off; all the bills had not come in yet, she said, and she must get her accounts straight before she could give him any details. Her next act was to pay a visit to her stock-broker: even with the three hundred pounds she was collecting from him, there would be a disturbing bill for Guy to pay; Isabel's extravagance had been shocking.

Anne telephoned to Helen to ask her and Guy to come and see the portrait, so one afternoon, soon after lunch, so that they could be sure of a good light, Caroline took them to the little house in Pembroke

Road. Anne led them up to the studio; the picture was on an easel at the end of the room nearest the door, and they all crowded past to see it in the light. Leonard laid down his brush and greeted them, then as he pointed to the picture, they turned round in silence. Caroline smiled expectantly at Leonard and Anne.

Helen gave a little gasp and clutched Guy's arm:

'The Sinn Fein colours!' she exclaimed in horror; 'Oh, how could you do such a thing?'

They all looked at her aghast: was she trying to be funny? But Helen was in deadly earnest; of course it was quite true, the picture was built up of green, white and gold, but only Helen could have thought of it like that.

'It's very lovely,' said Guy bravely; 'of course, he never meant . . .'

Anne looked ready to weep: 'It never occurred to any of us,' she pleaded; 'oh, do please try to look at it as a portrait, Helen.' She gave a despairing look at Leonard who had been gazing at them all in utter mystification; he shook his head and tapped his forehead gently, while the others were not looking.

Helen laughed bitterly: 'How can I? Of course, it's very like her, but the colour-scheme! It's the first thing that strikes one: I simply can't believe that it wasn't done on purpose. Caroline, how could you have let them . . .?'

Caroline's blushing head was bent in burning shame: how could her mother dare to disgrace them all like this. She felt she could never face Leonard and Anne again.

'It never occurred to me,' she blazed; 'I don't think of everything in terms of politics, but now that you've put it into my head, I'm rather glad!'

Guy threw a restraining arm round her shoulders, but Helen ignored the remark.

'You weren't going to exhibit it, were you?' she asked Leonard challengingly.

'The Hibernian Academy,' he replied grimly; 'but of course; if you'd rather I didn't . . .'

'Couldn't you alter it? Make the back-ground blue, or something?' She spoke brightly, as if she were trying to divert a headstrong child from some impracticable purpose; 'Then we'd all be satisfied.'

'No, by God I couldn't!' Leonard glared at her, roused to action at last; 'I suppose you think red, white and blue would be all right!'

'But it would be so *easy,* and blue . . .'

'Really, Helen,' protested Guy, terrified of what she might say next; 'you can't ask people to alter pictures. Don't you think you're making a lot of fuss about nothing?'

'Nothing! You call it nothing that my daughter's picture should be exhibited in those colours? Why, everybody in Dublin would be talking about it and I should be the laughing-stock of . . .'

'I shan't send it in,' said Leonard bitterly; 'you needn't worry.'

'But if you'd only agree to my suggestion,' persisted Helen, 'then you could send it anywhere.'

Leonard tore his hair with both hands: 'Of all the damned . . .' he began.

'Shall we go downstairs,' said Anne loudly, almost pushing Helen out of the room before her.

Guy and Caroline stayed behind for a moment.

'I can't tell you how sorry I am about this,' said Guy apologetically; 'you see, my wife feels these political matters very deeply, and sometimes she sees things that other people wouldn't notice. Personally, I think it's a brilliant portrait and I congratulate you.'

Leonard melted a little: 'Anne and I were so anxious for you both to like it,' he said; 'I'm afraid I was very rude—I have such a filthy temper: forgive me if I behaved unpardonably.'

'It is for you to forgive,' murmured Guy; they left the room awkwardly. Helen and Anne were standing silently on either side of the fire in the downstairs room.

'Come, Guy; we must go home.' Helen almost sprang to meet him.

'Won't you stay to tea?' said Anne, smiling; 'We needn't talk about the portrait.'

'Thank you so much, but we must get back.' Helen shook hands coldly with Anne and led the way to the door.

Guy held Anne's hand for a moment: 'I'm very sorry,' he said; 'I think it's a wonderful portrait; I was telling your husband.'

'It is good, isn't it?' There was a wicked little gleam in Anne's eye; she looked at Caroline's suffering face: 'Don't worry, darling,' she whispered, 'I know your mother can't help feeling like that: you mustn't blame her. Come and see us soon.'

Caroline nodded gratefully and they went silently down the step to the car.

'Well,' exclaimed Helen, spreading a rug over her knees, 'I never thought the Hendersons would turn out to be Republicans; it just shows you can't trust anybody, these days.'

'Republicans!' said Guy; 'what nonsense, Helen.'

'Mother, you're being quite impossible,' protested Caroline.

'Well, if they're not, they're fools: how could anyone in this country paint a picture like that and pretend there was nothing in it? No, it's no good; I've never trusted Anne Henderson since that Paris affair, and this finishes it; I shall never speak to her again. And as for him! You heard what he said about red, white and blue—you heard the contempt in his voice? He must be a Republican to talk like that.'

'My dear Helen, the poor chap was a little annoyed, to say the least of it.'

'I am *not* your dear Helen. Oh, I know you're all against me, as usual.' Her thin back was rigid; 'Anyway, I can tell you that if that portrait has to be shown with all Caroline's presents, you can get someone else to run the wedding for you: I shan't be there!' With this ultimatum, she drew the rug more closely about her and relapsed into blistering silence.

Nobody spoke again; Guy and Caroline stared out at the street in front of them, Guy huddled over the wheel, Caroline with her hands clasped tightly in her lap, biting her lips. The silence hurt; Caroline felt it burning into her, making her hot all over. She struggled to throw it off, but there was nothing to say. It continued, hostile and consuming, even when they reached the house. Guy left the engine running as he ran up the steps to open the door; Helen descended with dignity and swept into the hall, followed by Caroline, but she turned suddenly, nearly upsetting Caroline with her swift, unexpected movement.

'Won't either of you speak to me?' she demanded in a low, frightened voice; 'Am I a criminal to be treated like this?'

Caroline bent her head: 'What's the use: what do you want us to say?'

'Say anything, say you hate me, that I'm a bigoted fool; say anything you like, but don't put me out in the cold like this, I can't stand it.' She ended with an hysterical little sob.

Guy put a hand on her elbow: 'Helen!'

'That's not what I want: I don't want sympathy from hypocrites. I know you all hate me, even Isabel,' and she shook off his hand as though it might contaminate her; 'why can't you say so, instead of trying to keep up appearances.'

'My dear, I've never hated you, none of us have: how can you even think of such things?' Guy looked helplessly at Caroline, who was staring at the floor.

From the street outside came the burr-burr of the idling engine, an intrusive pattern of sound; it seemed to get louder, mocking them, drowning the power of speech. Guy shuffled his feet uneasily, and Helen spotted the movement.

'Go on,' she ordered; 'go and turn off the engine: my feelings don't matter, I know that.'

'Damn the engine,' said Guy explosively; 'you're being very unjust, Helen.'

'Unjust! I, who've been kept out of knowing anything about my own family for years and am the very last to know what's going on:

do you realise that I don't know a thing about any of you, except what I discover by accident? And you tell me I'm unjust! Go and turn off that engine,' she screamed, 'or I shall go mad.'

Guy ran down the steps and silence flooded back in at the door, to be broken by his returning footsteps. He closed the big door gently.

'If you don't know anything about us, Mother,' began Caroline slowly, 'it's your own fault. When we were small, if we told you anything about ourselves, you didn't like it and you tried to alter it, so when we grew up, we just gave up telling you. You couldn't change us by getting angry, and we wanted peace and privacy: it's no good telling people what to think, they've got to find it out for themselves.'

'So everybody in Dublin knows more about you than I do, and you run round to the Hendersons to confide in them behind my back; and a nice influence they've been! Oh, I heard what you said, that you were glad about the picture: you gave yourself away then, Caroline.'

'I was so angry then, I didn't care what I said.'

'But you meant it, all the same; so you've joined the traitors too!' She turned to Guy: 'I always knew you were one, but didn't think you'd taken Caroline away from me, you and the Hendersons between you. Now I've got nobody left—Isabel doesn't care.' She was calmer now, speaking with quiet deep bitterness, her thin face very white in the shadows, her eyes ardent with their consuming flame. 'I'm quite alone, I understand now, but I shall never give in, however much you despise and insult me. My loyalties cannot be exchanged.'

'We're not traitors, any more than . . .' began Caroline, but Helen held up her hand:

'Be quiet,' she commanded; 'nothing you can say will make it better now.'

With a glance of supreme contempt she turned and slowly climbed the stairs.

Guy and Caroline looked miserably at one another; he put his arm round her and led her silently into his study.

'Civil war,' he said, 'is war at its most sordid, and when it gets
into a house . . . !' He shook his head grimly. 'We were happy when
we were married, Caroline, can you believe that? Your mother and I
thought we could never quarrel; you and Isabel were conceived and
born in love and understanding; you grew up in bitterness and strife,
and there's nobody to blame: you can't give up your opinions for the
sake of peace, and in this country you don't get a chance to keep your
opinions quiet—something always comes along to blow them out of
you, and then you're in the soup. It's a desperate country!'

'It's the only place I want to live.'

'We all feel that, but we don't seem to be able to live in it together,
and that's where the trouble comes.' Guy began to laugh despairingly.

The house was unbearable; Caroline would have liked to take the
car up to the mountains and walk for miles, letting the wind rush
through her hair and into her lungs, but Guy was going out again
and wanted the car. If only she could get out of this house for good,
find a job and be independent; Brian O'Malley would give her a job
at any time. She went over to the telephone when Guy had gone:
she would ring up Brian. But suddenly she changed her mind; Guy
would be miserable if she went: she must stick it out until David
came home.

She wandered down to Trinity; there was a surging crowd of heads
round the notice-board in the Lady Registrar's office, somebody was
congratulating her. She found that she had scraped a First class in
French, a Third in Spanish; she knew she ought to feel pleased, but she
could only feel slightly sick; nothing seemed to be worth doing any
more. She went into the cloakroom and leant against the mantelpiece,
warming herself and watching the girls coming and going; stray ends
of conversation came to her:

'She's crazy about him,' 'I think I'll wear my blue,' 'The old brute
gave me a duck,' '. . . magnolia skin! My dear, I nearly said magnolias
didn't have spots.'

What was she going to do for the rest of the day? All these girls were going home after their day's work, they were looking forward to going home; she never wanted to go home again. A familiar face appeared: Nan. Nan caught sight of her at once and came rushing over; she was in the seventh heaven of delight because she had received a letter from Wully.

'Would you like to come to the pictures?' suggested Caroline desperately.

'Ooh, I'd love to; I love going to the pictures, but nobody ever asks poor Nan, isn't it a shame?'

'I'll pay'; Caroline knew that Nan was perpetually broke; 'after all, I asked you: I've got time to fill in,' she explained.

What a relief to know that she need not go home until the gong rang for dinner! Sitting in her plush seat in the warm darkness, beside this girl whom she disliked, watching a bad film, she almost enjoyed herself.

CHAPTER NINETEEN

The preparations for the wedding went steadily on. Isabel was having ten bridesmaids; she insisted on dressing them in expensive creations of gold lamé and their impecunious mothers were becoming perturbed about the cost. There were family arguments about the music and the hymns. Helen wanted 'O perfect Love . . . '; they had it at every wedding and of course Isabel must have it too, but Isabel would not hear of it; she hated that hymn, she said. The house was crowded with presents; Helen had to bully Isabel into writing grateful letters. Guy was consulted about nothing. Both Helen and Isabel seemed to shrink daily under the strain; Lady Millar paid a special visit to Fitzwilliam Square to tell Helen that she feared Isabel would have a break-down, but when she saw Helen herself, she was concerned about who would break down first.

The day came at last, the second Wednesday in March; the sun shone and the air was warm with spring. The trees in the square were beginning to put forth leaves, and the city pigeons cooed as they went through their courting ceremonies. Isabel sat up tensely in bed, to eat her last breakfast at home, white-faced and with dark bruises under her eyes. 'Come and talk to me,' she called through the open door to anyone who was passing, 'don't leave me alone.' She sipped at her coffee and nibbled a piece of toast, but could eat nothing. Guy slipped in to see her on his way down and shut the door. He sat down softly on the edge of the bed.

'Are you sure you want to face it? Tell me if you want to back out: it's not too late, even now.'

She covered her face with her hands: 'It is,' she wailed; 'I can't do it now.'

'I'll back you up, I promised you.'

'No, no. I can't get out of it now.'

'Pull yourself together; you needn't do anything. I'll tell them all.'

'No, no; leave me alone.' She turned her face to the wall.

'I'll take you right away; we'll catch a train before lunch.'

'I haven't got the guts.' For the first time she looked up.

'Yes, you have: with me to back you up.'

She took a deep breath: 'I believe I will! Give me five minutes. Can you come back?'

He nodded and was gone; the sound of his footsteps had hardly died away before Helen came in.

'Poor child, you look exhausted; try and have a little sleep.'

'I can't: I'm on wires.' She paused. 'Mother!'

'What, dear?'

'What would you say if . . .if I backed out of it?'

Helen's face went suddenly dead-white and she sank down on the edge of the bed. 'Do you want to kill me?' she whispered; 'think of the shame: how could we ever hold up our heads again? And all that money thrown away! Do you know,' she went on menacingly, 'that I've spent three hundred pounds of my own money on your wedding? I wasn't going to tell you that, but now I think you'd better know.' She dug her nails into the palms of her hands and bit her lips. 'You've got an attack of nerves, that's all it is, dear,' she said briskly; 'I was just the same.' She took one of Isabel's cold hands in hers and rubbed it gently: 'Think of all those people in the Cathedral, waiting to see you, and the bridesmaids, and Mike; think of poor Mike waiting there: what could you say to him? Oh, the humiliation of it!' She rocked herself to and fro, smitten with a sudden horrible vision of her enemy, Mrs. Joyce, saying to her: 'If you love your daughter, Mrs. Adair, you'd see that nothing else will do them, only to get married.' She pushed the thought away from her: how dared that woman come to torment her now! Whatever happened, Isabel must marry Mike today; she must be cajoled, bullied, shamed into doing it. Never mind what happened afterwards, there would be time to face that later; they could separate if they were unhappy, even get divorced, but she could never marry Denis Joyce until Mike was dead, for his Church would not permit that. Once married to Mike, she was safe from Denis.

'Every bride feels the same,' she went on, desperately trying to stimulate resolution in Isabel by the vigour which she forced into her voice; 'I promise you, darling, you'll feel all right when it's all over; it's only nerves, really, that's all it is. What a fool you'd feel tonight, if you . . . how could you ever face anybody again? And you'd never have another chance, remember that.'

Isabel fixed her with dark, suffering eyes: 'You're right,' she said tonelessly; 'I'll have to go through with it now.' She sat upright suddenly and beat on the bedclothes with her hands, her voice rising: 'Oh God, but it's awful, you don't know what it feels like!' Her eyes bored into Helen's face.

'Don't talk nonsense: you're getting hysterical. Pull yourself together.' Helen's mouth closed like a trap as she shook her daughter by the shoulders. Isabel's jaw dropped. 'You're behaving just like a temperamental actress,' went on her mother, 'and it's all nonsense. I won't have it: do you hear?'

Isabel quailed and collapsed on the pillows; Helen surveyed her there.

'You don't know your luck,' she said menacingly, and stood up.

There was a knock at the door and Doran came in, holding up the bridal bouquet:

'It's just after coming, Miss,' she announced beamingly.

Helen took it from her and held it against the wedding-dress, which was draped over a chair.

'Just look, Isabel; it's perfect, isn't it? All right, Doran, you may go.'

She waited until the door had closed again. 'Just think of yourself in that glorious frock, with this; my dear, you'll be the loveliest bride Dublin's seen for years.'

Isabel had been watching her wearily; 'Mm,' she said, without enthusiasm, turning her lip down slightly. 'You needn't be so worried, Mother, I'll marry him all right.'

Helen felt nonplussed: 'I think you ought to rest, dear; I'll leave you alone now.' She smoothed the sheet and pillow fussily:

'Comfy?'

There was no answer; she crept from the room.

Isabel pulled the bed-clothes up to her chin and stretched out her toes until they reached the end of the bed; Guy would be back in a minute and she would have to endure another of these awful struggles. She felt sick with nerves and her knees would not keep still. There was her father's quick step coming up the stairs, his firm knock on the door; she resisted the impulse to bury her head under the clothes and feign sleep.

'Well?' he said eagerly.

'It's no go.'

'You're . . .?'

'. . . going on with it.' She looked at him with terrified resolve.

He bowed his head: 'As you say,' and the door closed gently behind him.

Isabel lay back and blinked away the tears of self-pity; she felt furious with Guy for taking her at her word; if he had only begged once more, she would have given in; she had wanted him to beseech and implore. Now, she really would have to go through with it . . .

The Cathedral was packed; outside, there was a milling throng of citizens watching for the arrival of the bride. Old women with black shawls pulled over their heads, women carrying babies and surrounded

by a string of children of varying ages, small bare-foot boys, little girls
with streaming noses, young girls with waved, unbrushed heads and
made-up brazen faces, ancient and decrepit men, corner boys who
leant against the railings with a detached air, spitting over the heads in
front of them, flirting with the girls in their magnificent grandeur of
youth—all the neighbourhood was there to watch the show, enjoying
the premature spring sunshine, pushing, shoving to get a better place,
scolding, chatting and cracking jokes, ignoring the police who were
there to keep them back and pressing forward like an irresistible tide
whenever a car came into view.

'Oah, lookit; there's the bri-id!'

'G'way, thems only the bri-idsmaids; sure there's eight or ten o'
them, didjever see the like!'

'What's that they have on them, at all?'

'Lammy,' replied a confident voice; 'I saw it on the paper a-Monda
they was goin' to wear lammy. Oh God, they must be perished in that
old stuff!'

The bridesmaids were decanted from their cars and stood shivering
in the sunless porch, giggling nervously and clutching their crimson
bouquets; ushers came and went importantly; the organ played bravely,
filling in the gap. The bride was late; inside the Cathedral, people were
whispering and standing on their seats to see if she was coming. There
was no sign of her; they looked at their watches: ten minutes late—
something must have happened. Clergy peered anxiously into the
roadway; a car was coming.

Isabel sat erect, deathly pale, her unsmiling lips dark red; she stared
straight in front of her, not speaking to Guy, who sat beside her in
helpless misery. The car stopped and someone held the door open.

'We're there,' said Guy gently, a hand on her elbow.

Isabel stepped painfully out; she looked as though she might break
in two; she slipped her hand inside her father's arm and they began
the slow procession up the aisle; the bridesmaids fell in behind them;

someone whispered: 'Keep the pace down.' There was a tense silence
and suddenly the choir broke into the processional hymn. Guy
swore softly: they should have waited for that. He gave a sideways
look at Isabel; he had the impression that she was not really there,
he could not feel her hand in his arm and she moved as if she were
in a dream; at any moment she might stop, rooted to the ground,
unable to move backwards or forwards: what on earth would he do
then? Panic uncoiled within him, but he pressed it back. They passed,
barely moving, between the walls of people.

People leant out from their pews to look at them, and rage broke
loose in Guy: these foolish women, dressed in their terrible glad-rags,
yearning and simpering over the bride, what had they come to see?
He wanted to knock their faces in.

Isabel looked at the ground before her; she had not even raised
her eyes to see if Mike was there; the Best Man was turning round,
wondering why they were so slow; he whispered reassuringly to Mike.
There was Helen, standing rigidly, her huge hat covering her like a lid,
willing them to reach the chancel steps; there were the Millars, calm but
anxious, Emma Butler dabbing her eyes gently, Eileen Hunt and Alec,
the MacNamaras, everybody they had ever known. The clergy in the
chancel were like an ambush, quite close now. The Best Man drew Mike
out to meet them. Isabel looked up and, standing stock still, clutched
wildly at Guy's arm; there were still some yards to go and he could not
get her to move; a bridesmaid bumped into him from behind. People
were whispering, the clergy looked alarmed, Mike closed his eyes in
agony, Helen clasped and unclasped her hands, her head bent.

'Shall we make a dash for it?' whispered Guy; 'it's not too late, even
yet.'

Isabel did not reply; she shut her eyes, took a gasping breath and
moved forward again with slow, uncertain steps. They were there;
Guy released her arm and Mike took his place beside his bride.

She made the responses in a husky whisper, barely audible even to the clergy. The congregation was disappointed; people felt cheated if they had not heard the bride say: 'I will.'

At last it was over; Helen beamed from her seat in triumph and relief: Isabel was safely married.

'The Register!' she hissed at Guy; 'Take Lady Millar.' She held out her arm to Sir Horace, who led her gallantly away; she seemed to prance beside him, nodding and smiling at her friends, her huge hat bobbing foolishly.

'There was an awful moment,' whispered Lady Millar to Guy; 'I thought. . . .' She was very solemn; Guy nodded sombrely; he felt weak at the knees, as though he had been watching an execution. He was thinking of how he would have to face this cheerful rabble at the reception; he would have to be good-humoured and laugh at people's jokes, perhaps make a speech himself, when all he wanted was to creep into his study and be alone; then, when Isabel had gone, he would have to listen to Helen's self-congratulations: how lovely the child had looked—so frail, so dignified! How well the reception had been done: did he think the Millars had been impressed? A little hard core of purpose formed in his mind: he could not, would not endure it; he would go out and get drunk, royally, speechlessly, immovably drunk. The injustices of years were stirring, striving for liberation; he would release them all in one magnificent gesture.

Back at the house, he rushed Isabel and Mike into the dining-room for a stiff glass of brandy; Isabel looked as if she might fall down unless she were given something; then he sent them upstairs to stand and receive congratulations while he swallowed another glassful himself. He felt a little better; one more might make it bearable; he poured it out and drank it down quickly, grimacing at the thought that he was swilling his liqueur brandy like beer. He put the glass down on the table and made his way upstairs, laughing and talking with people on the crowded staircase.

Isabel stood like a statue; if anyone shook hands with her too violently, she might topple over; her hand, cold and stiff, was extended;

she murmured something as people grasped it and passed on, her face unsmiling and quite expressionless. Somebody tried to kiss her and she dodged the embrace.

'Will it work, Guy?' Eileen Hunt was at his elbow; he smiled at her in sudden relief: here was someone with whom he could be honest.

'It may—if she puts her mind to it. I did my best.'

'You look worried to death; I think it'd do you good to get drunk.'

'I'm going to,' he announced resolutely; 'I've already started.'

'Poor Guy!' She squeezed his hand and passed on. There was hardly room to move; the double doors into the back drawing-room had been opened, but there seemed to be no space, only a solid mass of people packed between the tables of glittering silver and glass; corks were popping and speeches had begun. Helen was enjoying her moment of triumph; she held a glass of champagne and listened to admiring comments with an almost dreamy look. Guy looked at his watch: not much longer now.

Isabel put down her glass and grabbed Caroline's arm:

'Come and help me dress.'

It was the first time she had asked her to do anything for weeks. They went up together to Isabel's little room; the lobby outside was stacked with suitcases and hat-boxes, shining new, already labelled: 'MILLAR—EUSTON via HOLYHEAD'. The going-away clothes were laid out on the bed; peach-coloured satin underclothes, beautifully made, a suit of ruby tweed, a tiny feathered hat.

Isabel looked desperate and ever so slightly drunk; she sank down on the edge of the bed. 'Oh,' she groaned, 'I do feel awful!' and she gave an elegant little belch, kicking off her white satin shoes.

Caroline could think of nothing to say; the whole thing had been a nightmare. She picked up the shoes and put them tidily under the dressing-table.

'Here, let me help you off with this.' She tugged helplessly at the veil, but Isabel ignored her and began to unfasten hooks and eyes; then she pulled at the little coronet of orange-blossom and it fell to the floor with the veil of priceless lace. Isabel kicked them into a corner, struggled out of her frock and, rolling it into a ball, hurled it upon the bed.

'There,' she said; 'now I feel better.'

She shook off the long white slip and stepped into the peach-coloured cami-knickers:

'"With all my worldly goods I thee endow": I'm going to be rich, Caroline, and that's something you'll never be. Don't you envy me? The happy couple, the blushing bride . . .' Her voice tailed off and she turned away suddenly.

'Don't,' said Caroline; 'I can't stand it.'

'Stand it! What have you got to stand?' She combed her hair in silence and adjusted her hat; the mouth in the mirror was turned down, the lower lip trembling like a child's.

Helen was coming; they could hear her, panting a little on the stairs; there were a couple of men behind her, coming to fetch the luggage. She poked her head in at the door, chiding them indulgently.

'Hurry, children; they're all waiting.'

'Just coming,' said Caroline quickly, hoping that she would stay out; she held open a dressing-case for the last-minute things and Isabel threw them in. The men banged about in the lobby and disappeared with the luggage. Helen came into the room:

'I must go down, darling; I'll tell them you're coming.' She smiled regretfully. 'Enjoyed it? It's been a lovely wedding, you should hear what people . . .'

Isabel stared through her mother and said nothing.

'I'll say goodbye to you now—I shan't be able to get near you downstairs.' Helen put her arms round Isabel's unresisting shoulders and kissed her on the cheek, 'Be happy, darling, promise me you will.'

'You'd better go, Mother; I'm coming now.'

'Yes, yes I must.' Helen gave one last look at her daughter and was gone.

Isabel stood in the doorway; there was no escape: behind her was Caroline, below were Mike and her mother; Guy would not help her now. She looked wildly round, holding on to the doorpost.

'I hate Mother,' she said with cold vehemence; 'Goodbye!'

'Goodbye.' Caroline was almost in tears; she caught hold of Isabel's shoulders and kissed her silently on the back of the neck. Isabel caught her hand in a sudden grip.

'Don't you desert me,' she begged; 'I've got nobody.' She bent her head and went stumbling down the stairs to join her husband.

CHAPTER TWENTY

Helen had everything arranged: she was going to leave Guy; not baldly and bluntly but, as it were, by degrees. She was not going to say to him: 'Guy, I am going to leave you: our life together has become intolerable.' Nothing so blatant as that. No, she was going to stay with Moira for a bit, then she would go to London; from there on to somewhere else, perhaps Harrogate; the doctor has advised Harrogate; her rheumatism had been very painful lately. She would just go on staying away indefinitely, gradually losing touch with Guy and the children until they had become accustomed to her absence; then she would announce that she was not coming back. It would be much easier that way, there would be no rows, no explanations or frantic scenes of attempted reconciliation; Helen was tired, desperately tired, and she needed to do things the easy way.

She sat in her bedroom, sorting things at her dressing-table. It was September 1929, and Caroline was returning from Butler's Hill that night so that there would be someone to do the house-keeping and look after Guy; she had been away since July and Helen had been thankful to be rid of her: so long as Caroline was in the house, she felt that there was a conspiracy of silence and politeness against her, intangible, indefinable, but horribly real. Guy, by himself, was silent enough, but alone with her he could not raise that barrier of antipathy which he and Caroline together seemed to be able to put up between themselves and her. She shuddered as she thought of the last six months, since Isabel's wedding: the loneliness, the boredom that she had suffered, it seemed that she had no friends left! Isabel was too busy, entertaining in her new house, to bother at all about her mother, and there was no sign of a baby yet, it was very disappointing; Helen was too frightened of her daughter to ask her outright whether she was hoping for one, but it would have been nice to knit little things, do some of the fine sewing at which she was excelled, plan nurseries with Isabel and feel that she was needed. Daughters always needed their mothers at a time like that, she assured herself.

Thank heaven she had some money! About four hundred a year of her own; that would keep her going in a small way at hotels, if she was very careful; she would not have to keep writing to Guy for money. She was determined to avoid asking him for anything; then she would not feel so bad about leaving him.

She went to the window and looked out; people were playing tennis in the Square, she could hear the whack of balls against the racquets and see white figures on the courts; it was the end of the season and the grass was very worn on the back lines; the evergreens were grubby after a drought of several weeks, the leaves on the plane trees were pale and dusty, and little eddies of dust were being blown about on the pavement by the breeze; the high brick houses stood, red and solid, glowing in the early evening sunlight. Very soon now, it would be that nostalgic hour when the wind has dropped, sounds are intensified and the dew begins to fall with the long shadows; when the shouts of the players only accentuate the loneliness of those who watch and listen and sit apart.

She shut the window and turned back into the room; for years she had listened to these sounds, looked out on those red, prosperous houses and the grimy shrubs, the green lawn and the summer dust; it was the last time. She began to sort again; she would need that and that and that; she would go straight to London from Butler's Hill, so she must take everything; it would mean a lot of luggage, but she must manage to get it out of the house somehow without Guy noticing. Three large suitcases were already packed, so why not take them down to Kingsbridge now, while Guy was out?

Like a girl making an illicit appointment with her lover, she flew guiltily down the stairs and ordered a taxi. Then she went up again, and lugged the cases down herself: it would not do for the servants to see them. She flung on a coat and hat and stood, hot and fuming with impatience, in the hall, her arms aching from the strain of carrying down the luggage. She could not stay still: if Guy were to come in while she was standing there, surrounded by suitcases, he would think she had gone mad.

She opened the door and peered out; there was no car in sight and hardly anyone was about, only a fat old woman dressed in black, wheezing painfully and sweating as she pushed her way along the street with slow, unsteady steps. Helen took one look at the intent red face and shut the door instantly: it was Mrs. Joyce. Helen stood trembling behind the door, indignation and resentment rising in a turmoil within her: how like the woman to choose just this moment to pass by! It was an interference, an invasion of her privacy. She waited a few moments, then opened the door again gingerly, only a little crack, sufficient to peep through; the woman should have passed now, and be safely in her own house. But no, she was standing still, holding on to their railings, *their* railings, mopping her face and gathering strength for the last few yards; this was intolerable, unforgivable impertinence! And here was the car, at last. Helen stayed peeping through her crack, waiting for her enemy to look up with a stare of curiosity; but Mrs. Joyce did not raise her head, she was too exhausted to concern herself with the comings and goings of her neighbours; she relaxed her hold on the railings and moved slowly on. Helen beckoned secretively to the driver to come and fetch the luggage, then with a swift look to right and left, she hurried into the taxi and they drove away.

In Stephen's Green, they passed Guy, returning from the Club; Helen cowered against the seat, eyes closed, as though that might prevent him seeing her, but he never even looked up; he walked steadily on, with a look of mild elation on his face.

As a matter of fact, Guy was feeling happier than he had been for many weeks: Caroline was coming home tonight. Back at the house, he hummed to himself as he washed his hands; he would go to Kingsbridge and meet her, the train was due in about twenty minutes. He went to the garage and took out the car; driving along the quays, he passed Helen's taxi on its homeward journey. She recognised the car and cowered again, horribly certain that in some extraordinary way he had found her out and was trying to follow her. Then, with sudden relief, she began to laugh weakly; of course he was only going to meet Caroline.

That night at dinner, Helen was almost gay; her liberation was opening out before her and she felt released, already on the wing. Guy smiled at her from the end of the table, giving her messages for Moira and Archie; he would get up and drive her to the station. She protested that it was too early, the train left at seven and she would much rather order a taxi; she was thinking of the luggage that she had left in the cloakroom and that Guy must not see. He insisted: it was stupid to get taxis when they had a car of their own.

'Please let me do it my own way,' she snapped; 'I should feel miserable if you had to get up so early.'

'Well, Caroline then.'

'Yes, I'll go.'

'No, no, no! Can't you let me make my own arrangements?' Her exasperation was so apparent that they gave in, mystified and a little hurt.

She went to bed early; she gave them her papery cheek to kiss:

'Goodbye; I shan't expect to see either of you in the morning.'

'We'll come down in our dressing-gowns.'

'I'd much rather you didn't.'

'Very well. Have you got plenty of money?'

'I cashed a cheque today.'

'Have a good rest, and don't worry about us, we'll manage beautifully.'

Helen almost laughed; she was never going to bother her head about them again; for their own sakes she hoped they would manage beautifully. She was free now, she had shaken them off. She experienced a moment of terror at this freedom: was it not a transition from one loneliness to another, even more hollow? She stood still, smiling sadly, looking round her drawing-room for the last time, feeling the pull of familiar things, longing for someone to speak one word of real affection to hold her back and break her resolution.

'Goodbye,' said Guy again; he looked as though he wanted to sit down and smoke his pipe; he was waiting for her to go. He went over to the door and held it open.

'Goodbye, child.'

'Goodbye, Mother.' Caroline was standing uneasily by the fireplace.

She went obediently through the door and slowly climbed the stairs to her lonely room. She heard the door shut behind her and later, through the floor, their voices and the sound of Guy's laugh; he had not laughed like that with her for years: if she had been in the room, he would not have laughed like that. She went on with her packing, glad that she was going.

The house felt quite different without Helen; Guy and Caroline began to enjoy themselves. He asked people back to sherry and told Caroline to have her friends to meals, so she invited the Hendersons and Brian O'Malley to dinner and they all sat talking far into the night. They gave a sherry party for Isabel and Mike, and their friends; Isabel was amazed; she had never thought of her father as being a sociable person.

Helen had been away for nearly three weeks when she wrote to say that she was going straight on to London; Guy handed the letter across the breakfast table to Caroline in silence, watching her as she read it; they both experienced a sense of deep relief, but neither would give it expression.

'Nothing like a long holiday,' said Guy guiltily; 'do her all the good in the world.'

'Yes.' Caroline smiled.

Guy opened the paper: 'Oh, my God!' he exclaimed; he sounded terribly agitated.

'What on earth's happened?' Caroline darted round the table to look over his shoulder.

It was the news of a financial crash, widespread enough to be really disastrous, even in that time of crisis.

'Will it affect us?' asked Caroline.

He laid down the paper, biting his lips and staring vacantly across the room: 'As far as I can see, your mother has lost every penny she possessed; I had a lot in it, too.'

'Lost? Really lost, for good?'

'Absolutely gone, as though it had been thrown into the sea; that's what it looks like. I must ring up Simpson and McAlister, they'll know what it's all about, I don't feel able to take it in somehow . . . must have another look.' He re-opened the paper, searching for reassurance and, finding none, pushed it away from him. 'This is a blow,' he said quietly, 'a terrible blow. If it's true—of course it's true, what am I saying? We shall have lost between eight and nine hundred a year, between us. I don't know whether we can go on living in this house, the expenses . . . We shall have to cut down drastically. I must think . . .' He put his hands up to his head. 'Of course we aren't ruined, I don't want you to think that, but I was beginning to think of retiring; I'm fifty-five: I thought perhaps at sixty, but there's no need for that, I should be good for another fifteen or twenty years.'

'Don't worry, Daddy; perhaps it won't be as bad as you think;' Caroline poured out his coffee and pushed it across the table.

'Four maids: couldn't we do on less, with only three of us to look after?'

'It's the stairs.'

'I know, but surely . . . Damn, I wish Helen was here to talk it over. You know, things haven't been too good lately, dividends down and the market at rock bottom; Isabel's wedding cost the hell of a lot of money, then there was what I handed over to her at her marriage; I gave her some of those very shares, they seemed perfectly sound then. I wish I hadn't.'

'It doesn't matter to her: the Millars are rolling.'

'I know, but I have a feeling that she might want something of her own, one day; anyway, I shall always feel awful about it—that I should try and make it good, or something. I think your mother will have to come back; this trip to London will be another expense. I'll go and see the stockbrokers and then I'll write to her. I won't be in for lunch, I'm lunching with a fella at the club. Don't say a word to anybody at present, will you? When was she going to London?'

Caroline glanced through her mother's letter again: 'Next week is all she says.'

'It'll be a terrible shock to her; I expect she'll come home anyway. Goodbye, Puss, and don't worry too much.'

He kissed her absent-mindedly and went out.

Caroline sat on at the table, drinking cup after cup of coffee and wondering how to save money; she could leave Trinity and ask Brian O'Malley for that job in his tweed shop; he had told her that it was hers for the asking, at any time. But she had a feeling that, if she did that, complications would crowd in upon her and she might never be able to escape. When she was with Brian, she could never remember what David was like; he was away and had been gone so long and, although she knew that she really did want to marry him, Brian's personality was so dominant that she was afraid of being carried off her feet. Brian was in love with her; he had often told her so lightly, with an astute look to warn her that any response on her part would make him show how serious he really was. So the thought of taking the job in his shop terrified her; she might find herself weakly agreeing to marry him, knowing that when David came home she would feel as if she had been trapped.

Doran came in to clear away the breakfast things, but when she saw Caroline, she made a discreet effort to retire; Caroline, however, wanted company.

'Don't go away, Doran; I've really finished.'

'I can come back, Miss.'

'I'm just going, really.'

'Very well, Miss.' She began to pile up the plates, silently, with an air of complete detachment. Caroline sighed: Doran was not going to talk; she folded Helen's letter into its envelope and went down to see the cook about the meals.

The autumn sunshine streamed into the dining-room at Butler's Hill, showing up every detail in the dark portraits, flooding the patterned carpet; it went shimmering over the polished table, it winked and gleamed on the silver and turned the marmalade in its glass dish into a flaming pool; Helen, who was a cold person, felt it warm on her back and stirred gratefully.

'I don't know what to do with you, Helen,' remarked Moira with dissatisfaction; 'three weeks ago, when you came here, you were as thin as a rake, as white as a sheet, and you looked as if you hadn't slept for weeks; I feed you up with cream and eggs and butter, send you to bed at ten every night and make you rest with your feet up all the afternoon, and you haven't put on a pick of flesh or got a scrap of colour. Don't you sleep?'

'Oh yes, pretty well.' Helen smiled guiltily.

'That means not at all.' Archie applied a lump of butter carefully to a corner of toast, covered it with marmalade and put it into his mouth just in time to prevent the whole edifice from collapsing stickily in his fingers.

Moira was looking seriously concerned: 'Will you have the doctor? I wish you would.'

'I will not, indeed; I never heard such nonsense,' snapped Helen with a return of her old spirit; 'I was just tired when I came here, but I'm rested now; I feel ever so much better.'

'Don't go to London: it's the most exhausting place I know; stay on here, for a bit anyway; you know we love having you.'

'Do!' echoed Archie; 'London's a filthy place; can't think why anybody goes there.' He spooned sugar thoughtfully into his coffee.

Helen was touched; 'I do love being here,' she faltered, 'but I've stayed such a long time already; may I think it over?'

The maid came in with the post and the local paper, and handed them to Moira, who sorted the letters, pushed some towards Archie and passed the paper to Helen.

Helen opened the paper slowly; there was so little news these days that she would have finished it long before either of the others had read their letters; then she saw the headline. It conveyed little to her at first, for no financial crash had ever affected her, but as she read on and saw the names of the companies involved, the truth began to dawn on her. She looked over the top of the paper at Moira and Archie, a terrified, desperate look, but they were engrossed in their letters. She began to read again, feverishly. It was unbelievable, it could not be true: nothing like that could happen to her! She must protest against such lies.

'Oh!' she said furiously; 'Oh!' But all the time she knew it was true, that all her money was gone, that her short liberation was at an end and that she would have to go back to Guy and to the life she hated so much as to know that she could not endure it.

Moira and Archie were staring at her, asking her what was wrong; she laid down the paper and pushed it away from her, knocking over her empty cup. Her eyes were full of tears, her lips moved but she could not speak; her hands grappled together and she made little dreadful noises in her throat.

'Oh my dear, what *has* happened?' Moira was beside her, an arm round her shoulders; she threw the paper to Archie:

'See what it can be,' she whispered.

Helen slumped down in her chair; Moira's face was white and terrified as they carried her in to the next room and laid her on a sofa.

'The doctor, quickly, Archie; I'm not sure she's not dead. Ask him if there's anything we can do till he comes.'

She felt horribly useless; other women, she thought, would have done something instead of just sitting there, watching. She went back to the dining-room to fetch the paper: she must find out what had happened. But when she read the news, she was still unsatisfied: Guy and Helen could not possibly be ruined, even if they had lost a good deal of their private means; he was a good architect and did pretty well. That cry of Helen's had not been an expression of shock or indignation, it had been a personal revolt against some private tragedy, some intimate, unimaginable horror. She looked at the paper again, but there was nothing else that could have affected Helen. Folding it away, she looked again at the figure on the sofa and averted her eyes quickly; Helen looked hideously pathetic with her open mouth and thin, lined face, a defeated old woman; yet, she was the younger by three years. Moira put her hand under the chin to close the mouth, but it fell open again, loosely.

Archie came back: 'He says to get her into bed; he'll be along as soon as he can.'

With difficulty, for she was unexpectedly heavy, they carried her up the stairs; Moira lit a fire and sat by it listening; listening for any sign of returning consciousness, for the doctor's car, for Archie to come up, for any reassuring movement in the house; when the logs in the fireplace fell in suddenly, she jumped.

The doctor announced that it was a stroke; they would have to get a nurse, he would make arrangements about that; there was no knowing when she would recover consciousness, if at all; the family should be told at once. He shook his head gloomily and departed.

Guy and Caroline arrived the next afternoon; Helen was still unconscious. Moira, worn out after sitting up all night with her, was supposed to be sleeping, but she came downstairs. The nurse had arrived that morning, an immense bustling woman whose personality so dominated the sickroom that the still figure in the bed seemed hardly to be present. When Guy and Caroline crept in, she was eating her tea, a hearty meal of bread, butter, jam and cake, with a boiled egg; she swept to her feet, exuding health and vitality, talking loudly with a strong country accent and laughing with such unaffected cheerfulness that they felt instantly reassured: nobody could die in such company.

Four days passed before Helen came to herself; the house had gradually become adjusted to the situation; nobody talked now in hushed whispers, nor tip-toed round the passages; they even laughed without a sense of guilt. The nurse came down while they were at dinner to tell them that Helen had opened her eyes and tried to speak; Guy rushed upstairs at once. He bent over the bed and took her limp hand in his, smiling, but her eyes closed and did not reopen. He felt foolish and embarrassed, but the nurse sent him away, telling him that he could not expect too much all at once.

Helen improved slowly; soon she was able to speak, but she would say nothing to Guy. When he came up to see her, she would close her eyes and keep them shut until he was gone. The nurse was scandalised; never before, in her experience, had she known a wife object so plainly to her husband's presence; she took Moira aside.

'It's a terrible thing,' she said in a shocked voice, 'terrible; I never saw the like. "Keep him away", she says to me, "Keep him away." And how can I keep him away, her own husband, and he such a lovely gentleman too, and so fond of her?'

Guy decided to go back to Dublin, and Moira agreed with him; then began a long discussion about money. He was worried about the Fitzwilliam Square house, which was quite empty, as far as the family were concerned, with four maids in it, doing nothing, looking after nobody and eating their heads off. Caroline must stay on with Helen, so there was only himself to bother about. Moira advised him to send the maids on holiday, shut up the house and live at the club; he should look out for a smaller, more convenient house outside Dublin: an invalid in a town house with four storeys was enough to make all the servants give notice at once. Helen and Caroline must stay on at Butler's Hill until the new house was ready. She paused for a moment:

'Will Helen mind moving?'   .

'I don't know, it's such a long time since she told me what she feels about anything. . . .' Guy broke off, conscious that he was revealing more than he intended, but Moira looked up sharply:

'Something awful's been happening to Helen—before she got ill; she was all closed up in herself and I couldn't get near her: Guy, what *is* it?'

He shrugged his shoulders hopelessly:

'I wish to God I knew; it's me and Caroline, partly; she's got it into her head that we're in league against her, hiding things from her.' He told her about Helen's outburst over the portrait. 'Since then,' he went on, 'she's scarcely spoken to me, except to ask for money for Isabel's wedding and to tell me she wanted to come to you for a holiday. I've tried to talk to her, but it's impossible. You know, when two people who have been fond of each other fall apart like that, it's only an insult when one of them tries to be nice to the other; the fact that it's an effort, that one's even consciously framing a remark or a question, and rehearsing it mentally, can't be concealed; there's a sort of cheerfulness in one's voice, and a determination not to wince at the rebuff, and you feel a fool, a nervous fool, twiddling your fingers under the table, longing to be spontaneous and natural, and quite incapable of it.'

'Oh, poor Guy; I never knew it was as bad as that.' Moira had tears in her eyes. 'And poor Helen, too; she's been her own worst enemy, all along. Let her stay here, my dear, as long as she likes; I think it will be happier for both of you. Sell that awful house and move into one you can afford, quickly. Make Isabel do the move for you, she's never done anything for anybody in her life.'

'Poor child,' said Guy; 'perhaps she would.'

'What do you mean, "poor child"?' Moira sat up indignantly; 'Surely to goodness, she's got everything she could possibly want?'

'Everything but what she really wanted,' said Guy sadly.

'Well, what was that?'

'The moon;' Guy stood up; 'and it was out of her reach. I'm afraid she thought I might have got it for her, but there are things that even I can't do. Goodnight, my dear; keep Caroline as long as she can be useful to you. I can't begin to tell you how grateful . . .'

'Oh, don't start thanking me. I know how you feel about Isabel; tell me, is the, er, moon still there to be grasped at, so to speak?'

'Yes;' Guy turned round at the door; 'that's the trouble.'

Reluctantly, Helen found herself getting better; she longed earnestly to die, but the strength that had kept her going for so long asserted itself and she knew that she was going to live; she lay there in her bed, with one arm and one leg stiff and useless, staring at the ceiling, the thoughts turning over and over in her mind.

I've no money, no money at all; I shall have to go back to him, to that awful life. They all hate me: why can't I die? I'm all right here, but it can't last; go back and see their faces, so polite and hard, all against me. Isabel against me, won't tell me anything, hard as nails; she's not happy: don't say that, don't say it; you can see she's not, only got to look at her face: don't say it, it's not true. She'll come to hate you, drove her into that marriage. Guy was adamant . . . couldn't do anything with him; I asked him, I did really, but he wouldn't hear of it. Leave it at the little cake-shop, that's what she said; I asked him, tried for a week. I hate that woman, holding on to our railings; pocketed her pride, she said; her son calls her Mammy, just think of it, Mammy! Common as dirt. She could never have been happy with him, better as she is. I said I had no private means, that's true now, not a penny. But the child's not happy: don't say that, don't say it. Why can't I die?

'Nurse!' That big bustling body, leaning over me, so clean and healthy, starched apron crackling, enormous meals. 'Nurse, keep him away.'

'He's been gone, Mrs. Adair, these two days: d'ye not remember? Come now, ye're half asleep; would ye like a nice cup o' tea?'

'Please.' Anything to be busy; 'prop me up.' Watch her boil the kettle on the fire, hear it humming and see the steam, like breath on a cold day; count the spoonfuls as she puts them in.

'More, Nurse; I like it strong; you never make my tea strong enough.' Almost in tears: self-pity. Nobody understands me, they don't know what I suffer. Mustn't see me like this, mustn't give in. No one's seen me shed a tear since . . . so long ago I can't remember. Chestnut trees nearly bare—must be October. How long have I been here?

'Nurse!'

'Not quite ready yet, Mrs. Adair; that old kettle's taking a powerful time to boil.'

'How long have I been here?'

'Arrah, let me think! It must be ten days now, but ye've missed nothing, the weather's been a fright altogether; nothing but gales of wind. Is yer hot bottle cold? Shall I give you another?'

No doubt about it, she's a good nurse, always knows what I want; clever hands; she doesn't try to put me off, either. Who's that opening the door? Can't be Guy, he's gone. Caroline; she's going to kiss me, and she hates me; they all hate me. Judas, Guy's Judas; so's Caroline: green, white and gold, and she said she was glad. Shut my eyes, she won't kiss me then.

'Well, Mother; how do you feel?'

'Not too bad.'

'Can I get you anything? Read to you or something?'

'No . . . thank you.' Shut my eyes again and she'll go away.

Fall asleep soon; horrible, nightmares: back in the Square, their cold faces watching me, hating me. Got to go back there, no money now, have to ask him for everything. I said I had no money, it's true now, funny; I tell you, Mrs. Joyce, I did ask him but he said no, wouldn't hear of it. Left it at the cake shop; for Mrs. Joyce, I said. That woman: driving me mad! Spent three hundred of my own, nothing left now; she nearly backed out, had to force her into it. Made her marry him, now she's not happy. She hates me: oh, don't say it.

'Nurse!'

She isn't there; never is when she's wanted; just like them all, only do what they're paid for. She's left me in the dark; there's that curtain flapping again; I can't stand it.

'Nurse! Nurse!'

Left the bell out of my reach; did it on purpose, knows I'm helpless. Like a great bird, that curtain, black wings flapping, hovering there in the window, waiting to get me. If I look away it won't pounce, can't if I don't watch it.

'Nurse!' Steps in the passage. Ah, a light! I'm panting, I can't breathe. It's gone away: only a curtain, all the time.

'What is it, Mrs. Adair? I was just fillin' the kittle for yer bottle; didja want something?'

'Only a light; don't leave me in the dark, Nurse. Draw the curtains, stop that thing flapping. Ah, that's better.'

Lie back now, plenty of light. They don't know the things I see in the dark. Must have light . . . light!

CHAPTER TWENTY-ONE

Christmas came and went; Helen and Caroline were still at Butler's Hill. The Fitzwilliam Square house was in the hands of agents; three young doctors were nibbling at it, their success demanding utterance in that final symbol of prosperity, a town establishment. Their poor little wives viewed the house with foreboding, dismally counting the stairs and peering into the servants' quarters, dark basement rooms with damp patches on the walls. That minute box-like appartment with no window but a small square hole looking into the kitchen was, the agent informed them, the butler's room, but of course in these days no one would dream of putting a servant into such a place. The wives took note and ear-marked it for a store-room. They quailed as they surveyed the stone-flagged passages and worn stone steps up to the ground floor, the endless stairs up to the bedrooms, the single bathroom, no bigger than a wardrobe, at the top of the house. Where could they have the nursery? Would Nannie leave when she saw the steps up which she would have to drag the pram after every walk, the eighty stairs up which she would have to carry baby, how many times a day? They counted on their fingers the number of maids they would need: cook, parlourmaid and housemaid; the cook would demand a kitchen-maid, Nannie a nursery-maid. It just could not be done, Nannie would have to manage somehow without help, for a kitchen-maid there must be: a doctor's wife must entertain. The burden of success was heavy; to prove that their husbands were making money, that money must be spent. They sighed and returned to their labour-saving homes to think it over. The hearts of two began to fail them; the third, realising that ambition must be satisfied, took the house.

Guy had taken a little place at Tallaght; a small old yellow-washed house with a couple of acres of land; it was a pleasant little place and he could drive in every day to the office. There was an extra ground-floor room which could be made into a bedroom for Helen, who would never walk again; it had a French window and her chair could be wheeled out into the garden. The doctor's wife had bought in some carpets, the Waterford glass chandelier and some of the massive furniture that would not fit into the new house. Guy and Isabel had tried to calculate just what they would need, what Helen would like to keep and which things she would not miss; he dreaded the day when she and Caroline were to arrive: Helen might take a sudden dislike to the house and say that it was impossible to live in.

By the middle of February everything was ready; the house was painted and furnished, the cook and a maid installed. Doran had announced that she was retiring from domestic service and would not go with them; her A'nt in the country had died and left her a little farm, but might she come back to help with Miss Caroline's wedding? Guy shook her warmly by the hand and promised that she should. The new house-parlourmaid was a buxom country wench with a strong willing body and no manners, engaged by Isabel. Guy had even arranged with a little man called Kelly to come three days a week, tend the garden and do odd jobs about the house.

Annie, the maid, banged about from room to room, lighting fires and puffing noisily at any speck of dust that caught her eye; Guy felt despondent when he saw her, face and apron smeared with blacking, her stockings wrinkled in a spiral down her legs: Helen would not keep her for two minutes. But in an hour she was a different creature, clean and shining with soap and water, her thick unruly locks restrained somehow behind a cap. He went in to inspect Helen's room for the last time; it looked very comfortable and homelike, the bed placed where she could look out of the window, a vase of daffodils beside it on the table with the little reading-lamp; the pictures from her old room were on the walls, her books on the shelves. The fact that she had taken all her other personal possessions with her had been a shock to him; he had first learnt it when Isabel had come darting down to the drawing-room in Fitzwilliam Square where he was having the carpet valued, and plucked at his sleeve:

'Funny thing: Mother's taken all her things away with her!'

'What sort of things?'

'*Everything.* Clothes, all the things she used to have on her dressing-table, letters, shoes, luggage—all except a few terrible old things she couldn't possibly ever want again. All her drawers and cupboards are empty!'

'Odd!' he said, and turned back to inspect the ink-stain that Caroline had once made on the carpet.

The suspicion gradually formed in his mind that Helen had meant to leave him; she had insisted that nobody should get up to take her to the train: was that because she had not wanted them to see how much luggage she was taking? He began to see light; it would account for her illness, her unwillingness to see him or speak to him, everything. He felt slightly sick: that she should hate him so much that life in the same house with him was unbearable! Yet, she had not protested when he had bought the new house; she was coming there. But with what loathing and repugnance, because she could do nothing else! She was penniless; and he was helpless; he could not afford to let her live by herself and she had never even hinted to him that such was her desire. Now, looking at the new room that had been prepared for her with so much thought for her comfort, he made up his mind that, once she was settled, he would not enter it without an invitation. This room should be her private little fortress where she could feel secure from invasion; otherwise, how could she, an invalid, protect herself from company that she abhorred?

He took out the car and drove slowly to the station; he had suggested sending an ambulance, but Moira had replied that it was quite unnecessary; they had bought a wheeled chair for Helen and this would travel with them; she could be lifted into it from the train and wheeled to the car.

Caroline squeezed his hand hard as he kissed her; she looked white and thin; probably she had been having a hard time, poor child; this journey, with an invalid, was enough to exhaust anyone. Nurse bounced out of the carriage, greeting him with enthusiasm, assuring him that the patient was none the worse for the journey; in two minutes she had the wheeled chair alongside the carriage, and Helen in it. There was, she announced, a lot of luggage. Rather grimly, Guy replied that he had been expecting that; they would need a taxi as well as the car.

Helen sat bent forward in her chair; she looked a sick and crumpled old woman. Her hair had gone almost white and her dark eyes had lost their smouldering fire. She would not look directly at Guy, but she extended her good hand stiffly to give him a stranger's greeting and the polite flicker of a smile passed over her face: after all, they were in public.

In spite of herself, she was pleased with her room; she murmured grudging appreciation of it to Nurse as the big woman put her deftly into bed. Nice big windows, a good fireplace that threw out the heat; very nice and comfortable, although . . . Her face settled into a grim mould of resistance: this was Guy's house and she had meant never to come back to him. Almost instantly she fell asleep.

Across the passage, in the small square drawing-room, Guy poured out a glass of sherry for Caroline:

'Here's luck to the house!' he said, and added: 'It's lovely to have you back, Puss.'

She held out her glass in response and took a little gulp, trying to smile, but it was no good; she put it down quickly and, turning to the mantelpiece, buried her head in her arms.

'Darling, what is it? Tell me what's wrong.' He drew her into a big chair before the fire and sat on the arm of it, stroking her long slim fingers.

'Do tell me what it is: perhaps I could help.' Guy's voice was grave and very gentle. Caroline sobbed and sobbed.

'Come on, Puss,' he whispered, handing her a huge white handkerchief. Caroline took it gratefully.

'It's nothing, really; I don't know what it is, but everything seems to have gone wrong . . . being with Mother makes me feel all dried up and . . . wicked, somehow; I can't feel anything any more, I'm just not alive: did you ever begin to wonder if you were made of stone?'

'Oh, my poor Puss! Do you know what it is—you're just tired to death. It's been a horrible time for all of us. I've often felt the same, it's no good blaming yourself. Listen to me: in another year, now, David'll be back and you'll be able to go off with him and forget all about it.'

'Oh!' she sobbed desperately, 'but that's half the trouble: I don't even want to marry him any more. I don't want to marry anybody, ever; I don't want anything. If only I could want something I shouldn't feel so miserable.'

Guy was completely nonplussed; this was awful.

'You write to each other?'

'Yes.'

'You haven't told him?'

'Not yet. But when his letters come, it makes me feel worse than ever, he's so terribly . . .'

'. . . in love with you?'

'Yes.' And Caroline wept again.

'And you think it's not fair to let him go on writing to you like that when you feel as you do?'

'Mm.'

'Well, I've got a suggestion: write a letter to him, telling him just how you feel about it, that you don't want to marry him and that you don't love him any more. Don't date it and don't post it; keep it locked up somewhere and, if you feel the same in three months' time, take it out, put the date on it and post it. In the meanwhile, write to him in the ordinary way; don't pretend anything you don't feel; your letters will probably be deadly dull, but that won't matter.'

Caroline smiled: 'Daddy, you are a dear.'

'Will that do?'

She nodded. 'I'll do it tonight.'

He gazed into the fire. I wonder, he thought; I wonder if she will.

CHAPTER TWENTY-TWO

Isabel sat in the drawing-room of her perfect house and twiddled her thumbs; she was at a loose end. For the first time for months she had nothing to do; the family were installed at Tallaght, she was of no further use there. There were no parties to plan, no visitors to entertain. All her friends were either away or having babies or occupied in some way that did not appeal to her. Mike had gone to Belfast for two days and she had not gone with him; Sir Horace thought that Mike was not concentrating enough on the business and had told him that, now he had been married a year, he must take a pull on himself. Isabel was discovering that her father-in-law was not quite such a fool as she had imagined.

The room had a huge bow front facing the Dublin mountains which loomed blue and exciting in the clear spring air. Long white velvet curtains shimmered to the floor to meet the white carpet that had been brought specially from London; massive square navy-blue chairs stood round the room, set off by cushions of a dusty, almost lilac pink. The lamp-shades were of the same pink, corded with dark blue, silken tassels hanging richly. The hearth-rug was dark blue and pink. Nothing jarred; everything was in keeping, tidy, orderly, new and modern. The single oil-painting above the fire-place had been chosen for its perfect relationship to the colour-scheme of the room. No books or papers were strewn around in homely disorder; there was nothing to show that the room was lived in and Isabel, breathing the restless spring through the open window, felt that the whole house was dead and stifling.

Upstairs, everything was just the same; what with the things they had brought back with them from America and London, and sent for to Paris, the place was almost a modern museum. Matt paint and gleaming chromium, brilliant leather and glistening fabrics, concealed lighting and exotic, coloured glass. The bathrooms were 'amusing', the little writing-room was 'witty'. 'My dear, how too, too marvellous!' exclaimed the guests as they fumbled for the hidden door-handles and guiltily wiped their shoes before setting foot on the immaculate carpets. 'Darling, how divine!' they breathed ecstatically as she showed them her peach and lichen-coloured bedroom with its pearly bed, shaped like a giant shell, and the adjacent bathroom with heated, mirrored walls and opaque glass bath that emitted a suffused glow from concealed electric bulbs. 'Too sick-making!' they apologised as they stained the scarlet leather chairs with gin and It.

Sir Horace mistrusted everything in the house; he dared not lean back in the tubular chairs for fear that the slender chromium would wilt. He never knew which switch to turn on, having once flooded the house with music instead of light. The white telephone sickened him, but what really finished him was the toilet fitting that played a tune and had caused him to leap in the air in horrified surprise; after that, he always felt the chairs before he sat in them, edged round the white carpet and would touch nothing until he was assured that it was harmless. Lady Millar was amused by the house, but asked Isabel doubtfully whether she did not find it a little difficult to live up to: did she ever dare to take off her shoes and make toast in front of the fire?

The first time Guy went there, he threw himself into one of the square navy-blue chairs and laughed till the tears coursed down his cheeks; watching Isabel, he expected to see, not a human being, but a body of glass tubes and cellophane. Helen had approved of everything but the expanding cocktail cabinet.

But now everybody had seen the house and all the surprises had been explored. The newness was beginning to wear off; people had dropped cigarette ends on the carpets, rain had leaked through the flat roof and made a dull stain on the shining, mirrored bathroom wall, the white curtains would soon need cleaning and one of her rowdy guests had chipped the edge of the black glass dining-room table.

Isabel twiddled her thumbs and fumed with boredom; the flowers were dead and there were only daffodils in the garden, cheap things that anyone could have. She really ought to go into Dublin and buy out-of-season roses to match the room; but she could not be bothered to drive in just for that, and she could think of no other excuse. There were new novels in the house; she ought to do some reading or her friends would get ahead of her, but this afternoon she did not want to read. She ought, she really ought to go to Tallaght and see Helen, but that was so depressing and she was depressed enough already.

Caroline might be free: she could fetch her and take her to the pictures and on to dine somewhere, and get her visit to Helen done speedily at the same time. She went to the telephone; but Caroline was going out to dinner already with Brian O'Malley; she was very sorry, she would have loved to come; almost any other day she could have managed it. But almost any other day was no good to Isabel; she put down the receiver moodily and stared at her elegant little feet in their neat American shoes.

There was nothing left to do but to return some of those calls; it would be a deadly afternoon but they had to be done some time. She might as well do some of the distant ones and enjoy the drive over the mountains: it was a perfect day.

'Stokes!' she called.

Stokes appeared in his striped jacket; he was the house-man, combined butler, parlourmaid and valet, odd-job-man and spare cook; he was an ex-Serviceman and limped from a wound received in the War.

'I'm going out. If anyone rings up, tell them I'll be in at dinner-time; ask them to ring up again then.'

'Very well, Ma'am.'

She watched him with antagonism as he went back to the pantry. She did not like Stokes; he was not like an Irishman at all, so rugged and sane and contemptuously silent. Mike had engaged him and thought he was perfect, but he made her feel that she was idle and frivolous. Whenever she spoke to Stokes, she was uncomfortably conscious of her blood-red nails and lips, her make-up and mascara; she always felt that he might suddenly call her Jezebel, denounce her and her friends and tell them that they were heading straight for Hell because they drank and enjoyed themselves and never went to Church. He was a fervent Protestant, Orangeman and teetotaller, and Isabel and her friends thought this was a tremendous joke; perhaps Stokes knew about that, but he never said one word to confirm her knowledge that he despised her and only stayed on in the place because he had to earn his living and jobs for ex-Servicemen were hard to come by.

She put on a hat and coat and set off in the car, her own car, given to her by Mike. She did not feel in the least odd driving over the mountains in high-heeled shoes and a veil. It was not a week-end, so there was little traffic on the roads; on a Saturday or Sunday there would have been car-loads of sleepy families out for an airing, hikers and cyclists, and loving couples in parked cars.

It was fun driving on a free road; head tilted back and a long cigarette-holder in one hand, she felt pleased with herself in her long low car; it was almost a pity that there was no one to see her. She was going downhill now, approaching a little larch plantation which covered the hillside as far as the tumbling river at the bottom. She saw a lone figure walking along the road a little way ahead, hatless, in grey flannels and a tweed jacket. She knit her brows in; a tiny pucker: there was something familiar about that back, the swing of the broad shoulders, the angle of the head: Denis!

He was about fifty yards away, walking in a fast, loose stride. She put on her brakes suddenly and almost stalled the engine, but he did not turn round. Her face was crimson and she could hardly breathe; she felt as if something that had been holding her in for months had suddenly burst and released her. Inexplicable tears rolled down her face and she forgot everything except that she loved Denis desperately, that he was here and she must talk to him. She drove on slowly, hardly able to see the road, and stopped beside him, leaning over to open the door of the car.

He looked up, surprised, and when he saw who it was, his jaw, dropped. Isabel pulled off her foolish little hat and hurled it into the back of the car, revealing the tears which were washing off her mascara in a grimy trickle.

'Denis . . . oh, darling! I've got to talk to you; get in.'

He gazed at her, stupefied; she had cut him dead for the last eighteen months, and here she was crying and telling him that she must talk to him. He sat down, still amazed and overcome, and took her hand gently.

'What the Hell's happened, Isabel? Don't cry now, dry yer eyes and wipe that muck off yer face. What's happened?'

She bent her head and sobbed as if her heart would break.

'It's you. Don't you see, darling, seeing you just . . . finished me.' She looked piteously into his face, her lip trembling, and held out her arms. 'I love you, I've never loved anyone else and never will; we've just got to be together: don't you see that nothing else matters?'

His hands gripped his knees, knuckles staring whitely through the flesh, but he would not look at her.

'Don't you still love me?' she faltered.

'Oh, my God!' he groaned, and gave in.

They clung mouth to mouth; wild fires leapt up and the tumultuous blood shouted in his ears.

'Come,' he whispered hoarsely.

He pushed open the door and led her urgently by the hand over the low stone wall, among the larch-trees, under the new fresh green, where the sunlight flickered in a dancing pattern on the ground; over a little rise to a small hollow.

The spring-scented breeze passed softly over them, the blue sky winked at them between the branches, even the little birds ignored them, flitting around and above, twittering their pleasure in the warm spring sunshine.

Annihilated, Isabel lay on the tawny larch-needles and sighed with absolute contentment; for the first time in her life she was herself, the person she was meant to be and not the creature that people and circumstances had tried to make her. She had escaped at last and she would never allow herself to be ensnared again. The courage that she had lost so long ago came flooding back; she had Denis now and she would never let him go, never return to Mike and her sordid life with him. Denis lay, face to the ground, one arm under his brow, and she half turned to run her fingers through his strong black hair, but he shook her hand away and turned an agonised face to her.

'I should have strangled you,' he said.

She gaped at him, frightened; he looked savage enough to do it there and then.

'But what's wrong?'

'D'ye think I'm in the habit of seducing people's wives, or what? Mike used to be a friend of mine. Supposing you have a child: are you going to pretend it's Mike's, for I'm not.'

'It won't be Mike's,' she said softly; 'I don't want his children.'

He sat up and glared at her: 'You married him and he's a right for you to bear his children: what in the world do you think you were at to marry him at all, if that's the way you feel?'

'I . . . I got hopeless; they were all against us—you and me, I mean, and I didn't think we could ever get married. So I thought perhaps if I married Mike I might forget about you.' She looked at him very humbly, on the verge of tears again.

'You knew I'd have waited for you for years, that I'd work like a slave to get enough for us to live on. You went and married Mike for his money, didn't you?'

She shook her head wildly, in a storm of sobs.

'And now, when it's too late, you come back to me?'

'It's not too late: you and I belong together, we've got to . . .'

He took her by the shoulders and shook her until her teeth rattled and she cried to him to stop.

'What did you think when ye married him: that you could walk out on him any moment the fancy took you? That you only had to get a divorce any time you liked? That's no way to marry a man. By God, if ye do leave him, he'll be well quit of you, though I suppose the poor chap'd eat his heart out if you did. And what d'ye think we're going to do now? Go back and pretend that nothing has happened, or d'ye think I'm going to run away with you and we can starve together somewhere?'

'Oh, don't be so beastly,' she wailed; 'you know you love me.'

'My God, if I didn't love you so much I'd hate the sight of you! Well, what are you going to do?'

She was disconcerted and a little angry. She did not want to be asked what she was going to do, she wanted to be swept off her feet and carried away by an irresistible wave of love into a new life where she and Denis would be always together, how and where did not matter. But instead of that, be had done nothing but abuse her and now he was becoming practical; it was mean of him and disappointing: this was not the lover she had dreamed about. She looked at him from under brimming eyelashes:

'Come back and have dinner with me and we'll talk it over; Mike's away.'

He guffawed harshly in her face: 'D'ye think I'm going to sit in his house and eat his dinner, after this? And then spend the night with you, I suppose, in his bed, and you'll lend me a pair of his pyjamas? Though, God knows, if once I got into the house with you there's no knowing what I mightn't do; when I'm with you I can't help meself.' He took her face between his hands and pulled it slowly towards his until their lips met, pressing her mouth until it hurt.

'Are you going to run away with me: are you?' His voice was low and husky, and her face lit up. This was better: this was love, life and adventure, hers to grasp at last; she nodded quickly, but he pushed her gently away and went on.

'You'll be poorer than you ever imagined it possible to be; you'll have to cook and wash up and mend and do the laundry; you'll never have any new clothes or go to the theatre or sit in a car for years and years and years. Our families'll never speak to us again, and no one we know will have anything to do with us. Even if Mike divorces you, I can't marry you, you know that. But if you come, I'll never let you down, I'll stick to you through everything, whatever the family says, or the Priests, even if it kills me Mother, as it very likely will. I've got the chance of going in with a fella in London and I was going to turn it down, but now I'll take it; it's worth—don't laugh, he said I might make a couple o' hundred the first year, if I was lucky. Will you come and live with me in a basement room in a London slum?'

Her enthusiasm suddenly cooled under this icy blast, but she rallied as she thought of the things that she might be able to sell: wedding presents, some nice bits of jewelry, things Mike had given her; after all, they were hers, whatever she did. But Denis was looking at her with one eyebrow raised.

'You don't bring even so much as a safety pin that Mike's given you, d'ye understand? Not a stitch of clothing except what's yer own from before ye were married, not a brooch or a ring, nor a ha'penny but what's yer own property.'

She pouted at being found out: 'Don't you trust me?'

'No, I don't, but I'll make an honest woman of you yet, even if I have to run away with you to do it. Are you coming?'

'But I haven't got *any*thing!' She thought of the money Guy had made over to her and cursed him for giving her dud shares. 'Must we run away? If you don't take that job we can meet as often as we like and nobody need ever know . . .'

He pushed her roughly away: 'Either you come away with me or I never speak to you again. I'll take that job anyway and get clear of Dublin, whether you come with me or not. Well, are you coming?'

The terror of being poor, which had always been her own personal horror, rose up like a wall in front of her; she could not see through it or over it; she could see only the meanness and the misery, the struggle and the fear. Her face crumpled into sobs again and her shoulders heaved as she turned away from him. She knew that she could never face it, but she had not the courage to tell him. She was afraid, eaten up by fear; afraid that he might kill her, afraid that she might, out of terror, agree to go with him, afraid to return to Mike knowing that Denis was out of her reach.

'Come on,' he said brutally; 'make up yer mind.'

He would kill her unless she said something; he would kill her if she told him she wasn't coming. She must escape, run away from him, get away in the car, somehow avoid this awful moment. She tried to stand on weak knees that would not hold her up, but he was beside her, supporting her and leading her back among the larch trees to the little narrow road.

'I see,' he said bitterly; 'you don't have to tell me. Go back and be the virtuous wife who wouldn't run away with her lover, but never admit to yerself that it was because he wasn't rich enough, that wouldn't do at all! Oh no, let it be because yer duty called you to observe yer sacred marriage vows: ye'll feel quite noble when ye've convinced yerself.'

She was crying brokenly; she sat down on the little wall and buried her face in her hands, trembling violently:

'I . . . can't drive: you'll have to . . . take me back.'

Obviously, she was unfit to drive; he helped her into the car and stepped into the driver's seat. She could not look at him: she felt smaller, more miserable, more despicable than ever before in her life. He drove off without a word and they slid down the little valley; still sobbing and trembling, she stared with blurred unseeing eyes through the windscreen at nothing.

They joined the main road, which was empty of traffic; neither of them spoke or would look at the other. Denis sat, one elbow out of the window, his great shoulders hunched, his face scowling and truculent. He drove fast, determined to compress this unlovely interlude into the shortest possible time. Isabel's intermittent sobbing exasperated him to the point of torture but he would not try to comfort her. He treated the car roughly, jerking it round corners like a disobedient dog on a lead. Climbing a steep rise, he kept to the crown of the road and changed gear impatiently near the top, but before the car had regained power an empty five-ton lorry came rocketing over the top, trespassing badly on the wrong side.

There was no time to dodge, no time for anything. Isabel winced and her feet stretched out to non-existent brakes as they met, head-on, with tremendous force in a grinding, roaring crash. A raging, hissing column of steam rose from the burst radiators as the two vehicles dug into one another in a hideous embrace, wrestled for a static instant and then rolled a yard or two down the hill, to settle heavily sideways into the ditch.

Denis slumped on top of Isabel, limply, with his full weight, and they both fell heavily against the door, which opened and spilled them into the mud and water at the bottom of the ditch. Isabel screamed; she was badly hurt and desperately frightened. Denis lay with his face in the filthy water, quite still; there were no bubbles. She pulled at his shoulder to raise him, but she had not the strength to keep him up and his head fell back again with a splash; with a desperate effort, she jerked him round so that his face was out of the water. Her head pounded where it had been knocked against the windscreen and she felt that her eyes were bursting. Gingerly, she climbed the bank, every movement making her gasp with pain. The lorry driver, she thought, must be somewhere about and she would make him help Denis. Her head reached road-level and she raised herself slowly until she was sitting on the grass edge; what she saw there made her give a little moan of despair. The body of the lorry-driver lay huddled in a pool of blood on the crown of the road; he had been flung through the windscreen, quite a long way away. Isabel was paralysed: no power on earth could make her go and investigate that motionless, twisted bundle.

There was not a sound to be heard except a slow drip-drip from the lorry that became slower and slower and finally ceased. Then she heard running footsteps; a labourer from a cottage beyond the hill had heard the crash; when he came up, she could not speak to him; she could only point.

'God,' he said; 'isn't that terrible!' He approached the body on the road and scratched his head helplessly. 'That fella's dayid, God rest his soul.' He pulled the body gently to the grass edge and tried to straighten it out.

'Down there,' gasped Isabel, pointing to the ditch.

He peered down critically as though he did not believe her; then, seeing Denis at the bottom, slid down the bank and bent over him. He looked up, closing his lips in a grim line, and shook his head slowly.

'What about yerself,' he said; 'are ye hurrt?'

She nodded painfully and sank her head in her hands.

'Is it a crack on the head ye got?'

'Mm, and all over.'

'Lookit, ye'd best wayit here while I go for help. There's Foley below has a car'd take ye to the hospital and ye could drop in at the Guards on the way; the barracks is on the road.'

She barked at him in sudden panic: 'Don't you leave me alone. Do you hear me, I won't be left alone.'

He scratched his head again, cowed by the authority in her voice.

'Ye might be here all night,' he objected, but she made no reply.

There was the sound of an approaching motor; the labourer stood in the middle of the road and waved his arms; the car, an ancient Morris, drew up and a man stepped out, a youngish man in a city suit and soft hat; he ran his fingers through his hair, pushing the hat to the back of his head.

'That's a terrible smash,' he said in awed tones; 'is there many killed?'

'Tew fellas dayid and the lady hurrt.'

'Do the Guards know?'

'Sure, it's only just after happenin' and there's not been a soul here, only meself.'

'Tellya what; I'll go down for the Guards and they can phone for th'ambulance or whatever they like.' He turned to Isabel:

'You'll best stay where y'are till the Guards have been.' He did not wait for an answer but got into his car and drove off.

It seemed an age before he returned with two young Civic Guards. They satisfied themselves that the two men were dead, then, notebooks in hand, they peppered Isabel with questions: When did it happen, how did it happen, who was driving, how fast were they going? She made no attempt to answer them, but sat with her head in her hands. They sighed and began again.

One of them touched her arm: 'Can ye tell us yer name?' he asked gently.

'Isabel Millar.'

'Mrs. or Miss?'

'Mrs.'

'Were y'alone?'

She shook her head.

'Was it yer husband was widger?'

She shook her head again.

'Was it the wan in the ditch? What was his name, now?'

She nodded and told him.

'Was he the owner of this car?'

So it went on, an interminable, shameful process; at last they had all the details she could give them. She was shivering with pain and shock and misery. One of the Guards looked at her with compassion.

'Sure, the poor girrl ought to be in hospital,' he said.

'The ambulance'll be here anny time now.'

The four men pulled Denis's body out of the ditch and laid it reverently on the bank.

'Isn't it an awful thing, a fine-looking young fella like that!'

'What'll ye do with the corpses?'

The word 'corpses' came through to Isabel from the murmur of talk: Denis was a corpse! For the first time she was really aware that he was dead and she stared at them all in an agony of horror. Another car and a lorry had come up, and there was quite a little crowd. She looked for one reassuring face, but they were all wary and embarrassed, respectful, compassionate.

'Oh, what'll I do?' she moaned, still staring at them.

One of the Guards tapped his forehead: 'It's the shock,' he announced to the rest, and they all turned away to look at the sky or the road, at each other, anywhere but at her.

'There now,' said someone; 'don't be frettin' Miss; ye'll be in the hospital in a minyit.'

But Isabel had passed beyond the reach of comforting words; she was unconscious.

CHAPTER TWENTY-THREE

'Come in, Brian,' said Guy; 'Caroline's still powdering her nose, or something. Come on in and have a drink.'

Brian's face wrinkled in its friendly smile: 'Well, thanks.'

'Annie!' shouted Guy from the hall; 'Bring three sherry glasses.'

'Yes, Sir.' Annie's unkempt head came round the door to inspect the visitor. 'Is it tumblers ye want?' she enquired in a hoarse whisper.

'No, no; little glasses—the one with stalks.'

'Oah aye!' And the head disappeared again.

The curtains were undrawn in the little drawing-room; outside, the blue Spring dusk was settling round the weeping ash tree and the yellow daffodils; lambs cried in a nearby field; cherry-blossom glimmered whitely against the old yew tree. Guy closed the french window regretfully.

'Perfect!' he said; 'a really perfect day. Why we lived in Fitzwilliam Square all these years when we might have had this, I can't imagine.'

He went into the dining-room to fetch the sherry just as Caroline came in. Brian took both her hands:

'Well!' he said; 'lovelier than ever!'

'Just the same, really.' Caroline smiled as he bent over her hands, pressing them gently together; but he did not kiss them; instead, he looked up into her face with an amused smile as he let them go.

'My, but it's good to see you again!'

Annie, red-faced and sweating, put down a tray with shaking hands.

'Is them the right glasses, Miss?' she whispered anxiously; 'I thought maybe you'd like the end of the fruit-cake, so I put it on the thray.'

'Thanks, Annie,' and Caroline began to laugh helplessly, looking at the tiny wedge of cake on its huge plate; 'but I don't think we'll need it; you can take it away.'

'What'll yez eat then, with that old stuff?'

'Nothing: we don't want any food.'

Annie retreated in bewilderment; the ways of the gentry were an enigma to her.

'I'm glad you're taking Caroline out, Brian,' said Guy, closing the door gingerly, a decanter in each hand; 'she hasn't had any fun for months. Dark or pale?'

'Pale, please. I'll take her to Jammet's and we'll make beasts of ourselves.' He turned to Caroline: 'Do you like oysters?'

'Love them; but I like lobster even better.'

'Bless your heart, you shall have both if you want them,' and Brian rubbed his hands joyfully.

'It does me good,' said Guy, stretching out his feet towards the fire as he settled back in his chair, 'to hear people talking about food as if they enjoyed it.' He looked wryly at Caroline: 'What are we having, Puss?'

She wrinkled her nose: 'Soup, meat and savoury: left-overs, cunningly concealed.'

'Come with us and have a party,' suggested Brian eagerly.

'Oh, Daddy, do!'

Guy scowled at them: 'I wouldn't dream of it, indeed I wouldn't. Spoiling your evening!'

'But you wouldn't; we'd love it.'

'Nonsense; go off and enjoy yourselves.'

But they begged so hard that finally he gave in. 'Run and tell your mother,' he said to Caroline, 'while I clean myself up a bit.'

Helen received the news a little sourly; it was not that she envied them, nor that she disliked being left, but she objected to Brian O'Malley. She had never met him, never even seen him, but he was a friend of Guy's and Caroline's and, as such, a menace. There must be something wrong with him if they liked him so much. Nothing of this was put into words; she hoped, rather frigidly, that they would enjoy themselves and not be too late coming back. This was a dig at Guy: she had not forgotten the night of Isabel's wedding, when he had returned in the small hours of the morning, very drunk.

She made Nurse wheel her chair to the window, where she sat in silence, peering into the dusk to catch a glimpse of the object of her disapproval; the little that she was able to see was unimpressive; a small broad figure with a loud laugh. As the car swept out at the gate, she told Nurse to draw the curtains.

The telephone rang, pealing out through the silent house; they could hear Annie pounding from the kitchen to answer it, then heavy breathing as she opened a chink of the door and summoned Nurse in an alarmed, husky whisper. There was a low-voiced consultation in the passage, then Nurse's voice at the instrument.

Helen knew at once that there was something wrong. 'Annie,' she called imperatively; 'come here at once.'

'Yes, Ma'am.' Annie's scared figure edged round the door.

'Who is it? What's happened? I won't be kept in the dark; something's wrong.'

'Yes, Ma'am,' said Annie meekly; 'it's Mr. Stokes; he says Mrs. Millar's afther havin' an accident.'

'She's dead, I know she's dead: why don't you tell me?'

Nurse's great body heaved past the cowering Annie, confident and reassuring.

'Nurse, Mrs. Millar's dead: tell me the truth.'

Nurse laughed: 'Ach, not at all! She's after having a little motor accident, Mrs. Adair, but she's all right; they just took her to the hospital the way they could keep an eye on her, like.'

Helen looked at her contemptuously: 'Wheel me to the telephone,' she demanded.

'There now, Mrs. Adair, don't be frettin', I tell you she's all right.'

'Stop lying to me.' Helen shook her good fist at her nurse; 'do what I tell you and wheel me to the telephone at once. If you don't, I shall get ill again, and you know the doctor said another stroke would kill me.'

Hastily, Nurse pushed the chair into the hall.

'Stokes?' Helen's voice was clear and firm; 'is Mrs. Millar dead?'

'Ah, not at all, Ma'am; she was a bit hurt and the Guards just sent her in to the hospital in the ambulance.'

'What hospital, what Guards? Give me the details at once.'

Stokes really knew very little; he gave her the names of the hospital and the barracks. Helen rang off.

'Nurse, ring up the hospital at once and tell them I want to speak to the house surgeon or the matron; no one else will do.'

Isabel, she discovered, was suffering from concussion and a broken rib. Although she was still unconscious, her condition was not serious. She would, the young house surgeon cheerfully assured Helen, be on her feet again in a few days.

'Now get me the barracks.'

Nurse fumbled with the telephone directory; something Stokes had said made her very unwilling to allow Helen to speak to the Guards herself.

'Would you not let me get hold of Mr. Adair first?'

'Get me the barracks.'

'. . . and he could talk to the Guards himself. All this is very bad for you, Mrs. Adair, ye'll be makin' yerself ill again.'

Helen snatched the directory from her and thumbed the pages with her good hand.

'Get me that number,' she demanded, pointing at it with her nail. Nurse had to obey.

They could hear the burring of the bell at the other end. At last a soft slow voice replied; Helen took the receiver firmly.

'I understand there was a motor accident this afternoon on the road near you and that a Mrs. Millar was hurt. I am her mother, Mrs. Adair: please give me all the details.'

'Oh aye, there was an accident at five-seven this evening; Mrs. Millar was taken to hospital. We rang up the address she gave us and the fella there said he would inform the relatives.'

'Was anyone else hurt: what happened?'

'It was a very bad accident; the car collided with a lorry and the lorry dhriver and the gentleman was with Mrs. Millar was both killed.'

'There must be some mistake: Mrs. Millar was alone. She told my other daughter this afternoon that she was going out by herself.'

'There was a gentleman with her all right.' The voice retreated from the instrument for a moment and came faintly from a distance. 'What was the fella's name—the young fella was killed in the cyar?' There was a confused murmur of voices, then: 'It was a Mr. Joyce, Ma'am, a Mr. Denis Joyce; he and the lorry dhriver was both killed outright; Mr. Joyce's neck was broke. He had an address in Fitzwilliam Square and me colleague here informed the family. Pause; 'Are ye there?'

Helen was not there; she was leaning back in her chair with the receiver held away from her for Nurse to take.

'Ring off,' she whispered; 'tell them that's all I want to know.'

She closed her eyes; her face looked horribly pale and pinched. Nurse wheeled her grimly back to her room.

'I'll get you into bed,' she said gently; she did not dare ask Helen to tell her where Guy was; she would wait up for him and tell him about the accident when he came in.

But Helen was not going to be put to bed; she was in full command again, sitting upright in her chair, two bright spots on her pale cheeks.

'Ring up Jammet's restaurant and get hold of Mr. Adair; tell him what has happened and give him the name of the hospital so that he can call there on his way back. Ask him to come home as quickly as possible: I will give him the details then. Then ring up Sir Horace Millar and ask him to get in touch with Mr. Millar in Belfast: after all, someone will have to let him know.'

Nurse stared at her patient with a new admiration and respect, amazed that her brain should be so clear and her handling of the situation so efficient. A capable woman herself, she experienced a pang of mortification that it should be Helen, the invalid, who had been the first to think of poor Mr. Millar, whom everybody else seemed to have forgotten. She vented her irritation sharply upon Annie and the cook, telling them to get Mrs. Adair's dinner quickly and not stand around like a couple of hens in a flood, the poor lady was starving for want of a bite of food.

Helen, however, was feeling better than she had felt for months; she sat upright, her head uplifted, a gleam of triumph in her eye. She was important again, in charge of everything, ordering people about; and Denis Joyce was dead! Whatever intrigue Isabel had been carrying on was over now for good and all; there was nothing more to fear. Unless Mike . . . supposing Mike was difficult? But he would forgive Isabel; he was devoted to her and would believe her explanation, whatever it was, especially now that the other man was dead. Poor Mrs. Joyce! Her lips framed the words in a whisper, but she could find no pity in her heart; satisfaction would not allow it. It was really providential, one could never have hoped that . . . she really must not think like that, was wicked to be so glad that anyone was dead. She bowed her head to hide the flicker of a smile although there was nobody there to see if she had laughed outright.

Annie brought in her dinner on a tray. Nurse followed, her telephoning done. Mr. Adair was on his way and the other two were coming with him; he would just call at the hospital and come straight out. Helen's lips gave a little smack as she finished her soup: she was enjoying her dinner.

But when Guy arrived, she was in a nervous frenzy: the publicity! Guy must do something to keep Isabel's name out the papers.

He and Caroline came in smiling and radiating that determined cheerfulness which is supposed to reassure the invalid: Isabel was all right, not badly hurt at all and Helen was not to worry. Guy had seen the doctor and Caroline had even been up to have a peep at Isabel.

'Pah!' snapped Helen impatiently; 'sit down; you don't know the half of it.' Eyeing Guy with a gimlet-like stare, she told them the story bluntly. 'And,' she added, 'you've got to keep it out of the press, somehow.'

Guy was looking intently at his feet: 'My God, what a mess,' he murmured to himself; 'what rotten, rotten luck!'

'They must have met just by accident,' said Caroline quickly; 'she asked me to go to the pictures and have dinner with her and I said I couldn't.'

But Helen was bobbing with excitement and exasperation. 'Did you hear me. Guy? You've got to get it hushed up!'

'But there'll be an inquest.' He stared at her calmly as though this were a complete answer. 'You can't suppress the report of an inquest: it's just one of the things that can't be done.'

'But everybody'll think . . .'

'Of course they will: what do you think yourself?'

'I tell you, it will kill me.'

'Poor child,' he said softly. 'Helen, did she ever tell you she wanted to marry this Denis Joyce?'

Helen shrank back suddenly into her chair: 'Me? No!' she hissed viciously. 'You know quite well none of you ever tell me anything.' She paused for a moment, breathing thickly; 'But if she had, I'd have . . . I believe I'd have killed her!'

'Which accounts for the fact,' said Guy drily, 'that she never said a word to either of us. But I knew, and you knew, too, really; didn't you, Helen?'

She had almost given herself away. She sat glaring at him, her breath coming in little short gasps. 'No!' she said vehemently, 'I never knew anything about it, except that she wanted him to come to the dance. I've never heard his name mentioned since, until tonight. I . . . I'd forgotten that he ever existed.' She gave a cunning, side-ways look at Guy. 'I thought . . . wasn't he going to marry Juliet Moore?'

He was watching her curiously, almost as if he thought she was acting a part. She stiffened: 'Well, don't you believe me?' she queried sharply.

'Of course I believe you. But I don't believe you were taken in by Isabel's story about Juliet Moore, any more than I was. I wish to Heaven she'd defied us all and run away with him before she married poor Mike!'

The claw-like fingers grabbed at one arm of the chair as Helen struggled vainly to get on to her feet; her eyes had become suffused and bloodshot and her face was congested, with a pale puffiness round the eyes and nose.

'You . . . you've declared yourself at last! A Republican and a Roman Catholic and you wish she'd married him. Get out of my sight, get out, get out!' Her voice had risen to a shrill scream and she went on babbling and muttering, incapable of forming words any longer.

Guy leant over her and took her shoulders gently: 'Helen, Helen! You've misunderstood me. Listen, you've got to listen: I should have hated it, I should have fought against it with all my power, done everything to stop it. But if she'd taken her courage in both hands and done it, I . . . believe we might have been proud of her in the end, and she might have been happy. That's what 1 meant when I said . . .'

She was struggling to shake him off: 'Let me go, let . . . go. Think I'm powerless! Get out, both of you . . . never speak to me again.' They could hardly distinguish what she said, her voice had become so thick and weak. Caroline pulled urgently at Guy's sleeve.

'Come away, Daddy; you'll only make her have another stroke. Oh, do come away; I'll get Nurse.'

'I want her to understand: she must understand.'

Helen was exhausted, but she made a final effort. Raising her bloodshot eyes to Guy's, she spat full in his face and relaxed against the back of her chair.

He let her go and straightened himself slowly, feeling in his pocket for a handkerchief. He turned to the fireplace and wiped his face carefully.

'Come,' he said to Caroline in a compressed, low voice. They left the room in silence.

CHAPTER TWENTY-FOUR

Mike was behaving well; he said nothing to anyone to indicate that he considered it odd for Isabel to be driving about the mountains with Denis Joyce while he himself was absent in Belfast; he visited her regularly at the hospital, sent her immense quantities of fruit and flowers, asked eagerly when she would be allowed to come home and told everybody that Denis Joyce was an old friend of his, poor chap. But he drank regularly and steadily from the moment he left the office until Stokes took pity on him and put him to bed at night.

He and Guy went to the funeral together; neither of them would admit that by going they hoped to allay some of the scandal that was being whispered round Dublin. They stood at the back of the mourners, watching the implacable old figure at the grave-side, head bowed stiffly; Denis's father looked a hard man. The young brothers, four of them, were slight, dark and handsome; all alike, and all like Denis, but on a smaller, lighter scale. Mrs. Joyce had stayed at home, too stricken to appear. Mike rocked slightly on his feet; afterwards, he and Guy lunched lengthily at the Club. Mike was grateful to his father-in-law for his wordless support. They talked of small things, casually, and drank a great deal of gin.

At home, Guy did not speak of Helen. He and Caroline tried to forget about her, but she was there, between them, forcing her presence on them; they could hear her voice through the door as she talked to Nurse, hear her bell ringing, her trays being carried in. Nobody came to see her. She sent no message to them, but every morning Nurse would ring up the hospital, enquire for Mrs. Millar and return with the news to Helen's room. When they went out they could see her in her chair at the window, watching and silent. When they came back she would still be there. She must have seen Guy in his dark clothes on the day of the funeral, but she made no comment.

Caroline did not tell Guy that she had spoken to her mother since the night of the accident; the interview had been painful and quite useless.

She had spent a sleepless night in cold rage against her mother; she made up her mind that in the morning she would make her sorry for what she had done to Guy, repeat to her what he had said, make her listen and wrench from her an apology for her behaviour. Never in all her life had Caroline been so shocked as by Helen's bestial little action.

Calmly, after breakfast, she asked Nurse how Helen was. Tired, but not ill, was the reply; indeed she was wonderful and it wouldn't do her a bit of harm if Caroline went in to see her; looking sharply at her, Nurse said that her patient was in far better form than any of them.

So Caroline knocked at the door and Helen, thinking that it was Annie coming to do the room, had cooed: 'Come in.'

Caroline closed the door and stood against it: 'Mother, I want to speak to you.'

Helen, lying back, propped up on a mountain of pillows, eyed her icily: 'Get out of my room, child. I told you last night I didn't want to speak to you again.'

'I'm not going till I've finished.' Caroline found herself blushing, anger pricking at her, hands shaking foolishly. 'You . . . you . . .' she began, and had not the least idea how to go on; everything she had been going to say had fled from her. She put her hands behind her back and clutched the door handle. Helen's eyes were shut and she looked almost as though she were asleep.

'You're so unjust to Daddy: I won't have it. He's one of the nicest people in the world, and . . . are you listening, Mother?'

There was not the slightest movement from the bed; the hands lay flaccid on the sheet, the closed eyelids did not flicker. Caroline went nearer.

'You're pretending to be asleep or faint, or something, but it won't work. I know you can hear me and you're going to.' Trying hard to control her voice, she told her what Guy had said the night before. 'Now are you sorry, Mother, you did . . . what you did?' She felt suddenly ridiculous.

The eyelids lifted at last and the smouldering eyes were fixed on Caroline.

'No: I'm not sorry. Now will you go?'

Caroline's eyes brimmed with burning angry tears: 'Yes, I'll go, and I won't ever come back into this room again until you've told Daddy you're sorry.'

One hand pinched the hem of the sheet into a little fold and creased it carefully, but the head never moved.

'That is what I wish.' The voice was quite calm and a little faint. 'One of these days I shall die and you will be glad to be rid of me, you and your father. Every night I pray that I may die before the morning, but I am still here and I can do no more; so the best thing is to pretend that I am not here and to let me die in peace. I wish I could go somewhere else, but I have no money now and that is impossible.' She sighed heavily and paused, giving Caroline time to feel stricken with remorse. 'Perhaps you don't know what you've made me suffer, all of you,' she went on, unutterable reproach in the quietness of her voice, 'when all I've done is to stick to my faith and my principles. Do you think I've deserved the treatment you've given me?'

'But what have we *done*?' Caroline felt hideously guilty, the more so as she could not raise even a flicker of genuine repentance. Everything that Helen had suffered she had brought upon herself, refusing every approach with a rebuff, condemning them because they could not see eye to eye with her.

'Done! We used to be Loyalists, but now you won't even wear a poppy on Armistice Day. You . . .'

'I think it's provocative and foolish, in this country, like waving a Union Jack in the streets. Why advertise and infuriate people? I buy one, but I won't wear it here: I would, in England.'

'Not wearing one classes you with the Republicans; everyone knows who you are, in Trinity and everywhere. If you knew the agonies of shame I endured when you went into Trinity without a poppy! And you only laughed at me—yes you did! And you ask what you've done: you've chosen your friends from amongst the set who are glad the British left, and your father only encourages you. Between the lot of you, you've betrayed every tradition I brought you up to and you wonder why I despise you!'

'Haven't we a right to our own opinions: can't we have principles too?'

'Your opinions are treachery: you have no principles.'

There it was, that was the root of the whole trouble. 'Oh!' screamed Caroline in exasperation, 'you're impossible to argue with. If you could only *see*!'

'Do you think I don't see? And when you find I won't think like you, you go and cut me out of your lives as if I didn't exist. Surely a mother has some rights? But no, and your father's the same. Isn't that cruel, Caroline, very cruel?'

'It wasn't meant to be cruel, it was only self-protection. We've got to live our own lives. It's dishonest to pretend you believe in things that have ceased to mean anything to you. So we went our own way: it was either that or we had to quarrel all the time.'

'It was meant to be cruel, to punish me for not being like you and blackmail me into submission. But I've never given in, not for one moment have I weakened. And even though I'm all alone, I don't care now: I'm proud you all hate me!' Helen's eyes were flaming.

Looking at her, Caroline's heart gave a great pound and all her rage fell away. She realised suddenly, with pity and terror, that she had been abusing a mad woman.

'But Mother, we don't hate you, we don't, we don't!' She had begun to cry hopelessly. 'Can't we forget about politics and be friends again, all of us?'

'Never! It's not politics, it's faith, it's my religion. Now go away and never come near me again, do you hear? Never.'

It was no use; weeping bitterly from mortification, pity, exasperation and a sense of utter helplessness, Caroline left the room, never to speak to her mother again.

The inquest had been postponed until Isabel, the only witness of the accident, should have recovered sufficiently to give evidence. Everybody dreaded it and longed for it to be over. It was a barrier to be passed before life could become normal again. The prospect did not encourage Isabel to get well quickly; whenever the subject was mentioned, she became almost hysterical, but eventually she was pronounced to be fit for questioning and the day was fixed.

Guy and Sir Horace went with Mike to back him up. Isabel sat, tense with nerves; not far away was the straight, stiff back of old Mr. Joyce. There were very few people.

It was not too bad, after all; the Coroner was a merciful man, concerned only with the facts. The worst moment came when Isabel had to explain why Denis had been driving the car. She took a deep breath and began: she had, she said, met him quite by accident on a mountain road and given him a lift; he had asked if he might drive the car, which was a fast one, but knowing that he was a very good driver, she had agreed. No, he had never driven that car before, but he was acquainted with all makes of cars; perhaps he had been a little careless, she was forced to admit, but the road had seemed to be empty and the lorry driver had come tearing over the crest of the rise on the wrong side of the road. Both men had been killed instantly, she added in a barely audible whisper, her lip trembling and shoulders quivering.

The Coroner hastily told her that would be all and called upon the labourer who had come running to the scene of the accident.

Isabel sat down and buried her face in her hands; all the time she had been speaking she had felt the piercing glare of Denis's father eating into her; he had watched her, sitting rigidly in his seat, his fine old head upright and grim. She knew he held her responsible for the death of his son and that he doubted every word she said.

It was soon over. There was a verdict of accidental death, an expression of sympathy to the bereaved relatives, and they were free to go. Guy and Mike each grabbed an arm and rushed Isabel into the street; Sir Horace trotted swiftly behind. They all piled into Mike's car and drove off at once, watched from the top of the steps by the prophet-like figure of old Mr. Joyce.

Isabel was to spend the day quietly at Tallaght with Caroline; it had been agreed that the less she was left alone at present, the better. So Guy picked up his car at the office and drove her out there; she sat shivering beside him, looking quite numb and worn out.

'You're over the worst now, old lady.' She gave him a doubtful, side-long glance. 'If you can hold your head up and go about as much as possible with Mike, of course, it'll do as much as anything to stop people-talking.' He paused and added gently: 'You know, I admire Mike a hell of a lot for the way he's behaved: he . . . he's very fond of you, child.'

She nodded miserably and stared out at the road.

Helen was sitting in her chair at the French window; she took no notice of them whatsoever. Caroline met them on the steps.

'Better go and see Mother, I suppose,' said Isabel doubtfully.

Guy and Caroline looked at one another.

'Yes, do,' said Guy quickly; 'she, er-won't speak to us any more, but she might like to see you.'

Caroline had a blazing fire going and glasses out on the table.

'Was it very nasty. Daddy?' she said; 'I thought you'd like a drink when you came back.'

He rubbed his hands gratefully: 'Drink?' he said; 'We can't afford to drink now, but I can't do without it at the moment, I don't know about you. No, it wasn't too bad; very few people. The Press was there, of course, and old Mr. Joyce; he's a very hard-faced old man—something Old Testament about him.' He hurried off to fetch the decanters.

When Isabel came in, they set her in a big chair, hedged her about with cushions, put her feet up and handed her a glass of neat brandy.

'Drink that one up quickly and then have another,' advised Guy.

She gulped and smiled wanly.

'Now,' Guy leant forward in his chair, 'before we dismiss this business altogether, there's just one more thing. Isabel, you ought to go and see poor old Mrs. Joyce.'

Isabel nearly dropped her glass; she stared at her father in terror, her eyes quite black in her white face.

'Oh no,' she whispered; 'not me: I simply couldn't.'

There was a long silence.

'Wouldn't it do,' suggested Caroline, 'if she wrote?'

He shook his head: 'We've killed her son. I'd like to try and put things right, so to speak, between the two families: there's too much bitterness about. Couldn't you bring yourself to do it, Isabel, in a few days? I know it's a big thing to ask, but . . . I feel it might make some difference if you could.' He waited, looking hopefully at her, and added: 'It might be some comfort to the poor lady.'

Isabel's face crumpled: 'I couldn't. I just couldn't.'

It was her final admission of cowardice; she felt a complete failure. Tears of self-pity welled up in her eyes: people always demanded from her something more than she could bring herself to do and it was always the same; she couldn't, she just couldn't. 'Very well,' said Guy firmly, 'I'll go myself.'

Two days later he drove along Fitzwilliam Square to the Joyces' house. It was a brilliant day with a biting east wind; the hawthorns and plane trees in the square were out in vivid leaf and the great lawn was thick with fresh spring growth. The Square looked its best in the spring: the trees and bushes had not had time to acquire their summer coating of grime, house painters were at work, windows had been cleaned and new curtains put up. He looked up at their old house as he passed, and smiled; the white net curtains were immaculate, the railings shone with new black paint and the hall door was now moss-green; a brass plate, burnished to look like gold, bore the name of the new occupant in the smallest and most tasteful of lettering.

He dreaded his interview; reluctantly, he climbed out of the car and rang the bell. The little maid who opened the door surveyed him with doubt and dismay: oh yes, Mrs. Joyce was in all right, but she didn't think she would see him; she was hardly seeing anybody, like, only Father Byrne and her sisters, Mrs. Doyle and Mrs. Tuohy; she was that upset, since the accident when Masther Denis was killed and not even a priest to say a word over him. Ye'd be sorry for the poor lady, ye would indeed: was it on business he wanted to see her?

He handed her a card: 'Tell Mrs. Joyce I should be most grateful if she would see me for a short time.' He smiled his charming diffident smile. She looked at the name on the card.

'Oah, glory be to God!' she said, 'it's well for ye himself is out! I never saw a man in such a state. If he knew you were, here I think he'd take a gun to ye!' She began to whisper like a conspirator: 'Come on inside a minyit, till I take this up to her.' She peered down the street before standing aside to let him in. 'Ye'll be outa this, please God, before he comes in. Oah, mercy on us, what'll she say to me at all, when I show her this?' Clutching the card tightly, she disappeared helter-skelter up the stairs.

Somewhere in the house a gramophone was playing dance music and a dog was barking; kitchen laughter ascended from the basement and from the garage at the back came the sound of a motor bicycle being started; it sputtered and died away. Standing there, in the dim hall that was the very pattern of the one that had been his own a few doors away, Guy had the sensation of being a stranger in his own home. There was the door that, in his old house, had led into his study, but outside it was an untidy coat-stand crammed with mackintoshes, overcoats and hats belonging to people he had never known. A couple of bicycles leant against the wall where the telephone table had been; the paint was scarred and battered on the walls. There was a savoury smell of bacon and cabbage, still lingering from the mid-day dinner. His own house had been quiet and orderly, but this one was vibrant, pulsating with the life of a large and active family.

The little maid came tumbling down the stairs: Mrs. Joyce would see him. She showed him into the chilly front drawing-room which was rigidly tidy; the ugly furniture was straight and stiff and the smooth cushions looked as if they had never been disturbed; there was a faintly musty smell. It was a dead room, never used. The maid had put a match to the fire, but the flame had not spread beyond a blackened patch of newspaper and had gone out. The double doors were closed, but through them he could hear cautious, laboured movements: the snap of a spectacle case, the relieved groan of ancient chair springs as a heavy body heaved itself up, a subdued gasp of exertion, the minute sound of hair being combed; then a chair being pushed out of the way on the carpet, and slow, painful footsteps.

Guy had lost the feeling that he was back in his old house; this ungracious flowerless room was not home. As he heard a fumbling at the door handle his courage failed him and he wished from the bottom of his heart that he had not come.

Mrs. Joyce was dressed in deepest mourning; an elderly dog followed her stiffly into the room and sniffed suspiciously at Guy. He held out his hand, but it was ignored; he received a formal little nod and a sharp blue glance.

'Wontcher sit down, Mr. Adair?'

Mrs. Joyce seated herself with dignity, smoothing her black skirt over her knees, and waited.

Guy bit his lip with embarrassment and sat on the edge of a high-backed chair; the rheumy old dog took up his place between them and stared into the chilly grate, trembling in his rigid limbs.

'Mrs. Joyce,' began Guy, and paused; but he was going to get no encouragement. Mrs. Joyce was watching him silently, her head on one side like an intelligent old bird.

'I don't want to distress you in any way,' he went on, 'but I do want you to know how deeply sorry we are, my whole family, about what has happened. Isabel was too . . . upset to come herself, and my wife is now an invalid and can't get about at all. I came, because I felt there might be some, well, some bitterness in your mind about things. I wish you would reassure me that there isn't. I didn't feel it was possible to express what I felt in a letter or I should never have intruded upon you.'

'Bitterness!' Her voice was harsh; 'isn't it too late to talk like that now, Mr. Adair? Eighteen months ago ye didn't mind about bitterness.'

'Eighteen months ago? I'm afraid I don't know what you mean.' His voice seemed so genuinely puzzled that she looked at him curiously. But she hardened her heart. He knew: he was only pretending to have forgotten.

'I'm talkin' of the time I went behind me husband's back to call on your wife,' she said bluntly, fixing him with an outraged blue eye.

'Oh, I'm sorry,' he said humbly; 'I'm afraid she never told me.'

'Mr. Adair, you're a good liar, but you can't deceive me: sure, I have the letter yet.' She was trying to get to her feet, her face red with anger.

He passed a hand over his face in complete bewilderment: 'Oh, please don't go. Do believe me, I haven't the least idea what you're talking about: what letter?'

'The letter she wrote, poor woman, after spendin' a week trying to get you to agree to lettin' my Denis and your Isabel get married. And you wouldn't hear . . .' She stopped, suddenly convinced that he really knew nothing about it.

He sat quite still and gaped at her, unable to think of a single word to say. Anger against Helen for her calculated villainy swelled up viciously; he felt that when he got home he would kill her. He saw a pair of hands before him, fingers outstretched to grip, then tightening inwards; brutal, murderous hands. With a sudden jerk of horror he found they were his own; he put them down quickly and grabbed the edge of his chair. He must think of something to say, and, now that the truth was out, his momentary impulse to murder Helen died away and he found himself pitying her and wanting to protect her from the hideous consequences of her action; nobody understood her as he did or could see how, in her warped mind, she thought she had done right.

But it was too late now to go back; Mrs. Joyce straightened herself in her chair:

'So she never told you,' she said hotly; 'may God forgive her, for I never can!' She took out her handkerchief and wept; then, falteringly, she began to tell him the story of her visit to Helen and the letter at the little cake shop. But Guy stopped her.

'Don't,' he said gently; 'don't tell me any more. The harm is done and there's no good going over it.'

She looked him steadily in the face: 'You would have let them marry, Mr. Adair,' she said, and there was no query in her voice. 'That's what she was afraid of.'

Guy shook his head: 'What makes you think I would have?'

'You'd have fought against it, but you would have given in, in the end. You're a merciful man, Mr. Adair, and you would have seen it was no good striving against it. I know you better than you know yourself.'

He bent his head and stood up to go: 'I should have done something: I knew they were in love with each other, but I waited for one of them to say something to me and they never did.'

'We were all to blame,' she said; 'maybe I deserved what happened; maybe it was my punishment for goin' behind me husband's back, but I did it for the best.'

'I would like you to believe that my wife meant it for the best, too,' he said quietly.

'Ah, but the pity of it!' She shook his hand warmly. 'Don't be sorry you came, Mr. Adair, for I'm glad. And will you give your Isabel a message from me? Tell her not to fret, poor child, there's no good in looking back. I thought I could never forgive her, but that's past now. It's late to wish her happiness in her marriage, but I wish it now: will you tell her?'

'I will, indeed.' Guy gave her a smile of genuine liking; she stood at the door, the ancient dog beside her, dabbing her eyes unashamedly and nodding to him as he got into the car.

He drove straight back to Tallaght, his mind in a turmoil. Helen would be at the window in her chair, when he got home, a book on her knee, watching; she watched the avenue all day, now, as though she feared that some enemy might creep up unawares and jeer at her. He felt he must talk to her, tell her that he knew about everything, that it no longer mattered . . .

He drove in at the gate and turned the car on the gravel sweep; Helen was not there, the window was empty. He stepped out of the car and stood for a moment, listening; from behind the house came the whirr of the mowing machine, the most peaceful sound in the world.

A white figure appeared at the door and came rushing out to meet him; it was Nurse and she was terribly upset.

'Oh, Mr. Adair, I have terrible news for you!'

Caroline? Isabel? His face went very white.

'Tell me what it is, quickly.'

'It's Mrs. Adair, Sir; she took another stroke after lunch and she passed away at ten minutes to four. We couldn't get hold of you at all, nobody knew where you were, and Miss Caroline's out since twelve and didn't come back since.'

Helen was dead; perhaps his hate had killed her in that horrible moment when he had made that murderous gesture with his hands. He felt guilty and ashamed.

'There now. Sir; sure it's a merciful release, when you come to think of it and all the poor lady had to live for.'

He could bear Nurse's well-intentioned condolences no longer; he felt none of the conventional emotions and he must spare her the shock of perceiving this; she was looking for tears and his heart felt like a stone.

He nodded and murmured something as he walked past her into the house. If only Caroline would come back! She was someone he could talk to without pretence. He went into the drawing-room and shut the door; nobody would disturb him here, they would respect his sorrow and wait until he rang or called. His sorrow! All he felt was that Helen had cheated him again.

He crossed over to the window and looked over the green fields to the mountains beyond. From behind the house came the whirr-whirr of the mowing machine.

CHAPTER TWENTY-FIVE

The kitchen cat picked his way fastidiously over the daisies towards the delphinium spires that stood so straight and grand and misty in the border; he had a nest there, the slightest of hollows in the dry earth, where he could lie under the broad-palmed leaves and watch the world with lazy blinking eyes on days when the dogs were out, or curl himself tightly nose to tail and sleep. He paused with uplifted paw, suspicious of the two slack figures lying in deck chairs under the chestnut tree. A white butterfly flitted aimlessly out of the flowers and wavered across the grass over his head; he watched it approaching, head turning as it came, and stood on his hind-legs to catch it in his paws; up, in a leaping movement, an arabesque of liquid blue-black fur in the sunlight. He missed it and held the upright pose for a moment, subsiding airily to yawn and resume his course towards his secret lair. He lay there, darkly, at full length, coral tongue curled at the tip and protruding slightly, yellow eyes gleaming from the shadows. It was hot and he was panting.

Moira smiled and sat up; she had been watching all the time. She glanced warily at Caroline and swung her feet furtively to the ground.

'What's wrong?' asked Caroline, sitting up.

'Oh dear! I thought you were asleep.'

'And you were going to creep off and do something without disturbing me.'

'I just thought I'd tell Minnie we'd have tea out here; after all, there are only about three days in the year when . . .' Moira looked as guilty as if she had been caught stealing. 'Well, thank you, darling, if you would. . .'

'You're *awful*!' Caroline turned round severely, half-way to the house; 'You never will learn that people like doing things for you.'

'And you never will learn that when you do things for me it makes me feel about a hundred, and paralysed at that,' retorted her aunt. 'Come back quickly, I want to talk to you.'

She relaxed in her chair, watching Caroline's disappearing figure in its grey-green linen frock, her hair shining like fiery gold in the sun, bare legs twinkling brown in white sandals as she ran.

'That incredible hair!' she murmured to herself; 'where does she get it from?'

She listened to the click and whirr of the mower, cutting hay, and the strident cry of a corn-crake retreating further and further into her dwindling domain which by the evening would be laid flat in shimmering sweet-smelling strips. Moira felt the regret of summer, of lovely things destroyed. Tomorrow, Paddy would come and shear the daisies off the lawn and she would tell him she was glad, that it had needed doing badly, when all the time she would be looking forward to next week when they would have grown again and she could look out of the window at the star-strewn grass.

'Now,' she said briskly, a little ashamed of her soft-heartedness as Caroline reappeared, 'I told you I wanted to talk to you. You know, it won't be very long before David's home again and you'll be getting married.'

Caroline sat on the grass and hugged her knees, chewing a daisy stem: 'Well?' she said warily.

'You are going to marry him, aren't you?'

'Did Daddy say something . . .?' She gave Moira a horrified look.

'No, darling; nobody said anything, least of all yourself; but I just knew. It made me ill to look at you, all last winter when you were here with your mother, getting whiter and thinner every day and not saying a word to anybody. You made it very hard for anyone to help you.'

Caroline blushed with remorse: 'It makes me miserable even to think of last winter,' she said; 'I don't know what happened to me.'

'I do,' said Moira gently; 'adoring your father the way you do, you couldn't forgive your mother for not feeling the same about him; and you tortured yourself because you'd lost all affection for her and she for you. When she wouldn't speak to you, it made you feel that you were wicked and heartless not to care more; and so everything became more and more awful and you got into a state where everything was poisoned for you. But you're on your feet again now, aren't you?'

'Yes,' said Caroline slowly; 'when Mother died, everything got all right again. Isn't that an awful thing to say, Aunt Moira?'

'No,' said Moira firmly, 'it isn't; we may as well be honest. Your mother was a fanatic and she nearly wrecked all your lives; she thought she was doing right, but she had a terrible creed—I never realised how terrible until she unburdened herself to me about you all one night last winter, the night before you left for Dublin. So I shouldn't feel guilty about her any more, if I were you: just try to forget, and when you do remember her, be merciful.' She smiled: 'Well, to go back to what we were talking about, what's going to happen to your father when you've gone?'

Caroline removed the daisy stem from her mouth: 'I know,' she said, 'it's a problem and I haven't had the heart to talk to him about it yet. I was wondering if Miss O'Connor would come back and house-keep for him.'

'He's going to be awfully lonely;' Moira stopped, wishing she had left that unsaid. Everyone knew that he was going to be miserable but there was nothing anyone could do about it. 'Would she come?' she added as an afterthought.

'I think she would: those kids she's been with must be getting quite old now.'

'And you think he could bear it?'

'He's going to hate it anyway, but I think it would half kill him if we got a stranger in to look after him.'

'Mm,' said Moira contemplatively; a tiny black spider had fallen on to her skirt; she held her finger for it to climb and shook it gently off, over the grass; as it fell, it wove, and stayed suspended from her outstretched hand. 'You know,' she went on slowly, watching the swinging spider, 'I don't think I've ever felt so sorry for anyone as I have for your father during the last year or two: everything's gone wrong for him, and he's such a dear, he doesn't deserve it.' She picked a blade of grass and wound the spider's thread round it, then laid it gently on the ground. 'However, that's neither here nor there; there's something else I want to talk about: David must learn something about farming. If you and he are ever going to live here, you'll be ruined unless he does. I'm not joking; it's terribly important.'

Caroline wrinkled her nose: 'I don't know how he's ever going to learn about farming in the Navy!'

Moira smiled: 'He can pick up a lot from books, but there's an awful lot he can only learn by experience. Of course, a good steward makes all the difference and we've been very lucky—Morgan's a paragon amongst stewards. Now I have a sort of plan; when you two are married, I'm going to make over part of the house to you, all for yourselves, if you'll treat it as your home and come here for your leaves; then David can get to know the place and the men, going round with Archie and Morgan, and find out how it's run.'

'To have this as home,' said Caroline; 'oh, how lovely!' She stopped short, aware that Moira's face was very serious.

'I want you to spend every minute you can here. You see,' Moira was speaking in a little dry, husky voice, 'it's more urgent than you think: Archie's got a bad heart. He may be able to carry on for several years, but on the other hand he might . . . go quite suddenly.'

'Oh, Aunt Moira!' said Caroline brokenly; she put out her hand to touch her aunt's, but they could say no more for a little procession was coming from the house; Paddy, carrying a wicker table, followed by Minnie with a laden tray, a folded cloth tucked under her arm.

'Was it here ye wanted it, Ma'am?'

'Yes, Paddy; and you'll bring some more chairs?' Moira's voice was perfectly steady.

Minnie was clattering with cups and spoons: 'Shall I wet de tea, Ma'am? De Captain and de gentleman was coming up to de house.'

'Yes, Minnie; make it in the big tea-pot, they'll be thirsty.'

Minnie turned to go, but half-way across the lawn she stopped suddenly, peering into the delphiniums in the border.

'Arrah, look at dat!' she exclaimed in triumph; 'if it isn't me old pussums! Come on now, me old doat, come on wid Minnie and I'll give ye a sup o' milk in the kitchen away from dem old dogs. Sure, dem old dogs'd devour ye!' She picked up the long black unprotesting body and carried it, hanging limply from the crook of her arm, back to safety, murmuring to it as tenderly as to a child.

The dogs came rushing across the lawn, thrust wet noses into Moira's hand and flung themselves panting on the grass; round the corner of the house came Guy and Archie, slowly, talking hard. It was all so peaceful, so friendly and so perfect that Caroline suddenly felt that she could bear it no longer. Blind with tears, she tried to get to her feet, but Moira's hand was on her shoulder.

'Don't go, darling; I'll give you time.'

That made it worse; Caroline felt humbled to the ground by the sight of such courage. She must get away and hide her shame and weakness. But through her tears she had a blurred vision of Moira's face, calm, strong and radiant, and there flashed upon her the certainty of what she had often guessed before, that her aunt was a deeply religious woman. From that face, Caroline drew the strength to control herself.

Moira kept the others busy, talking about the haymaking and making little jokes about Minnie's devotion to the cat. Minnie came flying out with the teapot.

'Are y'at home, Ma'am? Dere's visitors at de door.'

'Oh hell!' growled Archie; 'who is it, Minnie?'

'It's de Reverend Wilson, Sir, and Mrs. Wilson.'

'Yes, of course, bring them out,' said Moira quickly, giving Archie an amused little frown; 'and, Minnie, bring some more cups and chairs and things and cut some more bread and butter, very thin. Run, or they'll think there's no one in the house.'

Minnie turned and ran as fast as her stout legs would carry her.

'Now why,' complained Archie, 'on an afternoon like this, do people have to . . . Puh, Moira, you'll have to do something about that woman Minnie, she stinks.'

'Lend me a comb, Caroline darling, my hair's standing on end. It's a very hot day, she's not generally as bad as this.'

'Haven't got one, sorry. And my face must be awful,' wailed Caroline.

Archie regarded them with calm severity: 'I've never met anything like you women! Neither of you has a hair out of place, and as for Caroline's face, poor Mrs. Wilson wouldn't notice if she polished it. Here they are.'

Round the corner rolled a beaming, buxom figure in a huge green floppy hat and flowered sleeveless frock, followed by a diminutive black-clad husband, smiling deprecatingly.

'The female,' Archie announced solemnly to Guy, 'is more deadly than the male.'

They stood up with resigned and smiling faces to greet the rector and his wife.

'How are the children?' Moira asked Mrs. Wilson, when they had all settled down.

'Oh, having great sport today in the hay; all except Nan, she's gone to a tennis party at the Websters, you know, the new bank manager and his wife, at Kilbeg. They seem to be very nice, friendly sort of people. Their son is at home now, y'know,' she added significantly.

'I must call on them.' Moira always felt that she neglected her social duties; 'Caroline, we might do that tomorrow.'

'The next wet day,' murmured Caroline, hoping that Mrs. Wilson would not hear.

'It's a great pity you had to leave Trinity, Miss Adair,' went on the rector's wife; 'indeed, it's all I can do not to call you by your Christian name, for when Nan's there it's Caroline this and Caroline that until I can think of you by no other name. Nan says she misses you something terrible, you were always so good to her.'

'Indeed,' protested Caroline with perfect truth, 'I wasn't at all, I . . .'

'Ah, now, now! She says if it hadn't been for you she doesn't know how she'd ever have got through her first year, she was that strange!'

'Caroline's good to everyone,' said Moira smiling, 'although perhaps she doesn't always know it.'

'Nan says all the boys in College were mad about her, engaged and all as she was,' Mrs. Wilson rattled on; 'I hear Captain Hamilton's been doing great things in India,' and she gave a sly look at Caroline; 'getting the M.C. and all sorts of things on the North-West Frontier; Nan says she always knew he had it in him, although he used to be a quiet sort of a boy with nothing much to say for himself. There was a time there a couple o' years ago when I used to see his car passing nearly every day, I used to think he must be sweet on you, Miss Adair, but Nan says . . .'

Caroline was not allowed to know what Nan said, for the rector leant across to his wife and interrupted the conversation:

'Was it on Tuesday or Wednesday we heard about the . . .'

'It was on Thursday,' she replied with decision; 'I know, because I was getting the eggs ready to take in and Nan said . . .'

'There now, I knew I was wrong! It was on Thursday,' announced the rector with proud certainty; 'she never makes a mistake about the date.'

'Well, anyway,' continued Mrs. Wilson, 'old Sir Hercules is as pleased as punch about it and Mrs. Farrell at the Post Office says he sent him a long cable of congratulations that cost him over a pound,

even though he didn't put in the ands and ams and wills, fancy that!'
She suddenly assumed a tremendously arch expression: 'And when's
your young man coming home, Miss Adair?'

'Some time next winter, I think.'

'And I suppose you'll be married straight away? Nan says . . .'

So it went on; Moira smiled secretly at Caroline; they relaxed and
began to think of other things while this stream of talk swept over
them, until Mrs. Wilson rose suddenly to her feet, announcing that
with Nan not there, there was no knowing what the children would
be up to and she must go instantly.

'Come, Robert,' she commanded; and Robert stood up obediently
although he was in the middle of a discussion about the sexton's wages.

'Who drives?' asked Archie at the car, wondering which door to
hold open for the rector's lady.

'Oh, Robert's the driver! He wouldn't trust me at all,' she exclaimed,
revelling in the weakness of her sex. 'Oh, goodness gracious me, I nearly
forgot! Nan's having a little tennis party on Tuesday, Miss Adair, and I
was to be sure and ask you to come. There'll only be the Websters and
ourselves, and the curate from Kilbeg. Of course I know our poor court
isn't quite up to club standards, but still,' and she gave Guy a roguish
look, 'the young people seem to be able to enjoy themselves just the
same! Now do come, Miss Adair, won't you?'

'I'd love to,' lied Caroline weakly as they drove off.

Moira smiled at her comically: 'Was Nan a great trial to you at
Trinity?'

'She was the bane of my life,' replied Caroline with fervour.

Guy put his hand on her shoulder: 'Walk down to the sea with me,
through the Glen?'

She nodded: 'I think I'll just get a jersey.'

They set off, arm in arm, through the quiet wood; the heat of the
day was wearing off, but there was no breeze; even the birds were silent.

'Did Moira tell you about Archie—that he's got a dicky heart?'

'Yes. '

'He was telling me this afternoon; he's worried about David, that he may not want to give up his career, perhaps fairly soon, to settle down here. Have you any idea how he feels about it?'

'None whatever,' admitted Caroline unwillingly; 'we've never discussed it. But he's awfully keen on the Navy.'

'What's he think about this government?'

'I . . . I don't really know,' she faltered.

'And it'll be how many months before he gets back?'

'About six.'

'Anything might happen in between; you've no idea what a state Archie's in about it—not about himself, he says he's had a good life, but about the place. He's going to write to David and lay the whole thing before him; what worries him is the thought that David may come to hate this place for dragging him away from his career, or may want to leave it empty for ten or fifteen years. He feels Butler's Hill would die if it wasn't loved. You know,' he added gently, 'it's been his whole life, this place is everything to him.'

They were in the Glen now, walking slowly down the mossy path under the roof of translucent green. Through the funnel of trees at the bottom they could just see the water, shimmering calm in the open sunlight. Caroline stopped.

'It's my life too,' she said, almost in a whisper, looking not at him but straight beyond to the light; 'it always has been. When I was a child I used to dream about this place. When it was empty, after the house was burnt down, I used to imagine that I lived in it and was watching over it until somebody came back to live here. I think I spent more time here, in those six years when we never came near the place, than I ever did in Dublin.'

She had forgotten that Guy was there; her hands were slightly lifted, palms outward, in that gesture of salute that had come to her as a child. She was suddenly aware of him again and dropped her hands, shaking her head with a quick little movement as though to escape from her mood. She put her hand on his arm again.

'Do you know, Daddy,' she said with surprising fierceness, 'I really believe that if anybody else was going to come here but David and me, and I was going to be shut out, I'd hate them and want to kill them. If I knew that I could never come here again, something would die inside me. Am I very wicked?' and she smiled.

'Wicked?' said Guy; 'maybe! But thank God you do feel like that. If you can only induce David to feel the same!'

'I think he will,' she said slowly; 'he hasn't had to face it yet, but when the time comes, I think he'll choose this.'

They were silent until they reached the sea.

'By the way,' said Guy with an amused little smile; 'did you ever write that letter—the one to David.'

Caroline looked rather ashamed: 'When it came to the point, I couldn't do it. Look, the tide's out,' she was pulling at his arm; 'come and play ducks and drakes!'

She was like a child again, trying to make him hurry; he shook his head helplessly and allowed himself to be made to run.

CHAPTER TWENTY-SIX

Guy tried to persuade her to stay on at Butler's Hill when he went back to Dublin; he and Annie, he said, would manage beautifully by themselves, and the cook could do the house-keeping; one man who was out all day did not need three strong women to look after him. But Caroline was adamant; she was beginning to realise how very soon she would be leaving him for good, and she was determined to do everything in her power to make him happy while she could.

She hated leaving Moira, who was being so brave and gay and behaving just as she always did when she had no worries; and it cut her to the heart to leave Butler's Hill in the height of the summer, when the corn was yellowing in the fields and the wind blew the warm buttery scent of the gorse from the hills, the cloud shadows chased across the sea, turning it from green to purple, and the short summer storms passed over to leave the countryside glistening and gleaming in the sun. She told herself that it was no hardship; Tallaght would be green and pleasant, the same sun would shine upon her there, and the gorse on the Dublin mountains would be out in full glory.

Tallaght was pleasant, and Guy was grateful; he consulted her about everything, instructed her about money matters and asked her opinion of people. They went to the Horse Show with Brian O'Malley, who was making a name for himself as a sheep farmer and who was exhibiting a stand full of tweeds with great success.

One night, Isabel and Mike came to dine with them; they were both very silent and Mike was already a little drunk. After dinner, over the coffee, he turned to Isabel:

'Have you told them yet?'

She looked uncertainly from Guy to Caroline and back again: 'Not yet.'

Mike threw his head back: 'We're starting a family,' he announced, as though he expected somebody to deny it.

Guy noticed the 'we' and his eyes narrowed for a brief second.

'I'm very glad,' he said quickly; 'when's it to be?'

Mike's chin went even higher: 'Christmas.' He watched their faces, waiting for their brows to pucker in the effort of mental arithmetic, but Guy needed to do no sums.

'Splendid!' he said, rather more heartily than he would have wished, prompted by renewed admiration for Mike. 'So I'm to be a grandfather! Caroline, how'll you like being an aunt?'

Caroline smiled: 'Which do you want: a girl or a boy?'

'Strangely enough,' said Mike rather awkwardly, 'I think I'd like it to be a girl, this time.'

'Little girls are fun.' Guy spoke with conviction; 'they're so intensely feminine from the very beginning.'

'Yes,' Mike relaxed and smiled; 'that's what I think.' He looked greatly relieved.

Poor Mike, thought Guy; he could bear the thought of fathering Denis's daughter, but a son would be too much. In spite of all his gallant efforts, it was apparent that he had no illusions about being the happy father. Guy felt miserable: he and Helen were responsible for this. He noticed gratefully that Caroline was talking; he himself could think of nothing to say. Isabel looked frightened and unhappy; probably both she and Mike were secretly hoping that the child would be born dead.

Isabel was tired and wanted to go home. Guy raised his glass:

'Here's to you both!' he said gently, wondering what Sir Horace and Lady Millar thought about it all.

Mike fetched Isabel's coat and held it carefully while she slipped her arms into the sleeves; he was a little unsteady on his feet. Her bag was on the sofa, he picked it up and handed it to her. Not once did he touch her; he had held his fingers away so that they would not even brush the hair that fell in curls at the back of her neck as he pulled the coat up on her shoulders. Guy watched them leave the house; close together, immeasurably apart. If they were like that in front of other people, what must they be like alone together? He wanted to weep.

Aunt Emma summoned Caroline to lunch with her again; she had had a letter from Moira and was in a fever in case David was going to be difficult.

'You must use all your influence with him, dear,' she said helplessly. 'I do hope poor dear Moira is being careful of Archie and not letting him do strenuous things, row boats and so on. We must do everything we can to keep him alive as long as possible. I don't mean because of David only,' she added in confusion, 'but he is such a dear nice person one would hate anything to happen to him.' She herself, she said, would do her best; she was writing to David, pointing out to him in the strongest terms where his duty lay.

Caroline knew just what the letter would be like. Good, excellent Emma would cover many pages with her old-fashioned hand and Victorian sentiments, underlining important words and phrases invoking divine guidance and stating that her heart would break if he failed in his responsibilities. It would make David miserable.

'Oh, Aunt Emma, don't be cross with me,' she said quickly; 'but . . . please don't write to him like that.'

'Why ever not, child?' Emma's tone was irritable. 'Someone must tell him what he ought to do.'

'He's grown-up, he's not a child any longer: let him make his mind up himself.'

Emma stared at her as if she thought her mad; her face was red with indignation: 'But he might make it up wrong!'

'Listen,' said Caroline, trying hard to suppress her annoyance; 'I love Butler's Hill, but I'd rather it was taken over by the Land Commission and broken up into three-acre farms than that David should go and live there against his will. Don't you see that if he's pushed into it he'll have a grudge against it all his life? I want him to go there more than anything in the world, but I'm not going to say a single word to influence him. If he went there because we made him, he'd hate me before we'd been there a year. He must be free, Aunt Emma, for us ever to be happy together. And 1 believe in him,' she added, 'enough to know that he'll do what he thinks right without being told. Oh, do try and have faith in him too; you brought him up and . . .'

But Emma was in floods of tears. Suddenly penitent, Caroline left her seat and threw her arms round her neck.

'Don't be angry,' she begged; 'I didn't mean to hurt you; please, Aunt Emma, say you aren't angry with me.'

'I can't understand young people these days,' wept Emma; 'they've no gratitude and no sense of duty; they won't let anyone help them; they think we're all . . . old and . . . and stupid and useless.'

'No, we don't, you mustn't think that. David loves you and so do I. It's only that I think no one can make decisions for other people, even if they are young and inexperienced. Please, please, Aunt Emma, do believe me and don't send that letter to David.'

'Very well,' conceded Emma, still mortally hurt; 'but I can't see why I'm not to be allowed to give my own son advice.'

It took Caroline most of the afternoon to pacify her; she returned to Tallaght worn out, but triumphant.

Annie met her in the hall:

'There's some kind of a tallygram for ye, Miss Caroline.'

It was a cable from David: 'Coming home Christmas stop Can you fix wedding January stop Love you darling.'

She had a lump in her throat: he had been so excited that he couldn't wait to tell her the news, even by air mail. Oh, he was a darling! She felt that she would burst from sheer gratitude for being loved like that. Seizing the astonished Annie round the waist, she pranced her down the passage to the kitchen.

When Guy came in, she told him the news gently, over tea. He made a very good attempt to appear delighted.

'Well, I suppose we shall have to start making plans,' he said; 'where'd you like to be married?'

'What about Butler's Hill? Aunt Moira's longing for it to be there.'

'Of course, there'd be one big advantage in having it there.'

Caroline looked suspicious: 'What's that?'

'You'd be able to have Nan for a bridesmaid!'

'Daddy, you beast!' and she made a face at him.

'But seriously,' he went on, 'I don't think it would be a good thing, my dear. You can't ask poor old Emma to go tearing round the country in mid-winter, at her age; not that she's so very old, but she's not strong. And besides, there'd be a lot of expenses, fares and things to pay. I'm afraid, Puss, you'll have to be content with a small wedding, just relations and old friends; I can't afford a show like we had for Isabel.' He sighed, frowning unhappily.

Caroline kissed him: 'Don't worry, Daddy: I'd rather have it that way, truly I would.' She felt she would agree to almost anything that would take that worried look off his face whenever he talked about money.

He gave a sudden rueful little smile: 'You know, I'm jealous of David already: I'm sure he doesn't deserve you, Puss.' He gave one of her tawny curls a gentle tug. 'I think you're going to be very happy, you two, bless you both!'

He had not said a word about himself and what he would do when she was gone.

'And what's going to happen to you, Daddy?' she asked softly; 'Who's going to look after you?'

'Never mind about me, I'll manage beautifully.' He was turning his cigarette lighter over and over on his palm; suddenly he put it down firmly on the table. 'Well,' he said; 'I'm sure you and Moira have been plotting something: let me hear what it is.'

'We thought perhaps Miss O'Connor might come back . . .'

'I could give up the house and live in a hotel . . .'

'No, Daddy, live in a house; you'll be lonelier amongst a lot of people.'

He smiled: 'You know, you frighten me sometimes; you have an uncanny way of knowing things. Well, I'll think about it.'

Annie's head came round the door: 'Misther O'Malley.'

'Oh Lord!' Caroline stood up, an expression of horror on her face; 'he's taking me out to dinner and I'd forgotten all about it!' And she fled upstairs to change.

At dinner, she told Brian that she was fixing the date of her wedding.

'You don't say,' he said, and shook his head disapprovingly at her beaming face.

'Don't be so cross: you knew it had to come.'

'Sure I knew, but I always kidded myself somehow that it wouldn't, that you might get tired of that man of yours, or maybe just tired of waiting for him. We've had some good times together, haven't we?' He smiled his crooked friendly smile.

'We have indeed,' said Caroline warmly.

'My!' He looked at her regretfully, as though he were seeing her for the last time; 'how I'm going to miss you is just nobody's business; I've come to count on you, somehow.' He was leaning towards her, across the little table, but with a gesture of distaste he looked round the room at all the other diners and sat back. 'All these dam' people,' he said disgustedly, laying down his knife and fork; 'let's have coffee and go for a drive up the mountains. I want to talk to you: O.K.?'

She nodded. In a moment he had waiters flying round, fetching coffee, making up the bill, bringing glasses of liqueur brandy. He drank his quickly, as though it were a medicine, and waited impatiently until she had finished.

'Now,' he said, and shepherded her swiftly to the door.

His ancient Ford groaned its way up Grafton Street and out towards Rathfarnham, past the lighted, crowded trams that charged shuddering and banging along the streets. Out of the city it was chilly and very quiet and there was a frigid semi-moon.

'Frost!' he announced, sniffing the air as he put the car at the long hill past the Hell-Fire Club; 'we'll go to the top and back by Glencullen. Can you walk?'

'Walk? Yes, why?'

'We'll take a little walk at the top, up the Featherbed; do us good.'

'Oh, walk!' said Caroline with a little gurgle of laughter; 'well, I don't know, my shoes . . .'

He winced: 'Oh, my dear, when you say things like that it makes me just crazy.'

'I'm sorry,' and she smiled at him in the darkness.

'That makes it worse!' He plunged the car into low gear and they wheezed and whined up the hill in silence.

'Hallo: somebody up there with a light!'

'They want us to stop.' Caroline spoke quietly, suddenly carried back to her childhood and the night when she had been asleep in the great bed at Butler's Hill and the men had come to burn down the house. She knew what this was, just as she had known then: the I.R.A. were out drilling on the mountains and this was one of their sentries, posted on the road to prevent curious spectators from seeing what was going on.

'Don't make a fuss,' she added quickly; 'it's the I.R.A. They'll send us back again.'

'Blast them, they're doing this all over the place; they were at it round my place the other night. They would pick on tonight!'

He brought the car to a standstill as a voice from behind the flash-light shouted to him to stop. A dark figure approached the window and shone the torch in their eyes.

'Yez'll have to go back,' said the voice.

'Nonsense!' said Brian firmly; 'who the hell are you?'

'Let yous not mind who I am: yous'll have to go back.'

'This is a free country, isn't it? Can't I take my best girl for a drive in the mountains if I want to?'

'Most nights yez can, but tonight yez can't,' replied the voice patiently. 'Come on now,' it continued more roughly, as a second figure slipped out from the shadow of the hedge and took up its station at the opposite window; 'that's enuffa talk, turn her round now.' By way of inducement, he produced a revolver, a dark sinister little shape in the moonlight. 'D'yez see that?' he enquired; 'well, now ye know—or d'yez want me to use it?'

'Do turn round, Brian,' whispered Caroline; 'it's no good.'

He shrugged his shoulders. 'Damn you,' he said angrily to the voice; 'I suppose it's no good arguing with you if you've got a gun. Why can't you all stay quietly in your beds instead of trying to raise your bloody little army and destroy the peace of the country? What's the point of it, will you tell me that, what's the big idea?'

'Th' Irish Republican Army'll never lay down arms until we're quit o' the bordher and Ireland is united once again,' said the voice proudly. 'Come on now, willya? Me patience is exhausted, seewhaddimean?' He clapped the revolver against Brian's forehead.

'All right, all right, but put that dam' thing down.'

It took some time to manoeuvre the car round on the narrow hill and Brian was hot and out of breath by the time they were facing Dublin again. The man leant in at the window to give them a parting word of advice: 'I have the number of yer car,' he said threateningly, 'so if there's any throuble we'll know where to go. S'long,' and he waved them off.

'Well, I'm damned,' said Brian furiously as they slipped down the hill; 'you think you're living in a nice peaceful little country and you suddenly come up against this sort of thing. When's it ever going to end?'

Caroline felt strangely excited: here, in 1930, within ten miles of the capital, were men desperately organising themselves, unmolested, into an armed force opposed to the Government. The old bitter spirit of resistance that had been the curse of the British was still at work, wriggling and squirming under the surface, to rise and make war against the accepted order. These men refused to recognise the imperfect settlement of 1921; they were idealists, fanatics, enraged against the half-measures accepted by the majority and against the majority who had agreed to them. Ireland for them must be all or nothing: if the Northerners would not join the Republic, they must be made to do so. If the present Government was unwilling to proclaim the Republic, it must be put down. Anyone who opposed the Republican conception of a United Ireland was an enemy of the people. For sheer single-hearted tenacity of purpose, the I.R.A. were hard to beat: these men, out on the heather under the cold moon, were utterly ruthless in their determination to impose their will on every man, woman and child in Ireland, and on the English too, if they attempted to interfere, irrespective of creed, racial sympathy or political belief. It was the old old struggle, still going on.

'I can see their point,' she said; 'can't you?'

'Holy smoke!' he exclaimed in alarm, 'you're not a Republican, are you?'

'No.' Caroline began to laugh; 'I'm too reasonable: you could never be one if you could see anybody else's point of view. But all the same, however much of a menace they are, you've got to admire them in a sort of way. I mean, they're like my mother was, only at the opposite extreme: she was a diehard and everybody else was a traitor; however infuriating it was, you had to hand it to her for being honest. Well, it's just the same with them—they're absolutely hopeless to do anything with, but they're quite convinced they're right.'

'Yes, but my dear sweet angel, your mother didn't go about with a gun, shooting people who didn't agree with her.'

Caroline giggled: 'I think she'd have liked to.' She had a sudden, irresistibly funny vision of Helen sitting in her chair at the long window, holding a loaded revolver. 'Oh, I quite agree with you, they're impossible and their methods are inexcusable and they ought all to be locked up because they're a public danger, but I can't help having a sort of sneaking admiration for their unshakable idealism. Politics seem to have got so material, somehow.'

'All politics are material, honey; they always have been.'

'You're talking like a tired old man!'

'Maybe, but I see it this way. What causes a country to revolt against foreign domination? The fact that the foreigner can dictate what happens to the wealth, or the religion, or the land, or anything else you like to think of, of the under-nation. It's the interference in your way of living that you object to, your everyday business.'

'Interference with your freedom,' said Caroline hotly.

'What is freedom? Being able to do things the way you like. If you're taxed by a foreign nation, that's an assault on your freedom and you resent it and cry out that you're being oppressed. Isn't that material?'

'But even if the foreigners took nothing out of the country and made us all millionaires, I'd still want to get them out.'

'Because,' Brian pounded the driving wheel with his hands to emphasise his point, 'because they'd have the power to turn round and say: "that's enough now". It's their power over you that you'd resent; even if they didn't use it, you'd know it was there. And power is control of wealth. This Free State we're living in is no more free than Northern Ireland, which it so despises: Britain still controls it, even though it's got dominion status, sovereign power and all sorts of things that look just lovely on paper. The wealth of Ireland lies in the North, and the North is hand in glove with Britain; and that, saving your presence, is one of the chief reasons why your idealistic Republicans want to get hold of the North; we have the weight of population and we need the wealth of the North to balance it. As it is, our only bargaining power is in agriculture; we've got no industries, no raw materials. If Britain cut off her exports to us tomorrow, we'd be sunk; we've got no trade relations with any other country, worth talking about. There'd be no transport, no fuel, no bread—we don't grow wheat; there'd be meat and potatoes and bacon and eggs and milk, but no way of distributing them.'

'Britain needs our agriculture.'

'She could adjust that, if it came to a show down, by increasing her trade with the Argentine, Denmark and Holland. And then where would we be? No, it's no good pretending we can be independent as we are at present. That's why I have such an admiration for De Valera: he wants to make this country self-supporting. He wants us to grow our own sugar and wheat, make our own automobiles and furniture and face-creams; he's one of the few people who see just where England's got us. But even if he gets in at the next election and gets all his projects going full-blast, he still isn't out of the wood, because, England being our only market, our raw materials must still come from there too, unless we're willing to pay cash for them somewhere else. At least, that's how I see it,' and he shook his head gloomily.

Caroline had to smile: 'All right, you win,' she said; 'you can stop now.'

Brian burst out laughing: 'That I.R.A. fella sure did start something! Look, honey, we're right at your gate now and I haven't talked to you at all, only *at* you.'

'Come in and have a drink; there's plenty of beer.'

'Won't your dad mind?'

'Not a bit; I expect he's fast asleep. I tell you what we'll do—we'll go into the kitchen and cook ourselves some scrambled eggs.'

He rubbed his hands: 'Lovely! May I cook them?'

'You?' said Caroline, who rather fancied herself as a cook; 'do you know how?'

'Sure I know how! I'm a real sissy, I even know how to knit.'

They crept laughing through the dark and silent house to the little red-tiled kitchen. Caroline fetched things out for him and sat down to watch critically.

'Have you put in enough salt?'

'Plenny.'

'I'm sure they're going to be too sloppy.'

'You bet your life they aren't! Not dry, either; kinda half-in-half.'

In the end, when he produced two platesful of beautiful, golden scrambled eggs on toast that streamed with butter, she had to admit that he knew what he was doing. He even put the saucepan in the sink to soak.

'Now,' he said, triumphantly sitting down at the deal table, 'we can talk!'

'Well?' Caroline felt a little apprehensive.

He leant across, fork in hand: 'Are you really going to marry this guy?'

'Must you call him a guy? Anyway, I am.'

'I'm sorry, I just call chaps guys, I didn't mean anything. Listen here, couldn't you possibly think of marrying me instead? I do love you, honey; I've loved you ever since the first time I saw you, when I drove you to Anne Henderson's party, remember?'

'Yes, of course I remember.' She was looking at him with her head on one side, leaning a little back.

'You and I could do big things together, we've got the same ideas. If I had you and you had me, there isn't anything we couldn't do. You make me feel kinda . . . grand and able to beat the world.' He came round the table and stood behind her, one arm round her shoulders, speaking softly into her ear. 'When we were sitting there, having dinner, and you told me you were fixing the date of your wedding, it just came over me that I couldn't let you go without trying to get you for myself. I'm crazy about you—don't you love me a little?' He lifted a curl and gently kissed her ear.

'I do,' she said slowly, 'a lot.'

He took her face in his hands and kissed her full on the mouth.

'Oh, my darling: enough to marry me?'

She was on her feet and his arms were round her; her whole body tingled, pressed against his, exulting as they kissed again and again. He held her away from him for a second and looked wildly round the room:

'We must . . .'

But in that moment, Caroline knew that it was over. She sat down weakly on the edge of the table and gently disengaged his hands.

'No,' she said; 'we mustn't. Something happened to me then that I never meant you to know about.'

He was still breathing heavily: 'Caroline, you do love me. You've got to marry me.' His hands reached out to her again, but she shook her head.

'A year ago, I would have, if you'd asked me. I felt lost, somehow, as if I was crossing the sea and had gone adrift in the middle; David was so far away and wasn't coming back for such ages. But I've found out, now, where I am and I've nearly reached the other side and, when you're not with me, I know I don't want to be anywhere else but there.'

He stood up straight behind her, grasping her shoulders:

'I see,' he said huskily; 'oh, Caroline, and to think I could have had you!'

'We'd have been sorry. I'd have known I was wrong, really, all the time and it would have hurt us both, frightfully.'

He took a lock of her hair and rubbed it wonderingly between his fingers: 'Your hair—that lovely hair!' He bent down and brushed the top of her head with his lips: 'Can we be friends, honey?'

She smiled up at him: 'Always.'

'I don't know: it's dynamite, the way we feel about each other. We might forget you were married.'

'It takes two to forget.'

'You mean, it only takes one to remember?' He shook his head as though it were more than he could bear. 'You're a very lovely person,' he said gently.

She poured out the beer: 'Better eat up, it's getting late.'

His face wrinkled for a moment in its crooked smile as he went back to his chair.

'Damn,' he said; 'and I just hate cold scrambled eggs.'

CHAPTER TWENTY-SEVEN

Guy had declared that they must be mad, for there was a wind like the edge of a razor and patches of snow lay in the hollows of the hills, but all the same they had set off, Caroline and David, to spend the last day before their wedding on the mountains. Up here, it was colder still, and when she stood upright, the wind forced its way down her throat, knocking the breath out of her body, battering her face and trying to tear her hair out by the roots.

'Oh!' she gasped, and held out a hand, laughing helplessly.

'Almost . . . there now.' David himself could hardly speak.

At the top, they had to crawl the last few steps, ducking their heads to breathe; on the crest, among the huge dark rocks, they could not even see, for the wind battened their eyelids down; they retreated hurriedly down the lee-side to a hollow where they subsided gasping on the frozen ground. Caroline took her paralysed lower jaw and wagged it in her hand.

'I han't halk,' she announced gladly, with streaming eyes.

David pulled her on to his knee: 'You poor angel,' he said, and kissed her blue pinched face.

A shower of hail spilt over them, pricking their bare heads as they huddled together, stinging and smarting as the white stones bounced off into the heather.

'I think,' said David, 'we've had about enough of this joke; when the shower's over, we'll go back to the car.'

She shook her head like a dog, disengaging a little battery of hailstones that had become entangled in her curls.

'It's over now. Oh, look!'

The shower was moving across the mountain, down a valley between tree-clad hills, a tenuous sunlit veil, like a pillar of gauze, slow and unwavering. Fascinated, they stood watching it, hand in hand.

'It's ours,' she said; 'our very own; nobody else has seen it.'

'You have a private world.' His grip tightened on her fingers; 'Don't run away and hide in it where I can't get at you.'

'I'll always come back to you,' and she wrinkled her nose at him, 'as long as you're nice to me. Kiss me, darling.'

'My God, I'd bite you for that, if I didn't think you'd enjoy it! Oh, darling, I do love you!'

They clung together on the bitter mountain-side for a moment, then turned and went scrambling and sliding down until they were back on the road again and at the car.

'Where'll we go now,' said David; 'we've still got half the day.'

'We'll eat our sandwiches, I want to talk to you; then we'll drop in on Isabel and you can see the baby.'

'I hate babies—ones of that age. I suppose yours might be all right: they'd probably be funny, with red hair. I gather one doesn't comment on who this one's like.'

She looked at him sharply: 'Poor Isabel, Lady Millar's been beastly to her; she hasn't even been to see it and, of course, that makes everybody talk forty times as much. Mike's been grand, he's backed her up all the time, although he's nearly drunk himself silly in the effort. Sir Horace is all right, he's never said a word; he's a dear old boy, really. But I think she's a fiend: I mean, whatever she thinks privately, she might conceal it instead of making it obvious to the whole of Dublin that she doesn't think the child is Mike's. You'd think she wanted to make certain that their marriage goes on the rocks.'

'Mothers are odd,' said David; 'they'll endure untold things from their husbands without saying a word, but they're like cat and mouse with their daughters-in-law. I can imagine Mother being an absolute tigress if you started any nonsense, whereas ordinarily she's the mildest . . .'

'She's a darling, and she's been sweet to me.'

'Of course she has, you silly, how could she be anything else?'

Another shower of hail beat upon the car as they chewed sandwiches solidly.

'Listen,' said Caroline; 'what are you going to say to Uncle Archie about Butler's Hill?'

'Must I tell him tonight? Is that what this solemn family meeting's about? It's stopped me having my bachelor party.'

'I think so. In fact, I know it is.'

A little furrow came between his eyes: 'Just how ill is he?'

'The doctor gives him anything between five minutes and four or five years.'

'If he died tomorrow, would you want me to give up the Navy and settle down there?'

Caroline was wrapping her left hand into a little parcel with the corner of the rug.

'That's just one of those things you must decide for yourself,' she said, not looking up. 'Don't think about what I want: I'll go anywhere with you.'

'Always?'

'Yes, always.'

'Oh, my love!' His voice was broken; 'why do you love me like that? It makes me feel an awful cad.' He took her face in his hands and turned it towards him: 'Look at me.'

'Why?'

'I want to find out what you want me to do.'

'You won't find out anything;' she looked at him with a grey unwavering stare. 'Now, take your hands down, they're so cold I can't even think. Don't you see,' she went on slowly, stroking his fingers one by one, 'if I tried to make you do one thing or the other, you'd have the right to resent it all your life? It's your whole career and you must choose for yourself.'

'The Navy's a grand life,' he said regretfully; 'why can't Uncle Archie leave it to us to make up our minds when he's dead? He may go on for years—doctors often make mistakes.'

'Butler's Hill means more to him than anything else in the world; he's spent his whole life making it what it is. I don't think he was ever so happy as when he went back to rebuild it; that's why he can't bear not to know what's going to happen to it when he's gone.'

'You love it too, don't you? You thought I wouldn't find out, but you gave yourself away, my sweet: you should keep that dreamy look off your face. You want me to go there.' He drew her closer to him and gently shook her shoulders: 'Don't you? Own up.'

Caroline smiled at him, her mouth a little tremulous: 'I want you to do what you want,' she said firmly; 'come on, it's time we went to Isabel's.'

Another car followed them as they drove in at the gate; Caroline turned round in her seat to see whose it might be.

'Oh dear,' she said apprehensively, 'it's Mike and the Millars, and we can't possibly escape.'

Sir Horace came prancing up and wrung her warmly by the hand.

'Ah, the happy couple!' he exclaimed. 'Still determined to take the plunge, eh? Well, well, I wish you every happiness, I do indeed. I hope we sent you a decent present. Clara, what did we give these young people?'

'It was a lovely present,' said Caroline quickly, 'a pair . . .'

'Bah! Salvers. She always gives salvers. Not good enough, I'll send you a cheque tonight, you'll get it in the morning,' and he patted her hand kindly.

Lady Millar advanced, one hand upon Mike's arm; she greeted Caroline with cold severity and extended two fingers to David. The whole family, they were made to feel, was under a cloud and she was a wronged woman, brought here against her will and determined to make everybody suffer for it. When Mike smiled at them, she sighed heavily and released her hold on his arm.

'We've come to see our . . . er, the baby,' went on Sir Horace. 'Fine little beggar, by all accounts, nothing wrong with his lungs, roars with the best of 'em, hahaha . . .' He broke off, quelled by a withering look from his wife.

Isabel was at the door, smiling nervously and looking quite terrified. Mike gave her elbow an encouraging squeeze as she led them into her white drawing-room. Lady Millar looked straight through her and went over to the window, ignoring them all and staring out at the cold grey-blue hills. The others clustered round the fire and Sir Horace burst into jocular conversation, asking Isabel if she had a tubular cradle and a robot for a nurse. They laughed foolishly, feeling inexpressibly awkward and embarrassed. Isabel rang for tea.

Suddenly Stokes flung open the door and a starched and smiling nurse appeared with a white bundle.

'I'll take him,' said Isabel quickly, and held out her arms.

Lady Millar turned, but she did not move a step as the others crowded round the baby. A minute wrinkled hand wavered over the edge of the shawl. There was dead silence as they peered at the small red face with its wide solemn eyes.

'My God!' David gave a great shout of laughter that made the baby break into a wail of alarm, 'Mike, you old stiff, he's the image of you!'

Caroline gasped at his audacity: 'Yes,' she echoed gallantly, 'I never saw anything so . . .'

'By Jove!' exclaimed Sir Horace, 'I do believe you're right.'

'Like Michael!' screamed an incredulous voice from the window, 'let me see.' Overcome by curiosity, Lady Millar hurried across to inspect the baby for herself.

'So he is, Horace,' she cried excitedly, 'so he is. He's the image of Michael!'

Isabel sank weakly into a chair, the baby in her arms. Lady Millar bent over and kissed her.

'My dear,' she said humbly, 'forgive me; I've been very unjust to you. Will you let me hold him, just for a minute?'

Smiling, with a trembling lower lip, Isabel handed her the bundle and sat back to gaze at them all in utter astonishment at this development, the greatest piece of undeserved good fortune that had ever befallen her.

Her eyes sought Mike's, across the room, begging him to come over. Wonderingly, he came and sat on the arm of her chair. For a moment, she forgot that there were people all around them.

'Oh, darling,' she whispered.

Mike stared at her as if he could not believe his ears; she had never spoken to him like this before. He put his hands on her shoulders and turned her slowly towards him.

'Is it possible,' he murmured huskily, 'that you love me?'

She nodded, unable to speak.

He said nothing. He smiled at her and took both her hands; her lips curved tremulously in response; the smile spread into a laugh as he pulled her to her feet, and in a moment they were both laughing, leaning against each other for support.

'You wait,' he said as he sat her down again, 'till they've all gone!'

'There, there,' crooned Lady Millar, 'don't cry now, it's only your old granny, don't cry, don't cry.'

Sir Horace took out his watch and dangled it hopefully before the tiny puckered face.

'Goo goo,' he said, prodding the shawl gently, 'goo goo; listen, tick-tick-tick! Clara, I want my tea.'

After tea, David and Caroline settled for a moment, one on each side of Isabel's chair. They must go, they said. Arm in arm, the three of them went to the door. Isabel beamed at them.

'Bless you, David,' she said; 'bless you both: you don't know what you've done! I'm going to be happy at last!' And she danced a foolish little jig of pure delight on the doorstep.

Caroline turned to David as they drove out at the gate:

'Darling, you've missed your vocation: you're a diplomat!'

He grinned: 'I always heard that propaganda was a mighty weapon. Home?' he added, hesitating at the approach to a crossroads.

'Into Dublin,' said Caroline quickly; 'you must meet Leonard and Anne—they're my very best friends of all. You'll love them.'

Anne was sitting in a low chair by the fireside, toasting crumpets.

'Oh you darlings!' she exclaimed smiling, and stood up to move a pile of books from one chair and a marmalade cat from another. 'David, I am glad to meet you—I'll get Leonard, he's just come in.' Toasting-fork in hand, she wandered out into the passage.

'I've seen her before,' said David; 'one Christmas Day when we were kids: remember?'

'Yes, of course, and Cousin Catha . . .'

'I thought she was the loveliest woman I'd ever seen; she made me feel terribly romantic.'

'I've never seen anyone lovelier.' Caroline laughed and shook her head as David pointed back at her.

Anne came in with a tray. 'We're rather lonely,' she said; 'Olga's being such a success she couldn't get back for Christmas.'

'Is she happy?' Caroline turned to David: 'Olga's playing the lead in "Widow's Cruise",' she explained.

He was impressed: 'Is she now! We'll go and see her.'

'Happy?' Dreamily, Anne spread butter over a crumpet; 'I suppose she is, in a way. She's a self-sufficient sort of person and she's been very lucky—they want her to go to Hollywood now.' Head on one side, she looked at them for a moment: 'But she'll never be happy the sort of way you two are,' she added, a little sadly, 'she's too complicated and successful.'

'How's her Russian prince?'

'Still starving himself to send her orchids; my dear, he's only one: she's besieged by Russians and Poles and Scandinavians and

Frenchmen, and she won't have any of them.'

'Poor Olga,' said Caroline, not knowing quite why she felt sorry for her.

Leonard came in, rubbing his cold hands: 'Fire's gone out upstairs,' he complained; 'she neglects me,' he announced to David and smiled affectionately at Anne. 'So Caroline's got you back at last—you shouldn't go leaving her like that, it's not safe. I know of at least two broken hearts and half a dozen cracked ones.'

'Never again,' said David seriously, 'she's coming with me from now on, even if it kills her.'

'Caroline, did I tell you? You can see Leonard's posters in England now, in all the stations.' Anne was smiling proudly.

'Oh, I am glad! They ought to have been there long ago. If I ever have to live in England, d'you know what I'll do? I'll go down to the station every day and look at them and feel I've been home.'

'Which reminds me,' said David, 'that I haven't thanked you properly for Caroline's portrait. It . . . it's simply lovely.'

'The old red, white and blue,' laughed Leonard, and Caroline blushed at the remembrance of that terrible scene.

'It's going straight down to Butler's Hill, after the wedding, to be hung. And when Caroline's old and ugly I'll be able to look at it and tell people she really was like that, once.'

Leonard looked at Caroline: 'It was a purely selfish action,' he said; 'I enjoyed doing it.'

Anne was clearing away the tea things.

'Maid's out,' said Leonard; 'it's always her day out, every day of the week,' and he began to help Anne.

Caroline felt suddenly restive: 'We must go,' and she stood up.

'I've begun to remember all the things I've got to do; I shan't ever be able to be married tomorrow unless I stay up all night.'

'Wait a moment.' Leonard dived into a cupboard and brought out a decanter and glasses. Pouring out the sherry with a slightly trembling hand, he linked his arm in Anne's.

'Here's to you both: may you be as happy as we've been—I can't wish you anything better.'

'Somehow,' said Anne, 'I think they will be,' and she smiled her slow sweet smile.

'Thank you.' Caroline found that she could hardly speak, she was so overcome by their kindness and affection.

She turned back to look at them as she stepped into the car. They were standing in the lighted hallway, arm in arm; as the car drove off, Leonard drew Anne closer to him and the door closed slowly.

Caroline was very tired, and with the detachment that sometimes accompanies fatigue she watched and listened to them all at dinner and felt that she was not really there herself. She was aware of things unsaid, of Guy's feeling of utter lostness which he was making a gallant effort to conceal; of Archie, doing his best to keep Aunt Emma cheerful on one side and Miss O'Connor amused on the other, but all the time debating with himself inside that long narrow head what he was going to say to them after dinner; of Moira, gay and smiling, but worried to death about Archie, and of Aunt Emma who, however hard she tried, could not but feel that her son was being stolen from her and resent the resentment that she felt; Miss O'Connor smiled and nodded and talked, but she was thinking of the old days when she had lived with the family, when Helen had been there, and wondering if this was not too intimate an occasion for her to intrude upon, so she was secretly plotting an excuse to hurry away when she had peeled an apple and drunk the health of her little Caroline who would always be a child to her. David was the only one who had no secret thoughts; he was happy and looked it, confident that everybody was enjoying themselves as much as he was and quite unworried by the decisions he was going to be asked to make after dinner. Caroline smiled gratefully at him:

it was nice to have someone strong and untroubled who would keep her feet on the earth and prevent her from being swept away by the little currents of doubt and anxiety which were eddying round her. She wished that Mike and Isabel could have been there, just so that she could see them being happy, but Isabel was not strong yet and the wedding tomorrow would be quite exhausting enough for her.

In a sort of dream she listened to Archie making a speech and, a moment later, could not have repeated a word of it. Everybody was standing up and David put out his hand to make her keep her seat; people smiled at them behind raised glasses. She smiled back and David looked proudly at her and stood up to say something. Then it was all over and Guy was pushing back his chair and saying that they would all go into the other room together. They filed in and Miss O'Connor darted up the stairs. Doran, looking more ancient and fragile than ever, but beaming with delight, brought in the coffee and mechanically Caroline began to pour it out: milk but no sugar, sugar but no milk, black without sugar; she sorted them out slowly and David passed the cups round.

They were all collected in a wide circle round the fire, David beside Caroline on the sofa, Moira on the arm of Emma's chair, Guy and Archie leaning against the mantelpiece, sipping brandy and talking seriously in low voices. Archie looked round and decided that the time had come; he cleared his throat and Emma's voice trailed off with:

'I always think white chrysanthemums are so very . . . oh, Archie, I'm sorry.'

He smiled at her, so she finished in a loud whisper to Moira:

'. . . *funereal,* dear!' and sat back in her chair to hear what was to come.

'Now I want to get straight to the point,' began Archie, 'and I shall be talking to David and Caroline, but if anybody has something to say I shall be very glad to hear it.' He turned to David who was looking into the fire with an expression of regret at having to be serious when he was feeling so pleased and happy and wanted to talk.

'You were only children,' he went on, 'when Butler's Hill was burnt down and for some years your Aunt and I were very doubtful about the wisdom of rebuilding it, having no children of our own to leave it to; one doesn't build for strangers to inherit; but in 1926, when you came of age, David, we wrote to you to sound your feelings about it. We wanted to know whether, if we went back, rebuilt the house and got the place into the best possible order, you would be willing to live there one day, as the only Butler of your generation. If you had said no, we should have stayed in England, but your reply was encouraging, if a little indefinite: you said that in the end you would like to settle in Ireland, but that you hoped the question wouldn't arise for very many years. On the strength of that your Aunt and I decided to come back. We were neither of us old or infirm and we had every reason to believe that we could carry on there for a good long time before you would be called upon to make any drastic decisions.'

Caroline glanced at Moira; she was looking at the floor, her face in repose, dreamy and very sad, but she gave a little jerk and looked up to smile and shake her head as though she had been caught revealing things that she had meant to keep to herself. Archie sighed and went on.

'Now, however, I'm afraid the time has come when we must begin to think about what is going to happen next. My, er, prospects of being able to . . . er, to occupy Butler's Hill for more than a short time longer are bad.'

People shifted their feet uncomfortably and Emma opened her mouth as though to speak, but he held up his hand.

'This is a business matter and I want no sympathy,' he said with a grim little smile; 'my prospects, I say, are bad, and you may have to make your decision much sooner than any of us expected or intended. Now, I have a proposition to make.'

There was a little stir; Emma sat more upright and folded her hands in her lap; Guy edged the decanter along the mantelpiece to where

Archie could reach it; David pushed out his feet, crossed his arms and looked up enquiringly at Caroline.

'If you two will come and make your home at Butler's Hill now, I will make the place over to you without delay, on the sole condition that your Aunt and I can continue to live there in my lifetime. By this means, if we are lucky,' and he made a little grimace, 'you may be able to avoid the burden of death duties and, if you are willing, for I can compel you to nothing, you will also be able to learn something about estate management from me and benefit from my experience, instead of being forced to pick up what you can later on with nobody to advise or help you. But, legally and morally, you will be in control and in a position to disregard any advice I may be presumptuous enough to offer. I want to make one thing clear: if you come, the house will be divided and we shall live as two independent families—no young people, just married, should have to endure the company of their elders.' He paused.

The blood pounded in Caroline's ears. She wanted to shout out to Archie that they would come; she wanted to look at David and, with the impact of her will, compel him to accept; she wanted to cry. If she could do none of these things, she felt that she would burst.

David was scratching at a tiny stain on the lapel of his dinner jacket; everyone was looking at him, everyone except Caroline. He glanced at her, but she was staring into the fire as though it were the most important thing in the world.

'You mean,' he said, playing for time, 'retire now and turn farmer?'

'I do,' said Archie, and there was another silence.

Emma gulped and her hands fluttered vaguely. Caroline glared at her to keep her quiet.

'Yes?' said Archie.

Emma shot a desperate look of apology at Caroline: 'But what,' she faltered, 'are the poor children going to live on?'

There was a momentary titter and Archie smiled.

'I'm sorry,' he said; 'I'd meant to mention that. I'm afraid they won't be rich, but they ought to be able to live. Whatever rents there are will go to David and he'll just have to make the farm pay; he'll have to work like hell to knock a profit out of the land, but I'm convinced it can be done if you're young and interested and not afraid of work. The time for living like a gentleman on your rents and private income has gone for ever. Of course, when Moira and I are gone, he'll come in for our depleted capital. The household expenses will be shared, each side paying its way. The house itself should need no repairs for years, unless,' and he grinned, 'Caroline likes to have the bells repaired.'

David stood up: 'Thank you, Sir,' he said; 'it's a very generous offer, but I'd like to talk it over with Caroline before we make up our minds.'

'Yes, of course, of course,' said Archie quickly; 'talk it over between you. If you decide to take it, write to me from London and I'll have all the legal business arranged and drawn up by the time you come down to Butler's Hill at the end of your honeymoon. If you . . . er, make up your mind the other way, just write to me and we'll say nothing more about it. There's only one more point I want to make, and then I'll have finished: it's about the political side of it.'

Emma sighed loudly and shook her head. Archie went on:

'After the Treaty, many Unionists preferred to leave the country rather than live here under a Government for which they had no sympathy; others decided to stay on and make the best of it; some stayed on against their principles and took what I consider to be the dishonest course of living here and taking every opportunity of blackguarding the Government. In my opinion, you can never be happy or live honestly here unless you are prepared to swallow the fact that the British have gone *for good* and that the present Government represents the will of the people. We might prefer to have things as they were, but we are a minority and I think we can accept this Government without any disloyalty to our traditional principles. If you feel you can't, you had much better sever all connexion with the South and never come here again; that would be hard to do, for our lives have become knitted into the fabric of this country. But I think there is an opportunity here for us Anglo-Irish; we represent a tradition of which we have no reason to feel ashamed. Protestant, on the whole, land-owning and far from rich, we have honestly worked to improve conditions for the people; many of us fought for their independence. I think the country would be a lot poorer without us, and I think the Government knows it. If you are willing to live on your land, give employment on fair terms and co-operate in making this a decent country, I think you will be doing a far better job than if you become a political refugee and sulked in England.' He poured himself out some brandy and made for a chair.

'I remember,' said Moira softly, 'when Butler's Hill was burnt down and I brought you back to Fitzwilliam Square, Caroline, I told your mother that I thought we had lost our place in the country and that if we stayed on here we should be like aliens, besieged, because the land had turned against us. I don't think that any more: I think there's still a place for us here, but we can't take it for granted, as we used to do, we've got to work for it . . .' She broke off suddenly: Emma had begun to weep.

'I've never been called dishonest before,' she sobbed, 'but even after ten years I can't get used to the British having gone. I only stayed on here because I hadn't a friend in the world outside this country. Helen was like me, and Catha, but they're dead now and you've all changed. I'm a stranger, even here.'

David was beside her, leaning over her: 'But Mother, can't you see, they're right: you can't bury yourself in the past when you've got all your life to live!'

'For you,' Emma dabbed at her eyes, 'they're right. You're young and you have faith; but I'm too old, I can't change now.'

David turned to Caroline; she was sitting very straight, gazing at him with shining eyes. He held out his hands and she came over.

'We don't need to talk about it,' he whispered; 'shall we tell him now?'

She nodded. They turned and stood hand in hand.

'Uncle Archie,' they said together; 'we'll come!'